I0593819

DRAGON'S TRAIL

Joseph Malik

Published by Oxblood Books, Gig Harbor, WA, USA

Edited by Monique Fischer
Print cover design by Lynn Stevenson
E-book cover design by West Coast Design

v1.08.20180819

Library of Congress Control Number: 2017911975
ISBN: 978-0-9978875-5-6   paperback
ISBN: 978-0-9978875-4-9   hardback
ISBN: 978-0-9978875-0-1   e-book

Register at www.josephmalik.com for updates on new releases.

author@josephmalik.com
Facebook/Twitter: jmalikauthor

*For my beloved wife, to whom I turn
whenever I need a study in courage.*

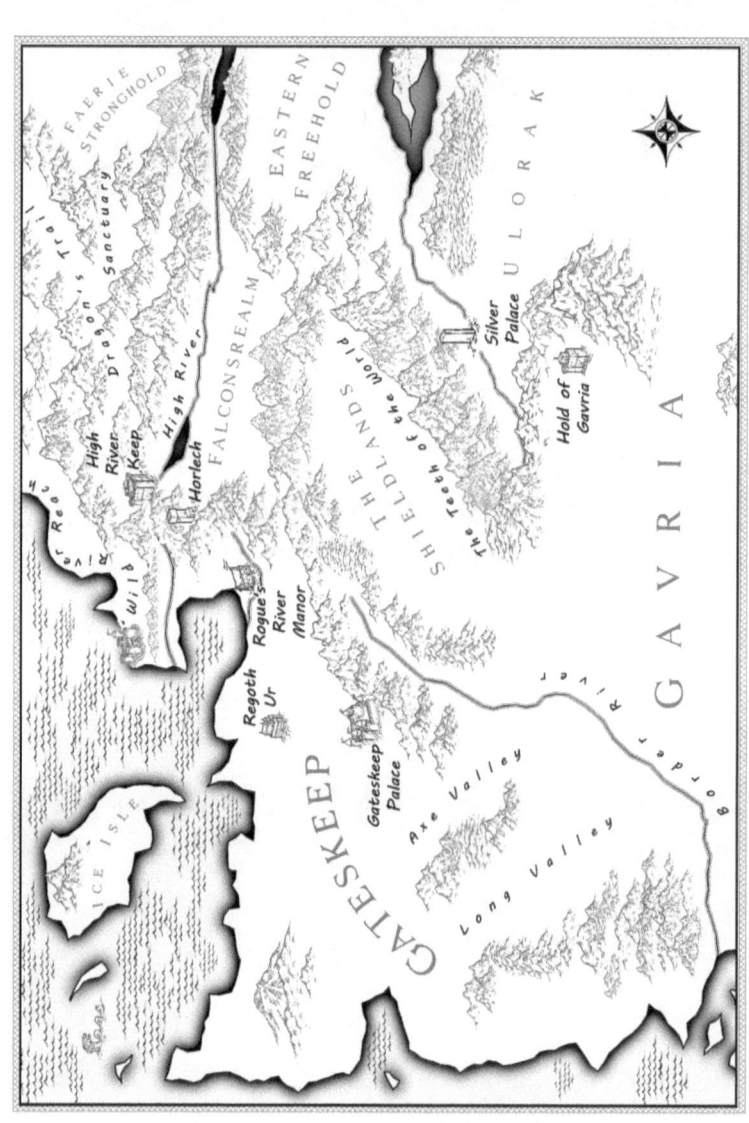

GLOSSARY AND CAST OF MINOR CHARACTERS

Adielle: Princess Adielle Riongoran-Thurdin, eldest child of the royal family, ruler of **Falconsrealm** and heir to the throne of **Gateskeep.**

Akiel: Prince Akiel of Corimann, a prince of the **Faerie.**

Albar Hillwhite: Eldest son of the patrician, ore-baron Hillwhite family. Betrothed to **Adielle.**

Axe Valley: One of two passages into **Gateskeep** from **Gavria,** and vice versa. Often a battle site between **Gateskeep** and **Gavria.** See map.

Damon Riongoran-Thurdin: Youngest member of the immediate royal family, second in line for the throne of **Gateskeep.**

Eastern Freehold: Furthest east nation, with easy passage through **Ulorak.**

Edwin Hillwhite: Brother to **Albar.** Duke of Horlech. See map.

Faerie: Northeastern neighbors.

Falconsrealm: Gateskeep's largest territory, a mountainous region traditionally ruled by the heir to the throne of **Gateskeep.**

Gateskeep: Northwestern country that includes Gateskeep, Falconsrealm, Ice Isle, and The Shieldlands. See map.

Gavria: The nation south of **Gateskeep.** See map.

Gbatu: Collectively, all the races and tribes of subhumans. There are over a hundred subspecies of *gbatu.* The most common species range from three to four feet in height and are lightly-furred, tool-using, and intelligent. They live in tribes which consider themselves to be at war with every other species in the realm, including each other.

Greatsword: A large war sword. Typically wielded two-handed but balanced for one-hand use. A late 14th-Century greatsword is Carter Sorenson's weapon of choice. A smaller, earlier version, the *gran espée de guerre*, is Jarrod's.

Guard's sword: The only heavy swords allowed to be worn within castle walls in **Gateskeep,** except by royalty, knights, and **riders.** Uniform in design with a heavy iron blade, steel edges, and a simple hilt.

Ice Isle: Gateskeep's northern principality and northernmost territory. Ruled by the second heir to the throne, Prince **Damon** Riongoran-Thurdin. See map.

Javal: Knight Captain Sir Javal Riongoran-Thurdin of Ravenhurst

Keep. Mentor to Jarrod Torrealday and cousin to Princess **Adielle** Riongoran-Thurdin and Prince Damon Riongoran-Thurdin. Orphaned by the battlefield loss of his father Duke Brannon Riongoran-Thurdin, Javal was raised by Lord Nor of Ravenhurst.

Loth of Hwarthar: General and Warlord of **Gavria.** He slew **Javal's** father at **Axe Valley.**

Rider: In **Gateskeep** and **Falconsrealm**, a title below true knight, merited by skill at arms or exceptional performance in combat. A **rider** will rise in social standing upon attaining knighthood. Knights often refer to each other as **"rider"** as a term of respect.

Rorthos Riongoran-Thurdin: King of Gateskeep.

Saxe: A cleaver-like, single-edged shortsword. Used primarily in the **Shieldlands** of **Gateskeep.**

Sheth: Colloquial name for a giant variety of *gbatu.*

Shieldlands: Southern territory of **Gateskeep.** See map.

Ulorak: A **Gavrian** territory and trading crossroads with the **Eastern Freehold**, Ulorak was originally a commonwealth of **Gavria,** though it was claimed by the **Eastern Freehold** once it fell into disrepair after the death of Sabbaghian the Black. Ulorak became sovereign under King Ulo Sabbaghian, and then became a **Gavrian** territory once again when King Ulo accepted appointment as Lord High Sorcerer of **Gavria.** See map.

DRAGON'S
TRAIL

PRELUDE

"The history of the sword is the history of humanity."
— Sir Richard F. Burton, 1884

In eastern Gateskeep, bordering the principality of Falconsrealm, the Tower of Horlech stands against all seeming odds, sagging and nearly fallen. From the top floors, the rift-strewn wildwoods and misty cliffs of Falconsrealm stretch out of sight in three directions.

Known to locals as Edwin's Folly, the Tower of Horlech slouches to the northeast atop a knob of rock and scrub, looking for all the world like a helm's crest bent by a debilitating blow. Year after year, Edwin's Folly stands; year after year, the townsfolk of Horlech wager that it won't. On the first day of summer, the town holds its Tower Day celebration, in which the previous year's losers pay their good-natured debts and wagers begin anew.

Inside the sagging walls of Horlech, on the eve of the celebrations a few years ago, a young sorcerer named Crius Lotavaugus advised the war council of Gateskeep.

A spindly shamble of a man, Crius Lotavaugus's tangles of hair and tight dark beard made his age indeterminate, but it was widely held that he was the youngest to ever hold the office of Lord High Sorcerer of Gateskeep.

He stood at the head of the great stone table in comfortable, if drab, attire: a long leather jerkin, a pair of silver necklaces, unremarkable trousers, and well-worn boots burnished with deliberation and care.

"War?" Crius asked. "And I'm only now hearing of this?"

Glances and convictions collided in the silence.

"A war is coming." Ravaroth Anganor, informally called Lord Rav, sat on Crius's right, rocking back in his chair. He wore his dark beard in fine braids in the manner of men of the Wild River Reach, and his clothes were rich with spring colors inlaid with silver across his prominent chest, which sported a general's brooch.

"Coming," Crius stressed. "War is always coming. But that's no reason to provoke one."

"The bloodline of the wizard Sabbaghian," said Lord Rav, "banished all these years, now walks the halls of the Hold of Gavria. They have put him on their war council."

Duke Edwin Hillwhite, who owned the crooked tower, was a gangly man with a mop of black hair and a broad jaw. He addressed the others at the table. "The Gavrians are buying up all our grain, and trading us gold, not iron, for it. What else could they be doing with grain and iron? They're building an army."

"And you raise your prices for iron just as we have to start equipping a larger force," said Lord Rav. "How convenient."

Edwin shrugged. "Demand is demand, General. I don't set the prices. The mines set the prices."

Lord Rav laughed to the others at the table, who joined him, before he turned back to Edwin. "They're your mines, boy! You're telling me you don't control them?"

"Not alone," said Edwin. His tone soured. "And don't call me 'boy,' again."

"You would do well to remain silent," Crius told the duke. "In fact, I'm not quite sure why you're in this meeting."

Edwin stammered, "This is my castle!"

"Granted to you in the hopes that you'd repair it," reminded Crius, "as you are the only man in the kingdom who can afford to." He made a show of looking into the corners and ceiling. "How's that going, anyway?"

Edwin fumed. "Do you know what's required to stanchion this place?"

"Indeed," said Crius. "I'm impressed that the knocking of your headboard hasn't collapsed the place entirely."

"No need to get sore just because I'm twice the man of any of you," said Edwin, folding his arms and straightening.

"If that were true," said Rav, "you wouldn't need your men to enforce it."

Edwin's arms unfolded. "Meaning what?"

"This is a garrison town," said Rav. "Those are soldiers' daughters your boys drag in here."

Edwin twitched. "You have no idea what I go through."

"Two or three a week, I'd imagine," said Crius. "You'd think this tower would stand straight of its own accord."

Edwin lunged at Crius across the table. It took three men to hold him back.

Lord Rav refilled his and Crius's goblets from a decanter of something reddish-purple and mercifully strong.

Edwin, still fuming, shook the others off and sat. "I should pummel you, you little bastard," he told Crius.

"And I should turn you into a titmouse until this matter is

concluded," Crius said. "You could still flap around and tweet all you want, and perhaps we'll finally find it endearing. But I'll refrain if you will."

"Is that what this is about?" Edwin asked the table. "The council called us here to discuss what I do in my bed, with my subjects?"

"No," said Rav. "But don't make us have to come back here to discuss it further. You will like that conversation even less than this one."

The room fell silent.

"Which brings us back to the matter at hand," said another general, named Lord Erlac, whose graying beard grew in patches across an array of scars that he stroked out of habit. "We hear rumors of an insurgency brewing in Falconsrealm."

"Finally, we get to it," said Prince Damon. Damon was a dark-haired noodle of a boy in fine clothing that was mostly white, including a white fur cape despite the sun outside. He was the prince of the distant Ice Isle, though it would be ruled by a regency council for a few years, yet. The Snow Prince, they were calling him.

"Let's discuss this," Damon said. "And what, Duke Edwin, did your brother find so important in Falconsrealm that neither he nor my sister could be here?"

"Prince Albar—" began Edwin, only to be interrupted by the Snow Prince.

"Albar," Damon hissed, pointing at Edwin, "is not a prince yet. My sister rules Falconsrealm. He never will. Those are points you'd be well-advised to remember."

"We've seen attacks on our border outposts in the Shieldlands," Erlac continued. "Supply trains raided, a ship burned along the Border River. And if you ask me," he turned to Edwin, "they're getting a pass from your brother, that power-starved, quivering milksop—"

"My brother is the heir presumptive!" Edwin shouted, rising. "He'll. . ."

"Go on!" Erlac yelled. "Finish that statement! I beg you. We would love to know what the Hillwhites plan to do once you've finally married into royalty. Enlighten us."

Crius gestured to Edwin that the table was his.

Edwin took his seat.

The scarred general continued, this time more quietly. "We know the forces at Gavria are sending liaisons to the court at High River." High River Keep was the princess's seat at Falconsrealm. "We don't know why."

Eyes turned to Edwin for a long moment.

Someone finally grunted.

"I've not heard of this," said Edwin.

A knight, clean-shaven and young in contrast to the others at the table, denoted by his gold horsehead pin as being a rider in the king's personal order, summarized the council's concern.

"All this aside, Gavria is building her armies," he said. "If Sabbaghian is their Lord High Sorcerer, then Gavria's next campaign may well be engineered by a foreign mastermind. We will have no references to this man's strategies, and no parallels to his experiences. We will need advisers. Not heroes, not warriors. Chancellors. For the duration of the war. If there is a war."

Crius took a moment to pinch off the bridge of his nose between thumb and forefinger. "What you're asking, sire—" his reasoning felt as unsure as the skewed walls around him, "— is to bring you demons. Demons to whom you will hand over your power, and trust to lead your armies against another."

Another young knight, still in his mail-and-leather riding gear, stood and slammed his fist on the marble inlay. "We said nothing of demons!"

Crius looked to the ceiling. "Careful, or you'll bring this

place down." After a moment watching the timbers and listening for creaks, he let out his breath. "Sabbaghian's son, this King Ulo Sabbaghian, was raised in the demon world. Brought here as a demon. Conjured, as any demon. That he is human is of little consequence. He is a demon. And he is not to be trifled with."

"You're scared of him?" asked Lord Rav.

Crius nodded. "As you all should be."

"What we want is what they have," said Lord Erlac, stroking his scars absently. "Only more of it."

"Master Crius," Prince Damon's voice was gentle. "Yes, this is what we're asking. I understand the dangers inherent in this course."

"Respectfully, Highness, I don't think you do," said Crius.

"I do," insisted Damon. "The true danger is the fears these men, these demons, would arouse. We will not speak of this outside this room. We'll treat them as we would any other adviser."

"The true danger is far greater than people's fears, highness," said Crius.

Damon blinked once, and, in a voice that belied his age, said, "Perhaps. But that's why we're entrusting the Lord High Sorcerer with this."

Crius looked to Edwin, who grinned. "Oh, if I could but slam the door behind you," said Edwin.

Crius's gaze roved the eyes of the others. None shied from him. "You'd already decided this. You had decided this before we even called this meeting."

"No one else can do this," said Damon. "If it's to be done, you'll do it."

Crius smiled, looked down at his hands, and nodded, tight-lipped. "Very well, Highness," he said. "I will travel, and I will bring you demons."

All agreed, and the council broke with murmurs of

conversation and the bangs and scrapes of benches.

Prince Damon wove his way over to Crius, shaking hands and clapping shoulders. Damon kept his voice low as he spoke to Crius away from the others. "What's this danger that we don't see?"

"The killing blow is so often the one that looks harmless," said Crius. "You won't know what the danger is, and neither will I, until it has us by the throat. This will not solve your problem with Sabbaghian, or with Gavria. This will complicate it."

"This will level the field," said Damon.

"It won't," said Crius.

"The war council says it will," said Damon.

"The war council hopes it will," said Crius. "If Gavria marches, demons won't matter. We'll need to rely on the same things we've used against them from time immemorial: iron and blood. Swords win wars, Highness."

Damon clasped Crius's folded hands in his own. "Then bring us demons with swords."

I

OVERTURE

"Fighting was fun; this was the thing. Fighting was tremendous fun."

— Ewart Oakeshott

T he Middle Ages had come to Camille Bay.
It was a rainy Memorial Day weekend. Spring seemed to have been and gone without a single hour of sunshine, and the coming summer held no promises.

Camille Bay, Maine, is a tiny Birkenstock town known for its artistic population and a never-ending slew of obscure exhibitions. Camille Bay is host to fantasy conventions, an occasional movie set, and the region's most prestigious glass-blowing school. She boasts several successful authors among her quiet inhabitants.

The particular way Camille Bay had chosen to draw the immediate world's attention today entailed a re-creation of a medieval fair in the market square, courtesy of several large Renaissance troupes.

Everyone in the town participated; participation is the town creed. The costumes ranged from casual passers-by in Robin Hood hats, to axe-bearing Norsemen and lace-ruffled Elizabethans. Woe, indeed, to the unwitting tourist, reluctantly handing over his Mobil card to a bearded Norseman in a bearskin cape and a leather jockstrap.

Crius's vision unclouded in an alley of Camille Bay.

With a fleeting sweat of terror he realized that this was not a world he'd expected and certainly not the world he'd visualized moments ago, standing an ocean of space distant in his chambers at Horlech with the Tower Day celebrations rampaging in the distance.

A granite sky spat mist over a fitful, intense gridwork, a hornets' nest as garish and searing as the sun even in the intense cold of the day. Everywhere he looked, the world seemed to explode with its own sprinting pulse; every color and edge exquisite in its squarishness and order. He smelled fish and seawater. An unsourced thrum slashed at him from nowhere.

He climbed to his feet on a hard black road. A fine road.

Roads were roads.

Roads hadn't changed.

There he stood on the road, crumpled, hands on his knees, awestruck at a piece of trash more bright and polished than anything he'd ever seen, a massive facet of a jewel blowing along the slate of the yard fences and the blacktop of the alley.

He watched it go, and the world tunneled into place in its wake.

Square homes built shoulder to shoulder sprawled up the hills away from the sea. At the end of the alley the road led up the hill, and also down to a calm harbor brimming with boats.

Away from the water, the town was bursting. He knew a festival when he saw one.

Festivals hadn't changed.

He pulled his hood up and struck out uphill, thrilled with

the quality of the road beneath his boots. The noise grew and his pulse quickened.

What a world! What an intense, bright, loud, fast world!

He stopped at a barrier and reached to warm his hand by its flashing lamp; he found light, but no heat. He touched it. He rested his hand on it. He giggled.

He took a slow look across the multitudes. Warriors in piecemeal armor, commoners in simple dress, well-outfitted courtiers.

Many things, it seemed, had not changed. More than he'd expected.

A mechanical animal, albeit an unkempt and mangy one, butted its way through the street, forcing noblewoman and barbarian alike to leap aside.

He found a space beneath an awning and watched the people pass. An occasional townsperson tipped his hat, someone clapped him on the back, and once a man dressed like a northern tribesman, ridiculously muscled, bumped into him, muttering in a language that was guttural, ancient, and simple.

Across the road, under the eaves, berserker donned hunting hat and woodsman donned horned helmet, and the two laughed at each other.

Two women in court dress emerged from a shop behind him, then threw bright rain jackets over their dresses.

Costumes. Nostalgia. Idealism.

He headed for the center of town, which bustled with demons with swords.

In the late afternoon, away from the noise and the rabble, Crius topped a range of sand and gravel mounds near the sea. He tripped, slid, and came to a rest at the feet of eight men and one woman, all clad in the local garb, not costumes.

Three men pulled the sorcerer to his feet.

"Let him go," snarled another voice, rife with the crack of authority.

Crius shook his clothes straight and took a look across the nine faces — or eleven, now, he saw — for there were two more men about to duel beyond the line of onlookers.

The woman, though, was the first to hold his attention. She was striking, petite but strong with black hair and eyes and olive-skinned. He laughed inwardly. She looked northern Gavrian. She was not one to bring before the Gateskeep High Council.

Beyond her, the young man with the sharp voice was bare-chested to the sting of the sea air.

With a ponytail and goatee the color of the wet sand behind him, he was on the small side of medium-sized, but his proportions were exaggerated with slabs of long muscle, cat-like. The most wondrous wicked scar, a mark of great pain and courage, graced the knotted muscles of his stomach. He stabbed his rapier into the sand, dropped into a full split, and leaped up again.

Crius knew the type.

He liked this type.

The other man was much larger, much stronger, red-cheeked and thick-bearded in a ruddy shirt and a black jacket. He whipped the jacket off and tossed it to one of his cronies.

Remorseless jaw. Fierce eyes. A warrior to be reckoned with.

But it was the young swordsman whose grin, brilliant as the moon, had snared Crius's eye.

Here, Crius thought, was a hero: this young rake flipping his rapier from one hand to the other, tossing it behind his back and over his head with a juggler's ease, all the while bowing smugly.

The grin faded, however, as his opponent was handed a

much heavier sword than his own and began limbering up.

Within a moment, both struck an *en garde*, and so began the challenges.

This was a grudge match. Unofficial, unsponsored, prohibited by a myriad of local statutes, and held well away from the main bustle.

The younger man spoke first. "I, Jarrod Torrealday of Knightsbridge, do accuse you, Harold Reynolds of Torrington, of the crime of rape. The victim, Lady Siriana, is present to substantiate the charges." With his weapon he offered her a salute that snapped through the air, and returned his attention to his opponent. Jarrod's voice became rocky and dropped an octave, and his happy-go-lucky countenance melted into an unforgiving glare. "How will you plead?"

The tip of his rapier was as steady as a star.

Crius was impressed by his professionalism. This was a champion's champion. This was the man he wanted. And left-handed, he noted. Rare, indeed.

"I protest my innocence," Harold replied tiredly, and spat on the ground toward Jarrod in punctuation. "And that, on you. I'll leave you with a story to tell."

"Well, then," Jarrod answered, "May God guide the true blade, sir. To the first blood?" Out went the right hand for balance, the right leg a bit behind, weight shifting to and fro.

Harold nodded, his mouth a tight line behind the beard. "So be it. First blood."

"Get him, Jarrod!" yelled one man from the sidelines.

"Kick his ass, Jarrod!" added another.

They crossed blades. Neither moved for the longest moment. Harold lunged.

Jarrod exploded forward in a whirl of flashing steel, and Harold crumpled and spilled into a knee-deep puddle, pleading his surrender as Jarrod stomped and beat him.

The blood-thirstier onlookers were disappointed. Though Harold's nose was smashed, his eye swollen and his beard dripping blood, the duel had lasted only seconds.

Jarrod disarmed him with a kick, his face quivering in fury.

Harold sloshed to his knees to find Jarrod's rapier pricking him not-so-lightly in the eyebrow.

"Give me your hand," said Jarrod.

"My h—"

"Your *hand!*" he screamed, his face reddening.

"Careful, Jarrod!" someone shouted.

Jarrod tossed his rapier well aside, took Harold's hand in both his, and twisted it. He pried Harold's ring finger back until it nearly disjointed.

"Tell me to stop," Jarrod growled. He bent it back further, and Harold yelped again. "Tell me to *stop!*"

"Ah, st—! Hey!"

"What?"

"Stop!"

Jarrod's lip curled over his teeth. "*Beg* me to stop."

Harold was breathing in panicked gasps, "*Stop!*"

He snapped the finger back. Harold shrieked. Stomachs wrenched. The Lady Siriana, whom Jarrod had been championing, covered her ears and spun away.

"Now, the next time someone tells *you* to stop," Jarrod snarled, "you just remember how *that* felt, you bastard. And you," he panted, "Will. *Stop!*" and he broke another one.

He shoved Harold back into the water with a foot on his chest and waded ashore.

He toe-flipped his rapier up into his hand, snatched his shirt from an onlooker, and left at a trot that in five steps turned into a sprint.

Siriana attempted to run after him, but one of Jarrod's supporters took her arm and held her back.

"Don't," was all he said.

"No, I gotta—" she attempted to push past him, but to no avail. "Lemme go!"

He put his hand on her shoulder. "Please, don't," he emphasized. "He doesn't want to see anybody right now."

Late into the night, Jarrod Torrealday lay awake in bed, unjumbling his thoughts.

Cars slashed by, the headlights making nightmares of the room's shadows. He turned on his side and listened to his pulse like so many marching feet.

His rapier hung from the doorknob. Headlights roamed over it again and again.

He wished he smoked.

The lights brought flashes: Harold's acceptance of the duel, Siri begging Jarrod not to hurt him, the conflict and the hatred in her face. The absurdity of crossing swords for a woman he'd met exactly once. Watching Harold warming up, the sloppy footwork and heavy lunges, the beer bottle he'd cast aside. The relief and the frustration of knowing deep inside there was no true danger. Sizing Harold up as drunk, and fat, and clumsy.

And being right.

He'd taken Harold apart in five seconds.

Harold and that ridiculous mammoth blade. *Way too much sword for you. Compensating for a deficiency in your . . . character?*

Touching blades; thoughts of Harold, and others, of Siri drunk and held down on a feasting table like part of the goddamn buffet.

And you still can't do anything right.

He picked up his phone, but his hand trembled too hard to

read it, much less use it.

The morning's breath in his throat, dry and ugly; a grip in his gut as a solid year of hell—still so fresh he could smell it if he lay still long enough—stampeded across the darkness. A delusional ex-champion with a rapier. Endless months of crying coaches and shouting lawyers. A kaleidoscope of TV cameras and microphones, a magnificent life vanished like sand through his fingers, and a girl, achingly beautiful, who might as well be a ghost now. All of it an utter screw-up.

And now this.

Crawling out, one Harold at a time.

He took a pull from the bottle of Lagavulin beside the clock, acidic and hot.

His own voice startled him. "What were you gonna do?" he asked the shadows. "Kill him, too?"

He flipped through pictures, finding a block-script quote by Rostand in *Cyrano de Bergerac*: "I feel too strong to war with mere mortals—*bring me giants!*"

He took another drink, longer.

It was time to move on.

Carter Sorenson traveled Renaissance festivals giving demonstrations on the history and tactics of the greatsword.

Nearly seven feet tall and so immensely muscled as to appear capable of pulling locomotives with his teeth, his head and goatee were shorn equally close and flecked with gray. He had played three years as a defensive end for the Patriots, and later had done quite well on the professional mixed martial arts circuit—facts that were well known throughout the Faire.

He regularly drew quite a crowd.

Carter was looking for Jarrod in the post-fair gala. Sunday mornings provided the last chance for browsing the artisans' tents. By noon the majority would be packing up in preparation for a return to whatever, in their lives, passed for normalcy.

While he didn't spy Jarrod, he did see Renaldo Salazar, one of Harold's cronies. Carter had heard that Jarrod and Harold had had a—what did they call it?—a *trial* the day before, which had ended with Harold in the hospital.

Renaldo wasn't a serious Renaissance enthusiast, but a fringie who liked to flaunt his physique in fur loincloths and matching boots. He was, however, exceptional with a longsword, and had given Carter a run for his money at several historic European martial arts tournaments.

Worse, though; after Jarrod became famous for killing a guy in a swordfight in Paris a couple of years ago, hordes of macho half-wits and dilettante sword geeks had formed illegal underground dueling clubs around the world. In these circles, Renaldo had made a name for himself. And it was no secret that he wanted a piece of Jarrod.

This, Carter thought, could be an interesting day.

Renaldo was pushing at a small young woman with olive skin and dark hair.

"Siri." He looked hung-over, or possibly still drunk. "I need to talk to you."

Carter started easing his way through the crowd, quietly, hands on shoulders.

Renaldo reached out to touch the small woman. She shrugged away from him. "Huh?" he persisted. "Look, let's talk about this."

Carter recognized her, now: the one all the fuss had been about. Word had it that Harold and his buddies had raped her at a feast a few months ago in Manchester, which, he figured, was why Jarrod had kicked Harold's ass. And good on him.

"I'll kill you." She shoved him in return. "I mean it."

Carter moved faster. "Lemme through. Move."

"You?" Renaldo countered. "You mean Jarrod. You bring him to me."

Her eyes were savage. "I will. I hope he cuts your eyes out. Get away from me."

"You tell him I said to find me. Anytime. You got that? I'm not Harold. I'll be ready."

She looked him up and down, pausing for a moment on his loincloth before shaking her head. "Where do you keep your wallet?"

"Bitch!" he shouted as she walked away.

Carter finished pushing his way through the crowd to Renaldo, and stood before him, eclipsing the sun.

Renaldo Salazar was big. Striking, chiseled, corded with muscle.

Carter was leviathan. Tanned biceps the size of footballs shoved at the rolled-up sleeves of his T-shirt, a vast expanse of black across which faux bloodstains marred the stencil GET UP.

A broad voice, freakish in its depth, sprang up through Carter's throat. "Is there a problem, here?"

Renaldo stepped back as Carter stepped forward. "My problem is not with you."

Carter grinned the merry grin of a Norseman cutting tulips with his favorite axe on a spring afternoon. "It is now."

The smile widened, its menace amplified by a gold canine tooth, its predecessor rumored to still be embedded in the skull of an actual ninja.

Renaldo's voice rattled from the hollows of his soul. "Find Jarrod. Tell him to come find me. And bring his blade," he swallowed the last part of the sentence, and repeated it for good measure.

Carter cleared his throat. "Get out of here before I make what happens next look like an accident."

Renaldo obliged and, in a moment, had vanished into the crowd.

Jarrod shoved his way through to Carter a moment later. "Did I hear my name taken in vain?" He was dressed in a leather jerkin and tights, the gleaming swept hilt of a heavy rapier adorning his side.

"Hullo, friend," Carter said to Jarrod with a slight bow. "Renaldo Salazar was just looking for you."

"I wonder whatever for? A pleasant day to you, my lord," Jarrod returned. "A thousand thanks."

Carter waved it off with a wide smile. "I enjoyed that so immensely, I should be thanking you."

"Carter Sorenson," said Jarrod, "may I introduce—"

"Siriana." Carter kissed her hand, bowing quite far to do so. "We've met."

"I thank you, as well, sire," she curtsied.

Carter dropped out of medieval vernacular as the crowd dissipated. "The fringies are out in force."

Jarrod shrugged. "Inviting the whole town doesn't help." Behind him, the Tin Man of Oz pedaled past on a unicycle. "I could do with less of this."

"It's going to be a long summer," Carter agreed. "You two headin' back today?"

Jarrod looked at Siri, whose nod told him it was about time to get going. "Yeah, I think so, in a bit. Why do you ask?"

"I'd maybe like to meet you for lunch," the giant offered. "We haven't talked in ages. You're still the fight coordinator over at North Coast, right? The Vikings-and-Indians thing?"

"That's on hold until next season." Jarrod's tone was dejected. "They haven't picked up my option yet."

"So what are you doing these days?"

"Jumped out of a building for FOX a couple of times."

"Jumped?" asked Carter. "Geez, I'd figure they'd just throw you."

"Funny guy," said Jarrod. "I did just finish a month of private lessons for Isabella Barnes."

"Isa . . . bella . . . Barnes?" Carter stammered. "Isabella freakin' Barnes. 'Disney's Izzy?' *Playboy?* Her?"

"Paramount is planning a Zorro spinoff. She'd be playing his daughter, the heir to Zorro's . . . whatever. Swordsman —uh—ism. Hero-ship."

Carter wiped his forehead. "Christ. I hate you so much right now."

"I only saw the initial concept," Jarrod assured him. "It may not go through."

Carter's tone was incredulous. "Can she fence?"

"She can, now. She has great wrists."

Siri rolled her eyes.

"I gotta say, sometimes I feel guilty getting paid," Jarrod admitted. "How's your gym?"

"Just sold it."

"Hey, I'm sorry."

"I'm not."

"What are you doing now?"

"Absolutely nothing," said Carter. "Taking the summer off. I was hoping to talk to you about the Viking thing, frankly."

"Interesting you should ask. I've got a slot for an assistant coming up this fall—assuming they pick me up."

"I'm looking for work," Carter admitted.

"How's the knee?"

"It's good."

"You're going to get knocked around a bit," Jarrod warned. "It's cold, muddy, long days, lots of bruises. But the money's good. They're shooting in Iceland in September. You'd love it. Ever have *Brennivin?*"

Carter grinned. "A course of antibiotics cleared it right up."

"So you're good to travel. Fantastic. You know Pete's Chowder House?"

"Down at the harbor, right?"

"Yeah. Meet you there, say, one o'clock?"

"'Twill be done, my lord." Carter bowed again, back in character despite his modern garb. "And my lady."

Jarrod's bow was much more composed: haughty, sharp, and arrogant, as was the medieval persona he chose to portray at these sorts of things.

"Indeed," he said, "I look forward to it. My lady?" he extended his arm, and the two of them vanished into the milling crowd.

In his motel room on the edge of town, Jarrod changed out of his medieval getup.

He picked up his new rapier. It needed to be swung. Thrusted with. Parried. Shoved into a hanging side of beef. Or Renaldo, whichever was more convenient.

This was a custom job, to his own specifications. Heavier than most rapiers, nearly a medieval knight's sword with a cage for counterbalance, the blade afforded more powerful attacks and better control in *prise de fer,* plus the ability to chop bone, always a bonus.

He swung it around the room, slashed the air.

Amazing weapon. Kinetically majestic, with the gleaming branches and rings above the handle. A strong swordsman's fencing blade. Not an Olympic blade.

He stood before the mirror in his boxers, struck an en garde, and flexed.

Fuckin' Olympics.

More shadowy figures yelled at him in his head.

How close were you? Five matches away? Three?

Lookin' good, though. Gettin' it back.

He unflexed at a knock on the door.

Jarrod stood before the door and paused. The knock returned. With the rapier behind his back, he unlatched, braced, and then carefully opened the door.

Jarrod recognized Crius from earlier, but it took him a moment. It nagged at him that he'd been tailed.

"Excuse me, sire." Crius coughed into a handkerchief. "I must have a word with you."

"If this is about the fight, I don't really want to talk about it."

"Understandable," the man admitted, "but I need a champion, and quickly."

Invisible fanfares rang over Jarrod's shoulder. "A champion, huh?"

"Yes." He tucked his handkerchief away. "The compensation would be, at the least—"

The horns fizzled, and Jarrod bit his tongue and shook his head. "Uh-uh. Forget it, pal. 'The art of fencing is not a harlot to suffer itself to be sold.' I teach for money. I don't fight for money." And with a grimace, he started to close the door. "Ah—goodbye?" was his way of warning Crius to get his foot out of the door, or he stood to lose the better part of it. "Nice boots."

"Thank you. Please, may I speak with you?"

"You are speaking with me." Jarrod's fingers drummed on the rapier's grip as he earmarked a troubling list of attributes: the shaky hands and foreign mannerisms, the intricate design of his staff or for that matter of his boots (and who logs that many miles in period boots, he had to wonder), the odd cut of his doublet, and the ornate necklaces in plain view. This guy carried the authenticity kick way too far, and Jarrod took him for one of the fringe elements who lived in their garb.

"I'd like to come in," Crius said.

"Maybe, in a moment," Jarrod promised.

"Please, sir. We need a champion."

"We?" *We* stuck in Jarrod's head. "You were 'I' just a moment ago. Or is that a royal 'we?'"

"Well, in a way, I suppose," Crius admitted, stroking his goatee and looking away in thought.

"Yeah? We're done, here." And at that, Jarrod closed the door and threw the bolt.

He donned black drawstring hemp trousers, and was lacing up his hiking boots when the knock at the door returned, much louder this time.

Sighing, he snapped the door open. "Look, friend—"

Pain burst through the left half of Jarrod's head and the world dissolved in neon tangles.

Renaldo Salazar stepped into the room, and drove an elbow into Jarrod's throat, following it with what should have been a world-ending kick in the nuts that Jarrod sidestepped out of muscle memory.

A lifetime of fighting exploded through Jarrod and he spun on his heel with a handful of Renaldo's jacket, hurling him onto the credenza and collapsing it.

He couldn't breathe, his throat cramping, and he started to shake.

Windpipe. Windpipe.

Jarrod picked up the phone, watching Renaldo over his shoulder.

He felt pain, but it was miles away. It felt like the point of the boot had torn his hamstring. The concern was the tightening in his throat.

He punched buttons. **9— 1—**

His eyes traced the letters below the keypad. They became

words.

> **FOR AN OUTSIDE LINE: DIAL "9"**
> **THEN "0" + THE NUMBER.**
> **FOR LONG-DISTANCE, PLEASE DIAL "0"**
> **AND AN OPERATOR WILL ASSIST YOU.**

Jarrod slapped down the contacts on the cradle.

Focus.

His brain refused to comprehend anything except the flares that were now going up, screaming for air. Panic was setting in; he knew he had only moments before things started shutting down. And then, God help him.

9 — No, wait. . .

0?

9?

Renaldo was getting up.

Jarrod met Renaldo's skull with the phone, hurling it into the back of his head and shattering the plastic case, and fell back against the wall, wheezing. Melting.

Renaldo grabbed the corner of the bed, heaved, and righted himself like a tall ship in a storm.

And it was then that Jarrod saw the sword at Renaldo's side. A longsword, with about a foot of handle, and the same ornate, branched guard as his new rapier.

Renaldo began sliding the sword — and there was a lot of it — out of the scabbard. "Let's go. You and me."

"Yeah, real fair," rasped Jarrod.

As he lunged for his rapier, all the way across the room, something blew through the door. Something brown, holding something red.

The brown thing knocked Renaldo out with the red thing.

Jarrod stared emptily through the haze that was his eyesight as Renaldo lay sprawled on the floor, on his side, arms askew.

Crius harrumphed, and tossed a fire extinguisher on the bed. "Such foresight to keep these in every hallway."

"On my swordbelt," Jarrod squeaked. "Med kit. There's a . . ." he fought panic at the sound of his voice, ". . . trache tube. You gotta cut me." The neon wrigglers were coming back, purple and orange, crawling through the edges of his vision as he found himself on his knees. "Oh, fuck. Cut me, man. Trache me."

Crius stared at him in incomprehension. "I'll talk you through it," Jarrod rasped. "Get my med kit. Hurry. Oh, fuck. Oh, f—"

The room flared white and faded.

Carter awaited Jarrod and Siri in the coffee shop of Pete's Chowder House, just up the street from the weekend's madness.

He heard sirens, thought nothing of it, and sipped his coffee.

Carter remembered long conversations and many demonstrations with a young Jarrod, even ten years ago, when Jarrod Torrealday was a smirking little slip of a boy, still in high school but an A-grade fencer with a solid grounding in Judo.

Back when Carter had sparred with the young Jarrod, he'd felt like he was standing on ice. Everything he hated about fighting a *judoka* in the octagon, coming back to haunt him in thirty pounds of mail with a blade that flashed like thought. Terrifying. Not just swords, either. Spear, axe, knife. Immense talent. With something sharp and a suit of armor Jarrod could, quite literally, whip anybody in the world.

When the rules were off.

The strict regulations for historical armored combat had frustrated Jarrod, and he hadn't placed well in tournaments. He'd dropped out of the medieval re-enactor scene and went on to win a junior World Cup championship in saber. Saber rules, he could do.

A few years later, as an undergrad at Duke, Jarrod had attracted attention by insisting that medieval armored combat and Eastern martial arts shared common ground. This was now common knowledge, but at the time, it had been heresy.

His blog posts and videos—Judo-flipping and leg-sweeping in full 15th-Century field harnesses with swords—had snared the attention of a director in Hollywood who flew Jarrod out to advise for a television series whose fight sequences, once produced, had raised the ire of pretty much every professional fight choreographer in the world simultaneously before becoming the new standard.

The years that followed brought magazine interviews and movie consults, capped with a History Channel special and a move up to 16th in the world in saber.

To say Jarrod had a gift was an understatement. Hailed as the Bruce Lee of medieval combat, he was, more than any other man, responsible for the recent revival in historical European martial arts. The cover of Sports Illustrated had called him *The Deadliest Man Alive.*

Then, the kid's fall from grace: Jarrod's dismissal from the International Fencing Federation on his way to the U.S. Olympic team amidst world-rocking scandal. A rivalry in Paris—a stupid thing, an argument over a girl—had escalated into a duel and left a world-class *sabreur* dead in the cold rain of the Latin Quarter.

The trial, the acquittal; nonstop coverage. *The Jarrod Torrealday Story* ran twenty-four seven. Young, handsome, promising, lethal. The media loved hating him. Rumor had it he'd even been offered his own reality show as the underground dueling clubs cropped up across the world.

Jarrod had resurfaced in Greece a year later, consulting for a sword and sorcery film with a laughable budget. A TV tabloid found him at a nearby bar, raving drunk. The resulting interview still spawned memes for a man at rock bottom.

Fifteen years older, Carter could imagine what Jarrod had gone through. Jarrod had hit his peak at age twenty-six, and then tripped over it and fell off the far side. Long goddamned way down, too.

But good on him for the Isabella Barnes thing.

Carter knew Jarrod would rise again, and it would be entertaining to see how.

He himself had had several peaks. College ball at Penn, then three years with the Patriots, and a blown knee in the playoffs at about Jarrod's age. A Master's in medieval history and a private school teaching job, coaching varsity through his years of rehab, and then a pretty good tour in MMA until the knee went out again. He'd walked—well, limped—away from teaching to chase a TV career that never quite materialized—a few neo-gladiatorial TV shows, even a short professional wrestling stint—before cashing in and starting his gym.

And selling it. What a pain in the ass that whole thing had become. So much hard sell, so little training.

And now he had a small nest egg, a trusty diesel pickup, and renters in the house. Time to figure out the Next Thing.

Maybe Iceland with Jarrod Torrealday. Why the hell not?

He checked his watch. One-ten. *C'mon. Punctuality.*

More sirens. Something big was happening up the coast. He checked out the window, saw no smoke, and finished his coffee.

At one-twelve there was a tap on his shoulder.

"Parking trouble? Oh, uh," he stammered, realizing that it wasn't the person he thought it would be. "Hi."

It was one of the Renaissance guys, leaning on a staff. He needed a shower.

Carter eyed Crius up and down clinically, then guessed.

"Dave Grohl stars as the moody young Gascon?"

Crius stared in incomprehension.

Carter made the metal horns with one hand. "Dude."

Crius returned the sign feebly, staring at his own hand for a moment, first. "Doo-ood," he answered.

"Exactly," Carter said. "What's up?"

"Jarrod," said Crius.

"He'll be here in a minute," said Carter.

Crius grunted once, politely begging to differ. "No, he won't."

His tone had unaccountably melted into something Carter couldn't quite nail down as malice, but a stern, out-of-place, grave-sort-of-something Carter instinctively knew he shouldn't like. He shifted his weight uneasily around the booth.

"Why—uh—hmm. What makes you say that?" he leaned back a bit in feigned curiosity.

"Jarrod needs your help," said Crius, telepathically driving it home with such emphasis that Carter stood and pulled on his battered Patriots jacket before he even knew why he was getting upset.

Carter unfolded a fiver and left it on the table. "What is it? Renaldo?"

"Yes. Hurry."

Carter cracked his knuckles and his neck, shook life into his head. His voice was alive, his hands itching. "Let's go." He was already heading for the door.

Crius followed, having to move quickly to keep up with Carter's broad stride, and grabbed Carter's hand.

"Hey, none of that," Carter pulled his hand away and pushed the door open.

There was a moment of distress when his hand didn't find the door, punctuated by a heavy blow to the crown of his skull.

"Ow! Ffff—!" He doubled over, holding his head with both

hands and swearing. "What the hell?"

From between his forearms, he could see that he had stepped out of Pete's Chowder house into a tiny, stone room, with a large desk. Thick timbers crisscrossed the ceiling, vanishing into darkness above him. He'd hit his head on one. "What the *hell*?" he re-iterated.

A fire glowed in a fireplace, though it was daytime outside a nearby window. With a flick of Crius's hand, it grew into a blaze of white flames.

Carter's mind scrabbled for an explanation as his heart sledgehammered against his chest. The throbbing in his head was Thor's hammer, hurled at him from way down his family tree. He slammed air into his lungs, looking about for something to hit.

The door behind them opened, and a soldier in a long shirt of black mail with a short spear entered the room. He babbled in a language Carter didn't understand, looking back and forth between them as he spoke. He aimed the spear at Carter.

Carter stepped up to him, hands in the air, fingers spread, and then he grabbed the spear, twisted it free, and wrapped the guy up as it flipped away and clattered. They grappled, Carter noting that the man must have been built out of bricks under the mail, quick and solid, until Carter tripped him backwards and ran him back six steps, full-speed into the wall.

Carter stepped back and left the soldier on the floor, groaning.

Yeah, I bet that hurt.

Carter drove a deep breath out through the thumping in his skull. He did this again, and his hands stopped shaking, at which point he picked up the spear and took a step back.

The wood in his hands was dense, smooth, and dark. The head was triangular instead of flat, ensuring a slow-healing wound. Gorgeous work. "All right," he growled to Crius, "Explain."

"You're going to feel disoriented," said Crius. "You've just made quite a journey."

Carter glanced around again. "Oh, ya think? What is this?"

"There's no need to harm anyone."

"I'll decide that. Start talking." The guard stirred, and Carter threatened him with the spear. "Don't fucking move." He'd ripped a fingernail on the mail and it throbbed.

Crius continued, "You feel threatened, and I understand. I brought you here the way I did because you wouldn't have believed any of this otherwise."

Carter looked around the room, at the stone walls and timber beams, the raging fire, this grunge-rock wizard's insane sincerity, and the groaning guy on the floor. Who, to be fair, had given him a better fight than he'd expect from any LARP-er.

And this spear, he thought, looking at it again. Sweet Jesus.

Across the room, a glassless window showed an expanse of sky, cloudless, with a gentle magenta tint that he unconsciously tried to blink away. The sun beyond was far brighter, the breeze through the window far colder, than Maine had been.

Carter stared out the window, squinting at the odd light. A black-armored warrior on a black pegasus glided into view maybe a hundred yards out, wheeled, and leaped away again. He moved closer for another look.

It was—blinking again—definitely a pegasus.

The rider was out there doing steeplechase in the air, just playing around, in what appeared to be the winged-horse equivalent of burning donuts in the parking lot. Past the rider he saw a long, low castle wall with fat, squat towers, and an ocean of wide plains beyond.

A horn sounded in the distance.

Carter leaned the spear against the wall, then walked over and gave the soldier a hand up to his feet. "Apologize to him for me," he told Crius.

The soldier grumbled something as Carter brushed him off and clapped him on the upper arm in the universal sign for *good game*.

Behind the helmet, the soldier—or knight, or whatever he was—smiled and shook his head, saying something that Carter accepted as a compliment. Carter put out a hand, and the man shook it, his gloved hand around Carter's forearm.

"He says his name is Sir Dar, he's a knight, and he hopes that I brought you here to teach his men," said Crius.

Carter turned to Crius. "Well, funny you should mention it. I'm a pretty good coach and I'm looking for work."

"Yes. I saw you with your big sword, yesterday, teaching. We would like to extend an offer of employment to you."

With those words, Carter realized that he wasn't hearing in his ears what he was hearing in his head, but rather, it was as if the scruffy kid was playing a subtitled movie in his mind as he talked. He only noticed now that this had been going on since Pete's Chowder House.

It seemed there was going to be a lot to take in.

Carter pulled out the chair in front of Crius's desk, antique, soft leather, immensely comfortable, and settled in before the fire. Sir Dar took his spear, put his fist over his heart and bowed to Carter, and showed himself out.

"Let's talk," Carter said to Crius, "but slowly."

II

MINUET

"Never give a sword to a man who can't dance."
— Confucius

J arrod awoke to a chill.

He smelled candle smoke, with an underpinning of wet concrete and cedar. A basement smell. A woodshop smell. And distant incense.

It was cold.

Swearing silently through a yawn, he opened his eyes. A turn of his head yielded surprisingly less discomfort than he'd expected.

Jarrod looked up into the candlelit crags of a face, stubbly, the lines engraved with concern.

It took him a moment. It was a face he recognized, but certainly not one he'd expected. Carter's face.

"You awake?" the voice seemed to seep from all corners of the room.

Jarrod closed his eyes again, tried to speak. Someone had stolen his tongue and replaced it with a hunk of steel wool.

Carter handed him a ceramic chalice of cold water. Jarrod sat up a bit and nursed it.

The room was generous, lit by wide candles in stone sconces and done in early—very early, he noted—medieval decor. Rough stone walls, bare timbers overhead, and a stack of split fat logs and a pile of dried cow flop beside a glowing fireplace. A wooden floor that looked splintery. A wolfskin spread-eagled on the wall, replete with dried, eyeless head. Rustic and simple, yet somehow rich: beams and boards were well cared-for, the bedsheets were soft and the furs covering him were real and thick, and the lone tapestry—green with a gold skeleton key superimposed along a white square tower in its center—was fine silk, heavy and bright, that seemed to glow of its own accord.

It was quiet. Wind rustled the skin on the wall. The fire snapped occasionally. If he concentrated, he could hear the burbling of a brook over stones.

"You all right?" asked Carter.

Jarrod tried to sit up further. Carter helped him.

"Good Lord," Jarrod groaned, stretching with great effort and *ow*-ing repeatedly under his breath. "How long was I out?" *Days? Weeks?* No bedsores.

"Beats me," said Carter. "You were out when I got here."

He yawned again. "How long have you been here?"

Carter sipped at a ceramic stein of something foamy he'd had near his feet. "Three days."

Jarrod stretched his neck and leaned forward to grab his toes beneath the furs. His flexibility wasn't greatly compromised. He'd been well taken care of. "Bastard Renaldo," he griped. "Beat the shit out of me. Could've sworn he collapsed my windpipe. Did they cut me?" He reached his hand to his throat, expecting bandages, and finding none.

Carter's tone was resigned. "I don't know."

"Where's Siri?"

"I don't know. Not here."

"We've got to find her—Renaldo—"

Carter cut him off. "Forget Renaldo. This is you and me."

"O-o-okay," Jarrod blew out a long breath. "Where are we?"

Carter stood, went to the far wall, untied one leg of the wolfskin, and pulled it back to reveal a deep arrowslit set in a stone wall two feet thick.

Jarrod moved to the edge of the bed for a better look.

It was raining lightly against the outermost lip of the arrowslit, smudging any details of the curtain wall a hundred yards further and a hundred feet below.

They were very high in the tower.

Past the curtain wall, the skies were dark with rain above a hundred wooden roofs that sprawled down the hillside, oozing smoke from their chimneys. The outer wall of the town stood at the base of the hill, its towers, vaguely round, reduced to blurs in the mist.

The quiet was infectious, the rain a blanket on the world.

"Wow."

"The Castle of Regoth Ur," said Carter, "in Northern Gateskeep."

"Do we have cell service out here?"

"I doubt it."

"Help me up. Wow, it's cold."

Carter handed Jarrod a folded black shirt from the end of the bed, and helped him to his feet.

It was then that Jarrod noticed Carter's outfit, which consisted of a gray cable-knit sweater with laces at the neck; a black cape trimmed with dense silver fur he couldn't immediately identify; molasses-colored trousers that appeared to be suede, hand-stitched and stiff; and fine knee boots that laced up the front, the tops turned out to show a fur lining that matched his cape. Atop the sweater peeped the stiff, silver-embroidered collar of a black undertunic that looked to be either velvet or heavy silk, quite expensive, he guessed.

He hadn't given the getup much thought at first, because nearly every time he'd seen Carter had been at a Renaissance fair, Guild event, or movie set. He was acclimated to seeing Carter dressed like he'd just stepped out of formation with Hengist and Horsa.

Perhaps most intriguingly, over the sweater Carter wore a sword and matching dagger on an authentic baldric, the sword's scabbard in a silver-embossed frog that matched the piping on his collar.

The frog, essentially a sheath for a sheath, was one of the telling signs that an actor, re-enactor, or consultant knew what the hell he or she was doing.

A scabbard tucked under a belt holds a sword handle at an awkward angle and renders it nearly impossible to draw. A proper frog is adjustable and angles the weapon's handle forward exactly at hand height. It was a small detail, and Jarrod was a details guy.

Jarrod was *the* details guy.

He stood with some effort—he was disoriented and hungry but he felt strong, all things considered—and pulled on the long shirt over the undertunic. The long shirt was black and either rough silk or soft hemp, and several sizes too large. It sported the same embroidered-silver collar as Carter's undershirt. He began rolling up the sleeves from below his fingertips. "Nice sword."

The sword was wide and he could tell it was heavy even in the scabbard, maybe thirty inches of blade with just enough leather-wrapped handle for two hands. "Where'd you get that?"

Carter grinned an unstable grin. "You wouldn't believe it, man. We are *through* the looking glass."

"How so?"

Carter leaned against the wall. Jarrod rubbed his muscles all over, partially to limber up, partially to warm himself. The more he moved, the less he hurt.

The giant sipped at his beer. "Welcome to Gateskeep."

"What the hell is Gateskeep?" Jarrod asked, not kindly. *A bunch of Burning Man rejects have built a feudal-era commune in northern Maine. They'll probably make me king.*

"As far as I can tell, it's the northwestern country of a small continent. They call this their world, but the map I've seen looks like a continent. We're in the castle of Regoth Ur, a short ride from the northern sea and a half-day's ride from the palace, to hear them tell it." Jarrod stared at Carter from hands on knees, and caught a pair of woolen trousers, coarse and gray, as they were tossed to him. "Pump your brakes. Start again."

Carter's voice was inattentive. "I dunno. It's another world. I don't know how. Maybe you'll get it."

"Another world, huh? Wow, these are scratchy," Jarrod commented, turning the trousers over. "And long. Jesus. Are there any breeches or hose over there?"

Carter tossed him a set of silk breeches. "Candy-ass."

"Yeah, yeah, yeah. I need a belt."

Carter rifled through the pile of clothes and tossed him a padded leather belt. The tooling was intricate, the clasp silver, the lining velvet, and the best Jarrod could figure, it looked expensive. It all did.

Jarrod cast a sidelong, wary glance out the window as he cinched the pants tight. There were no belt loops, but a braided rawhide drawstring. He tied the strings and secured the belt around his waist, then rolled up the cuffs. "So, I have to ask," he started.

"Go ahead," said Carter.

Jarrod slowed in his motions as he tucked and buckled the belt over the tunic. "Is this a reality show?"

"Not as far as I know."

"Yeah, bullshit."

"No bullshit."

"Bull," he repeated, "shit." The words sounded strange off his tongue.

"Hey, look, I'm sorry. But what I'm told is that there's another—ah, Earthling—here. I don't know . . ."

As Carter's voice roved on, something tugged at the edges of Jarrod's perception, the shimmer of reality that signals the ruin of the dream of a lifetime.

"I don't understand a lot of it, but he's on their side. The other side. There's a war. Or there's going to be. They're asking for our enlistment."

"In a reality show."

"No."

"Seriously. Because I've got lawyers. Good ones."

"Jarrod," warned Carter.

"Okay, fine. Enlistment. What'd you say?"

"I said hell, yes."

Jarrod rubbed the bedpost with his thumb. "If you accepted, then there's got to be more." Carter wasn't stupid.

And there was the nagging ache, again. The more Carter spoke, the more things seemed to shimmer.

"There's a lot more. They'll explain. But look, would I miss this for anything? I'm forty-three years old and I still have roommates. They're paying us for this."

"How much?"

"A lot. They're paying in gold."

Jarrod drummed his fingers. "Ooh."

"Yeah. I mean, shit," Carter said. "Amy's long gone—"

"I didn't know that," Jarrod interrupted. "I'm sorry."

"It's fine," said Carter. "But I have nothing going on. Me, you, Iceland. Why not here?"

Jarrod looked around, again. "Where the fuck is here,

exactly?"

"Gateskeep," said Carter again.

"Yeah, you said that. So, chamber pot? Garderobe? What do we piss in in 'Gateskeep?'"

"Ah, no. There's a trapdoor beside that barrel. There's an aqueduct that feeds the tower."

The trapdoor opened with an ornate iron handle, and from beneath came the sound of the stream he'd been hearing.

Jarrod didn't know anybody in Hollywood smart enough to think of an aqueduct system, much less build it into a castle floor by floor. He turned his back to Carter and relieved himself as he formulated his next question.

"I'm only going to ask this once, and I want your best answer:

"Is this for real?" they chorused.

The giant nodded his head sternly. "As real as it has to be."

Jarrod sighed. "That doesn't help."

"I'm not being flippant. The last few days it's been clear." Carter pointed at the ceiling. "They have three moons. One big one, pink and purple, with a *ring*. It's like a dinner plate up there. You can see it in the daytime."

"Aliens?"

"Technically, I guess, but not that you'd know it. Humans, horses—they have pegasi cavalry, and I've heard that they have dragons, ogres, goblins, elves, the whole . . . you know."

"You're shitting me."

"No."

"Come on. You're bullshitting me. This is a reality show. It's got to be." He craned his neck around the room. "Goddamn pinhole cameras around here somewhere. Come on. I'll play along. Just tell me what we're getting paid for this. Where's my agent? *Saul!*" he yelled. "Hey, Saul!"

"It's not."

"You're smiling," said Jarrod.

"Of course I'm smiling," Carter grinned. "You will, too."

"I swear to God," said Jarrod, "I will kick your ass. Somehow."

"I've been here three days, and I've had a pretty good look around. This is a working castle. It houses probably a hundred people. And everything works. I mean, the way it should. The nobles don't do the dishes. There is not a cigarette butt, or a beer can, anywhere." He ticked off on his fingers, "No canned food. No sugar. No plastic. No stainless steel. Everything in this castle is built by hand."

Jarrod looked out at the rooftops stretching into the mist. "What's with the city out there?"

"I don't know if I'd call it a city," said Carter. "But there's a good-sized village right outside the castle walls. These guys have a working feudal system. A whole country—a couple of 'em."

A thin layer of ice caked the surface of the water in a barrel next to the trapdoor. Jarrod broke it with the heel of his fist and washed his hands, then leaned close and drenched his face and hair and scrubbed vigorously, shivering and groaning at the cold. He pulled the shirt from his trousers and wiped his face with the tails.

"Countries," he grumbled, tucking the shirt in again. "Feudal constitutionalism, or are we still grinding along under privatized rule?"

"They're a lot more civilized about it than we were," Carter admitted. "Administration, standing armies, but there's a lot of friction between the crown and the estates, mostly a communication issue, the way I see it. Castles, petty lords. There's a king and a bloodline hierarchy, but the big decisions are made by guys appointed by the local lords to various councils that advise the royals. They have a War Council, a Trade Council, a Farms Council. You get the idea."

"Okay. Does it work?"

"Hell if I know. What I see is a pair of rudimentary nation-states, vastly overextended from their seats of power and with no hard borders. They're on the ragged edge of administrative collapse, and the outlying lands are in chaos."

"Big fun. Is there a church in all this?"

"I don't think so. Probably not, which would explain why it's so factious. Keep in mind," Carter said, sipping at his beer, "I've only been here a few days. The beer's good, though."

"That'll help," muttered Jarrod. "Though I doubt I'm up to date on all my shots."

"These guys are pretty clean," Carter assured him. "Not fastidious, but they bathe. Most of them, daily. They clip their nails, cut their hair, brush their teeth. The dogs are housebroken."

"That's handy."

"They seem to live pretty long, too. There are some seriously old dudes around here. Some of them have got to be pushing eighty. Maybe a hundred and eighty. Who knows?"

"We should be so lucky," Jarrod sighed. "I assume, from your trappings—" he motioned, "—they gave you some sort of honorary rank? A social standing?"

"Yeah. Chancellor."

"Which is?"

"As best I can gather, it's equivalent to a knight, more or less. It's not a martial rank, though. Non-landholding nobility. They call it a 'palace lord.' Not sure if that's a good thing or a bad thing, yet."

Jarrod grunted, and fought his way into a thick gray sweater-tunic like Carter's that was woven tightly and scratched his neck. He pulled the collar of the undertunic through it. "Nobility," he echoed. "So there's a class system? Caste system?"

"They have a robust working class," Carter said. "There's no mass production, so it's all artisans. The merchant class is better off than they are. There's a trade society, too, and some of them are rich enough to buy their own nobility. A couple of the merchant families have as much power as the royalty. Think of the Medicis, the Welsers. Patricians."

"Interesting."

"Very. You, they may knight," Carter supposed. "All you'd have to do is show 'em what you got. I bet they'd knight you in a minute."

Jarrod grinned inwardly at the praise, but tried to remain as stern and businesslike as he could manage. "And this is not a reality show?"

Carter wiped his forehead. "Jarrod."

"Okay, fine. Did they bring my rapier?"

"Yes."

"Where is it?"

"I don't know. I'm sure it's safe. We'll get it."

"Let me see that," Jarrod motioned to the sword at Carter's side.

Carter cleared the blade from its scabbard and handed it to Jarrod. "Everyone carries these in the castle. It's a standard design, but they're still not mass-produced."

Jarrod could see the weld lines in the firelight, the spine made from twisted iron bands hammered into a herringbone pattern with steel edges. Gorgeous.

Heavy damned sword, though.

"Armor?"

Carter spent the next few minutes running down the weaponry and armors he'd seen about. Jarrod winced at Carter's estimation of the technology as comparable to the Late Dark Ages in Europe: axes, spears, and mail armor augmented with iron and leather seemed the outfit of the typical soldier. The officers were better-equipped and the knights, better still. Distinct from medieval *chevaliers* in grandeur and function, and observedly distant from the concept of chivalry as Carter knew it, the knights of the royal orders were an elite contingent proficient in weapons and field tactics, trained-from-birth killers who pledged their lives to the king. Carter had mixed it up with one on his first day, wooden weapons and leather helmets, and was quite impressed.

"You didn't try him with your greatsword," Jarrod assumed.

"Ah, no."

Jarrod tried a few cuts through the air with the sword and flipped it around in his hand a few times. The piece, while functional and well-balanced, was heavy for its size and not entirely historically accurate. The wide blade shouldered out at the crossguard, with a deep fuller for half its length that lent it considerable forward momentum. It was a hack-and-smasher, built to break armor, or break a man inside his armor.

"Yeah, that's a beast, all right. What about shields?"

"I'm seeing center-held roundshields and some teardrops, great big ones. Not a lot of finesse, either. They're real crash and bashers. The swords are secondary. They mainly use spears and axes. The knights use swords, but they've had a lot more training than the grunts."

Jarrod stood five feet seven inches tall, and in fighting trim weighed in at just under a hundred and fifty pounds. "Yeah, how big are these guys?"

"Big," Carter admitted. "The knights, especially. I'd guess that the nobility has more meat in their diets. I'm seeing knights six feet, six-two. Big, wide guys. Lots of power. Some of the women in the lists are about your size, but, ah . . . I mean . . ."

"Women?"

Carter nodded slowly, quietly.

Jarrod looked up from the sword at the sudden silence. "Women fighters?"

The giant only smiled. A slow, broad smile.

It was infectious. "Oh, man, sign me up," Jarrod begged.

"Sign yourself up. Here," Carter handed Jarrod his boots.

Jarrod was thankful that someone had taken the care to bring not only his blade, but his boots, which were sturdy, leather-and Gore-Tex hikers. There was a practicality to the choice, a horse-sense that, to Jarrod, resonated with a medieval mind-set and further cemented the reality he was finding around him. "C'mon," said Carter. "I'm starving."

"Yeah, me, too." He rolled the words off his tongue. *Me, too. Me, too . . .*

It jarred Jarrod like few things ever had. A revelation that slammed him on the head nearly hard enough to knock his fillings out. The room spun.

Carter steadied him. "You okay?"

Jarrod stammered with a few awkward phrases, quietly, at first. What he was hearing in his skull were clicks and pops and nasal, alien vowels. His tongue was doing backflips in his head.

"Jarrod?" Carter asked again, looking into his eyes with considerable concern. "You okay?"

Jarrod shook his head, tangled hair falling from his hands in incomprehension. "Carter—"

"Yes?"

Only it wasn't *'yes'*. Not quite. A terse word, an acknowledgment. But what Jarrod heard was sure as hell not, *'Yes.'*

"We're not speaking English."

The Lords' Hall was nearly empty. It was between mealtimes, and Carter assumed the time by his best guess to be about two in the afternoon.

Quick math brought Jarrod an answer of fourteen stone

tables, each capable of seating probably a dozen people if they refrained from wild gesticulation. An old man in fine purple and black clothes sat at the end of a table alone, reading a letter and slurping soup from a wooden bowl and spoon. A boy in dirty clothes and two girls in simple dresses and aprons cleaned tables, and a pair of even dirtier boys stacked logs with some commotion by a wall-length fire pit. Coals glowed like a forge, blasting welcome warmth halfway across the room.

Carter led him back to the kitchens.

"Is it cool to just go back there?" Jarrod asked. The word he'd unwittingly substituted for *cool* didn't quite have the connotation he'd wanted, becoming instead more of an *allowed,* but his usage had less of a stern inflection, and a bit more spark to it. A raw language, brimming with barked profanities and innuendo.

The cook was a round woman of indeterminate age, in an unremarkable dress with a long blonde braid and a kerchief to hold her hair back. She had a cheerful smile, and greeted Carter with a curtsey. He bowed, as did Jarrod.

"Back again, eh?" she giggled. "I'll have some dandy ready in a moment. You know where the food is," she assumed, and went about grinding what Jarrod swore were coffee beans. They certainly smelled like coffee beans.

"Where did she get coffee beans?" he asked under his breath. Carter sliced and gutted a large yellow potato thing and ladled it full of gloriously thick stew. He handed it to Jarrod, along with an ornate wooden spoon, licking his fingers.

"Mmm, damn, that's good."

"You're not afraid of that?" Jarrod asked.

"I once ate a sandwich I found in a drawer."

Jarrod stuck his finger in the stew, wondering how long it had been sitting out, whether the meat was tainted, and what else was in there. There wasn't a refrigerator in sight, and he'd come down with strange things around the world by accepting food on the advice of his stomach instead of his brain.

The stew was hot enough to likely be sterile and smelled of alien spices and garlic. Lots of garlic. "Carter . . . the coffee?"

Carter made a point of stopping everything else he was doing. "I don't know. I didn't ask."

"Okay, I'll ask."

"Don't ask."

"Why?"

"Because it's rude. And you'll draw attention to yourself."

"Carter, there is no coffee anyplace this cold. Coffee doesn't grow in places this cold. Chicory, I'd believe."

"Dandelions," the cook replied from behind them. Though plump, she had a nimble footstep. "Roasted dandelion root," she admitted. "We call it dandy. Do you like it?"

"It smells . . . like something from our homeland that I'm very fond of," said Jarrod.

She smiled again, all dimples and motherly manners. "I took it you two were foreigners."

Jarrod rubbed his stubbly chin. "Ah, you could say that, yes. Forgive us our mannerisms, my lady."

Carter made himself a potato-bowl of stew similar to Jarrod's, and they took a seat at a near table.

Jarrod tore at the potato, which was sweet and slightly carrot-y. Carter could see the younger man's hands shaking, and put his own hand on Jarrod's wrist to steady it.

"I'm scared," Jarrod told his stew.

"It's okay, man. Hell, I *freaked*."

"Why us?"

Carter again made a point of stopping what he was doing.

"Why not you? What I've been asking myself for the past few days is, why *me?*"

Jarrod attacked his food, which was hot, oily, and heady with thyme and garlic and something he couldn't remember the name of that reminded him of Turkish coffee. The meat was stringy with a slight organ flavor—venison of some type. He was halfway through when the cook brought him a plate piled high with fried vegetable nests drizzled in butter and honey, and a cup of the dandelion-root tea. When his food was gone, Jarrod drained his tea—which was so like coffee that it could have been coffee, replete with cream and sweetener—and picked grounds from his teeth.

"You better?" asked Carter.

"I'll make it," Jarrod pushed himself away from the table.

"You want a beer? You've got to try the beer. They'll put a brewer in jail here for making bad beer."

"Good," said Jarrod. "But no beer, yet. I want to go talk to somebody and I want to be sober."

"Yeah, okay." Carter whistled, waking three large brindle bulldogs near the firepit. He set their plates on the floor, and one of the dogs lumbered up and trotted over. They left as the dogs took to their job.

Jarrod stood in the doorway, watching as the dogs mopped up the mess, and Carter clapped Jarrod on the back. "It's gonna be okay. I think you're gonna love this."

Carter pushed open the door. "Jarrod, this is Master Crius Lotavaugus, Lord High Sorcerer of Gateskeep."

Crius stood behind his desk and threw up the rock sign with grave formality. "Dude," he announced sagely.

"Roll with it," Carter advised, before Jarrod could even turn to ask.

Jarrod shook his head with a disbelieving smile. "We've met." He dropped to one knee with a flourish. "Sir, I owe you an apology for my rudeness and a tremendous debt for my life."

"An apology is hardly necessary," said Crius. "Your refusal to lease me your sword arm distinguishes you as a man of honor. Arise, sir."

Jarrod rose with the elation of a batter who's watched his line drive bounce off the foul pole into the left-field bleachers.

"Please, be seated. Are you well?"

"Thank you, sir," said Jarrod, sitting in a chair before Crius's desk. "I'm very well. Whoever healed me did fine work."

"Do you wish the Chancellor to stay?"

Jarrod looked behind himself. "Chancel—oh. Yeah. Yes. Please. Carter?"

Carter hulked by the door like an oversized palace guard. "Right here."

"Jarrod Torrealday," Crius knew his last name, and Jarrod could only assume he had been speaking with Carter at length. "Lord of . . .?"

"Knightsbridge," Jarrod answered. *Knightsbridge* was the name of his family estate in Connecticut. "My father would, uh, be Lord of Knightsbridge."

"Jarrod, Son-Lord of Knightsbridge."

Suddenly, irresponsibly, overwhelmingly, Jarrod wanted this gig.

He longed to tell Crius of his schooling at the *Academie d'Espée*, Paris; and at the Royal College of Arms in Cambridge; and of his junior World Cup saber title; and his black belt in Judo.

But he knew he wouldn't have to. The job was his. All his qualifications would come through revelation, as he moved across this, his Disneyland, like a hurricane.

"What we have—why you're here," Crius began, slouching back in his chair, "is the result of a most unfortunate turn of events. Unfortunate for our kingdom, mind you; not necessarily for you.

"This is—we are—the Kingdom of Gateskeep. How much has the Chancellor told you?"

Jarrod wanted the whole damned thing to buttress Carter's claims. "Not a lot. How far back can you begin?"

The sorcerer bit his lip in thought, scooted his chair around, leaned forward a bit, and sighed.

"Long ago, a race of beings—we called them The Demons—came to us. They had done what we had never done, what we had never allowed ourselves. They had developed, from our water wheels and fires, what came to be known as the New Magic. They knew, or claimed to have learned, why trees grow, why fires burn. They could create fire—any of them—with tools they all carried. They had tools to kill, tools to take the place of maps, tools for mounts, tools for light. Not unlike what I've seen of your world.

"The danger, we realized from the inception of our allegiance with The Demons, was that of power without discipline. Any fool among them could create fire, which we all know is the most dangerous element in existence. Similarly, any madman of their ranks could kill. Effortlessly. They had cast out their gods and taken their salvation into their own hands.

"This was The New Magic. The Demons' Way.

"Here, we train our strongest minds to bend the will of the Universe. We become the sorcerers and the healers. Understand, there is a tremendous amount of discipline a sorcerer must undergo. To inflict harm, to create malignancy in any form, is forbidden. It is schooled out through the rigors of instruction.

"The threat we sorcerers foresaw in the Demons' Way was similar to that of lit torches in the hands of children."

Jarrod found his mouth dry.

"A war erupted over the importance of this deliverance. So great was this war that the Demons themselves finally stepped in to make amends. Those of us favoring a life of technology for their descendants—to be trained in The New Magic—would be taken to your world, a sister world."

Jarrod took the moment of quiet to poke the anthill. "Earth, right? Is that why we speak your language?"

The sorcerer smiled. "Our language was taught to you by a particularly gifted sorcerer—a telepath—while you rested."

"The same guy is tutoring me, Jarrod," interrupted Carter. "You wouldn't believe how fast you can pick up a language when your teacher's telepathic."

Crius smiled again. "And though I would observe that you speak quite well, your command of our language will increase if you choose to study further, and you'll become more familiar with our language the longer you stay. As it is, you'll make do."

"Carter said something about ogres, goblins . . ."

"Yes. The *gbatu.*"

Jarrod found that the word brought a crawling prickle up his spine and a childish hatred of shadows. "What's a gbatu? And shit, that's hard to say." The *g* was a ghost; a glottal stop before the *b*. The name felt practically vomited. On top of that, the word *gbatu* he somehow associated with fear of the dark.

"Gbatu are the lesser races."

"Lesser? That's not really a word we use where I come from."

"Less than human, more than animal. Some are common, some are rare. Some were . . . mistakes."

"Jesus."

"You are here because it was learned by our intelligence organizations that the Gavrians—"

"Gavrians?"

Crius held up a finger to freeze the conversation, and, reaching behind his desk, picked up a wide scroll which he unrolled across his desk. Jarrod saw it was a large, intensely detailed map.

Carter was right; it was a continent. The countries— kingdoms, regions, whatever they were—were not delineated with drawn borders. Most of the towns and cities, he noted immediately, lay along rivers.

Aqueducts. Plumbing. Fresh water.

Civilization.

"You are here. The castle of Regoth Ur, in the Gateskeep Northlands. To the north of us lie The Wilds, and beyond the sea lies Ice Isle, our northern principality, ruled by Prince Damon."

"To the east is Falconsrealm," said Crius, "also our principality."

Falconsrealm, Jarrod noted, was a snarl of geologic badassery where several mountain ranges came together and upthrust. Falconsrealm was isolated, lightly-populated, and a real bitch to reach from its mother country.

Ripe for the picking.

"Falconsrealm is ruled by Princess Adielle, heir to the throne of Gateskeep, eldest child of King Rorthos and Queen Adrassi. They're Riongoran-Thurdins."

"I should probably be writing this down," Jarrod mused.

"These are the Shieldlands," said Crius, pointing to a wide, flat plain dotted with towers and villages, below Falconsrealm. "We fight Gavria for it about once a generation or so."

"Who rules those?"

"Those are the border lords I was telling you about," Carter interjected. "It's the Wild West out there."

"South, but yes," Crius nodded to Carter and continued. "The lords of the Shieldlands are sworn to Gateskeep. Our beloved king lives in The City of the Gate, at Gateskeep Palace, here." He struck the map lightly with his index finger. Gateskeep Palace was a hand's length across the map from Regoth Ur, bumped up against a line of mountains.

"South of the Shieldlands is Gavria, our southern neighbor. Most of Gavria is mountains and arid lands. Gavria has mines, so they trade with us: gold, iron, salt."

Jarrod interjected, "Iron and gold? Dear God, what's their military like?"

Crius nodded slowly. "Their armies are vast. Professional. Armed to their balls. We've been fearing war. Moreso, now, with a spate of recent developments."

"And these new, uh, developments, involve us."

"They do."

Jarrod felt like interlacing his fingers behind his head and kicking his feet up on the desk, but refrained. "Let's have it."

"There has been a recent appointment to the Gavrian Parliament. He's one of yours."

"Mine?"

"From Earth," said Carter.

"Yes," agreed Crius, "and blood son of one of the most black-souled malefactors to ever walk this world."

Jarrod gave that what he deemed an appropriate span of respectful silence. "I," he said quietly and with deliberation, "am going to want every last detail."

"Four hundred years ago, his father, a sorcerer of tremendous power, seized the throne of Gavria. He is still renowned as the most powerful sorcerer who has ever lived.

"He didn't hold the throne long. He and his entire family — wives, children — were put to death. Gavria wanted an end to the bloodline. Gavrian forces tore down his palace and his lands fell to ruin, swallowed by the Eastern Freehold.

"Legend has it — and we now know it to be true — that one wife, bearing an unborn son, escaped to your world, with much of the family fortune. She wasn't pursued, for your world is in the psychic backwaters of the universe and the forces of magic don't flow easily there."

"Four hundred years ago."

"For us. Far shorter, we fear, for your world. The dread son is of Carter's approximate age. A native of your country, of the metropolis of—wait—New York, yes?"

"New York," Jarrod confirmed. The word was a spear of daylight. "So, what, then? She learned English? Got a day job? Sent him to parochial school? Come on."

Carter shrugged. "Hey, it's been known to happen. Land of opportunity."

Jarrod put his head in his hands. "And he's from New York. Tell me he's no one I know."

"I can't answer that. We do know that he returned to his father's lands twelve years ago, and he has proven most enterprising. He has built a magnificent palace on the ruins of the last and has amassed a considerable fortune. He's quite brilliant in the ways of commerce."

"Most of us are," Jarrod admitted, omitting *compared to you, I'm sure.*

"His country is Ulorak," Crius tapped the map, showing a high country ringed with mountains in the northeast corner of Gavria. "They declared themselves sovereign from the Eastern Freehold some years back. He is King Sabbaghian the Silver."

"King," grumbled Jarrod.

"And sorcerer. He would have possessed limited powers in your world, but here his magic would be amplified a hundred times. By all reports, he is many times the sorcerer I am."

Jarrod looked back at Carter. "Oh, that's great," he breathed. Carter only nodded. "Anything else?" Jarrod asked.

"Ulorak has recently become a Gavrian protectorate, and King Sabbaghian is now *Lord* Sabbaghian, High Sorcerer of Gavria."

"Gavria, your neighbor whom you think is preparing for war. The guys with all the iron and gold."

"With the appointment comes a seat on the Gavrian War Council."

Jarrod shifted in his seat. Princesses. Monsters. Rising

Joseph Malik

armies. Exiled sons of evil sorcerers returning to claim dark thrones.

"And you want us to, what? Stop him? Kill him?" It didn't sound as convincing as he'd hoped it would.

"Counter him," said Crius. "We know nothing of his patterns and processes. Our greatest fear, of course, is that of power without discipline. Our sorcerers don't kill—even Gavria's—we're trained not to. We use sorcerers in battle, but to control the elements, frighten the horses, raise rivers," he recalled something untold with a fond smile for a moment, "and suchlike. This man lacks internal controls. But more to the point, we have no idea what he might do. You'd be advisers here. Carter, at court, and you, Jarrod, on the field."

Jarrod licked his lips and braved, "Isn't that backwards?" he jerked a thumb at Carter, "He fights for a living. I just teach."

"I have seen you fight. You are our choice."

"That wasn't much of a fight," Jarrod admitted.

"And what impressed me, quite frankly, was not just your ability with a blade, but that you displayed fairness and integrity, and in victory you showed decency and restraint. Carter has assured me that you are one of your homeland's greatest swordsmen, and that you were recently chosen to champion your entire nation. I have no doubt that you will make an exceptional advisor."

"We'll see," said Jarrod. "What's involved?"

"For you? Admission into a royal order."

"You mean knighthood?"

"Not quite. We have a specific rank for those who have been accepted into an order on merit of arms. You'll be a 'rider' for the order, a knight without lands. The title of rider is normally given by a knight officer for heroism on the battlefield, or skill at arms in a tournament. It can also be awarded directly from the king himself. This will be your case; you'll be a King's Rider."

"I don't, um, ride particularly well."

"It's only a title," Crius assured him. "You'll study hard under a patient knight, and be his sergeant so that you may learn our tactics, our weapons, our strategies—and help us understand your own, of course—and in a year, perhaps sooner, you will receive full knighthood and with it, a commission. Once you're commissioned, should necessity arise, you'll be on the field, commanding. The crown equips you with everything you need. Weapons, squires, a handsome spending allowance—"

"White horse, shiny armor?"

"Our armor is black, and our finest warhorses, as well. But we can arrange the other marks of your station—inclusion in a royal order, eventual rank and knighthood, and the adulation of beautiful maidens everywhere.

"After the threat has been neutralized, if you wish to remain, we can discuss a court appointment or a charge of land. You will be welcome to stay as long as it suits you."

Jarrod wrestled with a breaking smile.

It was hard to remain seated, so he took a knee. His legs quivered as he bowed his head and put his fist on his heart. "I owe you my life. But there are, um, difficulties, involved here. I have responsibilities back home."

"Such as?"

An uncomfortable pause followed as Jarrod received a rare, bird's-eye glimpse of the universe and his place in it.

Responsibilities wasn't a word he normally associated with himself. He'd spent his twentieth summer alone in the Utah desert "seeking perfection through the art of the sword." All he could really attribute to himself was a healthy trust fund and a recent history of waking up drunk somewhere in Europe.

Further, his responsibility to the next six months' made-for-Canadian-TV fight sequences seemed to collapse under its ostentatiousness like a giant sculpture made of Cheez Whiz. And it occurred to him that he hadn't yet even found a space for his fencing school.

Crius sensed his hesitation. "You have your own lordship at home. I understand. If, after your oath is fulfilled, you wish to split your time between your world and ours, we can arrange that, too."

"You can do that?"

"Once you're a lord here, you'd have your castle and lands, and your own sorcerers on retainer. We'll just make sure we assign you one who can make it happen."

"Could I go home for a few days and square away my affairs, maybe grab a few things?"

"Yeah, me, too," said Carter quickly.

"Of course."

"Where do I sign?"

From behind his desk, Crius produced Jarrod's new rapier in its scabbard. "There's nothing to sign. You'll need this, I assume."

With a wide grin, Jarrod stood and accepted the weapon and fastened the belt around his waist. He drew it partway, pressed his thumb down on the edge, and squeezed a trickle of blood into his hand, then stuck it out. Crius shook it.

Carter drew his own sword and did the same, shaking hands with them both.

Jarrod said to Crius, "I want a tour of the castle. Also, I need to see your forge." He motioned to Carter. "I want to meet the guy who made that sword. And Carter, I'll take that beer now."

Ending and starting a life simultaneously.

Jarrod disabled his Facebook and set his email accounts to auto-respond: A one-year gig in Europe, last minute. Working under an NDA. Direct all professional correspondence to Saul Scheinberg, Esq.

A long conversation with Saul Scheinberg, Esq., involving copious and bilateral use of the word *frankly*. The trust would pay the mortgage and insurance on his cottage in Connecticut. Saul would also contact the motel regarding a series of strident voicemails about a bill being refused by Visa as "suspiciously excessive."

He leaned back in his desk chair and ran through everything he needed to do, scribbling notes, punching out the occasional email.

Fencing students can pick up with Brandt Buxton over in Hartford, but goddammit Brandt, I want 'em back in 12 months. Recommend somebody to take the Iceland gig. Somebody who's not Brandt. Empty the fridge. Shut off the gas. Pawn the damned cat off to my sister at Trinity. Call the alarm company. Get the Audi towed back here. Garage it and drain the fluids.

Get a dental checkup. Just to be sure. No goddamn way are they coming at me with pliers and brandy.

Get a tetanus booster.

Call Siri. Explain. Somehow.

And then . . .

Pack.

The tour of the castle had given him some idea of the local fashions and level of warfighting technology. The visit to the forge had cemented his resolve to go home and get his own gear.

The smiths had a pretty good grasp on how to produce steel, that infinitesimal and oh-so-magic Goldilocks zone of carbonization between malleable wrought iron and brittle cast iron. He'd seen charcoal-packed iron slowly baking in ovens and bars of cooled blister steel in the smithy, and knew everything he needed to know: simple shear steel.

The shear steel process made good steel hideously expensive

and the realm of only the most elite smiths, who kept their processes of quenching and annealing as secret recipes to retain a competitive edge.

Because of this, the quality of any steel he'd find in Gateskeep would be hit-and-miss, and some of what they called steel would probably be iron of one type or another. There was really no way for anyone less than a materials scientist to tell how good a smith's sword was until it either shattered, bent, or successfully took off a hand.

No, thank you.

He'd asked the smith a couple of quick questions describing a Bessemer-type blast furnace and might as well have been asking the guy to align the front end on his Audi.

Never mind. I thought you were somebody else.

A fifty-gallon military-grade rolling footlocker, waterproof with oversized wheels and a locking lid, would be his arming trunk. It had accompanied him around the world; it would accompany him to another. He spent an hour scraping and clipping baggage claim tags and stickers.

He intended to stack the deck as egregiously as he could in his favor, and as a professional Medieval weapons expert he was one of maybe a thousand men in the world with the hardware hanging in his living room to do it.

The swords and daggers on his wall array and in his arms locker were not props, nor stainless steel wall-hangers bought in some tobacco shop at a mall. Jarrod's weapons were immaculately-balanced artisanal killing tools and works of 21st-Century metallurgical genius.

From his wall, his centerpiece: a four-foot greatsword, technically a *gran espée de guerre*, a broad-shouldered, gleaming, deadly son of a bitch with a spatulate tip and a robust edge designed to shatter bones under any mail it might not cleave. At just over three pounds, a two-handed blow with it would split an unarmored human being in half, and a blow to an iron helmet would leave a man playing with blocks and making goo-goo noises for the rest of his life. The sword was so large overall that its burnished leather scabbard had an integrated baldric designed to either hang off his shoulder or buckle around his waist.

His second choice was the closest thing in his arsenal to what they'd be packing in Gateskeep: a reproduction of an 11th-Century single-handed arming sword with a long blade, a stippled and filigreed handle and crossbar, and an ornate ring pommel. Light and agile, its subtle taper and forward balance made it a smash-and-cutter like the *gran espée de guerre*. Unlike his big war sword, the edge was razor-honed for use against a man in light armor or none at all. The stippling and filigree ensured a good grip in a leather glove, or in a sweaty — or bloody — hand. An edge sharpened to such a degree would part a silk scarf with a slash, but would roll over if struck against plates of iron. It would be his sidearm.

He threw an assortment of plastic training weapons, plus a couple of daggers and a set of brass knuckles, into the big trunk, then put two more swords into a locking rifle case.

Two roundshields; one big, one small. A third — a full-body teardrop — for the hell of it.

Armor was tough.

A house decorated with suits of armor on half-mannequins and nothing exactly right; everything from a muscled Greek cuirass to black-and-red fantasy leather with fluted dragon scales, even a custom 15th-Century man-at-arms harness, fully-articulated in engraved case-hardened steel, breathtaking in its detail and painstakingly fitted to him at no small expense.

Half a morning staring at armor, cup after cup of coffee growing cold in his hand.

He packed several layers of armor.

He stuffed a leather and canvas pack with clothing that

looked more or less nondescript, ripping the tags.

An entire overnight bag crammed with medical gear. What little camping gear he owned. An oilskin Stetson. A big, leather-bound, steel flask of bourbon. Two thick blank books and several pencils. Translations of manuals of arms with lots of pictures; something to talk about with the other jocks.

He'd had a pair of bespoke cigar-colored leather trousers made in Italy. He showered, scrubbing till his skin was red, and dressed in the leather pants, a long-sleeved polypro undershirt, and a black cashmere turtleneck.

He ordered two grinders from a place up the street and ate both over the rest of the afternoon, swearing, unpacking, looking at things again, and repacking.

And last, in a locked waterproof plastic case, a four-inch Springfield XD in 9mm with tritium night sights, a paddle holster, and two nineteen-round magazines of 147-grain Federal HST hollowpoints. An ugly, blocky little gun and even uglier bullets, designed to expand under hydrostatic pressure into six-pointed claws the diameter of dimes. They would leave immense wound channels and blow skulls wide open. *When all else fails.*

He threw in two boxes of 124-grain FMJ hardball because he had it.

He hoped to hell he wouldn't have to shoot a hundred and thirty-eight people.

He secured the trunk and the rifle case with heavy-duty Master padlocks and secured the keys to everything around his neck with a length of paracord. He fed a second set of keys onto a split ring in a pouch on the arming sword's belt.

Jarrod was sitting on the footlocker, the *gran espée de guerre* over one shoulder, chasing the second grinder with a big glass of bourbon and ice—last meal, after all—when his doorbell rang. He answered it to find Crius Lotavaugus standing in the rain.

"Please come in," Jarrod said.

Crius entered and took a look around. His eye fell on the man-at-arms harness, still on its mannequin, and he strode over to it. "This is spectacular. Is it steel? It's steel."

"It's steel," said Jarrod, omitting any mention of case hardening and high-strength alloy as much as he wanted to gush about the suit's metallurgy. "Will I need that?"

"Let's hope not."

Jarrod dropped ice cubes into two glasses and poured three fingers of rye into each. "Do you want to go through my gear?" he asked as he handed one glass to Crius, "I want to make sure I'm not, uh, cheating. Somehow." The words sounded stupid out loud.

"You're facing the greatest sorcerer our world has ever known," said Crius. "There is no cheating."

"I'll hold you to that," said Jarrod.

Crius sipped at the rye. His eyebrows rose and he saluted Jarrod with the glass, swallowing hard.

He was looking at a wall of framed pictures of Jarrod: accepting a fencing trophy before a huge crowd; delivering a spectacular kick in a *savate* ring; young and beardless, holding a Golden Gloves belt with his face beaten all to hell; smiling with his friends in armor; and a few framed magazine covers including a collage of teen tabloids featuring Jarrod with a starlet he'd been dating at the time. Crius spent a long time staring at a framed *Sports Illustrated* cover with Jarrod's face beside the handle of a sword.

Crius swished the rye around his mouth slowly, smiling. He motioned to the *Sports Illustrated* cover. "What does it say?"

Jarrod clenched his teeth. He'd been toying with taking that fucking thing down for two years, now. "It calls me 'The Deadliest Man Alive.'"

"Are you?"

"Arguably."

Crius nodded and took another sip. "Good," he decided.

"Bring what you think you'll need," said Crius, finishing his drink. "And if something remains here that you require, we can always send you back for it."

Jarrod downed his drink. "I'll hold you to that as well."

"As you should."

Jarrod took his glass.

"Are you ready, Son-Lord Knightsbridge, King's Rider of the Order of the Stallion of Gateskeep?"

Jarrod slipped the bottle of rye into his pack and lashed down the top, and wondered with ice in his gut what Carter was bringing.

"I'll never know."

III

FUGUE

"It is of the highest importance to know how to wrestle, since this often accompanies combat on foot."
— Baldassare Castiglione, 1528

"Crius, you're jesting!" the knight cried from the next room. "Me?"

Jarrod listened intently. It sounded as if the knight had a good argument going. "You know of my track record with sergeants. If he's of any value to you . . ."

Three pages loudly set Jarrod's arming trunk, shields, and duffel down in a room across the hall, and nodded as they headed out.

And Crius's rebuttal: "He's to aspire to knighthood, and command. His Majesty has admitted him to the Order of the Stallion as a King's Rider, and therefore, he is your charge."

At this point, the two strode back into the anteroom, the knight throwing up his hands, professing his helplessness.

"I don't need this, Crius. Give him to Ilywyn!"

"He's a capable warrior, and a crafty thinker, and you're one to talk, Sir Javal!" Crius finally accused, grabbing the man by the arm and spinning him around. He shoved a folded letter into Javal's hand. Javal broke the wax seal and read it, his eyes flicking back and forth to Jarrod.

"You're jesting," he said. "Or the king is fucking with me."

Javal was rail-thin and tall, Anglo-European in appearance with dark hair and gunmetal eyes. Jarrod figured him for a fit forty, for though his movements were quick with the strength of youth, his eyes and mouth harbored intense lines.

He was clad in black woolen trousers with cross-garters to high on the thigh, and a drab linen tunic with the sleeves shoved up to his elbows. His face was angular and clean-shaven and quite handsome, with a challenging jaw that could have merited a Gillette endorsement. His hair was black and wiry and for the most part clipped above his ears, though its cut was so ragged it looked as if he'd done it himself in a tantrum. His posture was ramrod; his hand gestures broad and foreign.

And what hands, Jarrod thought: broad, scarred fists and thick forearms crossed with red and pink tracks of wounds long healed. All four knuckles and the wrist bone of his right hand were freshly scabbed over and a bit swollen, as if he'd been in a fistfight just the prior evening.

"Of all people, I know you hate taking on a new sergeant," Crius continued, quite sympathetically, "We need a knight to train him who is loyal to the crown, and none is more loyal than you. Make a rider out of him."

Javal kicked his heel. "All right. But look at him," he turned fierce eyes on Jarrod. "For hope's sake, look at how *small* he is!"

Jarrod straightened to his full height and nearly said something.

"This matters?" Crius asked. "*You* were knighted at fourteen winters. Or have you forgotten? Dreaming of a lifetime of chasing dragons and maidens, how many suits of armor did we have to build you as you outgrew them? How old was Sir Morgan when you led —"

"*Hey!*" Javal snapped. He stiffened, regained his composure.

Crius let it go, having made his point.

"Now, I want you to take him with you when you leave today for castle duty at High River. You will groom him for command. He's to be an adviser to the king."

"Yes," said Javal. "I read that part." His voice was incredulous as he looked Jarrod up and down.

"He is his nation's—and possibly his homeland's—finest swordsman."

Jarrod shrugged in response to the look Javal gave him just then. "And at the moment," Crius continued, "the king has made him a King's Rider, and the Crown will present him with anything you think he needs. He goes with you, for a year."

Javal's shoulders sank. "A year."

"Jarrod, you are to take orders from this man. He is your superior, and your mentor. And Javal, Jarrod is not a squire, he is a King's Rider and your acting sergeant. Your actions today disappoint me."

Sir Javal mumbled an apology. Crius harrumphed, wished Jarrod good luck, threw him the rock sign, and bowed out of the room.

Sir Javal looked Jarrod up and down. "What's that, your salute?"

"Pretty much," Jarrod had to admit.

Javal made the sign and looked at it, turning his hand over and grunting.

He handed Jarrod the letter. "This makes you a member of our order. Keep it safe."

"Sure," said Jarrod. He tucked it into a small purse on his swordbelt.

"Give me your sword."

Jarrod shrugged the *gran espée de guerre* off his shoulder, cleared it from its scabbard, and handed it over, hilt-first. Javal stood the massive weapon upright in his hand and struck the pommel, checking the balance and the fitting. He let out a low whistle. "Solid steel?"

"We don't make our steel the way you do," Jarrod told him, and held out his hand to have the sword back. He set the tip on the wooden floor and carefully put his weight on it, bending the blade past a 45-degree angle, then let it snap back to true and handed it back. "We can harden the spine differently from the edges."

Javal eyed down the edge and muttered something profane. "Can you use it?"

"Yes."

"Do you care to qualify that?"

"Gladly," Jarrod said. "All the nations of my homeland hold a competition every four years. I was selected to represent my nation at the most recent one."

"Did you win?"

"I was disqualified for killing another competitor outside of the match."

Javal finally looked impressed. "Over a woman, I hope."

"In fact, yes."

"So you've already killed a man. That's good. That's one less thing I have to worry about. And now? What do you do now?"

"I teach future competitors. You could consider me my nation's master trainer." It wasn't far from the truth. He had a former student who was up for an NCAA saber title and he'd taught *Zera, Barbarian Queen* everything she knew.

Sir Javal sighed. "We'll see what we can do with that. Do you ride?"

"Not by your standards, I'm sure."

Javal leaned back and tapped his head against the wall three times, swearing.

"So, in my homeland," Jarrod trod carefully, "We have many orders of knighthood. There is ceremonial knighthood, royal knighthood, orders that work as professional military guilds or fraternities, if you will, and we have even had orders that have functioned as their own private armies."

"And?" Javal asked.

"Well, which are we?"

Javal stared at him for a moment. "You don't know?"

"I just got here," Jarrod said. "I was told that I would be admitted to this order. I'd kind of like to know what it is."

"Look—uh, Jarrod," he began, clumsily. He sat down on a wooden chest and leaned his head against the stone wall and closed his eyes.

"The Order of the Stallion," he began again, "has, well it has the highest—how do I say this?—turnover rate, of any of the orders. What I mean to say, is that a knight of the Stallion has absolutely the shortest life expectancy of any of the chivalrics.

"We are Gateskeep's wandering servants, the king's eyes and ears."

"A royal order, then," Jarrod deduced. "A military order."

"Indeed. We are, in our own right, the swift hand of the king, above and beyond the embodiment of the ideals the other orders are sworn to. We fight on all fronts. Part of our pledge is to weed out evil within the ranks of the other orders, and we are sanctioned to do anything—*anything*—our quests, and our oaths, require."

"Special Operations."

"Interesting turn of phrase. Yes. The other orders hate us, and fear us, yet they envy us. We are the smallest in number, and the most feared. We killed the last known dragon around these parts. Every knight in the kingdom answers to us."

"Okay."

"You're my sergeant. Most sergeants aren't members of an order, but they hope to be. As a King's Rider, you're a probationary member of the Order of the Stallion, made so at the king's request. The good news for you is, only the king himself can remove you from the order. I'm short a sergeant, as it happens, and for you, a sergeant's billet is a good way to train you.

"The question I have is, what do I need to train you on? I've never heard of you. I have no idea what you did to win your warrant from the king—*the king!* Crius tells me you're the champion of a land I've never heard of, and you tell me you're disgraced. All you have is a letter from the king and a sword that's worth more than my manor."

"It's a start," said Jarrod.

"That it is. I hope you know what you're doing."

"I know I can't undo it."

"You stand an excellent chance of getting killed within the next year. Are you prepared to die?"

"Not needlessly," Jarrod admitted.

The knight bit his lower lip as the words left Jarrod's mouth. He perused them for a long moment, running them back and forth across his mind.

"Brave words," he decided. "Well then, sir, let's see what you brought, and then we'll take you down to Master Argyul's and see how much training you need."

"What the hell is that thing in your mouth?"

"Baby's little pacifier." Argyul was the sword master's name, and he laughed heartily at his own wit as he kicked clear a space in the straw of the gymnasium.

Jarrod flipped his mouthguard sideways with his tongue. When inserted, it gave the impression that his teeth were filed to points, with long vampiric white fangs when he smiled. "This is to keep him from knocking my teeth out," said Jarrod.

"Good thinking. You'll need it."

Jarrod wore a black horsehide motocross jacket with a matching leather skirt, which was a custom job with padding and carbon-fiber plates riveted beneath, attaching to the jacket with heavy buckles. His longer mailshirt would cover the skirt completely but he didn't wear it here. He did wear motocross gloves and heavy workman's knee pads, steel-toed work boots, and a padded mail mantle and hood, all in black. He flipped the hood over his head and tightened the drawstrings.

Jarrod had watched Javal's dislike for him dissipate as the knight had gone through Jarrod's gear, concluding that Jarrod was a rich lord in his homeland. The coat of plates Jarrod had packed—a magnificent thing of burnished harness leather tanned to a deep whisky color with sandwiched plates of ultra-high molecular weight plastic—brought a string of curses that Jarrod had never imagined; the modified motocross jackets he used as gambesons even more.

Jarrod explained away the plastic and carbon fiber as materials that grew in his homeland. Javal knocked on them, tried to flex them, and pushed at the padding behind. "Fine, fine," he'd said.

Javal had been especially taken with fencing manuals, of which Jarrod had brought several. The knight seemed physically relieved to see the pictures, and mentioned that he was eager to see Jarrod fight.

After playing with a heavy plastic training sword for a few minutes, Javal had agreed upon its use in sparring, and also mentioned that he wanted one himself. Jarrod had told him that he'd only brought the one set of training weapons, but gladly gave him a nice Gerber multitool with a spring action built into the pliers. Javal had thought the metal snap on the knife's leather belt case was particularly slick. He now wore it on his own swordbelt, which was a simple, double-wrap affair.

Jarrod had brought a hand-and-a-half training sword, which he now bore against the castle's master trainer.

Argyul was armed with a wooden sword a little shorter and heavier, with a heavy glove on his hand. He wore no armor except for a heavy leather jerkin and leather knee guards.

He was taller than even Sir Javal, barrel-chested with a potbelly and wide arms braided with muscle. He was old enough, Jarrod assumed, to be Javal's father, but he moved with a bounce in his step and a focused heft to his shoulders that Jarrod had seen in enough aging martial arts masters to know that this was not a man to be fribbled with.

Jarrod flashed his fangs. "This'll be fun," he assessed.

Argyul obviously had to be able to whip the arrogant young bucks—like Jarrod—easily and embarrassingly, or he'd never command their respect. He had power and explosiveness in his build, which made sense, because he likely couldn't match someone with Jarrod's grace and youth in any sort of enduring engagement.

Jarrod concluded that the old badger probably knew every dirty trick ever imagined, and had imagined quite a few of his own.

It was time to go to school.

Javal handed him a mail glove, for the right hand. Jarrod put it on over his leather gauntlet. Javal muttered, "That's for the sword hand. Turn it inside out."

"You've never read Fabris," said Jarrod.

"One of those books you brought?"

"Yes."

"I intend to," said Javal.

Argyul beckoned.

Jarrod and Argyul stared at each other for a good five seconds, neither moving.

"Looks like a frightened mouse," Argyul commented. "Aggression's not your strong point, is it, mouse?"

Jarrod tongued his mouthguard sideways. "I'm wondering how you want to do this," he said carefully. "Are we going full-speed? Light contact? Touch sparring? I don't intend to kill you. I can crack your skull with this pretty easily, though."

"Ha!" barked Argyul. "Can you, now?" He stepped forward and tentatively touched blades with Jarrod.

Jarrod engaged with a flash of motion and a *kiai.* Argyul's sword clattered across the gym.

"I can," said Jarrod, and fitted his mouthguard.

A page walked up and handed Argyul his sword again.

Sir Javal was now standing, Jarrod saw.

The swordmaster darted in. Jarrod swept up the blade with his own, slipped a foot behind, then locked elbows and wrenched Argyul off-balance, spinning him several steps away.

The heart and soul of Judo may be The Big Throw, but the most jarring throw in Judo, and also in *savate,* is the foot sweep. Jarrod's grandfather had learned it from a Japanese-American soldier in North Africa and taught it to Jarrod as a way to deal with schoolyard bullies. Twenty years later, Jarrod regularly threw armored opponents, even the massive Carter, with it.

Argyul got his weight back under him, growled deep in his throat, and charged at Jarrod with a feint and a quick lunge. Jarrod countered with a coulé, the swords sliding against each other, but he missed the touch and Argyul was big and they ended up locked in a wrestling match, which Jarrod didn't want. Argyul, much bigger, threw an arm around his neck and kneed him in the ribs and then in the face, which Jarrod managed to block with his elbows but the savagery of the blows startled him. *We are not sparring,* Jarrod thought. *He is trying to put me away.*

They disengaged and Jarrod swept Argyul's feet as he backpedaled. Argyul landed on his tailbone, heavy and hard.

"Slippery little bastard," grumbled Argyul, getting up.

Jarrod said, "Do you want to go that hard? Let's be clear, I don't intend to harm you."

The sword master assumed a safe distance and scrutinized Jarrod again, then put up his blade and crouched a hair lower. "Don't worry about me."

Jarrod nodded. The black blade whistled as he saluted and dropped into a guard. *This is me, not worrying about you.*

Argyul stayed just out of long attacking distance, blade covering the high inside line in *tierce,* slightly extended, body almost square. But Jarrod had seen that a thousand times. Standard play against a short southpaw. With a stomp and an *"Et la-a!!"* Jarrod tore into him.

Argyul seemed more ready this time, and the conversation of the blades began.

Argyul's bladework was an amalgam of techniques familiar to Jarrod, but none that he had ever seen used together. He was attacking and defending as if his wooden sword were a double-edged blade. It wasn't quite rapier fencing, not quite longsword combat.

His attacks were long, straight, and simple, which Jarrod expected from someone his size. Like many tall swordsmen, Argyul's strides were overly large—covering distance quickly was to a taller fighter's advantage—so Argyul's composure went to hell for a moment whenever he was forced to change direction.

During the initial exchanges Jarrod keyed in on the older man's predilection for semi-circular parries and cutover attacks, noting also his Marozzo-esque bent toward anticipatory maneuvers, his overuse of *tierce,* and his general lack of pointwork except for a near-textbook Agrippa thrust delivered by throwing the shoulder forward and slipping the rear foot back. Jarrod adjusted for all this, deferred to Fabris to wring the most mileage from the off-hand mail glove, and pressed the attack. He thwarted the parries with doubles, over-utilized envelopments just to prove that he could, and built his fight around a series of elaborate feints which he knew from past experience raised all kinds of hell with guys who anticipate.

In a real fight he'd be nicking the edges of the blade by now, but he tried to keep his parries below the balance in case Argyul brought it up.

Argyul didn't bring it up. He was too busy swearing.

As Jarrod accelerated his attacks to twice their pace, blade darting and whirling and clacking against Argyul's, sometimes with one hand, sometimes with two, it became clear to the entire room that the mouse was in full control of the fight.

Jarrod bulled him across the gymnasium, then stepped out of attacking distance, made some space in the straw, and beckoned the swordmaster in.

Argyul brought his most fearsome attack yet, their blades banging and flashing so quickly that even Javal had to squint to see.

After driving Argyul across the gym yet again, and demonstrating that perhaps no one in the world could match the rapid-fire pace and unorthodox attack vectors that were his hallmark, Jarrod closed to a clinch, grabbed Argyul's blade with his mailed hand, and twisted it expertly, smacking the swordmaster under the wrist with his pommel. The sword spun toward Sir Javal, who threw himself out of the way as it banged off the wall behind him.

Argyul punched Jarrod in the face.

Jarrod counterpunched an eyelash later, two heavy jabs and a heelkick to the thigh to shove Argyul out of range, and tossed his sword away, shucking the mail glove as Argyul recovered.

I'll see your fisticuffs, and I'll raise you la savate.

Argyul rushed in with an overhand punch, flat-footed and chambered over his shoulder. Jarrod leaned back to slip it, and as Argyul's fist whistled past, Jarrod cocked his front leg and just missed his face with a knife-edge snapkick. Argyul stumbled back.

Impressed swearing erupted from the onlookers and everyone moved in for a closer view.

Jarrod shuffled in, now in a boxer's stance—narrower in the feet, fists up, elbows guarding his sides—and popped him again with the jab, stepping back smartly to slip the counter as Argyul threw another haymaker and missed.

Jarrod jabbed again, heavier, reeling the bigger man back.

Argyul reached out and pawed to block the next jab, then shook his head and spat blood after Jarrod's left cross snapped his head back. Jarrod followed it up with a roundhouse kick into Argyul's guard that staggered him, but Argyul didn't go down.

Jarrod bobbed. He weaved. He feinted with the jab. Argyul's fist whistled through the air at the edge of his nose yet again.

Jarrod deduced that they didn't have boxing, here. At the least, fisticuffs may never have been raised to the art to which it had on Earth. Argyul's punches were crude, telegraphed, and easy to dodge.

Granted, if one of them connected, it would lay him out flat with X's for eyes.

They may not have had boxing, but they sure as hell had wrestling, Jarrod concluded, as Argyul charged in low, hit him with an expertly-placed shoulder, and locked his arms around Jarrod's waist trying for a classic Greco-Roman takedown.

Jarrod slid to a sprawl to counter and they grunted and slithered and whirled, and suddenly Argyul's feet were in the air and he was going over Jarrod's hip. Jarrod *kiai'd* as he drove Argyul into the floor, braking him with both hands still on the jerkin and careful to drop him flat on both shoulders, then cocked his left fist to deliver a finishing punch which he never threw.

They don't have Judo, either.

Jarrod stood over the sword master and held his hand out. In a moment or so Argyul took it, and Jarrod helped him to his feet.

"Thank you," Argyul said to Jarrod.

"The pleasure was mine, sir."

Argyul motioned to the page, who brought both their swords.

Javal bowed to Jarrod, his fist over his heart, then raised the rock salute.

Argyul grinned at Jarrod. "Damn, son. Let's do that again."

Just before dusk, Jarrod and Sir Javal ambled, horsebound and fully armored, down a wide, muddy forest path. Jarrod was having a bit of a tough time with his horse, for this beast had a nastier temperament than anything he'd ever ridden. Every now and again, the black mare would snap her head up in a vain attempt to bite at Jarrod, and Javal would reach over from his own mount and rap her on her head with his mailed fist.

"Keep your knees on her, stronger. Show her who's in charge."

Jarrod locked his knees down. "I think she knows who's in charge," he grumbled, "And it ain't me."

They moved at a smooth, rolling gait that he was unfamiliar with; a little faster than a walk, a bit less than a trot. It jarred him less than any horse he'd been on before.

His gloved hand fell time and again to the rawhide-laced grip of the spear knocking against his leg.

The world was mud and fog and cold rain.

Javal's traveling armor was a long black shirt of heavy-gauge mail slitted up to the crotch for riding, with twin gold braids — fourragères — designating his rank tied through his mail at his shoulder and looped under his right arm. His helmet, also black, had a hinged visor slitted for his eyes. He wore it open so that the rain dripped off it onto a leather gorget and mantle and a thick fur cape over his shoulders.

On a black riding horse, Javal led a massive black Friesian with a powerful neck — his destrier — that Jarrod swore was the biggest horse he'd ever seen. Tethered to the destrier but far behind was a sturdy brown pack horse who shouldered Javal's spare shields, heavy weapons, food, tools, and bivouac gear. Behind the brown pack horse was a second, spotted pack horse hauling feed and all of Jarrod's gear including the massive arming trunk. The trunk and rifle case had taken some work to mount, involving a lattice of poles.

Jarrod wore a shirt of ultra-lightweight titanium chainmail with a black nitride coating over his heavier jacket, which was thick pebbled horsehide with padding and carbon-fiber plates. He wore a stout leather gorget over the mail, Merrill trail boots, Gore-Tex gaiters, and his oilskin cowboy hat. The thick woolen trousers he'd first gotten from Carter when he woke up here were soaked through already, but still warm.

He was really glad he'd brought the gaiters.

He'd been given the spear; the rest of his gear was his own. The *gran espée de guerre* hung from his saddle, which had a built-in frog though it was on the wrong side for him, and the helm from his man-at-arms harness — a great T-faced Barbute with a high crown and a locking faceplate with a cruciform grille — hung from its chinstrap around the hilt of the big sword. A hood of titanium mail matching his shirt and stitched onto a cashmere cap was stuffed inside, a small carabiner on the bottom buckled around the chinstrap of the helmet to keep it from falling out.

He was concerned about the amount of damage that a year in the rain would cause his gear. He had brought the titanium shirt as traveling armor mostly due to its corrosion resistance. It didn't hurt that it was as tough as a steel shirt twice the weight. Similarly, the horsehide was as water-resistant as leather gets, but he'd brought a jug of Neatsfoot oil and a one-pound tub of Vaseline because damn, it rained a lot here.

Jarrod knew his gear was a game-changer and on the one hand he felt a bit like he was cheating the system. On the other, he had the feeling that fair play and sportsmanship would likely go out the door once people started trying to take him apart with axes. And Crius had insisted that nothing would be considered cheating.

"I am going to your homeland," said Javal, looking over at Jarrod, "And buying a shirt of that mail."

"It never hurts to have good gear, sire. But without mindset, knowledge, and practice, the best gear in the world is just dead weight."

"Good words," said Javal.

The worst part, Jarrod knew, was going to be the first week or so. He was immensely physically fit, but he was not a horseman. There was going to be a hellish period coming up shortly, he was certain; probably starting once they made camp tonight.

Jarrod straightened up in the saddle and braced himself for trial by ordeal.

"So, we're off to castle duty?" Jarrod cleaned his nails with the tip of his knife as Sir Javal gnawed the knuckle off a rabbit bone and spat it into the coals.

"Allegedly," the knight answered. "At Albar's. He hates having the Order of the Stallion around. We make him nervous."

"How so?"

"There's much going on in Highriver. Gavrian emissaries coming and going. Lots of spies. Even a few knights, I hear, have turned their loyalties. That's why I chose Highriver."

"Great."

"The last two knights of the Stallion stationed there met with grisly ends. The unfortunate Sir Rinan, last assigned to Highriver? Fell on a pitchfork. Three times."

"Really."

"Mm hm. And in his own bed, fancy that."

"Yee-owch," Jarrod agreed. "So, we're going there to check things out."

"Yes. This will be a great opportunity for you."

"Opportunity? I thought I was going to be some sort of field adviser, or somesuch."

Javal pulled a potato off its spit and set it in his wooden plate. "Oh, you will. But you've got a thing or two to learn first." He blew out a laugh, "At least I don't have to teach you how to fight. But I'm supposed to make a knight out of you. You need to learn how our military works, and most importantly why. Lucky for you, I'm really good at that. And we won't have to spend the whole summer beating each other up. Unless, of course, you want to." He flashed his teeth, his eyes mischievous.

Jarrod reached into his pack and pulled out his flask. "Drink?"

"Absolutely."

Javal took a pull, swished it around in his cheeks, and nodded appreciatively.

"Good stuff," he said as he handed the bottle back. "Really good stuff."

Jarrod took a swig and corked it.

"I'm out," Jarrod said. "Good night, sire."

Full and sore, Jarrod went to bed. He had brought a lightweight, ripstop hammock with integrated mosquito netting and a rain fly, a RidgeRest pad, and a three-season sleeping bag. He'd slung the hammock between two trees, unrolled the pad along the bottom, and opened the sleeping bag into a duvet. His weapons trunk rested beneath the hammock and the rifle case on top, both on the lattice of poles to keep them out of the mud.

"And that's how your people sleep?" Javal asked.

"When we're traveling light," Jarrod answered. *As far as you know.*

Javal spread his own bedroll at the base of the cedar tree and settled loudly upon it, leaning his armored torso against the trunk with a creak and a thud. He then threw his own tarp over himself. "You're an unorthodox man, King's Rider Jarrod, but I think I like you. Sleep easy."

"And you, sire. Who's taking watch?"

Javal closed his eyes. "It's not necessary. The horses would wake us."

Jarrod was beginning to doze when he heard the rattle of armor. He looked out to see that Javal was laughing quietly to himself.

"Sire?"

"No one's taken Argyul to the mat in years."

Jarrod walked out from the tree line and tossed Sir Javal the roll of parchment toilet paper. "I could sharpen my sword with that stuff," he griped.

He hadn't thought to bring his own.

On the plus side, it had stopped raining. It was still overcast, though.

He was itching for a look at the ringed moon Carter had told him about.

Across the camp, Javal was readying his riding horse. He tucked the roll into his saddlebag without comment. Jarrod washed his hands in the water from the now-cooled kettle, using a chunk of soap fragranced with flowers that Javal had tossed him. The soap was handmade but stamped with a logo of some type.

A soap industry is a good sign.

He had brought a couple of bars of soap just in case, in a leather dopp kit.

He dumped the remainder of the water into the coals and hung the kettle on the pony, tucking the shovel back into his pack just as it began to sprinkle again.

He and Javal had had a hell of a time mounting Jarrod's arming trunk. It weighed nearly a hundred pounds, and rested on four poles that buckled onto a simple saddle. The trunk was strapped down tightly onto the wooden cross-braces, lengthwise along the pony's back. A suit of high-impact plastic practice armor in a duffel bag—which Javal hadn't yet seen—was tied down just behind it, and Jarrod's backpack hung off one side, supported by the straps through one of the poles of the lattice. However, it was a sturdy, muscular pony with a good sense of humor and didn't seem to mind the attention or the load.

His horse had a few things to say about his climbing on, however.

"Hey, up yours," he snarled, and clapped his gloved hand onto its nose to steady it. Its teeth clomped where his fingers had been a moment before.

Swearing, he grabbed the saddle and swung up as she moved aside, and he managed to get up as she kept turning in a circle away from him. She reached around to bite at him, and he met her skull with the flat of his boot.

That pretty much settled it. He kicked her around the edge of the firepit and out the path they'd forged, back to the King's Road, ducking branches and plunging through the dense undergrowth not two meters from the pack pony's tail.

Here, in the Gateskeep Northlands, the trees grew to be ten feet in diameter, and the undergrowth, off the marked trails, was virtually impassable for all but the hardiest and best-armored.

Jarrod commented on this.

"The Faerie Stronghold is worse than this," Javal spoke from what sounded like experience. "A hundred times worse. And the Faerie use the trees as their sentries. The vines are alive, and the thornbushes, if so commanded, will open up and swallow an intruder whole. They'll sting you to death."

Jarrod shivered as their mounts skittered down the shallow embankment to the road.

On the road, where the canopy opened, it was raining in sheets. Jarrod beat his oilskin hat into shape and put it on, raising his voice above the downpour. "And this is summer, is it?"

"In Falconsrealm," Javal returned.

A caravan of several wagons was weaving its way down the road ahead of them some fifty yards to the south.

Javal kicked his mount to a lope, taking the pack horses with him. Jarrod's horse was quick to follow the others, and he caught up as the train of horses slowed to pace the caravan.

The caravan's four guards, in black quilted armor with spears and leather helmets, looking soaked and ragged, saluted.

Javal exchanged a few words with the leader of the wagon train, and offered his and Jarrod's support as far as Beggar's Creek, which the merchants accepted. One of them tossed Jarrod an apple, which was green and wet and hard and more or less exactly like a hundred apples he'd ever eaten.

Jarrod spent the next several miles watching Javal four

horses ahead, blurred in the downpour, his dark cape sad with rain. And then he'd take a bite of apple and think back to school buses, autumn afternoons in New England, and old girlfriends, and then a blast of rain would jar him back to the immediacy of the chill, and the rain dripping from his beard, and the mud spurting from the hooves of the pack animals.

Back and forth, bite after bite, mile after mile.

He finished the apple and raised his hand for another.

Gateskeep's walled capitol, The City of the Gate, sits high atop a grassy knoll with her back to the Falconsrealm Mountains.

The mighty square towers of Gateskeep Castle look out across a rolling sea of rippling grasses and farmland, and on the misty horizon the jagged mountains which border Falconsrealm, blue and purple and capped with snow year-round, are a reminder of the motherland's isolation from her principality.

Jarrod and Javal had crossed into the city nearly at sundown. It had stopped raining and it was actually getting colder. Jarrod thought he could see the outline of the moon Carter had mentioned. It made his heart jump and he wished the night would clear.

Sir Javal noted to Jarrod that allied knights didn't have to pay city tariffs, and demonstrated as the sentries at the barbican waived the "entrance tax" and the two were let into the city proper.

They rode past a maze of thatched cottages and longhouses on the outskirts of town. As they neared the town center, the cottages turned to wooden houses. Soon the wooden houses became houses of stone, and smoky taverns, and darkened shops and lit apartment dwellings reminiscent of gingerbread dioramas, the twisting streets mostly deserted save for a few knots of haggard-looking men scurrying home from a day's late work and an occasional itinerant dog, black and brindle bulldoggish monsters.

The middle of the city was quiet and the world smelled of food. A boot-slapping tune spun along on a gentle breeze that smelled of roasting meat and frying garlic as they rode past a tavern. Jarrod's stomach roared so loudly that he swore it rattled his armor.

Nearer the inner wall of the city, where a central barbican would lead them to the great keep, the wooden houses turned to rich manors set more widely apart and walled separately, their gates decorated with heraldic banners that flapped and rustled as if competing for attention.

"This is the gentry's quarter," Javal pointed out. "Most houses here have their own troops on the grounds to defend them if the city's overrun. Of course, we've never been overrun," he admitted with a good deal of pride. "This is a great land, Gateskeep. Rich, and vast. King Rorthos is well-learned in the cultures and sensitivities of our various peoples."

"Probably keeps them from knocking him off," Jarrod concluded.

Javal shrugged. "Real, ruling power lies in the legislative body and the advisory—the palace lords and the High Council. They're the ones who are constantly having pitchfork accidents. The people here love their king. There'd be riots if he was to meet with an untimely end, and besides, it wouldn't put an end to his reign. His daughter stands to inherit the throne someday, as you probably know."

"I've heard of this," Jarrod acknowledged. "She's Prince Albar's, ah, babe."

Javal sighed, long and slow. "Yes, Albar's babe," he agreed.

Sensing a touchy subject, Jarrod dropped the matter, and a

quarter of an hour later they arrived at the main gates to the keep.

"Incidentally, what are we doing here?" Jarrod asked, as they were let through.

"Getting a decent night's sleep," the knight replied.

Jarrod had been to castles. He knew a big castle when he saw one.

No Cinderella Special, Gateskeep is squarish and massive, with thick walls and fat square towers that give her a squat, broad-shouldered appearance. The keep is squarish as well, and the great tower's silhouette can be seen for a day's ride.

The night had cleared to a cold wind as they'd traveled the last half-mile through the city. The moon, a full tenth of the horizon, was a deep, French lilac pink with soft stripes and splotches and a slender pale ring, casting magnificent slate shadows.

Jarrod saw very well by the moonlight.

Sore and stiff, Jarrod had to follow a page up eight flights of stairs, in heavy wet clothes plus armor and weapons, before he was led to his room in the keep. Four pages behind him carried his equipment.

The girls, and there were a lot of them, noticed the new guy with the entourage carrying his gear. He caught half a dozen unabashed smiles as he climbed the stairs.

He noted that there seemed to be many more women at this castle than at Regoth Ur. They dressed in clingy, embroidered silken gowns—lace-up sleeves and spring colors seemed the fashion—and some of the older women wore ornate affairs in richer colors.

Castle girls, Jarrod deduced, must have amazing legs. The

girls he'd seen here were willowy, even the shorter ones, and they all moved with an athletic grace. Which made sense; there were a hell of a lot of stairs to be negotiated in the course of a day.

That's why this feels so weird, he thought. Everyone's in garb and there are no fat chicks.

His apartment was small, a single room with a fireplace and an attached water closet with the trapdoor. He heard running water just like he had at Regoth Ur.

The furnishings were sparse but rich—he was sensing a theme—and included a wide bed heaped with quilts, a leather armchair with a footrest, and a mannequin-like wooden torso in one corner for his armor.

I'm gonna need more mannequins.

He set a log on the coals and blew until flames engulfed its underside.

The page had lit an array of candles over the fireplace, and also a thick, bright candle in a sconce beside the bed. Jarrod shed his armor and arranged it properly, hung his jacket over the arrowslit to dry, changed into a set of hemp pants, and set his trousers near the fire. He stared out at the lights of the city beyond, the rooftops glowing, the ring of the moon throwing light against the sky and blotting out the stars above.

He tried to imagine the intensity of the fear that shadows could cultivate when you grew up in a world that rarely saw true darkness.

He'd asked Javal about the moon and they'd discussed it at length, but it was difficult; the last few days had been overcast so there was no frame of reference, but also because after a thousand years nobody had ever bothered to do anything more than keep track of what it did.

One thing that it did, which freaked Jarrod out when he really thought about it, was every hundred and four days it would disappear along with the sun, turning the world pitch black for just over six days straight. He'd learned that they called it, creatively enough, The Dark.

These guys, he decided, really sucked at naming stuff.

He stared at the moon while he warmed his aching ass by the fire, wincing as he dabbed tea tree oil into the blisters on his thighs. The canted ring of dust scattered into the starlight and silhouetted the hills on the horizon. The sense of enormity clobbered him.

We're orbiting that thing, he figured. Or it's a binary planetoid system. Either way, I will bet what they're calling the moon is orbiting the sun.

He reminded himself to break out a blank book tonight and start doodling to see if he could figure it out. Then he decided it didn't matter.

What matters, he told himself, slowing his breathing, is this: you are no longer standing on a dirt clod orbiting a very ordinary star in the Orion Arm of an unremarkable galaxy in the backwaters of the Virgo Supercluster. You are standing on a different dirt clod, orbiting some other very ordinary star, only God knows where, and you have work to do.

He figured he felt much as Coronado must've, looking out over the Grand Canyon for the first time; or perhaps Neil Armstrong stepping on the moon.

Neil Armstrong went home again, he reminded himself. The Conquistadors burned their ships.

Plus, Neil Armstrong was first. Somebody else beat you here by twelve years. And he's a king by now. You've got some catching up to do, Sergeant.

He rolled the phrase *The Dark* around in his head a few times and realized that the words for *dark* and *dead* were identical. He needed a drink.

Sir Javal rapped on his door and let himself in. "Are you all right?"

"Overwhelmed, sire."

Javal handed him a folded black article of clothing, atop which was something small and gold; a brooch in the shape of a horse's head. "Your cape and rider's pin. The page will show you to the baths."

The baths were in a round, one-story building adjacent to the keep. Steam surged up into the night from slits in the ceiling.

This, Jarrod recognized, was where it all came together. A hot bath with mineral salts, and a scantily-clad girl rubbing soap into his hair and massaging his shoulders. Her name was Ryana, and she was one of the tall, willowy types he'd been keen about earlier in the evening. She was marvelously put together, sinewy and doe-eyed with hands like stones and an interest in up-and-coming knights.

Javal was in the adjacent tub. "How long can we stay here?" Jarrod asked, gently kneading the aches from his thighs as the girl poured a bucket of hot water over his scalp and massaged it in.

"At Gateskeep?" Javal's words slurred. "Just tonight."

"No, I mean in the baths."

Javal grinned and splashed water at him. "You're done. Out."

Jarrod stood, and Javal stared.

"That's a hell of a place for a wound!" Javal exclaimed.

Now the bathing girls were staring.

Jarrod looked down at the long scar on his stomach. "I told you I've put my time in, sire."

"Not that," said Javal, gesturing lower. "That."

"Oh, that." His circumcision. "Yeah. It's a rite of passage among my people."

"For going through that, I should knight you right now."

Javal waited with his hands folded patiently outside the feasting hall's double doors. His hair was still damp, and he was again clean-shaven and looked freshly scrubbed. He wore a V-necked leather jerkin with gold embroidery on the sleeves that matched the silver embroidery on the edges of Jarrod's cape. Over this he wore a red shirt of what Jarrod figured was either fine hemp or rough silk, a gold horsehead pin prominent on his chest holding his gold officer's fourragères under his arm. Behind him, the nobles' hall was bursting its seams with revelry.

Jarrod was clad in drawstring hemp pants and a black cashmere sweater over his black velvet warrior's tunic and a long-sleeved polypro shirt beneath, with his black and silver cape secured with his rider's pin, and leather trail runners. It was getting cold, despite being summer. The women he'd seen on his way down to supper were wearing stoles of fur and silk.

Javal opened the door to the bedlam and let Jarrod through first, and there, spanning the hall, were perhaps a hundred people, some brightly dressed, some looking quite plain, the majority in every shade of regalia in between.

The food was coming in plates and piles, and the myriad smells sent Jarrod's feet wandering. "So, where do we sit?"

"There's a member of our order over there," Jarrod didn't see where Javal was pointing, but it was of little matter, because Javal steered him down the stairs and through the tables. "Privilege of being my sergeant," Javal said at that point. "You get to eat with the nobles." He flashed such a self-satisfied smile that his teeth gleamed. He raised his voice above the flute and drum, "King's Rider Jarrod, this is the gallant Knight Lord Sir Durn." Javal stopped before a bald, bearded, beady-eyed gorilla of a man who rivaled Carter in height and exceeded him considerably in mass. Jarrod guessed him at six and a half feet tall and the fitter side of three hundred pounds. College lineman big. Professional wrestler big. *That guy would pound me into the ground like a fence post.*

Sir Durn extended his hand, saying, "Please, sir. Share my table."

And Jarrod then sat, excusing himself to the other side of the table where, being left-handed, he could eat with less difficulty. He was sitting beside Sir Durn and before Sir Javal.

Sir Durn began to snicker.

"Don't sit there," said Javal.

"What?"

"He's a foreigner," Javal explained, reaching over to slap Sir Durn across the top of his head. He told Jarrod, "It's—" and then started to laugh, himself.

"What did I miss?"

Javal started again. "Here, friends and comrades sit side by side, the better to keep the levels of conversation down."

Durn shrugged. "Only lovers sit across from each other at a meal."

"Where are we?" Javal asked, inquiring as to the status of dinner. Jarrod shifted over to the other side of the table, red-faced.

"Third course. You just missed the pastries." As Sir Durn spoke, a wooden plate and a silver goblet were set before Jarrod by a page, and the goblet filled by a willow-waisted, large-bosomed blonde girl blushing at his stare. She winked and vanished, giggling, into the mayhem.

"Oh-oh, that's trouble, that one," Durn laughed, clapping Jarrod on the shoulder with a beefy hand and thusly shaking him from his trance. "You Northers like your own, eh, boy?" and at that, he elbowed Jarrod in the ribs and laughed, "She'll eat a man alive."

"Indeed," Javal added with a wry smile, "Barbarians. You're better off with the bathing girls."

"Yeah, I wanted to talk to you about that."

"You should've seen him," Javal laughed to Durn, "Figured he'd kicked off right to the afterlife."

Durn shoved Jarrod, "You have to die pretty well to earn an afterlife like that one."

"Okay," said Jarrod. "Humor me here, because I'm from out of town. But where I'm from, that girl's father would be chasing me down the street."

"Where are you from?" asked Durn.

"Knightsbridge," Jarrod answered, and took a long slug of wine. It was fruity, rose in color, and potent. He tasted strawberries somewhere under the alcohol, and the honeyed kick of mead in the aftertaste. Home brewed. Good stuff.

"Never heard of it," said Durn. "No offense."

"It's far from here."

"Too far for my tastes," Durn laughed, "If you don't have bathing girls!"

Jarrod explained showers and plumbing as best he could.

"A heated waterfall in your privy? And you do it all yourself? It sounds so . . ." Durn searched for a word.

"Unsatisfying," offered Javal. "They have an interesting salute, though. Watch this."

Jarrod grumbled quietly as the others at the table learned to throw up the horns. He returned to the subject he was most interested in. "So there are no problems here, with girls rubbing soap into nude soldiers?"

Javal and Durn shrugged at each other.

"Sir Durn, if that was your daughter—" Jarrod started.

"I'd be thrilled," Durn admitted.

"I'm gonna need more wine here." Jarrod motioned for the serving girl to refill his goblet.

"There's nothing immoral going on in there," said Durn. "You'd be a fool to think of doing anything like what you're thinking. At least, in the baths," he joked.

"My people are a lot more . . . private," was the word Jarrod settled on. Of course, that was discounting internet pornography, popular music, tabloid shows, sexting, racy Facebook pages . . . It occurred to him that he shouldn't have mentioned it, but the dichotomy suddenly struck him: he was from a society that managed to be lascivious yet very, very private about it.

"Those girls are on their way to becoming healers," said Durn. "In the baths, they learn their way around a body. They see injuries from drill and sparring, and sometimes even from the field. They'll straighten your neck, and tend your welts, and hell, some of them will even stitch you up if they're far enough along. They'll call a wizard down to heal you if necessary."

"So it's a professional relationship," Jarrod assumed.

"It has to be," said Durn. "If they happen to catch the fancy of a young rider — or better still, a knight or a lord — in the course of their work, then all the better, I say. It's not like everyone in the damned village gets to soak in the garrison baths."

I can get behind this place, Jarrod announced to no one, and raised his goblet. "A toast to the garrison baths."

Durn laughed, clapped Jarrod on the shoulder, and reached for a meat pastry, which he plopped on Jarrod's plate. "You need to eat," he said, grabbing Jarrod by the bicep. "Not bad, actually." Jarrod bent his arm and flexed, and Durn slapped him on the back as the muscles shoved against his hand. "You'll do. So, in Knightsbridge, what gods do you pray to?"

"Here he goes," another at the table groaned.

"We have one big god who handles everything," said Jarrod. This brought a roar of laughter.

"Might leave him too busy to answer your prayers, huh?" said Durn.

"Yeah," Jarrod agreed, "He gets busy. What about you? Who do you pray to?"

"We have many gods, but they're busy, too," said Durn. "I pray to the soul of my father."

"My grandmother," offered another. "A wise woman and a great wizard."

"My grandfather. Died in battle."

"My grandfather, died on his grandmother," joked another, punching the knight next to him, who shoved him in return.

"Relatives," Jarrod acknowledged.

"Why not, eh? They know the answers, now. They like us— we hope. Wouldn't steer us wrong, and they're always watching."

"What about you?" Jarrod asked Javal. "Who do you pray to?"

Javal grunted, "No one listens."

They talked and joked and ate late into the night, until Jarrod had so stuffed and pickled himself, he opted to make his exit while he felt he still could.

And once outside the hall, the many flights of stairs loomed ahead of him like El Capitan.

He stared up at them for quite some time, judging exactly how he was going to do this.

"Hmm . . ." one step, then another, and *there* was the handrail. "Oh, that strawberry wine," he told no one. "Holy ship, am I wrecked," he muttered, completely giddy that the pun carried on his new tongue. He panicked momentarily as a pair of hands—soft, small hands, he found—wrapped around his waist, and gave him a heave up to the next step.

"Ah, oh, it's you." It was the Northland girl, the wine server with the spectacular bazongas he'd been sporadically flirting with all night. "Hey, I can do this. . ."

"No, you can't," her voice was a stern, sober contralto, all the opposite of her giggling demeanor from an hour ago. "Let me help you."

"Damn fine idea. You wanna just g—" get under my arm, yeah . . . Can I just get to the handrail? he begged silently. I'll be okay once I get to the handrail. No, the handrail's over there . . . ah, hell. "Okay, I give up," he slurred. "Have your way with me."

She sounded slightly amused, saying only, "You've outdone yourself, sire."

"Haven't I, though? Hey, are we here, already?" he wondered, looking behind him at the stairs spiraling into darkness as they stopped for a moment on a landing.

"No."

"Oh."

"Here, make a right."

"Where we goin'?"

"We're going to bed."

"No, no, n—" he shook his head and nearly fell, "No. My bed, is way the hell up *there*," and he pointed obliquely toward the roof and pursed his lips and nodded.

"Perhaps," she admitted, "but mine is right through here."

Jarrod staggered into the nobles' hall for breakfast a good bit after dawn, squinting and cringing at the din. Javal whistled for him, and Jarrod stumbled through the breakfast bedlam and took a seat on his mentor's left. Crockery clapping on tables rang like gunfire through his head.

Someone poured him a cup of dandy, the roasted dandelion-root coffee. He stared at it, saying only, "What a night."

"I'll say. You enjoyed yourself?"

Jarrod only grinned. Grinning, though, made the din louder. "I feel awful," he admitted as his grin faded.

Javal cut off a big slab of ham and helped himself to it. "Good."

"You're just cranky 'cuz you didn't get laid last night."

"As far as you know," the knight admitted. "Ah, what wouldn't I give to be twenty winters again."

"Twenty-*eight* winters, pal. And it's been a great couple of days. Can we talk?"

"We're talking."

"I was pretty drunk, but she, uh, she said something about the moon taking care of, you know."

"I do?"

"The whole kid thing."

Javal waved it off. "It's decent of you to be concerned."

"Yeah, where I'm from, that doesn't work so good."

"You don't have to worry."

"Uh—"

Javal appeared impatient. "Trust me on this."

"And that works?"

"Do you see me with children in tow?"

Jarrod looked around. "I haven't seen any children at all, come to think of it."

"This is the palace," said Javal. "This is not a place for children."

"Good," said Jarrod.

"You don't care for children?" asked Javal.

"Not particularly," Jarrod admitted. "Man, these women are gonna kill me."

"They might," the knight agreed.

A handful of small speckled eggs were placed on Jarrod's

plate. "Meaning?"

The knight cocked his head and chewed thoughtfully. "Pick your companions carefully. If word of your excesses gets out, a dear friend of one of your casual acquaintances may be waiting for you with a dagger some night. It's unlikely, but it's been known to happen."

"Ah," Jarrod wiped his nose with his palm. "This is a weakness."

Javal shrugged. "There are worse weaknesses. Were I you, I would stay off the liquor. It's a hundred times more dangerous than debauchery. Besides, it rots your liver, sharpens your temper, and softens your reflexes."

"So, I can quit drinking so much, and still—?" Jarrod made the more explicative half of an obscene gesture.

"Certainly. I do."

"So, what's on the agenda for today?"

"I spoke with Crius this morning."

"Crius? He's here?"

"Not exactly. You and I have a great deal to discuss."

"Such as?"

"Let's finish breakfast and suit up. I'll tell you on the road."

The sun rose over the fog-shrouded great tower of the Hold of Gavria, and cast feeble rays through the east-facing window of a lavish apartment in the uppermost floor. On the sill, a raven's grating caw disturbed the sleeping form of Ulo Sabbaghian.

He rolled over with a snarl. His eyes, nuclear blue under a tangle of black hair, flicked to a paperweight from the nearby desk. It flew across the room, smashing the bird off the window sill.

He found that this expenditure of energy served only to wake him further, and he shoved the quietly snoring form of his bedmate. His voice was slow, grating and inhumanly deep. "Get up."

"Milord?" asked the girl, rubbing her eyes.

"Close the shade," he hid his face in his armpit. His skin was toffee stretched taut over ripples of muscle, scarified into a quilt of patterns and symbols. "Then go, and tell the Chancellor I want a larger shade for that east window by nightfall. Go!"

Three sons and fourteen daughters had been born to Lord Sabbaghian, but the inherent gift of their father's magic ran strongest in Ulo's veins. Banished to Earth shortly before birth, Ulo Sabbaghian had learned that he could accomplish magic at an early age, and spent the better part of twenty years developing his tricks—the press had called them gimmicks—until he could build a meager show business career with a devoted cult following.

Arriving in the Gavrian outlands—arguably the Eastern Freehold, depending on whom you'd asked at the time—and summoned by a pair of neophyte sorcerers on a dare, of all ridiculous things, he'd learned of his father and his true lineage. More, though, he found himself suddenly and immensely powerful. He brought and dispelled storms, saw through animals' eyes, and communicated without words across distances to others who also held the gift. He carved a small fiefdom out of the wasteland that had once been his family's hold.

Refugees from a border war, given haven in return for work, rebuilt his father's castle with the dark rock that had composed half his lands at the outset. They were decent, rugged people, and he'd been good to them. He could inflict pain as easily as he relieved it; knock a house down with the same effort as he could bind its mortar with blessings. His people loved him, for he blessed their homes with strength and their animals with health, and the crops had been excellent year after year. Perhaps it was truly his magic. Perhaps the spirits of his ancestors smiled upon him.

Perhaps—and he personally thought this the case—he was just one wily son of a bitch who had stumbled into a power vacuum with three thousand years of knowledge to his advantage and the loyalty of several tribes of hard-working and likeable people.

The castle went up quickly.

He used the rock to build roads and bridges through the muddy wastelands that bordered his keep, eventually reaching farming villages claimed by no lord.

He instituted the concept of civil service, employing the locals to build and maintain the roads as part of their feudal duties.

Within a year, the roads from the villages reached the mountain passes that connected the Gavrian outlands and the Eastern Freehold. Roads brought trade. Trade brought wealth enough to gild the black palace in silver, gleaming in the sun, a beacon to traders clear to the Eastern Freehold. Wealth brought men to guard commerce as traders traveled the black roads for a fare. Mercenary guards became a paid police force, who became lords, whose forces became the foundation for an army, and he himself became a king, ruler of the new nation of Ulorak.

The Eastern Freehold had moved on him five years ago, but he'd used the small army he'd built, hiring retired Gavrian soldiers to train a large, if rudimentary, militia. With sheer overwhelming numbers, some clever leadership, and the ability to control the weather, he'd handed the Eastern Freehold its ass. At the deciding battle, the Freeholders had been forced to slog uphill through torrential rain and knee-deep mud, reaching Ulo's forces exhausted before a single blow had been landed. The ensuing slaughter was so massive and one-sided that the people in neighboring villages had used Freeholders' bones to build their fences and tilled the bodies into their soil, which became some of the most productive on the continent.

Ulo had handed control of that province to his commanding general, a blood-under-his-nails type named Elgast who'd had the outpost at the battle site rebuilt with Freeholder skulls mortared both into the outer walls and into a beautiful throne made of the dark black rock. Lord Elgast of Skullsmortar, atop his grisly throne, drank liquor distilled from fields fertilized with Freeholder corpses and kept the neighboring militaries lying awake at night.

Ulo thought it was all a little heavy-handed, but had to admit the man had a knack for getting his point across.

Word traveled of the powerful sorcerer in the silver palace bordering the Eastern Freehold—as well as his Lord Protector on a nearby throne of skulls—and the Gavrian Parliament decided that his fledgling nation of Ulorak was in fact a state of Gavria and demanded back taxes.

He'd met their emissaries with a delegation of his own, bearing not only his back taxes in gold, but also a contingent of nubile whores and several casks of Skullsmortar Whisky as an apology for his oversight.

It had been twelve years since Ulo had first arrived, twitching and shitting his pants in a thaumaturgic triangle in a forgotten corner of Gavria, and he was about to receive appointment to Lord High Sorcerer. Not bad work if you could get it.

The girl, a concubine reserved for visitors and nobility, stooped to pick up her gown, to which he snapped, without looking, "Don't dress. Your work here is hardly done."

"Yes, milord."

"Hurry back," he ordered, and shoved his face further into the bed as she dropped the gown, tied down the shade, and scampered from the apartment. He knew that once he awoke, he would have much work to do. He pulled the feather pillow over his head and swore softly.

"Ulo, son of Sabbaghian, Lord of Ulorak," a huge voice accompanied an intrusive blow against the doorframe. It seemed to Ulo to only have been a moment, but in fact, it had been some minutes since his companion had left.

"Enter," Ulo growled. He'd been *King of Ulorak* until just recently.

"My lord, I am General Loth, Lord of Hwarthar." The visitor was a bull-necked, ponytailed warrior dressed in the crimson tunic and black jerkin of a Gavrian soldier. He knelt in the doorway, his head bowed in respect. "I am a High Warlord of the forces amassing here in Gavria, and am assigned as your personal retainer by His Eminence, King Xaxarharas."

Ulo opened one eye from under the pillow. "Bullshit. Where's Elgast?"

Lord Loth was still. "I await your orders, my lord."

Ulo's voice was sour. "Where is Lord Elgast?"

Loth arose, effectively blocking the doorframe. "Lord Elgast has been relieved, and is returning to his lands. I am your retainer while you're at court, my lord. So it is ordered by King Xaxarharas."

Ulo lifted the pillow. "The king?"

Like most Gavrian warriors, Loth was copper-skinned and thick-browed, with a blocky build and a heavy forehead. His eyes were the color of tobacco and set unusually distant from each other, as if his fighting skills would be augmented by a widened field of vision. His jaw, clean-shaven, was emotionless.

His hands were leathery and broad, his dark forearms slashed with scars and his left hand, Ulo noted, had lost the last joint of the thumb. He wore a sword and an axe at his belt side by side, the sheaths ornate but not jeweled. Gold embroidery denoting awards, campaigns, and marks of rank decorated his jerkin.

"No orders yet," said Ulo.

"Then are you getting up, my lord?"

"No," said Ulo. "I've got a few things I want to do first."

"Call for me, my lord, when you need me." And touching his fist to his forehead and snapping it out in the Gavrian salute, Loth spun on his heel and disappeared from view.

Ulo chuckled silently, pleased with himself, and with his new bodyguard, as the concubine returned.

She stood silently before the bed, averting her eyes and awaiting his word.

And at that moment, the shimmering feelings that had taunted Ulo since his arrival began to turn to certainty. Certainty that after his years of toil, the great wheels were turning for him again, and that this fragile, obsolete world truly had no idea what it was in for.

Later, in the Parliament's war chambers, Ulo sipped at a mug of herb tea, eyeing the others in the room with cautious interest.

Like most Gavrians, Ulo Sabbaghian was tall and muscular. His kingdom of Ulorak—now a state, he had to remind himself— was a rainy, fertile, high country; he wore sandals and light, loose clothing of silver and black tied up with cross garters, and a dark silk cape with a hood that was usually up because there were no sunglasses here and the Gavrian sun was fucking relentless.

Sabbaghian The Silver, the Gavrians called him.

His skin was the tone of most Gavrians; on Earth he would have been regarded as American Indian were it not for his electric blue eyes. His hair was long and straight and black, parted in the center with a wisp or two in his face.

Ulo radiated quiet and calm. He was a mountaintop among men.

Directly to Ulo's right, Loth crammed his mouth with hot sausages and tea.

Kaslix, Lord High Chancellor of Gavria—and until recently, the leading contender for Lord High Sorcerer—opened the wide oaken door with a wave of his hand, as he often enjoyed doing, and greeted Ulo, Loth, and the other warlords and members of Parliament with a shallow nod of his black hood. The door slammed shut behind him, and all was silent for a long moment as the echoes faded.

"I would like you all to welcome our newest court advisor," said Kaslix, "Master Ulo, Lord of Ulorak, son of Sabbaghian the Black. But this is not Sabbaghian the Black. This man is Sabbaghian the Silver."

"He's still a Sabbaghian," grumbled Parliamentarian Rute, a thin, grave man with a long black beard and purple robes.

Kaslix continued, "He has returned not to avenge his father's persecution, but to aid us in laying the foundation for our next undertaking.

"Though his family name has been bane to our lips, we must forgive this, and interpret with broad minds all he has to offer. The War Council has chosen Sabbaghian the Silver as our next Lord High Sorcerer."

Before Ulo, the plates and mugs were cleared away, and the maps unfolded.

"And that's a pegasus," Carter said to no one in particular. "Yep. Sure is."

The pegasus was bigger than most horses he'd seen. It kept

its wings, raven-black and massive, tucked close to its body as the rain battered them. A stablehand led it around the corral while two others readied a massive saddle with a whole hell of a lot of straps.

Daorah Uth Alanas was the commander of the Royal Mounted Air Guard. Tall and tough with a tangled black bob and a muscular neck, she was an immense presence. Her face was honest and athletic; her nose, tan and freckled, had been badly broken and never set. She wore a shirt of black mail with twin silver commander's braids on her shoulder.

"Carter Sorenson," he introduced himself with a hand out.

She took his hand, locking her hand around his wrist, and nodded an acknowledgement. "I know. Commander Daorah Uth Alanas, Royal Air Guard."

Carter got as far as "Commander Day—" before being interrupted.

"I appreciate that you'll have trouble with our names. Daorah."

"Daorah," Carter bowed, and kissed her gauntleted hand.

Iron. Sweat. Horseshit. Leather.

"And it's 'Commander' if anyone's around."

His eyes went to the gold-filigreed scabbard at her side. "Right," he admitted under his breath. "How do we do this, Commander?"

It had been a long, long time since Carter Sorenson had been afraid of anything.

Carter looked down and wiped his blurry eyes, and saw the broccoli-tops of the forest whizzing by beneath his feet, the clouds so far overhead not moving at all, and saw that they were near the tops of the trees and moving at a respectable clip. The huge black wings of the pegasus whapped loudly, weirdly, against the sky, and a biting wind whistled around the edges of Daorah's armor.

He concentrated on the armor. Looking down, he realized, freaked him out.

Her armor was expensive-looking with ornate leatherwork, heavy black chainmail, and a high-crowned iron helm. He smelled moldy, oniony, fermented sweat and the blood-taste of iron, and as he put his hands around her breastplate she raised her voice.

"You're belted in!" yelled Daorah. "You can't fall! Let go! Let go!" she repeated.

Carter let go, and grabbed at the saddle instead. His legs were folded back on themselves in a wide kneeling position he'd only seen in yoga; the saddle rode above the wings. It felt hideously unstable and it was killing his knee. "Where are we going?"

"The Manor at Rogue's River! Just over those hills!" She pointed toward the horizon, to a rift of carpeted hills which was coming up at them really damned fast.

She guided the pegasus down as they topped the hills and skimmed the treetops. As they came upon a clearing, Carter could see a stone manor, really more like a small castle, nestled in the trees beside a foaming, roaring river that carved a sharp cliff from the hillside.

They dove. Carter's stomach, much wiser than the rest of him, stayed at a hundred feet for a while and judged the gap, then rejoined him when the pegasus braked and backwatered, its wings hammering against the wind.

Carter crashed against Daorah, righted himself, and apologized.

They set down with a *c-c-clump*, and the pegasus whinnied and snorted its dislike of having to carry the extra weight.

They had landed beside the stables. Daorah dismounted, then reached up and unbuckled Carter.

Carter patted the pegasus behind the saddle. He became dizzy when he found a warm, trembling, sweating creature under his hands. No machination, no hallucination.

No explanation.

After a moment of fawning over the beast, he slid off, easy on the knee, remembering enough to dismount on the right—the same side she had used.

"I, ah, didn't mean to—" Freak out up there. She's not listening.

Three pages had appeared, and she wasn't paying any more attention to him. She was ordering them to take care of her beast, to prepare baths and rooms and lunch for the two of them, and to alert the concierge that the Crown's charge had arrived, and half a dozen other things he didn't get all of, but a good bit was about armor.

"I'm sorry," she breathed as the pages ran off. "What?"

"Nothing, Commander."

It was around noon, after a bath and breakfast and a few calisthenics, when Carter jogged out to the front gates of the manor to meet Daorah.

She was dressed conservatively in a white tunic with half-sleeves and loose buckskin trousers, her sword around her waist on a wide, gold-embroidered baldric with a long dagger beside it. Carter figured her ten years younger than his forty-three years— maybe even Jarrod's age. She was six feet tall, and had the worst haircut he'd ever seen, broken ends and ragged spikes jutting in all directions. But what she lacked in cheesecake she compensated for with striking power: earthy, hungry, rough-and-tumble. Carter liked her on sight.

It was early summer, the sky bright with a few lazy clouds, the big ringed moon prominent overhead, casting a slight pinkish hue that he was sure no one else noticed, and the temperature was perfect. Carter's tunic of straw-colored hemp was unlaced at the chest and rolled up to his forearms, tucked into his breeches.

Daorah looked him up, and down, and up again, and her eyes settled on the sword hung on its baldric across his back.

Carter had brought as much of his own gear as Jarrod had, but his was on a wagon, slowly headed north.

"I took a look at your sword earlier," she said. "Impressive."

"It's just tool steel," Carter said, failing to add, *Five grand worth of hand-tempered L6 with a Bainite spine and a Martensitic edge. Any bad guys might as well be wearing aluminum foil.*

Carter's greatsword was a late 14th-Century design, smaller and slimmer than a Claymore but massive by any standard. It was a foot longer than Jarrod's *gran espée de guerre,* five feet pommel to tip, just under a foot of which was hardwood handle with a polished steel egg for a pommel and a graceful, curving crossbar. Above the crossbar was the *ricossa,* a squared, blunt section of blade wrapped in leather to match the hilt, which served as a left-hand grip for close-quarters fighting. The weapon was built from L6, an industrial tool steel used primarily in band saw blades, which can be hardened to an extreme degree while retaining magnificent durability and super-hard edges.

"Show me," she said.

Carter moved the baldric from across his back to over one shoulder, and rested his hands at his sides. In a single motion, he shrugged out of the baldric and cleared the sword, then snapped it with both hands into a fending guard, dropping the scabbard and belt in the grass with a jangle.

In the trained hands of a man Carter's size, the greatsword

appeared graceful and agile. A small crowd gathered as he moved through the major defensive positions with it.

In the right hands, a greatsword combines the strengths of spear, poleaxe, war sword, and rapier. It can parry spear thrusts, pierce breastplates, cleave helms, split mail, rend shields, lop the heads off of spears, and dissuade a charging warhorse. The hardened steel pommel doubles as brass knuckles for infighting. Levered in a series of teardrops and circles, it could hold off multiple opponents, or hold and defend a battlefield position.

The sword weighed less than six pounds, meticulously balanced so that he could wield it with one hand if necessary. He demonstrated this, too, including a spear-type thrust holding it by the pommel to maximize the reach.

He showed them how to fence two-handed using the *ricossa.*

When he had finished, the crowd applauded. He bowed, sheathed the weapon, and hung it across his back again.

"What is that weapon?" asked a bearded man with a heavy war sword at his belt, a sword a good foot and a half shorter than Carter's. He was powerfully built and hyper-alert, with fierce blue eyes and a heavy brow. Carter noted the scars on his hands and arms.

"It's called a greatsword," Carter replied. "It's from my homeland."

"I've never seen one that large. Could you train me with that?" the man asked.

"Gladly," said Carter. The man introduced himself as Master Gronek, the master at arms of the castle.

Carter nodded and stuck his hand out. "Carter Sorenson. Uh, Chancellor. Come get me tomorrow afternoon. I'd be happy to show you."

Gronek declined the hand, but put his fist over his heart and nodded in the Gateskeep soldiers' salute. "I'll leave you to it."

"Nice guy," Carter noted. Daorah grunted in agreement.

"So, that pegasus of yours," said Carter. "Do I get one, too?"

She laughed, and he sank.

"They pulled me from my command to train you," she grumbled. "We see the field from above. Since they want you making strategy, they figure I'd be the best one to show you how everything moves down here."

"Well, thank you," Carter said, buckling the sword around his shoulder. "You're making a great sacrifice, and I appreciate it."

She dropped on her hip and jackknifed, taking his legs out from under him.

"Ow!" He winced, rubbing his elbow where he'd banged it on a small rock. "Man, what the —?"

"Get up." She was already on her feet again.

Carter stood, eyeing her carefully. "What the hell was that for? And watch the knee." He swept grass from his stubbly head with a flick of his hand, and straightened the blade on his back.

"Never trust anyone," she gave him his first lesson. "You're going to be a Chancellor, counsel to the king, and you're probably going to be the most important figure in this war. So you never trust *anyone*. Least of all someone close to you. Besides, your balance is pitiful."

Carter slowly widened his eyes. "Is that so?" He dropped back into a fighting stance, knees bent, his fists up in a Muay Thai guard. "You just try that again," he dared with a nod.

Commander Daorah folded her arms and stood back. "No one in their right mind would attack you, now."

Looking dejected, Carter lowered his hands a bit. "Oh."

"You're going to get used to being hit off-guard," she was saying. "At your size, no one's ever going to fight you one-on-one, much less face-to-face." She took a step forward and looked him over again. "So first, we'll work on alertness, and today, I'll ensure you're passable at swordsmanship. Though it certainly seems you are. Eventually, we'll teach you to fight three-to-one, five-to-one, and even ten-to-one."

"I thought I was going to be commanding. You know, strategic-level stuff."

"Yes," she said. "And a lot of people are going to want to kill you over it."

The sun was feeble and cold above the Hold of Gavria. Ulo dunked cookies in his tea as he perused a journal written by his father during the last days of his reign.

A knock at his door jarred him; he'd been on edge since beginning the book some days ago. He took a slow breath, then another for good measure, and telekinetically opened the door without looking up.

The newcomer's presence in the room was so massive and grave that Ulo didn't have to turn from his reading to know when the man had entered the study.

"You would be?" Ulo asked, still not looking up.

"Mukul."

"And?"

Mukul was beside the desk, now. "Your time would be better spent learning of the early days of your father's life. You already know how it ended."

Ulo marked the page and closed the book. He knocked hard on the desktop. "Out."

A barely-dressed Gavrian woman scurried from under the desk and left the room in a flash of dark skin, long hair, and jewelry.

Mukul watched her go as Ulo adjusted his robes and looked his visitor over.

Mukul was southern Gavrian, toffee-skinned and wiry, not particularly tall, and older than Ulo. His tunic was fine purple silk, inlaid with gold threads and padded at the shoulders, and his feet were sandaled, gnarled, and black. His hair was gray at the temples and clipped short in the style Ulo had become accustomed to seeing on warriors. His right hand was crossed with scars that disappeared into his sleeve. "You're a soldier," Ulo remarked.

"Once," said Mukul. "I commanded the legions at Axe Valley in the Succession Wars, some years ago."

"And now?"

Mukul gestured broadly. "They come to me for advice."

"'They?'" repeated Ulo.

"All of them." It had the ring of a boast. "Most of the War Council, at one time or another."

"Who pays your retainer?"

"The Crown."

"And you don't find that that clouds your judgment?"

"Do you?"

"Not yet," Ulo admitted. "So, you're here to peddle your services?"

"Do you need them?"

"I don't know."

"That's a refreshing answer from one with such close ties to Parliament."

"What sort of things have you done? What's your most recent accomplishment?" A wind skittered through the arrowslit, rustling parchments on the desk.

Mukul let the moment pass before answering. "You."

"So, what's your end?" Ulo pulled his cloak tighter. They stood on the top of the great tower, and the wind carried their voices away from the sentry on the far side of the roof. "You didn't bring me here for nothing."

"I didn't bring you here," said Mukul. "I simply opened the door for you. Whispered in a couple of ears."

Ulo shook his head slowly. "You shouldn't have had to do that. I've paid them enough damned money. The way they're acting, it's as if I'm supposed to be wowed by the novelty of it all."

"Are you?"

He shrugged. "Sure."

"This doesn't impress you?"

"Impress? No. I built a nicer castle than this, faster. I'm richer than any of these men. My army did what theirs couldn't. My family history alters my place in things. On its own merits, however, I fail to be impressed with Gavria."

"What would it take to impress you?"

"More than you've got."

Mukul grunted. The wind blew the hair on the left side of his head upright for a moment. "How would you know what I've got?"

Ulo was careful to keep his thoughts tucked close. He spoke even more slowly than usual. "You're a warrior who no longer fights, who earns his keep as an advisor."

Great mists of rain hung from the horizon. The wind brought the smell of damp dirt.

"Yes."

"You wouldn't be coming to me now, unless there was something I could do for you. And it's something that you don't want anyone else to know, or we'd be discussing this somewhere where we wouldn't get rained on."

"As I said, you're shrewd."

They were silent for a while.

"There is something you can do," said Mukul, as the first drops of rain pelted them. "I need a voice in Parliament. You've done well, but you need to learn our political system so you can work within it. You have talent, but it would take you a lifetime to learn how to survive at court. I am offering my expertise."

"At what cost?"

"Friendship."

Ulo barked a laugh. "That, I do not need."

"My friendship, you need."

"You mean *my* friendship, *you* need."

"That, as well."

"And what does our friendship bring me?"

"Everything you can't buy," said Mukul. "Respect. Power. Your family's name no longer whispered in hushed tones and used in stories to frighten children."

Lightning flashed behind Ulo, and thunder slammed through the world.

"So, what, exactly, is the problem with Gateskeep?" Ulo asked, speaking to the war council. "Are their armies better trained?"

"I'd say yes," Loth spoke to the disagreements of the other warlords. "Face it, Hanmin," he addressed the eldest, "They run tight, textbook formations. They excel at breaking offenses. Their infantry is brave and solid. We counter this by hitting them with more armor, but you know they're more disciplined."

"That's purely academic," another warlord interjected. "Taking the Shieldlands creates a situation wherein we must use a small, mobile contingent to hold a space a week's ride across. It's improbable that we can hold that much land once we take it.

Gateskeep's armies are the last of our problems. We need manpower to instill order. We need soldiers in every hamlet and farm before we move into Falconsrealm."

"You don't have the soldiers," Ulo stated. "So, what do you have?"

"Well, as you know, ores—gold, silver, steel, and their end products—are our major exports."

"If by yours, you mean mine?" Ulo corrected.

"Ulorak is now a territory of Gavria," said Parliamentarian Hanmin, balding and fat. "I'd suggest you remember that."

Ulo stared at him for a moment and let it pass.

Loth spoke. "We're still short of manpower. We haven't a tactician who can hold Falconsrealm with our numbers."

"You do now," said Ulo.

The room went quiet.

"Are you suggesting we use your army?" said Mukul.

"If I had an army that could beat Falconsrealm," said Ulo, "would I be paying taxes to Gavria?"

Loth spat his drink across the table.

"I need to arrange a meeting with the heir presumptive of Falconsrealm," said Ulo. "This Lord Albar Hillwhite."

"He's the heir presumptive," said Hanmin dismissively. "He has no actual power."

"He's the heir presumptive," corrected Ulo, "so he has a tremendous amount of power. His power is not obvious, so it's nothing your feeble mind is able to appreciate."

"Watch your tone, wizard," said Marghan, Lord High Inquisitor.

"Arrange the meeting," said Ulo.

"You expect him to give us his country?" asked Hanmin.

"I expect him," said Ulo, "to listen to reason."

Jarrod Torrealday was doing his time in hell.

They'd been out of Gateskeep for four days. The joyride was over.

Aside from the bumps, bruises, and saddle-soreness, he had a crushing headache from muscle fatigue in his back and neck, and dozens of patches of skin rubbed raw under his ever-sweaty armor.

Adding to this misery was a case of hay fever he'd contracted as a result of his body's reluctance to adapt to new surroundings, which had now turned to a full-blown case of allergic sinusitis. On top of everything else, something he'd eaten had crippled him with the trots.

Even Sir Javal had to sympathize. Rather than taking the twenty-day trek around the mountains, through the Shieldlands, dropping in on local lords and training Jarrod along the way, he chose instead to negotiate the trails leading through the passes, spotted with snow even in summer but leading into High River's backyard.

Regardless, Jarrod's vacation had been utterly ruined by the time they limped into High River.

Jarrod hadn't been saying much the last few days, mostly because he found his answers terse and his temper shorter than it had ever been in his life.

There had been moments, however.

That morning's sunrise from the summit of Hellweather Pass, at the border of the Falconsrealm wildernesses, had come at just the right time to convince him not to hand in his spear.

And now they were riding up the King's Road, having skirted the length of High Lake, and proceeded through the gentry's quarter at High River City, far below High River Keep.

The lake—the headwaters of High River—was long and slender and deep, and split the city in two, East City and West City, one on either end of the lake with a handful of manor houses along the shores between them on either side. Jagged cliffs carpeted with evergreens stretched up and away into pinnacles that scraped fog down from the clouds.

Javal had told him that civilization was repeatedly brought to its knees every thousand years or so in an event they called The Cataclysm: earthquakes, tidal waves, gouges in the ground swallowing entire cities, mountains belching fire. He figured Javal was exaggerating. Something had to survive, he knew, or they'd all be living in caves. But he guessed that the massive moon tore the hell out of the planet.

He wondered what the oceans were like.

The road from High River City became hideously steep as the horses plodded up toward the great keep. It took nearly an hour.

As they rode under the barbican, Jarrod's neck craned to wonder up at the towers. Beyond the gatehouse lay an immense curtain wall in either direction, spreading for acres up a soberingly steep hillside of waving grasses. Further up was another wall, much higher, and beyond that was the keep in all her broad-shouldered glory: two mighty, broad towers in the near corners and at a far corner a smaller tower, dizzying in its height, its crenellations silhouetted against the forested drop of the box-canyon and the sawtooths and spires beyond.

"Wow."

"Yes" was all Javal said.

It was a long ride up to the inner barbican, at which point they crossed a stone bridge bridging a gully filled with large and splintery rocks.

Jarrod managed a half-wave to the many guards peering down upon them. "Hiya," he muttered. His mind was on food, with all his pains sapping his energies. Ah, yes. Food. And a long soapy bath to wash the sweat from his blisters.

Javal whistled for his attention. "Stop here, Jarrod," he called. Jarrod pulled the mare's head back (the two of them had just recently established where authority truly resided) and swung down, adjusting his swordbelt. He swallowed the pain as his legs shot slivers of black glass into his eyes. *Dammit, you're here!*

They entered the great keep, clapping each other on the back. Javal handed him a few *well dones* and assured him that the hardest part was over. "We'll get you healed up in no time, rider." The ground floor of Highriver was a three-story anteroom lit with narrow windows and torches that vanished into the distance down each wall, and adorned with ornate tapestries denoting the chivalric orders and allied cultures. The floor was rough stone and a wide flight of stairs corkscrewed up the right-hand wall.

"Sir Javal, Son-Lord of Ravenhurst, Captain, Order of the Stallion," Javal introduced himself to the guards, pulling off his helmet and headgear and tucking one into the other. "This is King's Rider Jarrod, Son-Lord of Knightsbridge. We report for castle duty."

The guard looked them over.

Javal raised his voice a bit. "Did you not hear the word 'Captain?'"

The guards made a hasty salute.

"Let me guess," said Javal. "You're here on scutage."

It was then that Jarrod noted that the guards seemed neither particularly fit, nor disciplined, compared to Javal.

"Yes, sir," said one. "Lord Farmond of Wine River hired us."

Javal nodded. He pointed to the twin gold braids around his left shoulder. "These," he said, "mean 'Captain.' One silver is 'Lieutenant.' One gold is 'Chief Lieutenant.' Two silver is 'Commander,' and two gold," he pointed to them again, "'Captain.' Make that mistake again, and I'll beat you unconscious. You at least train with us, yes?"

"I will, sir."

"That's the right answer. Alert the chamberlain that we've arrived, and get some valets to haul our gear. We've got quite a bit, so bring several. We'll watch the door."

"Yes, sir."

As the guard left the doorway, Jarrod asked, "Scutage?"

Javal's voice was low and serious. "Knights can hire mercenaries to stand in for them at castle duty, as long as they pay a tax in addition. The money paid to the mercenaries is called scutage. It's a major flaw in our security."

"I imagine so."

"It was bad enough that the border lords used to send the fools that pass for their local knights," said Javal. "Now even they don't bother to show up for castle duty, and their lords send these idiots instead. We say nothing of our missions or objectives to anyone outside of our own order. Is that clear?"

"Absolutely," said Jarrod. "You know, Carter said something about the border lords. Kinda rough out there, huh?"

Javal shook his head. "Lawless. Most of the lords of the Shieldlands took their keeps by force of arms, and it's ongoing. The estates out there might as well be small kingdoms, waging ten-man wars with their neighbors."

"Shit."

"Shit, indeed. Teenaged thugs and paunch-helmed robberbarons are the only troops standing between us and Gavria right now."

At that moment, another guard across the antechamber bellowed, "Attention, all! The heir presumptive, his grace, Lord Albar Hillwhite!"

"Speaking of paunch-helms," said Javal, kneeling. Jarrod dropped to one knee as well, and set his helmet in front of him.

A small knot of men wound their way down the stairs to the

main floor, laughing and talking loudly. Three were men in riding armor, fine silver mail over buckskin or suede; two of these were in spectacled Norman-style helms with mail hanging from the eyes and horsehair plumes, and the third, a head taller and half again as broad as the others, was bare-headed and sported a black topknot. There was also a hooded figure in silver and black who walked silently behind the warriors with a ponderous gait; and last was a blade of a man Javal's age, quite well-dressed in a bright yellow tunic and black cape, with a shock of dark hair and a pinched face that would have been handsome had it not been so intense. He seemed to be dominating the conversation.

As the knot neared, Javal's smile melted and his face went ashen.

His voice a hiss, the knight ordered, "Don't look up. And whatever happens," he said this last emphatically and with clenched teeth, "Do. NOT. Draw."

Jarrod, obeying but not understanding, averted his eyes. "Yes, sir."

The party wove its way over to the door. Jarrod fought the itch to look up with all he had.

"—well, quiet journey to you," the pinched-faced man was saying, "And I, ah—" his voice quickly trailed into nothingness as he saw the two kneeling knights by the doorway. "Yes. Quiet journey," he concluded.

On his way past, the tallest of the armored men slammed Jarrod's ear with his shin hard enough to level him and send his helmet skidding across the floor.

Jarrod regained his feet, slurping at the shooting pains in his head.

The knight muttered a gruff apology, snorting, "Oh, excuse me, sire!" with his hand on his heart. This brought hoots and taunts from his seconds.

Jarrod's temper supernovaed.

They tangled, crashing and bashing and cursing at the top of their lungs. Javal leaped to his feet and roared Jarrod's name, both a reprimand and a warning.

For Javal had recognized the tallest of the knights.

It was General Loth, High Warlord of Gavria.

Javal was working out how he would explain to Crius that Jarrod had been killed only a few days into his training until, in a spectacular moment, Jarrod rolled Loth up onto his shoulders and flipped him into the stone floor hard enough to rattle the entire castle.

The world stopped on its axis.

Somewhere outside, a bird sang.

Heads turned from Loth to Jarrod and back amid a growing murmur of profanities as it occurred to everyone in the room that Jarrod might have just killed the most feared warrior in all of Gavria with his bare hands.

Jarrod spat a mouthful of blood and put one hand on his swordhilt as he addressed Loth's seconds. "Are any of you tougher than him?" He nodded toward Loth, still not drawing.

Even a couple of Falconsrealm knights backed up a step for good measure.

Loth rolled to his feet, groaning, wincing, and nearly doubled. He staggered to a horse stance, then drew his sword and held it before him with both hands as he straightened up. His voice was pained. "Nice trick. Try that with a sword in your hand, boy."

"Okay," Jarrod offered, half-drawing.

"Jarrod!" yelled Javal. "Do not draw!"

Loth menaced with his sword, which was big, heavy, unornamented, and, Jarrod knew because he owned one almost identical, specifically built to fuck up the exact armor he was wearing right now. "Earn your spurs," Loth hissed.

"Rider!" shouted the loud man in yellow. The prince, Jarrod

realized. "That man is a guest of the crown!"

"So am I," Jarrod growled.

Loth's blade dropped a hair. "Who are you?" he demanded.

"I'm the guy who just knocked you on your ass," said Jarrod. "Or were you not paying attention?"

Javal stepped between Jarrod and Loth, his hands out in either direction. "Enough."

Loth was salivating, his eyes intent on Jarrod. "Away, Captain, or I'll run you through."

Javal's eyes were calm. "So be it, sir."

There was an awkward moment.

"I swear!" Loth warned.

Jarrod spoke quietly, "Captain, I can take this guy."

"I believe it," said Javal. "But take your hand off your sword. That's an order."

"Captain!" ordered the rat-faced man. "Get that soldier under control!"

"He's a King's Rider, not a soldier, and go back to your knitting, Alby," said Javal, still locking eyes with Loth, "This is man's work. Go on," he told Loth. "Run me through, so the rest of us can see you hanged."

"Hey, just apologize," suggested Jarrod, to Loth. "You apologize; I let you walk."

"Rider," ordered Javal, "Shut up."

In another moment, every available guard surrounded Javal and Loth, and had formed a wall between Jarrod and the warlord. "Get behind me," one muttered under his breath. Another clapped Jarrod gently on the shoulder in commendation. "Nicely done, rider."

Loth sheathed his blade. "Another time," he assured Javal.

"Assuredly," said Javal.

"And you," Loth challenged Jarrod through the crowd, "I need your name."

"I'm Jarrod of Knightsbridge!" shouted Jarrod, having to stand on tiptoes to be seen over the wall of black-armored Falconsrealm troops separating them. "And you owe me an apology!" he added as Loth and the others departed.

"Sir Javal!" shouted Albar, "Control that soldier!"

"Jarrod, form on me!" Javal pushed his way through the troops and stood face to face with Albar.

Albar beckoned the knights closer to him. "Arrest that soldier," he ordered, pointing to Jarrod.

Jarrod spat another mouthful of blood and put his hand back on his swordhilt. "Easy, Jarrod," said Javal. "Belay that order," Javal growled at the troops. With his helmet off, every knight knew who he was.

Javal's chin was even with Albar's nose.

"You get that soldier under control," Albar repeated, pointing at Jarrod.

"Oh, he's under control. Frankly, you're lucky he didn't decide to kill your—" and here his voice dripped vitriol on the word, "—*honored* guest."

"That man," Albar's voice quivered, "is an ambassador."

Javal cleared his throat, and spoke quietly. "This man," he pointed to Jarrod, "is a King's Rider."

Jarrod bowed.

"If you have an issue with his actions," said Javal, "you can take it up with the king. I doubt you'd want that, though, unless things have changed around here recently."

Javal turned to push his way through the crowd, Jarrod on his heels.

"Oh, and Alby?" he turned back. Jarrod noticed—boy, did he notice—that Javal failed to address the heir presumptive by his title. "You realize we've arrived early. I'm certain you'll take comfort in our extended presence here." He wiggled his eyebrows mischievously.

Javal muttered under his breath as they rounded the first turn in the grand stairway. "You just made your life exceptionally difficult."

"Are you suicidal?" Javal asked as he shucked his mail.

"That's an odd question," Jarrod admitted.

"It's a serious question. He would have killed you. Or worse: if you'd killed him, you'd be hanged tonight. I told you not to draw your sword."

"I didn't draw my sword."

"You were about to!" Javal reprimanded. "And you would have put yourself in a position that would have ended in your death, one way or another."

"You need to teach me the rules around here, Goddammit." Jarrod grumbled.

"I will. And until I do, you do exactly what I say. Let me see that," Javal put a thumb on Jarrod's swollen jaw. Jarrod lurched upright and snorted in a deep breath at the comets that tore through his head as the knight prodded.

"Whew," Javal estimated, "Is that where he kicked you?"

"Ow! Yeah."

"That must hurt like hell. Are you missing any teeth?"

"No, I'm good," Jarrod said. "Who was that motherfucker?"

"Wow. Good word," Javal said after a moment's thought. He unbuckled a legging and tossed it aside before continuing, in lower tones, "That motherfucker was Lord Loth of Hwarthar."

Jarrod bent at the waist and shed his mail with a grunt, a thunk, and a jingle. "Means nothing to me," he admitted quietly, standing upright again.

"He killed my father."

Jarrod was silent for a moment. "I'm sorry," he finally said. He hated hearing that people had died, for he never knew what to say. He didn't wholly believe that anyone ever knew quite what to say.

"Don't be." Javal blew his cheeks out at the memory. "He slew my father on the field, quite honorably. I can draw no animosity there.

"Loth's one of the finest warriors in all of Gavria, maybe in the world. I myself have met him on the field half a dozen times. Last I heard, they'd made him a general."

"A warlord? Wait a minute. He's a general from Gavria?" Jarrod's words were hasty and slurred with confusion. "Why didn't you take him? Why didn't you let *me* take him?"

Javal shrugged. "He's here as a guest of the crown. That makes him as good as a citizen.

"For one Gateskeeper to slay another is murder. We could have dueled, but I had no reason to—and truth be told, I doubt if I could take him in a duel." Javal sighed and shook his head, laughing quietly. "I can't believe you threw him on his ass."

Jarrod swelled with pride.

Javal continued, "If we were at war, things would be different. But we're not at war with Gavria. Well, not yet," he added with a knowing grimace.

"So, what's he doing here?"

Javal was silent.

"That's treason, isn't it?"

"Breathe a word to that end and you'll be much worse than dead."

Jarrod put a hand to his head. "What's our move?"

Javal had an answer for that. "We watch. And listen. The king's eyes and ears, remember?"

"And, on that," Jarrod brought up another point, "Why is it, you don't have to call Prince Albar by his title?"

Javal underhanded his other legging ungracefully onto the first, and, bared from the waist up, ran his fingers through his hair time and again to dry the sweat. There was not a wasted ounce on him anywhere; his muscles rippled like leaves in a slow breeze. "Well, as many people tend to forget—Albar included—he's not a prince yet.

"I've known Alby since we were boys. He's not of royal blood, much as he thinks he is. He's a Hillwhite."

"I'm going to guess that's a patrician family," Jarrod said.

"Yes. The Hillwhites could buy Gateskeep Palace outright if they wanted," Javal grumbled. "But I'll not address him as royalty until he marries. Frankly, I think he's a complete ass, and I'd not have a qualm about beating the feathers out of him. Of course, once he's prince, I'll have to kiss his bedslipper," Javal sat down on his armor chest. "That's the way of things."

Jarrod nodded in forlorn agreement. "So, what's next?"

"We'll get you to a healer. Clean up your face, and I'll show you where."

Two floors above their rooms, Javal asked Jarrod, "Have you ever been kicked by a horse?"

"Not yet. The day is still young, though," he admitted. "Why do you ask?"

"Anything similar?"

"I once hit my head bungee-jumping."

"Bungee-jumping?"

"Bungee-jumping. Yes."

"Bungee-jumping." Javal fed the word to his mouth a few times. "We'll think of something." He pushed open a heavy door.

"Durvin?"

Inside was a wooden cot with a feather mattress, a desk with a human skull and various sorcerer's doohickeys—mortar and pestle, vials, candles, the usual stuff Jarrod pretty much expected to see in a healer's chambers; one wall was composed almost entirely of books, and a bleached human skeleton hung near the arrowslit. In a moment, a tangle-headed youth in a wrinkled tunic entered from the next room, rubbing sleep from his eyes.

"My lord? Ah, Sir Javal. Good to see you, again. Another arrow wound from an outraged father?" He looked the knight over. "You don't seem to be—Ah."

Javal winced off the assumption as Jarrod quipped, "Discreet, all right."

The knight's voice was an arrogant hiss. "Tend to your own wounds, boy."

The healer, Durvin, took Jarrod's swollen jaw in his hand. "Hold still, sir. Hmm. Punched? Clubbed?"

"Alertness training," Javal stated, his tone authoritative. He turned his voice to Jarrod, "Right?"

Jarrod shrugged. "Sure."

"Also, he has the season's fever, and an infection of the bowel that makes him weak."

"Hmm. All right. Sit you down, on the cot, sire."

Jarrod sat. The boy handed him a vial of something gray, thick, and nasty-looking to hold, then went to rummaging through his desk. "So, what was all that bustle about out there? It sounded like a fight."

"A bully getting his comeuppance," Jarrod grouched.

"Good to hear. When it turns black, drink it all," he instructed, then turned around to face his patient, "And trust me."

In one hand he held a small stick resembling a conductor's baton, and in the other, the skull. He chanted something incomprehensible, again and again and again, and Jarrod saw the contents of the vial in his hand begin to swirl and darken, though it was only slightly warm to the touch.

"Drink it, sir." The healer touched Jarrod's jaw with the wand-thing and Jarrod tipped the vial up and downed it.

He found the vial's contents lukewarm, and tasting of smoke and licorice.

"That's pretty good," he admitted.

He immediately felt his sinus troubles disappear, and the throbbing in his face, and his gut-ache, simultaneously and with such urgency, they left him with a void of sensation that made his head reel.

"Better, sir?"

Oh, yes. "My God."

"And mine. Come back at dawn, every day for ten days. Don't be late."

Javal promptly thanked the young healer, and steered Jarrod down the hall.

"What'd he do to me?"

"Just magic."

"No," Jarrod was adamant. "I mean, did he just numb me? Or did he actually heal me?"

"What's the difference?"

Jarrod waved his hands in frustration. "Big difference. Am I still sick, and I just don't notice?"

"Do you want to be?"

"No. I want to be healed."

"Then you are."

The concept peeked around a corner at Jarrod and thumbed its nose at him.

Jarrod spoke slowly. "I can't be better, and not better. Am I asymptomatic but still sick?"

"That is what I'm saying. Right now, your body doesn't know the difference. Under Durvin, you'll *feel* healed almost immediately, and you'll heal quickly because of it. Healers like Durvin are a tremendous asset. They'll stop the bleeding and send you right back onto the field and under the stress of battle—trust me—you won't know the difference."

"I don't know if I like that thought."

Javal shrugged. "There's nothing to like or dislike about it. It simply is the way it is."

After another pensive silence, Jarrod bit his lip and nodded. "I don't understand."

"Neither do I. If we did, we'd be sorcerers."

"Well, I feel better, that much is certain."

Javal clapped him on the shoulder. "Good. What is 'bungee-jumping,' anyway?"

"This is ridiculous!" Jarrod cried, slipping and falling to his knees for the umpteenth time. The calf on his shoulders bleated loudly and urinated, dousing him. "Ugh! C'mon!"

Javal was fifty feet ahead of him, jogging effortlessly down the trail. "Come, Jarrod! Only another league or two!" he laughed.

Jarrod knew the drill. Come autumn, that calf would be a hundred pounds heavier, and he'd be able to run the entire hunting course with its weight on his shoulders.

Swearing a loud string of rugged English monosyllables, Jarrod arose and ran. The calf voiced its concerns about this entire operation. "Oh, and you shut up!" he warned it. "I don't like this any more than you do."

Javal, of course, was now fifty yards up the path, and about to vanish from sight. As he did, Jarrod shouted, "If there's a camera crew up there, I'm gonna kick your ass!"

"Set the calf down." Javal was waiting in the middle of the hunting grounds. Four huge marble pillars sat in the midst of a grassy clearing, in no particular pattern. Jarrod noted that a fifth pillar had long ago toppled and broken. The large moon with its slender dust ring was high in the sky opposite the sun, adding an odd pink hue that, to Jarrod, sharpened all the corners of the world. Wherever he was, it was a gorgeous planet.

Obediently, and quite cheerily, Jarrod knelt and swung the calf from his shoulders. It wandered off, not far. "I stink," he warned.

"Yes," Javal agreed. "Here, we can talk."

"Talk, huh?" Jarrod stretched his hamstrings against an apple tree. Standing, he could squeeze his shin within three inches of his forehead, straight up over his head like a dancer.

Javal whistled low in appreciation of the feat, then walked over and sat on one of the fallen chunks of marble. "Yes. Talk."

Jarrod tossed him an apple. "Hey," he called. Javal was mooncalfing as it arced toward his face.

With the pointed disinterest Jarrod would attribute to a Zen master, Javal caught it with an indifferent flick of his hand.

"That was him, today," he announced, rubbing the apple against his trouser leg.

Jarrod leaned away from his foot momentarily. "What?"

"King Sabbaghian. He was with Loth at the Keep."

"How do you know?"

"I can tell a foreigner just by his walk. You didn't see him?"

"I didn't look."

"He didn't want you to," said Javal. "That wasn't Loth's style, kicking you to the ground like that. That was King Sabbaghian behind him. He wanted a diversion. He made his exit during the fight. I'm pretty certain he knows who you are. I don't know how, but, ah—Good ol' Alby," he nearly laughed. "The look on his face—he figured we wouldn't be here for twenty days, yet. Oops! Order of the Stallion's here." Then he grumbled, "It actually wouldn't surprise me if Albar tries to kill us both."

"He hates us that much, huh?"

Javal took a bite of the apple and chewed thoughtfully. "Albar has a chance at something great. He doesn't want us to muck it up. I hate to think this way, but he has a lot to gain by siding with Gavria if things go badly for us.

"You see, Princess Adielle rules Falconsrealm. Alby's family rules nothing, though they control a great deal of the trade in Falconsrealm. They're ore barons.

"When they marry, she'll still rule, and Alby will merely be an ornament. He won't have any more actual power than he does now. Oh, we'll all have to salute him, but," he set the apple beside him on the rubble, "If he, if . . ." he stammered for a moment or two, re-organizing his thoughts. "I believe that Gavria is going to enlist Albar's aid, and eventually they'll use him, and those allied to him, to claim Falconsrealm. I don't believe they can do it without his help. They've been trying to take all of Falconsrealm for a thousand years, and they just don't have the resources to hold it. But if they can enlist the Falconsrealm chivalry, and the mercenary hordes of those loyal to Albar—and there a lot of nobles loyal to Albar, never underestimate him—they can launch the principality into essentially a civil war, and overrun it in the midst of it all."

"What does Al—? I see," Jarrod answered his own question. "And Albar becomes prince. Or king, or whatever, if the secession succeeds. A-hah! The succession of the secession," he punned merrily. "Da-dump."

Javal lobbed his apple at him. "Wiseass. You must be feeling better."

Jarrod ducked it with a laugh. "Much. No, but I think I understand.

"No, wait," he said. "Check that; I don't. Where's the princess in all this? I'd think she'd be pretty torqued if it goes down that way."

"I'd guess there's trouble in paradise. I'll be surprised if the wedding happens, and if it does, frankly—and don't breathe a word of this—I don't expect her to live a year."

"I'll kill that motherfucker."

"She's my cousin. You'd have to get in line."

"Wait—you're royalty?" asked Jarrod.

"It doesn't leave this glen," said Javal. "My father was brother to the king. I'm fifth, but really more like tenth, in line for the throne." He ticked off on his fingers, "Adielle, Damon, either Albar, or Damon's wife when he marries, any children between any of them, then me after all of them. I don't want it. I set it aside to join the order."

"Jesus," said Jarrod under his breath.

"Very few people know, especially among the soldiery. I don't want them thinking they're being ordered around by a man like Albar. When you meet him, you'll understand.

"Another thing: I worked my way up through the ranks. Never forget that. Once you're knighted into the Order of the Stallion, any consideration for commission will be strictly on merit. Your lordship, your lands, your family, your wealth, all get set aside because of what we do. The other orders, not so much."

"I won't say a word," said Jarrod. "What does Gavria get out of helping Albar take Falconsrealm?"

"Long Valley, the Shieldlands, the fertile lands. They wouldn't have to pay us for their food. And those on the Gavrian War Council get their names sung around the fire for the next fifty or hundred years, until we kick their asses and take it back."

"Doesn't Gateskeep already have farmland? That whole area

north of Long Valley."

Javal winked at him. "You're sharp. Our people wouldn't starve, not even close. But the lords of the Shieldlands would be killed, and once we don't have to trade with Gavria, Gateskeep would lose its primary source of iron and gold. Our wealth is in the Shieldlands. The Hillwhites control most of the silver for Falconsrealm, and what iron Gateskeep has."

"Well, shit," Jarrod said. "If Gavria takes the Shieldlands, the Hillwhites control the war. If they control the money and the iron, they could effectively hand Falconsrealm over to Gavria with a handshake. If they decide they don't like us, we're in a lot of trouble, my friend."

"They don't like us," said Javal.

"Then we're in a lot of trouble," said Jarrod.

"You grasp complex things quickly. I'm going to enjoy training you."

"Let's keep going. Tell me about King Sabbaghian."

"Oh, yes," said Javal. "King Ulo Sabbaghian, ruler of Ulorak. Lord Sabbaghian, now. They're calling him Sabbaghian the Silver. He's a Gavrian. Raised in your homeland."

"Crius said that. I remember now."

"I think I only know what you already know. He's the son of a great sorcerer. Some say the greatest that ever lived."

"Naturally," Jarrod muttered under his breath. "So, this guy's a sorcerer too?"

"And a good one. He probably wasn't much to speak of on your world, but here . . ." as Javal's voice trailed off, Jarrod fought back a shudder. Javal said, "I imagine Gavria is just as scared of him as we are."

"Yes, but they're giving him a seat on the war council," said Jarrod. "When he becomes Lord High Sorcerer, his power is only going to increase. He's now part of the problem. At least, that's how I understand it."

"You're probably right. But he's heavily guarded, hence Loth's presence. I imagine Loth's true mandate is to slay him if he gets any ideas.

"Usually, our fail-safe with regard to Gavria is to have members of our spy network assassinate the masterminds of the enemy's campaign, and then we counterattack as chaos ensues. However, Loth's presence—and Loth is of value to *us,* now, in his duty as Sabbaghian's shadow—negates this. We can't get an assassin near him because of Loth, and we can't kill Loth because he's the only thing keeping Sabbaghian in check. That's why I didn't duel with Loth this morning, or let you."

"So you figured this all out while we were kneeling, there?"

Javal arose, and said, "Yes, and I'll teach you to do it, as well. Get your calf."

"Northboy!"

"Whoo-ee! Hair like a pretty girl!"

"Arms like a pretty girl!" joked another. Jarrod received a clap on the back from Javal and went to stand with the twenty or so other knights, riders, soldiers, and hopefuls. This was not free sparring; this was military training for field soldiers. Toughs in piecemeal armor sent from the remotest keeps puffed out their chests and licked their lips with faux bravado. Knights were designated by steel spurs and cloak pins; officers by shoulder braids.

Mercenaries on scutage were conspicuously absent, Jarrod noted.

He wore his battered practice armor over a bull-rider's vest. This armor was the most protective thing he owned—maybe moreso than the man-at-arms harness he'd left behind—and was the least authentic: a cuirass and pauldrons of black high-density polyethylene cut from chemical barrels with memory foam glued behind, the whole belted together with scalloped lames for his upper arms and broad hanging tassets to cover his hips and upper legs. He had leggings to match. It was crude, lightweight, ugly, and damned near bulletproof. He carried a dented sugarloaf helm under his arm and his larger roundshield. He hoped that the dings and slashes on his practice armor would give him some street cred. He'd left his rider's pin off; he didn't want to get his nice cape muddy.

"Do you think you have enough armor, boy?"

Sir Dahl, a knight whose sigil pin Jarrod didn't recognize, was today's instructor. Jarrod noted the animosity between several of the younger soldiers.

"We'll see, sire," said Jarrod.

Sir Dahl picked a tall, raily student with an open-faced helmet as his dummy and, using wooden swords, went on to demonstrate a combination low feint and cutover.

He demonstrated a few more times. Jarrod paid little attention, checking out the others in the stable. Basic stuff. He knew two dozen variations on the maneuver already.

He was looking for the biggest guy he could find, partially to show them that he was not to be screwed around with, and partially to see where he truly lay in the order of things.

Combat athletes on Earth fight in weight classes because when it comes down to grunts and bruises, the larger combatant always has the advantage. Jarrod had seen a nature special about a starling using its maneuverability to fight off a hawk, which was all well and good; on the ground, however, a larger fighter has physics on his side.

From watching pairs of warriors sparring earlier in the day, Jarrod had already gathered that the majority were brute-force fighters. Fights were ugly and awkward with a lot of crashing, a lot of bashing, and a lot of knocking the other guy around and making an opening in his defenses.

It all made sense to Jarrod, and he'd expected as much: swords rarely pierce mail, so armored combat would be a matter of breaking his opponent into pieces inside his armor or wearing him down, not out-fencing him. Good odds presented themselves that the bigger fighters would be the better fighters.

Or at least, he reasoned, the bigger fighters would be held in the highest regard.

He didn't have to look for long. The one who'd christened him "Northboy" was one of the biggest—at least tallest—and a rider with a swan pin. He pushed the others aside and squared off on Jarrod as the circle broke up.

He wasn't as big as Carter, though. And Jarrod could give Carter a long, unpleasant afternoon.

Jarrod pulled on his helmet and buckled the chinstrap. He had his longest practice blade with him. He'd swiped his articulated gauntlets from his field armor and he wore them here, over a set of Persian-style leather bazubands.

"Nice gloves," said the big fighter.

"Tell your mother," said Jarrod. "Maybe she'll make you a pair, too."

Hoots and catcalls from others who'd assembled.

"Ready, Northboy?"

Jarrod smacked himself in the helmet with hilt of the sword a couple of times to seat it, and replied, "I have a name, good sir."

The rider settled into a stance, behind a large roundshield. "So? You won't remember it after this, anyway." He carried his weight a bit too far back, and might as well have announced that his first move would be a deep, low lunge.

Jarrod took his usual stance, reversed, blade forward and low, the shield close to his hip. "You will." He bit at his mouthguard, seated it, and they saluted.

The lunge came, deep and low and quick, followed by a fleche. Jarrod pivoted and the fighter ended up behind him, swearing as the tip of Jarrod's blade skipped off the back of his helmet.

"Nearly," the fighter commended. "You're fast."

"Faster than you," Jarrod grinned as his opponent engaged and pressed, swinging hard. Jarrod's shield interposed and he relaxed, gauging a rhythm and limbering up. The big guy wasn't quick, but he covered well and made good use of his reach, making counterattacks difficult. He was driving his blows hard and using the edge of his shield to knock Jarrod around. Which made sense; a big enough guy could bash his way to a startling degree of success.

Okay, chump. Let's go to school.

Jarrod fused the tip of his blade to the inside edge of his shield and closed in.

By doing this, his sword functioned as a second shield, in a manner that also kept his sword hand protected.

He had theorized—and, at one time, written—that this was the reason that Viking-era swords had had no crossbar.

He'd met with a great deal of pushback in historical circles regarding what he was about to do.

He moved forward with sword and shield together, rotating the sword along the shieldrim in quick slashes: first along the inside, then flipping the shield backwards—a trick that can only be done with a center-held roundshield—and slashing along the opposite side. The shield kept his blade out of sight the way a pitcher keeps the ball inside his glove until he throws.

Speed is a function of perception. Jarrod's opponent had no idea if the attack was coming on his left or his right until the moment the blade appeared, and with three-quarters of the visible motion removed, Jarrod's blows seemed so quick as to appear magical. The tall rider couldn't attack or even counter, because he could only guess where Jarrod's sword was. He retreated under a string of shouted profanities.

Someone whistled, and the fighting around them stopped.

Sir Dahl weaved his way over to Jarrod, tapping shoulders to move the others. *"You!"* he pointed at Jarrod.

Aww, crap, thought Jarrod.

Lu-u-u-cy, you got some 'splainin' to do.

"Your name?" asked Sir Dahl.

Jarrod let his sword down. "King's Rider Jarrod, Son-Lord of Knightsbridge. Sorry, I—"

"Shut up."

"Yes, sire."

"Hoy!" he shouted across the group. "Form a ring! I want you to see this!"

As the others formed a circle, Sir Dahl said, "Do it again. Just as you did."

Jarrod toed the rider's sword out of the mud and tossed it over to him. The rider caught it and Jarrod motioned for his opponent to resume the position he'd had.

Once again, Jarrod began his semicircles, at half speed.

"Hold, there!" Sir Dahl spoke loudly as Jarod froze.

Sir Dahl addressed the crowd. "This! Right here! Two things: first, his sword hand is not vulnerable. Not at any point.

"Second, the shield obscures the enemy's vision. This is excellent. Excellent," he directed the second *excellent* at Jarrod. "The enemy can't see where the next attack is coming from." He looked at Jarrod and asked quietly, "What the hell is this sword made of?"

"It's native to my homeland," Jarrod said. "Same as my armor."

"Good stuff," he commended, then addressed the crowd, "With your sword against the shield, you're effectively using two shields. You can be much more aggressive."

"If I may, sir?" said Jarrod. Dahl nodded, and Jarrod addressed the crowd.

"Instead of the usual give-and-take," Jarrod demonstrated, hitting the rider's shield with his sword and then smacking the rider's sword with his shield, "You are attacking nonstop." He pushed sword and shield together and moved in. "If your opponent hasn't seen this before, he has no choice but to back up."

Sir Dahl continued, "This is an ancient technique. A master's technique from the Lost Years. I've only seen this in manuscripts, but it's a great trick to have in your arsenal. I want to see each of you perfect this by next practice."

He turned his attention to Jarrod again as the clacks, grunts, and shouts resumed and the group went back to sparring.

"Very well done, King's Rider Jarrod," he commended. "You're Sir Javal's charge?"

"Yes, sire. His sergeant."

"You're the one who threw Loth on his ass?" Sir Dahl asked under his breath.

"Yes, sire."

"I shouldn't have had to ask. I'm Sir Dahl of Iron Fields. Do me a favor and help them learn this. Just walk around and help, yes?"

"Absolutely, sire," said Jarrod.

"Rider Saril, Son-Lord of Red Thistle, Order of the Swan," said the big rider, blade down and walking in close.

"King's Rider Jarrod, Son-Lord of Knightsbridge, Order of the Stallion. Nice to meet you."

"Likewise. Where'd you learn that?"

"I figured that out on my own. It seemed to make sense."

Saril shook his head in amazement. "I want you as my training partner."

Jarrod grinned. "Maybe later. I've got work to do."

"I hated you this morning," Saril admitted from a bath next to Jarrod's. Jarrod lay back and let the bathing girl pour hot water over his head, reveling in the release from his shoulders and neck.

He intended on getting a bath every evening. The girl had hands of stone as she went to work on his back, soaping by incidence as she worked the knots out. The heat and the massage wrung the last of the day from him.

A rider's entire day, he found, was devoted to war-making in some capacity. Regulated fight practice had been just a small part of the morning. The remainder had been spent drilling in maneuver warfare, primarily moving in various sizes and types of formations, and learning counters to expected Gavrian tactics. This part, since he was being groomed for command, he watched more than participated.

He'd gone for a nice long run before lunch; killed another hour or so while digesting by bullshitting with other soldiers and riders and dreaming up various dirty tricks, and yet another hour attempting a few of them; he'd thrown iron bars for distance for a while to strengthen his cutting blows; shown Javal and a couple of others the basic hip throw and a proper rear naked choke; gone a few rounds using the boxing gloves with Saril and a tough as hell burly kid with zits named Bevio; and as the day wound down he'd watched as many of the larger fighters attempted to lift various heavy objects while others wagered on the outcomes.

"You work hard," Saril noted. "You were sweating as hard out there as any of us. Even though you're obviously a master swordsman already. I mean, you could whip any of us. I know, because I can whip any of them, and you can whip me."

"On a good day," Jarrod admitted. "Don't sell yourself short."

"Oh, I don't," said Saril. "I won the Rider's Tourney two years ago in wrestling and swordfighting both. But you can do them both at the same time. You fight with your damned *feet.*" The group had been extremely impressed by Jarrod's *savate* skills. "Your opponent has to watch not only your sword, but your shield, your elbow, your fist, your feet, even your head—every part of you is a weapon. And still you outwork me," Saril finished. "I like that. I don't understand it, but I like it."

"Eventually," Jarrod said, "we all run into someone we can't outfight—someone more skilled, or more heavily armored, or greater in numbers. In that case, you'd better have another plan, and every moment you get behind the sword may give you a new option."

Most noteworthy to Jarrod was the skill chasm between the knights and the soldiers. Most of the knights of the royal and martial orders had literally been raised in the saddle and with swords in their hands, with the benefit of expendable family capital to hire trainers. They were good on their feet, they had excellent technique and solid fundamentals, and were immensely fit lifetime athletes. They were the seasoned professionals. There were, however, precious few of them. Maybe one warrior in twenty by his math, and most of them were instructors.

The riders—those who'd earned a place in a chivalric order through skill at arms—were gifted amateurs and many showed immense talent. These were the local-boys-done-good, the minor-leaguers on their way to the pros once they refined their skills. Most riders, and many of the older soldiers, were sergeants. Sergeants answered to the knights, and the soldiers and border knights answered to the sergeants.

The border knights were the problem.

A knight with no royal order affiliation was effectively an infantry private, albeit a poorly-trained one. Even if he or she had been granted a piece of land by the local border lord, a border knight's social standing and military rank was negligible.

This led to friction.

It was a symptom, as Jarrod understood it, of the way the border lords were overstaffing their ranks to gain advantage over their neighbors: handing out private knighthood and a few acres of tillable land to anyone who could carry an axe. Some border knights were given whatever land they could run the rightful owners off of. A few were only teenagers, hardscrabble and mean-faced.

These border knights, though, were gods compared to the rent-a-knights in on scutage, most of whom had substandard gear and little to no formal training. Two kids from the Shieldlands, filling in for a pair of border knights that a lord couldn't bother to spare, had been sent to castle duty without mail. They fought in helmets and quilted arming jacks with leather pieces tied at the shoulder and elbow.

Every last one of the soldiers, and even the border knights — and Jarrod had to give them this — had heart. The kind of heart that Jarrod had seen in boxing and *savate* opponents who would scrape themselves up off the canvas spitting blood, only to slam their gloves together and do it again. These people were tough. And tough, he knew, goes a long way.

Fighting with axe and shield in Falconsrealm, Jarrod had learned quickly, played much the same formative role as baseball in America. Whereas many American adults can catch a ball in a glove and crush a forty-mile-an-hour meatball over the plate, most Falconsrealm and Gateskeep boys — and more than a few girls — could put up a good enough fight with an axe and shield to make anyone worry.

The royal knights were primarily shock cavalry. The riders and sergeants were infantry force multipliers. And the soldiers and border knights were the grunts, getting the hard work done.

"So, who was your teacher?" asked Saril.

"I had many different teachers. My original weapons weren't the, ah, war swords. I learned wrestling and dueling when I was younger."

"The way you move the sword around its balance, I'd think you were used to using a much lighter blade. Am I right?"

Jarrod nodded. "Where I come from, we do non-lethal ritual dueling with long, thin swords. No armor."

"And yet you know how to fight with a roundshield. Well enough to teach us the ways of the ancient masters."

Jarrod shrugged.

"They're grooming you to become an officer. From rider to officer. Directly."

"So they tell me," Jarrod admitted.

"Where do you come from?"

"Knightsbridge. A long, long way from here."

"What, across the sea?"

Jarrod smiled as another bucket was poured over his head. He closed his eyes and laid his head back on the edge of the tub, feeling the blood sprint through his body. "And then some."

It was late in the evening two weeks—twenty-six days—later.

The locals measured weeks in eighth-phases of the big moon, thirteen days apiece, and referred to them by their numbered days. Each season was one hundred and four days, or one moon, long, starting after the six-day period of The Dark, which made for a slightly longer year than he was used to but all in all it lined up pretty well. Jarrod had gone one step further and broken the season into thirteen, eight-day weeks just to keep himself sane, drawing a calendar in one of his blank books. He called the first day of the lunar cycle Monday, and added an eighth day which he referred to as Sabbath. On Sabbath he didn't train, using the day instead to rest up, rub out his bruises, and practice his yoga, and claimed it as a religious affiliation. No one took any truck with it.

Jarrod and Saril were skipping down the stairs two at a time toward the feasting hall when a vision of medieval loveliness appeared before Jarrod as he rounded a corner. He grabbed the banister and swung along it to let her pass.

A soft beauty radiated from her cascading dark hair and gentle eyes, and her smile stunned him as he stared, awash in lilacs.

"Wow," Jarrod gasped, wrenching his neck as she turned to look back at him. Her friends turned also, and giggled.

He hurried to catch Saril. "Saril?"

"Forget her."

Jarrod looked back again, but the girl had disappeared around the corner of the stairwell.

"How can I?"

"Trust me."

"What, is she trouble?"

"Like you cannot imagine. She's a sorcerer."

"And what's wrong with that?"

"Ask Sir Urlan."

Jarrod knew Urlan. Tall, thin, cranky. The son of a palace lord on the Gateskeep High Council, Urlan was a landed knight who stood to inherit Three Rivers Manor. He had a gang of cronies around him at all times, and was a dapper young man, a smart dresser, with great charm and influence, and a hell of a lot of money. From fight practice Jarrod knew him to be a good swordsman; aggressive, but not particularly tough. He complained of his bruises loudly and often accused other fighters of employing "cowardly tactics." He got angry at fight practice a lot.

"Him?" Jarrod stammered. "What does she see in him?"

"They were betrothed when they came of age. Their parents arranged it, I believe. Shortly thereafter, she learned that she could read minds."

"And then she found out what a prick he is?"

"Precisely."

"So, you're saying no way."

Saril leaned against the door to the feasting hall. "Fall in love with a telepath. Let me know how that goes for you."

"Erm," said Jarrod, thinking it over.

"Not only that, but Sir Urlan's seconds will beat you to death. He's still pretty sore about it. Are you coming in?"

"Ah, I'm expected to dine with Captain Javal tonight." The Lords' Hall was one floor below the feasting hall.

"How did you get that assignment?" Saril wondered. "No offense, sir, but what did you do, precisely, to become Sir Javal's charge?"

Jarrod clapped him on the shoulder. "They came to me."

It was a black and rainy early morning. On the nights when it rained, it was *dark*. Jarrod was already used to the moon's illumination; it soothed the world and his dreams here were vivid and feature-length.

He was in his kimono and silk long johns, powering through *chaturanga* and waiting for the fire to warm the room, when he was greeted with a knock at the door to his chambers.

He tied his hair back and opened the door.

The girl he'd seen the day before—the dark-haired mind-reader who smelled of lilacs—smiled at him. It wasn't a toothy, ravenous smile, but an awkward, girlish smile.

"You're up early," he admitted.

In the firelight, dimpled and coltish, her hair in a sideways ponytail, she looked half-formed and childlike. He was a lousy judge of age and hardly anyone here kept track of their own age anyway, but he figured that, back home, he wouldn't have been able to date her for at least another year or two. He felt flustered and weird about having been attracted to her earlier. First glances and all that, he decided. Given time, though, she would be a stunner.

One thing he had noticed was that there were few children here; at least in the castles. He supposed their parents kept them on leashes at home, and, he thought, rightfully so.

Her voice was lower than he would have expected. "I'm Daelle," she said. "I'm your language instructor. Is this a good time?"

Jarrod couldn't suppress a smile at the degree to which the Universe was putting the whammy on his morning. "Hello, Daelle. Jarrod, Son-Lord of Knightsbridge. Uh, I need to put some clothes on. Please, come in."

He walked over to the water barrel, dunked his head and toweled his hair and face, and pulled on his leather pants, shedding the kimono for a tunic and a hooded cardigan. "I guess this will do."

The uniform of a royal chivalric off-duty was "warrior blacks," a short, simple black tunic, normally of silk but alternately made of velvet or wool for colder days, with the silver lord's brocade at the collar, and trousers of any type tucked into durable boots. Javal had arranged for Jarrod to receive three of these outfits, but the clothes were still at the tailor.

Jarrod had taken Crius at his word that the Crown would supply him with everything he needed, and commissioned a second pair of leather trousers, but they weren't finished yet either. Jarrod was also having a fourth tunic, of velvet, made large enough to fit over one of his motorcycle jackets, without the skirt, because he could already smell court intrigue and he wasn't going to be the one left without a chair when the music stopped.

"There is no hurry," she said.

"There is always a hurry," Jarrod corrected her, digging through his trunk looking for a belt. "How long, uh, do you expect this to take?"

"That depends on you," Daelle replied. "Which do you prefer? We can sit somewhere and I can give you lessons, or, if you'd rather, I can accompany you through your day and help you with translation when you need it."

"I'd prefer that," Jarrod admitted. "I'm kind of pressed for time. I still don't know my way around, I've got fight practice after breakfast, I have to pick out a horse, I'm going for a run at noon—" He managed to stop himself before saying, *and I'm kicking your ex-boyfriend's ass after lunch*. Jarrod stared at her for a moment. "I'm sorry. I didn't mean any disrespect."

"How do you mean?"

"What I was just—wait a minute. I thought you could read minds."

There was the laugh again, and the smile. "Not from here. I have to have physical contact."

"That's interesting." *And handy to know.*

"I used to be able to read minds from a distance," she said. "But I conditioned myself to only read when I'm in contact."

"Why is that?" Jarrod wondered aloud, buckling on his swordbelt.

"There's much less crying this way."

Jarrod looked her in the eye for a moment, then strode over and offered her his arm. She slid her hand into the crook of his elbow, and he smiled at her. "Shall we?"

"It may not be the best idea, having that girl on your arm all day," Javal acknowledged. "Sir Urlan is not taking it well, and he's got quite a temper on him."

She was three tables away, and laughing, when she caught Jarrod's eye yet again.

Jarrod licked at the head of his beer. "Yeah. He made himself my sparring partner this afternoon, the moment after I walked in with her."

Javal laughed. "Oh, no. How did that go?"

"He was enthusiastic," Jarrod had to admit. "He dented my helmet a few times."

"Keep your distance from her. You and Urlan will be around sharp implements and doing dangerous things."

"What am I, nuts? She can read my mind. Imagine if we— uh, yeah."

"Oh, I have," said Javal. "And I'm sure he has, too."

Jarrod waved his hands. "She's too young for me."

Javal peered over at her. "The hell she is. But it's probably better that you think so. Be careful that his seconds don't catch you alone some evening and kill you."

"For holding her hand?"

"You need to be very, very careful. He's a friend of Alby's, and you don't need any more trouble from him either."

Javal and Jarrod stood at a large and detailed sand table built around a mock-up of High River Keep. Scores of miniature wooden figurines dotted the tiny landscape.

Javal arranged the Gavrian figurines, painted silver, into a tight phalanx and moved them toward a line of Gateskeep figurines painted black. "Shield wall. Spears behind. Your move."

Jarrod arranged the Gateskeep figurines into a long box formation, four men abreast and six deep, and set them against the Gavrians.

"Correct," said Javal. "Now, suppose your formation doesn't hold. What then?" He moved the Gavrians to envelop the box.

"Send their armor home and pass it on to their younger brothers."

"That's about the size of it," Javal admitted.

Javal moved up a second formation of Gateskeep forces, arranging them in an inverted chevron. "Call up a second squadron if you have it," he instructed. "Sometimes, things fail. You can do everything right and still lose men. Formations crack, swords bend, your lead man trips and breaks his leg ten steps short of the shield wall. It happens. You will fail. Just keep going."

"I can do that. Believe me."

Twenty days' ride to the south, Ulo and Mukul were having their daily walk on the top of the great tower at the Hold of Gavria. "You certainly seem to understand the way of the gbatu," agreed Mukul. "I've fought against them my entire life. We'd have defeated them centuries ago if they were completely useless."

"I made that point to the War Council."

"Warriorhood is a calling of honor, Master Sabbaghian. You'll infuriate every man who's ever carried a sword if you enlist the gbatu."

"You make it sound as if I'm offering the snarling little

bastards full commissions. I'm saying we distract Falconsrealm, that's all. They're cheap, they're mean, and they're expendable. We give them second-rate hardware and turn them loose in Falconsrealm and Gateskeep to tie up their forces while we move north."

"And what happens after we take Falconsrealm? We've got a new country to run, boiling over with armed gbatu."

"They're never going to attack an entire army. They'd never attack a fortified outpost. They'd be skirmishers. As long as we retain superior force of arms, they're useless. The key is to ensure that Falconsrealm takes too long to learn that they're wasting their efforts."

"Will they be?"

"If we do this my way."

"If, indeed."

"Make it happen."

"You know," said Mukul, "you could make it happen. I'd be powerless to stop it."

Mukul wandered away, looking for a windbreak where he could light his pipe.

Carter knocked Master Gronek's wooden blade away with his wooden greatsword, hooked him outside his elbow with the pommel, and tripped him to the ground.

Inside his battered Corinthian practice helmet—a true anachronism, modeled after a design from a thousand years before the Middle Ages but with perforations below the eye-slit—and his hardened black leather armor, Carter was a historical train-wreck, equal parts Roman gladiator and Batman. Engraved *cuir bouilli* armlets, metal-splinted leather legs with cuisses that wrapped around his hamstrings, and hanging leather-backed steel tassets completed the ensemble.

But he was kicking ass.

Argyul rushed in behind a teardrop shield, his wooden sword in a high guard. Carter dropped back a half-step and levered a tremendous blow into the bottom point of the shield, using the momentum to counter over the top and skip the blade off Argyul's helmet.

"Good," said Argyul, stepping back. "Dammit."

Carter choked up on the greatsword, falling into a fencing guard using the *ricossa* as Gronek closed with him again.

"Aren't you tired, yet?" Daorah asked.

Gronek tangled with Carter, who wrapped up the blade with his own and threw him several feet away, then kicked another fighter in the shield, bowling him over.

"I don't stop when I'm tired," he told her. "I stop when it's over."

"Do you stop when you're hungry?" she asked. "Lunch is ready."

The fighters broke for lunch, and Carter pulled off his helmet. "I'm always hungry."

"After lunch, you have riding practice. We still have to find you a horse."

"I'd rather have a pegasus." He needled her about it constantly because he knew it got a rise out of her.

This time, for the first time, she smiled at the crack. "One step at a time."

Jarrod ran his hand along the horse's flanks. "He's blue," he said.

The Falconsrealm heavy saddlers were the size of Friesians, sixteen hands, with thick necks and heavy hindquarters. Jarrod still didn't entirely trust them. Stories circulated of a stablehand losing an arm to a horse bite two years ago.

"A roan," said Javal. "Very rare. And expensive. I'm surprised they gelded him."

Jarrod had never seen anything quite like him and he knew for damned sure that nobody else had one. The roan wasn't exactly blue; he was more charcoal-gray with shadows of black, but the light from the daytime moon gave him a bluish tint, even with the storm growing in the south today. The lighter coat spotlighted the slabs and knots of muscle in a way that a black coat wouldn't. It made him all the more stunning.

He was also the largest horse Jarrod had ever seen, as tall as Javal's great destrier and even thicker through the neck.

Falconsrealm knights held to two schools of thought in the choosing of a steed for battle. Some knights preferred light, fast draft horses, still bigger than their riding horses but compact and quick with feathered hooves, for skirmishes and quick flanking maneuvers. Others preferred massive, powerful destriers like Javal's that functioned essentially as heavy armored units replete with steel-shod hooves and blankets of mail and coats of plates.

Jarrod was going the tank route. He could ride well enough to do a couple of simple stunts, but he hadn't grown up on a horse and he was fairly sure he'd break his neck on a fast-mover. Plus, he figured that if he and Carter both had someone on their shoulders in a chicken fight, Carter's team would have the advantage. The concept, he felt, carried through.

But it raised a question.

"How the hell would I get up on him in armor?"

Javal ran his hand over the horse's buttock. "We'll get you up there. Look at those hips. Wow."

"You're right about the hips," said the trainer. "Let me show you something." He led the roan to the far side of the corral, where two stablehands had hung a pig carcass swaddled in mail from a gantry.

The trainer lined up the horse with the pig a few feet behind its tail, then smacked it on the ass. "Ho!"

The horse caught the armored bundle with both rear hooves, sending the rope past horizontal. As it swung back and hit the horse in the hindquarters, the roan jumped forward and kicked again. Organs spilled out through the mail into the dirt as the pig swung back in an arc.

"Enough," the trainer told the horse, walking it forward.

"Buy this horse," said Javal.

The trainer brought the horse around again, and they gave him another look-over.

The simple fact, Jarrod reminded himself, was that most Falconsrealm horses were black.

He hated the thought of doing something that no one else did; he had a tough enough time adapting already. The last thing he needed was his enemies thinking *I can't believe that asshole is on a blue horse.*

"He's expensive," said the trainer. "Not because he's a roan, but because he took us forever to train. He's impervious to pain as far as we can tell, and he's not afraid of anything. Not the whip, not any of us, not even the other horses."

"Is he pretty smart?" asked Jarrod.

The trainer looked at Jarrod, then at Javal, then shook his head. "No."

"Really," said Jarrod, looking into the horse's eye, which was huge, brown, and simple. "You hear that, fella? He says you're not smart."

"I'm not gonna lie to you, sir. He's dumb as they come, maybe the dumbest horse I've ever met. But if you'll beg my pardon, you don't want a smart horse. You want a simple horse.

A smart horse will see a battle and tell you to go fuck yourself. Because you guys are all crazy, and a smart horse knows that. It takes a dumb horse to do the things you ask him to do. With all due respect, sir."

"That might be the worst sales pitch I've ever heard," Jarrod admitted.

"I don't want you to come back here asking for your money back, telling me your horse is stupid. I'm telling you now. This horse is stupid. But he's as brave and as tough as I've ever seen. He will carry you through the gates of hell if you ask him to."

"If you don't buy him, I will," Javal told Jarrod, walking around the horse the other way, "I'd have to sell my summer home, though, I'd bet."

"You might, sir," said the trainer. "We've got a lot into him. He just took so long to train. He's ten; we've had him five years, sir. *Five years.* The plus side, though, is that he's good on all his commands by now. But we're not letting him go cheap. A couple of border lords have their eye on him, but they can't quite cough up the money just yet."

"Money's no object," Javal assured the trainer. "This man is a King's Rider. Jarrod, buy this horse. Right now."

"You'll take a promissory note from the crown, I trust?" Jarrod asked.

"With pleasure, sire."

"Done," said Jarrod, and shook the trainer's hand. "I'll send a man around this afternoon with it. What's his name?"

"Horse," said the trainer. "You want to give him a name, we'll start working him with it."

Jarrod looked the horse in the eye. He didn't care if the roan wasn't smart. He could use some dumb luck, anyway. Able to kick a man in half, and completely clueless about the amount of danger he'd be in. They clicked.

"Call him Perseus," said Jarrod.

Over the next two weeks, Jarrod kept a professional distance from Daelle and made it a point to talk to other girls around the castle, which he found was no problem, being a foreigner and the best swordsman in recent memory.

He put in long afternoons getting to understand Perseus.

He'd had some instruction in horsemanship back home; as a stunt coordinator for sword and sorcery films he at least had to know how they worked. Now, however, he got into the finer points not only of horsemanship, but of caring for, saddling, and armoring an animal that weighed three quarters of a ton.

For the first week, he was terrible at remembering everything—a strap not cinched again after Perseus blew out, mail barding or the coat of plates not tied in just right at an arming point—and he'd have something fall off the damned horse ten seconds after getting into the saddle and kicking him into gear. Real tough to look badass with your horse's armor dragging in the dirt.

Of course, that was when he could get up into the saddle at all. Perseus was so tall that when Jarrod ordered his own custom war saddle with right-side frogs for his warhammer and *gran espée de guerre*—the first thing he'd done after leaving the royal stables having agreed to buy Perseus—he also ordered it built with knotted leather braids that dangled down the flanks from either side of the saddle horn. He had to grab one of these in both hands to pull himself high enough to get a foot into the stirrup.

He also had to mount his horses from the right side, opposite everyone else, so as not to tangle up his arming sword. Perseus didn't seem to mind but many other horses did, some going so far as to side-step while he tried to swing up.

The war saddle had a short coat of plates integrated fore and aft over the skirt and it strapped in two places around the belly, with iron rings at each corner to tie into barding. More than once he'd forget to snug something down and end up pulling the damned saddle sideways, busting his ass. A few times he'd brought fifty pounds of armor or more down on himself.

At a weekend course in horsemanship at the Hollywood Stunt Academy, Jarrod had learned to do a flip into, and out of, a saddle, but on a fourteen-hand Arabian that was one thing; it was a fool's errand in thirty pounds of armor on a horse the size of Perseus. The seat of the saddle was above his head. They were impossibly huge animals. A knight leaping into his saddle was Hollywood bullshit.

The trainers were decent to Jarrod, though. He wasn't the first rider to come from a city, and he wouldn't be the last. He was getting better day by day.

No one made fun of the big blue horse. He actually got compliments on owning a roan. That helped.

On the downside, Perseus required a larger stall than other horses, and he was going to be a logistical nightmare on the road. It would take a second stout pony to pull a cart just with his food, water, and barding; a barrel with a day's supply of water took two strong men to lift. *Christ, my horse needs his own horse.*

He ordered a cart.

And two good ponies.

And he started making notes of which stablehands he'd consider bringing along on the road if need be, because damn, once he bought a riding horse he would be traveling with four horses and a cart; his own circus.

The romantic image of the lone knight crossing the vast and arid wasteland on his trusty steed involved a remarkable amount of artistic license.

He didn't see how he'd get Perseus out of the valley. It was half a day's ride to the far end of the city across the lake and he'd have to stop to feed the damned horse just to get that far.

They were pals, though. All the bumps, bruises, and false starts were bonding time. He'd find a way.

When he, Daelle, and Javal arrived at the gymnasium one morning long after they'd all concluded that Jarrod had, in fact, smoothed things over with Urlan, Jarrod found few of the smiles, handshakes, and rock signs he'd grown accustomed to. In fact, the mood overall was quite sullen and apprehensive. He expected that someone had died, or perhaps war had been declared.

He pressed through the ring to find Albar in the center of the gymnasium with a courtsword. A sharp, heavy courtsword, not one of the oil-slaked, blunted iron practice blades.

Albar was not in armor. He was, in fact, nude from the waist up, though he had heavy boots on, and loose trousers. Albar was slender and undefined.

Jarrod took his arm from Daelle and strode out to the middle of the gym.

"I'd draw, were I you, sir," Urlan recommended, from the crowd behind Albar.

Jarrod spoke evenly and firmly. "If you have a problem with me, Sir Urlan, you can settle it yourself. I'm not fighting this man."

Albar kicked clear a place in the straw. "Mortal combat is allowed during peacetime. You've insulted me, sir. And Sir Urlan as well. I demand you pay for it."

Jarrod cleared his throat. "For starters, sir," he said, "I have not insulted you."

"Your very presence," said Albar, "insults me."

"Be that as it may," said Jarrod, "I have no intention of killing you."

"And you won't, I assure you," Albar menaced with the blade. Urlan offered Jarrod a courtsword of roughly equal length. Jarrod waved it away, instead snugging down his bazubands and pulling on his gloves, and drew his arming sword. Those in the room who hadn't seen it before took an apprehensive breath as the blade threw beams into the dust motes across the gym.

"Seriously, sir," said Jarrod. "Put that thing away or I'm going to find a new scabbard for it."

Big words, but he was glad he had the medical kit on his swordbelt.

"Alby," said Javal, "When he kills you, it will make him very unpopular with your future wife."

"He won't kill me," Albar snorted.

Jarrod's voice was level. "Says you."

"Jarrod," ordered Javal, "do not kill the heir presumptive."

Jarrod muttered out of the corner of his mouth, "Can I just hurt him a little?"

"Suits me," said Javal quietly.

"This is your big answer, huh?" Jarrod asked Albar from behind his sword. "This just locks it all up for you. You can kill me fair and square and I'll finally stop embarrassing you in front of your good friends from Gavria. What's that all about, anyway? You and our enemy, just hanging out, holding hands and strolling in the gardens together."

"You die," growled Albar.

"Bring it, Skippy," said Jarrod.

Javal stepped aside. Albar lunged.

The courtsword was light, deft, and lethal. Jarrod parried, pivoted, and let him pass, taking the offensive and driving him back several steps at the end of his range.

Jarrod's sword was longer, and with the bazubands he had considerable reach on Albar. He kept his parries forward of the balance. He had no intention of getting cut.

Jarrod broke his attack.

Albar moved through a couple of guards, just out of long attacking distance. He was definitely Argyul's student, heavy on his feet and deliberate in his motions, and—Jarrod found with a couple of quick, probing attacks—with the same predilection for anticipatory maneuvers.

Albar charged. Jarrod feinted, enveloped, and slung Albar's sword far off to the weak side. He placed the tip of his sword at Albar's eye as Albar recovered, the bigger man wildly out of proportion and stance, Jarrod showing the room—and Albar— that he easily could have ended him, or given him a really great scar.

Jarrod broke off, struck a guard, and waited as Albar composed himself. "You need to stop this, right now," Jarrod advised as Albar fell into a guard, grinding his teeth, rattled.

Urlan drove into Jarrod from behind, knocking him forward with an elbow. Albar charged again, fast and straight, lunging.

Jarrod parried the courtsword, double-stepped to get his balance, lunged at Albar driving him back, then spun and slashed behind him. The tip of the sword opened a wide hole across Urlan's shoulder, missing his neck only because Urlan had flinched.

Albar lunged again, dropping into the same Agrippa thrust that Argyul had used—long and heavy and potentially lethal, but static and oh-so-slow to recover—and Jarrod side-stepped, countered hard, enveloped again, and this time, as Albar slid back to his guard, Jarrod followed him back, got the bind, and punched him in the mouth.

This was not a boxer's snappy cross, but a fight-ending overhand whose center of effort lay a few inches behind Albar's skull. Albar hit the floor hard, his head bouncing off the planks. His sword clattered away.

Urlan was pinching off the wound in his shoulder.

"You got any other bright ideas?" Jarrod asked him, menacing with his sword.

"Nothing comes to mind," Urlan admitted.

Jarrod turned his attention back to Albar, who spat a lot of blood carefully into his hands. "Kill me," he drooled.

"No chance," said Jarrod. "But you will quit fucking with me, sir. I am here because I have work to do."

Jarrod turned to Javal, and sheathed his sword as four of Urlan's sergeants leaped on him from behind and took him to the floor. When they were all pulled away from each other, one was unconscious, one was weeping, and another was coughing up blood. Jarrod's face was a thing of nightmare, swollen and smashed.

"Come on!" Jarrod roared. "I wanna fight some more!"

It was Javal and several knights who had broken up the fight. "Show them out!" Javal put his hand on Jarrod's shoulder. "Jarrod, enough."

"Never," Jarrod rasped.

IV

ACCELERANDO

"Everyone has a plan 'till they get punched in the mouth."
— Mike Tyson

J aval sat alone long into the night, toying with a dagger in his left hand and a pen in his right. A candle, burned to a fat stump, leaked wax off the side of the desk.

He read over what he'd written. The knife flipped in his hand, twirling and pirouetting with the flame's light. He harbored no thoughts of harm; he was simply more comfortable with blades than with quills.

Master Crius,
Greetings from your eastern neighbor.
You should trust that I follow your orders, and the Crown's, unquestioningly. I am honored by being charged with Jarrod's training. I will fulfill my duties to the best of my ability. I must admit, however, that I question your judgment in the choice of King's Rider Jarrod of Knightsbridge for the position he has been promised.
Rider Jarrod exemplifies such self-destruction and recklessness that

I believe he harbors a death wish. I would be hesitant to promote such a man to knighthood, much less a command rank. In his defense, I must admit that he is already an exemplary warrior in his own right. I do not exaggerate on this next point: Jarrod is as skilled in combat as any man I've seen, and he is possibly a match for any man alive. However, I believe the consistency with which he puts himself into dangerous situations, coupled with the hesitation he displays in actual combat, would present a liability on the field and

He bit his lip. The knife crawled through his fingers to balance on the back of his hand, then dropped into his grip.

". . . and I don't know if I can keep him alive that long," he muttered to no one.

He crumpled up the parchment, pulled another, dipped the pen, began to scribble furiously.

In a moment he stopped and read, and the knife began its dance anew.

⌒

"Crius?"

Crius was still awake in the front room of his chambers, tinkering with a spell mnemonic and a glass of brandy.

General Daral was an old warrior from the north, wiry and scarred and wearing his white and yellow beard in braids. He sat tiredly and took off his cap. "We need to talk, you and I."

"Please."

Crius poured him some tea.

"Thank you. Do you remember Sir Daran of—oh, I forget. Sir Javal's second from two summers ago."

"I do. Met his end with a *sheth* on a hunting expedition, yes?"

"Five sheth," Daral corrected. "Sir Javal saw his end coming, a year before anyone else. He told you, remember?"

"I do. This is regarding Jarrod of Knightsbridge," Crius assumed.

An ugly quiet drove itself like an adze between them.

Crius yanked it free. "That was a fair fight. Albar challenged him."

"And lost."

"Yes."

"Jarrod of Knightsbridge is dangerous," said Daral. "He's uncontrollable. And unpredictable."

"All the more reason we need him."

"Explain."

"I agree with Sir Javal's assessment: Jarrod suffers from an appalling hubris; nearly an expectation that the world be laid at his feet simply because he is a skilled warrior.

"But that same hubris, from my observation, affects everyone in Jarrod's homeworld.

"The son of Sabbaghian is going to be commanding the Gavrian forces, likely with the same abandon we see in Jarrod. To understand Sabbaghian, we need to understand Jarrod. When we can anticipate Jarrod, we can anticipate Sabbaghian. So we need to watch Jarrod. We need to learn from him. You don't think we're going to give him any real command on the field, do you? Sir Javal is teaching him so we can learn what someone from his world might do with an army. We have Sorenson in Rogues' River, under tutelage from Commander Daorah Uth Alanas, for the same reason. We will compare notes and cross-reference with Sorenson's mentors as the summer progresses. Come fall, we will have at least a cursory profile of Sabbaghian's patterns and processes. We will put them in advisory positions, and we will use them to beat Gavria."

"So we are not teaching him," Daral's brow furrowed. "He is teaching us?"

"Precisely. And we will be in his debt for it."

"That makes much more sense to me," General Daral said. "How is Javal with all this?"

"Sir Javal wrote me a wonderful letter the other night. He has sworn to fulfill his obligation."

Jarrod awoke in his bed, in his chambers. His ribs had been clamped with bandages and his right eye was swollen shut.

"So when it really comes down to it," said Javal, pouring two goblets of wine on the bedside table, "You're a coward."

Jarrod squinted at him through his good eye. "How do you figure that?"

Javal handed him one. "You hesitate."

Jarrod rose to a sit with considerable effort. "I didn't think I did."

"You did. You could have disarmed Alby and beaten him unconscious. You should have. Maybe given him a good scar or taken an eye, too. And you should have killed Urlan for what he did.

"Loth, as well. You threw him down, you waited to see if he got up, to see if you'd done enough. I should have known it, then."

"You told me not to draw against Loth."

"I was wrong. You should have killed each of them, right there. This is the right thing. This is what a warrior does."

"It's not what I do," said Jarrod.

"No!" Javal shouted. "It's not! *That's the problem*," he hissed. "You're either lazy, or you're afraid."

"I'm not really sure I'm up to getting my ass chewed right now. Could you come back later?"

Javal wasn't amused. "You are a war horse, Jarrod. As fine and strong and brave as they come. But when someone threatens you, you fight like a little baby goat, shoving people around hoping they leave you alone. Quit being a child about it. You're going to get us all killed."

More quietly, he continued, "You have a greatness inside of you. Men like Albar, men like Urlan, they see that greatness, and they hate it, because they haven't figured out that greatness in others doesn't diminish greatness in self."

"You have this. . ." here, he searched for a word, and failed, ". . . thing, a gift, inside of you. You are, with a sword, what King Sabbaghian is with his magic. We've never seen anything like it. No one has. A man like you comes along once in an age. And for some reason, you hate this thing that makes you great. And that makes men who lust for greatness even more furious because you *have* what they want, and *you don't want it.*"

"I screwed up with it," said Jarrod. "I used it to kill a man, who didn't deserve to die."

"That's not a judgment you can make," snapped Javal. "He drew a sword on you, yes? Over a woman? This man? This is the man you speak of?"

"Yes," said Jarrod. "He lost his footing. He hit his head and he died."

"So he killed himself," said Javal. "He should have been ready. He should have had his feet under him."

"He did. It was wet."

Javal shrugged. "Did he know you? Did he know what you were capable of?"

"Absolutely."

"Then he knew the consequences of fighting you. He came at you—*you*, of all men!—with a sword. He was prepared to die. Maybe he wanted to die, and needed you to do it for him."

"Jesus," said Jarrod. The thought had never occurred to him.

"Suicide by Jarrod," he muttered.

He let a moment pass, muttering under his breath in English.

"It took everything," he told Javal then. "It destroyed my life. It destroyed my career. The woman I loved left me. My father still doesn't speak to me. I became a—" they had no word for *meme*, "—a national example of failure."

"A man with your gifts? A failure, for killing a man in a fight?"

"My people don't understand," said Jarrod. "Most of us don't fight anymore." He suddenly remembered a thirty-year-old man, bearded, tattooed, learning to box in his gym, who'd broken down sobbing the first time he'd caught a heavy punch to the face. "We've forgotten this part of ourselves. We don't value it. Our world only has a handful of warriors left."

"That's a tragedy," said Javal.

Jarrod downed his wine. "You have no idea."

"Your gift didn't ruin your life," said Javal. "The man you killed did. And your nation's misunderstanding did. And look, you're here, now," said Javal, gesturing around him. "The greatest warrior in the world, with no one disputing it. Not even me, and *I* was the greatest warrior in the world until you came along."

"Sorry."

"There you go again. *Don't be sorry!* What do you have to be sorry for? Wine, adventure, the king's own two hands propping you up, beautiful girls wetting their linen when you walk by, an entire nation shitting itself in fear over you. This is a bad thing?"

"That man you killed did us a favor," Javal said. "If you hadn't killed him—or if your nation had at least the brains of a horse between them and made you the hero you should have been—you wouldn't be here, now."

"I never really thought of it that way," said Jarrod, refilling his goblet.

"You should," said Javal. "Because it's true. We need this thing that you have. We need you to use all of it, right now. It's not enough for you to kick ass in the courtyard, to teach us to swordfight and wrestle. It's not enough for you to punch a man like Albar, and to let an asshole like Urlan blindside you, or to let a man like Loth live. We need you to be big. Bigger. Do you understand? The stuff of songs."

"Epic."

"Epic. Yes. Be epic, damn you."

"Yes, sir."

Javal picked up his goblet. "Consider that an order. Now get some rest. Swords win wars. I need you whole as soon as possible."

Jarrod awoke in candlelight. Someone was dabbing at his eye with a damp cloth that felt like an ice pick in his brain.

He grabbed the hand and pushed it away. "Please don't do that."

"I am so sorry," said Daelle, whose hand it was. "Jarrod, I am so, so sorry. I didn't mean for you to—" She took a deep breath.

"Don't worry about it," he groaned, closing his eye. "I need a good ass-kicking every once in a while."

"It took four of them to do it," said a large knight wearing an Order of the Stallion pin. He stood at the door, one hand on his sword.

"Sire," said Jarrod.

"Pleasure," said the knight. "We figured that bag of shit would be coming for you while you slept. It seems like the only way it would be a fair fight."

Jarrod smiled. "Is Sir Urlan okay?" he asked Daelle.

"He'll live," she said.

"Mm."

Daelle perked. "That fight is the talk of the town. You beat the prince."

"He's not a prince yet," Jarrod grumbled.

Moments passed. Her next words were hesitant, girlish. "This was because of me."

"No," said Jarrod. "You were an excuse. They'd both been looking for one. I am screwing this whole thing up," he grumbled, shaking his head and staring at the ceiling. "I should just go home."

It was then that Jarrod noticed the cup on the table. It wasn't the cup that Javal had left, but one of the tall agate cups that Falconsrealmers used for wine and fine drinks. This one, the color of honey and blood, had spiderwebs of silver across it.

"I brought this for you," she said, handing him the cup, which he was disappointed to learn was empty. "I wanted to show you this."

"It's beautiful," he said. "Thank you."

She put her hands on his, around the cup. "When we break a fine cup, we take the pieces to a jeweler, who repairs it with silver. Do you see?" she traced the lines. "It's more beautiful now, more precious, because it was once broken."

Jarrod turned the cup over in his hands.

"You are broken," she said. "But you are healing. What you're doing for us? What you're doing for the king? All of it, lines of silver, my lord. To work with that silver, it takes heat and time and a steady hand. Sir Javal is that hand.

"I've seen your mind," she said. "I know your loss. I don't understand the world you come from, but I understand the enormity of what happened to you. I do. I've been in your head, my lord, and I've seen it. Your life was amazing. You were a hero. You were a champion. You were robbed of your glory, and your love, and all the trappings of your greatness. Nothing can bring that back, but you can be greater, here, than you ever were."

"I need to quit letting you in my head," Jarrod muttered.

Her voice faltered. "Do you want another tutor?"

Jarrod took her hand, and told her no.

A few days' ride to the southwest, near the Rogues' River Manor, Carter rode fast.

Here, west of the Falconsrealm Mountains, the sun was a forge. He was bare-chested, treating his muscles to a carcinogen-free tan. Daorah wore a light linen tunic, revealing when doused with sweat, sexy as hell and screaming her head off in the middle of a clearing as Carter thundered through, leaping his horse over fallen logs and juking to miss rocks and holes. It was a big horse, a powerful horse, a stepping-stone to a pegasus.

He raised his greatsword as he approached a head-sized squash on a stick in the middle of the clearing, sliced at it as he rumbled past, and missed it entirely. "Son of a bitch!" he roared, and reined the horse to a stop.

"You're not concentrating," Daorah walked up, and he swung down. "If your timing is off, you'll nick the wing. You will both die."

"I don't understand—" Carter stammered, then went silent. He put his hand on the horse's flank, felt it heaving. The key, he knew, was in aligning his own body with the horse, and that was a thing that a man raised here, riding for thirty years, could do. But he couldn't. "I don't understand how you keep it all coordinated. I can't even do it on the ground. The wings are a third thing you need to keep in mind? I don't know how I'm going to do that. I really don't."

"You'll figure it out, or you'll die," she said. "We can all do it. You learn. It's a dance, that's all. You just need—" her voice trailed off.

There, with the sun behind him, hands twisting on his enormous sword, she realized that she was looking at a man who could, one day, be a king. And she shook her head in silent rage and heaviness, for she knew that this beautiful, brilliant man, hero or no, could be marked for death by jaundiced, petty nobles whose hearts he'd stricken with the same awe.

Carter sighed. "Yes? What do I need?"

Her eyes locked with his as she untied her tunic and pulled it over her head.

Carter swore the sun got louder.

Daorah had a dancer's body, powerful and veined with sinews and slight curves of compacted muscle. Her breasts and stomach, lithe and rock-hard, were crossed and puckered with scars. It made her all the more amazing.

"Wow," was all he could say.

She took his hand from the sword and laid it on her cheek, cupping her jaw, a simple movement, intensely intimate, and as he tightened his grip ever so slightly he felt her breath catch. She did the same to him, her fingers probing, finding a perfect fit on the cabled muscles of his neck.

"What do I need?" he repeated.

She pulled his face to hers. "You need a different kind of riding lesson."

"Do you have a woman back home?" asked Daorah, her head on his chest.

"Oh, now you ask," joked Carter. She shoved him playfully.

"No," he said. "Not anymore." There was no word for *divorce;* rolling the idea around in his head, he noted that their word for *marriage* was a derivative of their word for *path,* and *husband* and *wife* were masculine and feminine forms of *traveler.*

They also had no word for *cheerleader.* Thank God, he thought.

"So, does this change anything?" Carter chewed thoughtfully on a stem of grass as Daorah rested her head on his chest again.

"Must it?" she asked.

"God, I hope not." Sheathed in sweat, dirt ground into their knees, it had been equal parts high school make-out session and bar fight. He was glad there wasn't a bed for miles; they'd have driven it through the wall.

"Such a relief," she said. "I'd like to think it wasn't just a diversion to skip your lesson."

"And here I thought this was part of it."

"Oh, it was. As soon as we get our wind back, we'll get you back up on the horse." Here, she turned to face him, her voice steadfast, "And don't you go thinking that I'm going to be any easier on you from here on out. I'll probably be rougher with you, even," she traced his nose with one calloused finger, then poked him on the end of it to make her point.

His eyes uncrossed as she pulled the finger away. "Who cuts your hair?" he squinted in distaste as he pulled a ragged lock to its length.

"Oh, ha-ha. Yours'll soon look the same, you handsome man," she foretold with a judging grin. "It gets knotted up in your coif. And during battle? It becomes so matted with sweat and caked with blood that you have to cut the clots out. It's called a fighter's cut. All warriors have it."

Carter was confused by this logic, and, as usual, it showed. "So, why not just shave your head?"

"Vanity," she replied without hesitation. This brought a spirited laugh from the giant.

In a moment, after contemplating her answer, she laughed, too. "I guess that does sound silly."

He had to agree.

"I've got three links of mail embedded in my brain-pan," she announced proudly. "And you know what?"

Smiling at her outrageousness, the giant shook his head and prepared himself for anything.

She exploded in peals of laughter, "They're all hooked together!"

He didn't even know why he found himself laughing. He was just ridiculously happy, on a sunny afternoon untold light-years from home, his arm around a nude Amazon, comparing old scars on a post-coital high.

His laughter trickled off, as did hers.

Here, a million miles away from the cheerleaders and the screaming crowds, I find her.

He was sure this beat the hell out of Iceland.

As he stared, he saw her eye distracted, flitting at first, then altogether, and she raised a hand to freeze the moment.

"What?" he mouthed.

"Get dressed!" she hissed, reaching for her clothes.

"Wh—" Carter did as he was instructed, pulling on his breeches as she tossed them to him.

"Sheth. Four, maybe more." She threw on her tunic—backwards, but in her haste it didn't matter.

Carter knew a sheth was the largest of the gbatu. He'd never seen one, but he understood they were ogrish and murderous. "I thought you said they didn't come this close to the manor." He was still fumbling with his belt.

"They don't. Definitely not hunting, they won't," she muttered as she pulled on her breeches and then her boots.

Carter was quite a bit slower in dressing, and in fact had only his breeches on and one of his boots half-laced when above him, eclipsing the sun, a red-skinned foot planted itself on the log just over his head.

Above them, the sheth was fumbling with its loincloth under a tangle of armor.

Still unseen, and not taking his eyes off it, Carter reached out his arm to Daorah, who handed him his greatsword.

He bit his upper lip and coiled, flashing his eyes once at her for affirmation.

She rolled clear as Carter roared to his feet, plunging the blade through a sheet of mail, center mass. The super hard steel crunched in his palms as it butchered its way through the iron links, and the blade sank until the torn mail twisted up around it.

The sheth stared down at him, and in a long and hideous moment Carter got his first look at the ruling caste of gbatu.

The sheth was easily eight feet tall stooped over and four hundred pounds of gristle and bulk—all the misdirected anger of the world stuffed into an array of armor, belts, weapons, and fur. Its arms were hairless and the width of Carter's thigh; near its knees, immense hands ended in wicked black nails.

The undershot jaw sported yellowed tusks. Its eyes, huge and slow-blinking, squinted through the daylight.

As Carter stared up into those eyes, and it stared back, his soul quaked with the uncertainty one feels having riled a madman.

With a bellow, the beast fell on him, and Carter had his hands full with a snarling, biting, wrestling, eight-foot nightmare infinitely stronger than he was.

Carter ducked under a haymaker, then locked his arms around its head and kicked its legs out. The neck snapped, and it went limp, heavy as the world. He stepped clear and let it fall.

He'd practiced the move a thousand times—taught it a

thousand times more—but had never used it. It was a dangerous move, a lethal move. An illegal move.

A handy move.

Even on something this size, the neck couldn't support the body's weight.

He grabbed for the sword and yanked. It came free after a couple of hard pulls.

He stared at the gore on the sword and his hands, then back at the body as it twitched.

He began to shiver.

Until he saw two more leaping over the log, fully airborne, these two in helmets and armor, with weapons drawn and fangs bared, each sailing through the air and charging him at a loping run.

Carter's lungs and arms surged. His back straightened, his muscles tautened, and he spit into the palm of his right hand and cleaned the blood away on his pant leg. He roared a wordless challenge as he braced the sword at his side like a spear.

He was about to remind the world why God still built Norsemen seven feet tall.

One of the sheth had a flail, really just an eight-inch iron cylinder at the end of four feet of chain; the other wielded a huge sword of a type he'd never seen before, two blades welded together at the tang and at the tip, the size of an ironing board with space for two or three more blades in the hollow between.

Carter, for all practical purposes as large as either, charged them both.

They roared; he roared.

Carter snarled up the flail around his blade and ducked low, not breaking stride, as the cylinder whooshed and rattled by his head. From two steps away he launched off both legs and met it with a forearm.

The full-body check was his greatest gift; the ability to time flex and release, to become a three-hundred-pound whip-crack. Carter had knocked men unconscious, broken helmets, and once nailed a fullback hard enough to give him amnesia.

He leaped in the air as the sheth went over, driving both feet onto its chest, feeling bones snap like muffled gunshots under the armor.

Carter backpedaled in his guard as the second one closed.

It was as big as the first one he'd fought, but in a curtain-sized shirt of square metal scales held together with strips of mail, and an ornate helmet painted with fierce, exaggerated eyes and teeth.

Carter and the sheth crossed and uncrossed blades twice, testing each other, before it rushed in. Carter sent the huge ironing-board blade out of line and reversed across its face with both hands. He felt the steel bite, saw the shiny metal revealed under the bluing and paint, and he stepped through, pivoting hard, going for its left ear, leaning in and swinging for the fences. It ducked but not enough, a fat dome of metal from its helmet spinning in the sun as it crumpled.

Hell of a sword.

And a shitty helmet.

Carter faced the other, which had found its feet and drawn a long knife. It moved in a protective crouch but spat a chunk of bloody flesh and ivory at Carter's feet in what could only have been a boast. Carter had checked it so hard it had smashed out several of its own teeth.

Carter nicked off a piece of finger, circling. It snarled and barked, opening and closing its hand to beckon him in.

It grabbed at the blade and lunged at him with the knife.

Carter let it have the sword. He took the knife hand at the wrist, snapped the arm backwards at the elbow, cleared the knife, and jammed it into the mail under the broken, jutting arm.

He took the greatsword by the ricossa and wrenched it away,

then drove it through an iron plate high on the chest, feeling the metal scrape, feeling it skip off the ribs, feeling it mire and finally hit the armor on the far side. The sheth struck at him, wildly powerful. It screamed, it gurgled, it grunted.

He slammed the handle from side to side, severing everything, until it collapsed. The jangle of armor was determined and brief.

There was another dead one, pinned against a tree on the far side of the meadow with a broken sword through its mouth; near it, a clawed forearm twitched in a patch of crimson-slashed daisies. The sporadic grunts of the dying sheth nearest him echoed with those of an unseen other, no doubt bleeding to death in the tall grasses. Daorah was nowhere to be seen.

"Daorah!" he called, wiping his tightening forehead with his biceps. It came away smeared with bright blood. The last one had clawed out a wide funnel of meat from his arm and it bled thickly.

Daorah appeared from the tree line, nude from the waist up, wiping her sword with her shirt. "Look at this," she told him. "Come here."

Carter followed her to the corpse of a sheth. He was unsure of what he was supposed to be looking at, so he asked.

"The armor," she said.

It was the same armor he'd noticed on the large one that he'd killed. "Nice."

"Oh, yes," she agreed. "Look, here," she walked over to one of the corpses in the field. He followed, and looking at the body, now he noticed a difference. This one's armor was a haphazard collage, many suits of armor tied, sewn, and riveted together into a jerkin.

"That one," she assessed, jerking a thumb back toward the big one with the scale armor. "They don't wear armor for its protective value. It's a trophy. See? This one," she pointed again to the closest corpse, "He's killed four humans. Two in mail, one in brigandine, and one knight, probably, for the leather armor."

"Okay. So we need to find out who's missing."

"Yes. For starters." She walked back over to the largest one. The lesson wasn't over yet. "So where'd he get this?"

"You're asking me?"

"You're the adviser to the king."

"Hm. Could he have made it?"

"They don't make armor. They don't even cook their food."

Carter scratched his head. "Someone made it," he assessed.

"Right."

"Could he have killed someone my size?"

She glared at him like a cat with its ears back. "There is no one 'your size.' Besides, he couldn't fit in your armor any more than you could fit in mine."

"So, someone out there's making armor for these things."

"That's a Gavrian helmet. Gavrians use iron plates set in their mail like this. Not all of them, but their knights do. Gavrians rivet their mail, and this crap is just pinched shut. It's cheap, and weak, but still, where'd he get it?" She bent to work the helmet off. The head beneath was equal parts warthog and bridge troll.

"Christ, that thing is ugly," said Carter.

"They're far prettier dead." She turned the helmet over, looking for a manufacturer's mark. "Are you hurt?"

"Tired," Carter said.

"Good. Let's call it a day. Get its legs."

"Jarrod?"

It was Javal's voice at the door.

It was well before sunrise, and though the room was lit from the moon and the coals in the fireplace, it was still nearly freezing.

Jarrod untangled himself from the spectacularly defined limbs of a visiting girl from Longvalley named Eothe.

"Hey, sire," he said.

He kissed Eothe on the forehead and rolled out of bed, apologizing. She mumbled something and buried her face under the pillow.

A frank conversation with a healer some weeks back had brought up what Jarrod intended to make the lynchpin of his entire experience here: the wonderful, wonderful moon.

Reproductive cycles were in lock step with the big stripy bastard that took up a tenth of the horizon, and women were only fertile every hundred and four days. Because humans here reproduced much more slowly than their counterparts on Earth, Mother Nature had never seen fit to introduce venereal diseases as a method of *de facto* population control. The practical upshot of this was that Jarrod now found himself in a world where shaking the sheets had become a competitive sport.

"I'm sorry, rider," said Javal. "It's important."

Jarrod tied his kimono, slipped on his moccasins, and met Javal in the hallway, closing the door and shivering.

"Who's in there?" Javal asked.

Jarrod rubbed his arms to warm up. "Eothe."

Javal's brow furrowed. "Eothe, the singer from the banquet? Well played, rider."

Jarrod brushed his hair back. "I'm only banging girls from out of town from now on. This way, when their boyfriends want to kill me, I'll at least see them coming."

"I can't argue with your logic."

"What's up?" asked Jarrod.

"A report from Regoth Ur. Attacks by sheth."

"Okay. That happens."

Javal had a note in his hand, and he referred to it. "Your man Carter dragged back quite a trophy: a sheth in a coat of plates and a helmet."

Jarrod looked at the note. He couldn't read most of the words but someone had sketched out the armor. "Well, that doesn't make any sense."

"Right."

"Are they sure it wasn't just horse barding, cut to fit?"

"Boy, that's good," Javal admitted, turning the sketch sideways and back again. "According to this, it was armor. Coat of plates, arming jack, everything."

Jarrod was now fully awake. His heart raced. "Who the hell would make armor for sheth?"

"Who'd pay for it?" Javal asked. "That's a lot of iron."

"Well, we know who has iron."

Javal looked down the hallway both ways, saw that it was clear, and leaned in to Jarrod to whisper regardless. "This is something new," he whispered. "This is something you'd know about, yes?"

"Yes and no," said Jarrod. "I'm familiar with the concept but I had nothing to do with it, if that's what you're asking."

"Absolutely not. Can you advise the lord's council?"

"When?"

"After breakfast."

"This is brilliant," Jarrod told Sir Dahl and the others at the Chambers On Nine, a large, lavish meeting room that overlooked the valley and lake far below. "If you want to knock out a militarily superior adversary, you first need to distract them. Get them looking the other way. Classic misdirection."

"This is how you fight, where you come from?" asked Sir Dahl.

"Pretty much," said Jarrod. "Look, you don't have big armies here. That's why you don't have mooks."

"Mooks?" asked Javal.

Jarrod tried again. "Flunkies. Meat shields."

Javal choked on his wine.

"You have soldiering as a profession, here," said Jarrod, "Because you can't afford not to. Your soldiers have to be as effective as possible, as highly-trained as possible, because you don't have very many of them. In my homeland, countries have armies in the millions. A thousand-thousands," he offered, since they had no word for *millions*. "Historically, in my homeland, armies have had units of marginally-skilled, low-paid soldiers whose only job is to absorb damage and hold ground. They're what we call mooks."

Javal let out a breath. "Who gets that job?"

"People with nowhere else to go," said Jarrod. "You don't have that here. You can't; you don't have the manpower. But that means that Gavria doesn't have the manpower either. Unless, of course, they've been reproducing like crazy. Anyone been there in the past twenty years?" He looked around the table.

"Seriously? Nobody?"

No one said anything. "Okay, look. There's no way they could possibly have more sex than us, right?" He looked at Daelle, who blushed and giggled. "I mean, come on. Really? We've got to assume that their population density is roughly equal. So, what do you do when you don't have manpower?" Jarrod asked.

He took a quill, dunked it in ink, and made a dot on a piece of parchment. He dunked it again and drew a circle around the dot. "You *augment*. We call it a force multiplier. My people do it with numbers. Here in Falconsrealm, we do it with training. Gavria does it with steel. They're arming the gbatu to try and divert our attention. They have the steel to augment the gbatu and make them into something we have to worry about." He looked to Albar.

"Why are you looking at me?" said Albar.

"I'm asking you, sir," said Jarrod. "What do you think of this?"

"I think it's preposterous," said Albar. "There's no possible way this happened."

"Do you think Regoth Ur lied about this?" asked Javal.

"No," said Albar. "I think this is a fluke, a freak occurrence. If it was happening at the scale you're proposing, we'd have seen it, here."

"Oh, no," said Jarrod. "That's the thing, sir. We wouldn't see it. Look out the window. You've got this mountaintop that we're on. Below here is the lake, in this deep valley with cliffs on all sides, and a town on each end. There could be an army of sheth on the other side of those hills behind us, or even right down the road, and you wouldn't see it from here."

"He's right, you know," said Javal.

"And what?" asked Albar. "They're going to lay siege to us? The gbatu? They can't even fight in a line."

"They don't have to lay siege," said Javal. "They just have to tie up our forces and stretch us thin. While your best knights are running down armored sheth in the corners of the mountains, Gavria marches right up the road and knocks on the door."

"That's what I would do," said Jarrod. "I'll tell you what, sir," he said to Albar. "If you start sending patrols deep into the mountains around here, they'll run across sheth in Gavrian armor within a week."

A couple of war council members grumbled.

"That is one thing we will not do," said Albar. "If we start hunting for phantom sheth knights, then we will certainly be left undermanned. I will not see that happen."

Jarrod ground his teeth and let a long breath out through his nose.

"Nothing changes," said Albar. "We never speak of this outside this room. The last thing we need is panic. Or more, as you say, misdirection."

The Gavrian War Room was a bedlam. Men jumped from the table, yelling and pointing.

"Enlisted the gbatu?" Loth shouted, lunging at Ulo. Ulo stood, and with a sweep of his hand knocked Loth over from five steps away.

The room settled. Loth rose.

"Anyone else?" Ulo asked.

No takers.

Ulo looked to Mukul, who rolled his eyes and threw up one hand.

When the room had settled, Ulo sat, and sipped his tea, treading carefully. "I've been driving those little bastards out of my lands since the day I arrived. Gbatu, by their nature, fear an even fight. They fight us only when they outnumber us."

"*Idiot!*" Loth added.

"That's how you win," said Ulo.

"You're mad," Loth grumbled. "And you're a fool."

Ulo sipped his tea. "By your logic, perhaps."

"By any logic!" Loth shouted.

"By arming the gbatu in Falconsrealm, giving them rabbits to chase while we move northward? Your problem is solved."

"What about Hillwhite?" asked Marghan. "We were of the impression that you were working with him."

"I am. Hillwhite likes this plan better. His hands are off this. Nothing leads back to him."

"So we take the risk," said Kaslix.

"And we get the reward," said Ulo. "Falconsrealm and the Shieldlands, as part of Gavria. Ruled by . . . I don't know. You decide. I don't care."

The room went quiet.

"How long have we been at war with gbatu?" Ulo asked.

Loth spoke. "Since the world began."

"And they're still a problem, right?"

This brought hesitant agreement.

"Why?" asked Ulo.

A long moment passed with no one saying anything.

"Numbers?" someone ventured.

"Resourcefulness," offered Loth. "When they're cornered — when they *must* fight — they can be fearsome."

More nods and beard-pulling.

"So we arm them," said Ulo. "We armor them. We turn them loose in the far quiet corners of Falconsrealm — the deep places — and when Albar sends his legions to rout them, they'll have to fight. They'll fight hard. Falconsrealm already has a war on its hands, though it doesn't know that, yet. While their troops are occupied we move north, through Ulorak, along the Teeth of the World."

"The Eastern Freehold will never —"

"The Eastern Freehold," said Ulo, "Won't raise a hand. I've got a champion watching those passes from a throne made of their generals' skulls."

Hanmin made a religious gesture. "You're mad. He's mad," he told the room.

"No," said Marghan. "I want to hear this."

"We buy off the lords of the Shieldlands," said Ulo, telekinetically picking up several troop markers and sliding them across the great map on the table. "We skip Axe Valley, we skip Longvalley. We stage at friendly towns and keeps, and when the weather clears, we cross the mountains and walk into

Falconsrealm."

Much conversation.

"It could work," said Loth.

"Once we have Falconsrealm," said Mukul, "we'll have the rest of the Shieldlands. We won't even have to fight for them."

"It will work," said Marghan. "And now, it seems we have no choice."

"We use my ore to continue to arm the gbatu," said Ulo. "My iron, my smiths. Hillwhite buys the arms from me, at my prices. You tax me on it."

"Done," said Hanmin.

"I'm heading back to Falconsrealm in the morning."

"What for?" Loth demanded.

Ulo smiled. "It turns out the Hillwhites are just as resourceful as the gbatu."

In a straw-strewn corral, barefoot and filthy, his feet frozen and knuckles swollen, Jarrod circled Rider Henck of Blood River.

"Come on," Jarrod said. "Keep your hands up."

He healed quickly here. Organic food, lots of sleep, daily massages. And magic. Sweet, sweet painkilling magic. His bruises had faded and he was strong today. Still a bit sore when he moved wrong, but he was having a pretty good morning.

It surprised Jarrod that a martial people such as Falconsrealm would not have developed a distinct style of unarmed combat. Very few of these men wrestled better than schoolboys, and those who did employed only the most rudimentary forms of catch wrestling; not one of them knew how to employ any manner of advanced throw, bar, or sweep. Nor did they box, nor use their feet for more than occasional kicks to the shin or groin. When they grappled, they were strong and they fought dirty—butting heads, kneeing, and clawing—but they had no technique to speak of past headlocks and brute-force takedowns. Quick boxer's jabs, snappy blocks, hip throws, and leg sweeps vaulted Jarrod through wrestling practice—here, any sort of unarmed combat was called "wrestling"—and quickly earned him an even greater level of respect. He'd known it was only a matter of time before he'd be asked to teach.

Every now and again he'd whip out *la savate* and really give them something to ooh and aah about. Kicks to the face, he'd discovered, were really cool to Gateskeep fighters. As was the rear naked choke.

But at the moment, he was teaching Henck to keep his hands up.

Jarrod popped him with a quick jab. Henck pawed his hands out and pulled his head back, and Jarrod hit him three more times, lightly, moving around him.

"*Parry*, dammit," Jarrod growled. "Don't engage the punch. Keep your head down and your hands up. Tuck your elbows in and get your weight on your back foot. Your arms are your shield. You don't reach out to catch a sword with your shield, do you?"

Henck made a lunge and Jarrod dodged it as the pain from his ribs, still tightly bound, sparked through him. He threw a knife-edge kick up into Henck's guard, something Henck could parry easily if he did it right.

Henck's tight guard and upright facing absorbed the blow, and he moved in, a grin splitting his dirty face.

"Excellent," Jarrod commended.

And just like that, overconfidence consumed Henck. He charged at Jarrod, hands outstretched, and Jarrod stepped aside, ducked low, and drove a heavy left hook into Henck's side that left him on his knees in the straw holding his stomach and gasping. The onlookers laughed, and more than a few feigned the injury.

"Don't get cocky," said Jarrod. "Who's next?"

"Maybe you can teach me something," came a voice Jarrod recognized far too well.

It was Javal, stepping over the fence and peeling off his shirt. The other fighters cheered, and Javal tossed his boots aside and rolled up his trouser legs.

Jarrod beamed. "Welcome, sire."

Javal bowed. "Rider." He kept his hands close, his feet a little inside his shoulders. He moved on the balls of his feet, cat-like, and his weight seemed to float three inches off the ground.

"I never thought a dancer could teach me how to fight!" jeered someone.

"You're going to have to face me in a moment," Javal warned the faceless heckler.

Jarrod smirked from behind his left fist. "Don't count on it." This brought catcalls and hoots.

Javal, Jarrod noticed, had been paying attention these past few weeks. He led with a flurry of punches and low kicks. Jarrod stayed close and met each with a sharp block, amazed at the musculature of Javal's forearms. It was like blocking an iron pipe. Javal threw reaching punches that had a swordsman's shoulder-thrust behind them, which left him overcommitted, but his fists were fast enough and hard enough to make Jarrod cautious.

Jarrod returned, and took a few hits about the face and ears and a handful to the body, but backed Javal sufficiently away that he could throw a spinning back kick to get range. He left the ground, driving it a bit too hard, showing off, and Javal stepped in and clobbered him with an elbow dropped across his ribs which left Jarrod lying in three inches of mud.

"Ow."

"Get a healer," Javal ordered anyone. "Jarrod?"

Jarrod rolled to a crouch. "Fine. I'm fine. Damn, that hurts."

Javal's voice was low enough that Jarrod doubted the others could hear. "If I ever see you trying that in a real fight, I'll kill you myself."

Jarrod groaned, straightening upright. "Shall we continue?" he asked, formally.

"Are you well enough?"

Jarrod shrugged. "It doesn't matter."

Javal bowed again, and struck his guard.

"Captain? King's Rider Jarrod?" the voice was dense with authority; Jarrod turned to see a thin, clean-shaven, serious man in fine golden clothes—a royal chamberlain, he recognized—standing at the edge of the corral. "Present," Jarrod announced. Javal saluted wordlessly.

"Clean up and report to the Chambers On Nine."

Jarrod arrived at the Chambers On Nine with Daelle to translate—it was a matter of state, after all—and Javal was waiting for him at the door. A meeting was well underway from the look of the table, which was cluttered with parchments and half-empty wine goblets. Jarrod recognized a few faces around the table—Albar, Chancellor Pitney, and several men he'd seen before at the Nobles' Hall. He wasn't quite sure why he and Javal had been requested to the meeting until his eyes fell upon the hooded figure in silver and black at the head of the table.

Ulo.

The man who was undoubtedly Ulo had a knight in silver armor standing on either side of him. Their helmets were of Gavrian design which Jarrod had seen on Loth's seconds so long ago: spectacled half-helmets hung with mail from cheeks to chest like massive silver beards. Their cuirasses were long vests of plates—steel, he bet; not iron—connected with bands of riveted heavy mail. They wore simple but large iron pauldrons and mantles and all their armor was heavy, beautifully-crafted, and expensive. Their forearms and upper arms were covered in red leather.

However cheap iron might have been in Gavria, Jarrod deduced, they didn't have forges, either; at least, none capable of producing sheets of steel big enough to make breastplates or pauldrons.

But that didn't change the fact that Gateskeep was going to take it in the shorts if they had to fight these guys. A pissed-off man in that much steel and iron would be a real pain in the ass.

He regretted not bringing his man-at-arms harness.

He was exceptionally glad, however, that he'd brought his war hammer. It would work wonders against Gavrian armor, especially the pick side. And the *gran espée de guerre* would be able to break an arm or a rib under that armor, or possibly knock the guy out with a clean headshot.

It would take a lot of effort, though. Yow. He would get tired really fast if there were more than a few of them. He made it a point to start running more.

Loth was apparently not on this trip.

Daelle quietly informed him that these were Gavrian dignitaries, discussing the season's upcoming trade.

He remembered hearing that this meeting was coming. From the bleary eyes and sets of grinding teeth he observed around the table, he could tell that it wasn't going particularly well.

"Ah, Captain Javal, King's Rider Jarrod," announced Pitney. "And . . ."

"Daelle," said Jarrod. "My translator."

"I'm glad you could join us."

"I know little of trade," said Javal.

"You'll fit right in," grumbled one of the Falconsrealm

nobles.

"Allow me to introduce," said Pitney to the Gavrian side of the table, "Sir Javal, Son-Lord of Ravenhurst, Knight Captain of the King's Order of the Stallion, the senior field officer of our forces. And his sergeant, King's Rider Jarrod, Son-Lord of Knightsbridge."

Javal and Jarrod saluted, fists over hearts.

"Captain, our guests have asked specifically that the two — ah, three — of you dine with us."

"We'd be honored."

"Well, then," Pitney announced. "To the Great Hall."

The council broke, with the usual banging and scuffing of benches. Not much was said among them as they filed for the door.

Javal went to the table and picked through the parchments, skimming them.

Ulo sidled up to Jarrod. His voice was deeper and slower than Jarrod expected, monotone and calm, with a haunting subtone that reminded Jarrod of Tuvan throat singing. *Definitely going for the spooky evil wizard shtick,* Jarrod noted.

Ulo's first words were, "I thought you'd be bigger."

Jarrod looked down and shrugged. "This was the only size they had left."

"I trust you'll join me at my table."

Looking into the hood, Jarrod could just make out the dark features, high cheekbones, and shrouded, electric blue eyes. Ulo looked Native American, shamanistic. And a little bit nuts. *Okay, yeah. He's terrifying.*

The sword on his belt had a ring below the crossbar for his finger; a trigger for surgical precision. The handguard was a simple bar in the shape of a D. The sword rode in a silver-inlaid scabbard with black jewels. "They let you in here with that sword?" Jarrod asked.

"You don't trust me."

"Right," said Jarrod, motioning toward the door. "Walk ahead of us."

As they wove down the stairs, Ulo's hood turned to watch a particularly hood-turnable girl going up the stairwell.

"Yeah," said Jarrod. "That happens a lot around here. Mind the step," he pointed, and as Ulo stumbled forward, Jarrod caught him with one arm.

"That stair is twice as high as the others," said Jarrod, taking Daelle's hand.

"What's the point of that?" Ulo's voice was so calm and level that he appeared disinterested.

"If you're in a helmet, you can't see it, and you bust your ass."

"But you all know it's here."

"Of course."

"Smart."

"It's not a new concept. We did it on Earth. In Europe, they paint the trip steps bright—" He didn't have a word for *orange*. Daelle had to translate *orange* as "fire." Ulo got it.

"I never knew that."

"Now you do. Gavria doesn't do that?"

"Not as far as you know," said Ulo.

"Well played."

Ulo's laugh was quiet and slow. And weird. "I've been waiting to meet you."

"Likewise."

"How's the head?"

Jarrod shrugged.

"It was . . . nothing personal."

"I would've done the same. Trip step," he warned again.

At the next landing they were at the Great Hall, which was smaller than the Lords' Hall and used primarily for entertaining visitors and, as Jarrod had learned the week prior, throwing raging holiday parties that lasted for days.

Jarrod and Ulo took seats at the head of a table at the front of the room. Wine was poured into tall agate chalices, and a plate of stuffed mushrooms was set into the space between them.

Ulo took one with slender fingers and pulled his hood back.

Jarrod had known a Kazakh fencer with skin nearly as dark and green eyes, but never anyone with skin as dark and eyes as radioactively blue.

Ulo continued in English, speaking more quietly but still with the eerie, grating overtone that made Jarrod's teeth ache. "Do you understand," Ulo asked, pausing to take another mushroom and pausing again to savor it, "the ramifications of the deal you've been offered?"

Jarrod told Daelle to excuse them. She did, and Ulo watched her walk away a little too long for Jarrod's liking.

"What deal?" said Jarrod. "And she's a kid, asshole."

At this, Ulo smiled. "You're a sorcerer, training for knighthood."

"I'm not a sorcerer," said Jarrod, "I'm a stuntman."

Ulo stared a hole through him. "A joke," he said slowly.

"Maybe."

Ulo was visibly uncomfortable. "But you're here to kill me."

"I have no interest in killing you."

"None?"

Jarrod shrugged. "Keep talking, we'll see how this goes."

"We are two scorpions in a jar. Our masters will shake our jar sooner or later."

"I don't have masters. Keep your hands where I can see them," Jarrod advised, as Ulo reached into his lap. His hand reappeared, holding a napkin, and he daubed a corner of his mouth.

"You don't appreciate the danger you are in," Ulo began.

"Story of my life," Jarrod admitted, picking up his wine.

"You have no rights here. You have no ability to stop anything that your superiors decide to start."

"So you say. Go on."

"Let's suppose that you discover nefarious doings far over your head."

Jarrod set his chalice down. "Let's."

"Do you think there is some court of appeals, here? A United Nations floor to air grievances? Have you even seen a court of law in this world?"

"Come to think of it . . ." He shook his head after a moment's reflection. "No. Not really. Huh."

"There are no courts here," said Ulo. "Not as you'd know them. No one has ever derived any concept of individual justice here. The moral order that you take as axiomatic is an artifice."

"I am not drunk enough for this conversation."

"Laws here are laid down by the rulers at their whim, and upheld by auxiliaries. This is why there are no real laws in any of these realms. Well, one law: the strong rule."

"Lucky for me."

"You need to take your ideas of right and wrong, and go home. Now."

"I don't see that happening," said Jarrod. "Maybe they *need* a judicial system. Maybe they need somebody to stand up and tell them that we hold these truths to be self-evident. You know, and all that."

"I thought so, myself, once."

"And?" asked Jarrod.

"I became king. Not president."

Jarrod gave it a respectful moment. "Point taken."

"They've never read Plato's *Republic*. They've never heard the Sermon on the Mount. The very concepts that your perceptions of right and wrong are based upon are completely alien to these people."

Jarrod drained his wine, snapping his fingers at the server and pointing to the empty. "Keep going," he told Ulo.

"The 'justice' you're fighting for—"

"—I didn't think I was—"

"You are," Ulo assured him, "is an artificial virtue that's necessary for a society that doesn't exist here. Your concepts of right and wrong are a function of the voluntary agreements of a nonexistent social contract."

"And?"

"And you're just going to make people mad."

"Looks like it's working."

"Except here, there is nothing to stop anyone you anger—not just me—from throwing you in a dark hole with your eyes burned out and leaving you there until everyone forgets about you. Which won't take as long as you think. So if this develops into a war—"

"You mean when," Jarrod corrected.

"*If* this develops into a war," Ulo repeated, "Thousands of people are going to die. You are powerless to stop it. You'll be swept up into the machinery of war and spat out on a bloody field someplace, if you're not snatched away in the dead of night and buried alive. A bit of an ignoble end either way, don't you think?"

The mushroom plate was pushed aside and another plate, piled high with sausages around a pot of mustard, was set between them.

Jarrod smirked. "I can't be the first person to have trouble taking you seriously."

"You could be the last."

"Are you threatening me?"

"It doesn't have to come to that."

Jarrod dipped a sausage in the mustard and bit off a chunk. "So, All You Are Saying, Is Give Peace a Chance?"

Ulo had a slow, intriguing smile. "You are sorely outmatched," Ulo said. "My bloodline goes back a hundred generations here. You are out of your element, and if there is a war, thousands of men are going to die, and one of them is going to be you. And if you start sticking your nose where it doesn't belong—which is your order's stock in trade—you won't live to see a minute on the field of glory."

Jarrod swallowed, cleared his throat and stuck out his hand. "You know, we got off to a bad start. I'm Jarrod. I didn't get your name."

Ulo continued, unphased. "They are giving you what you want. Enjoy it."

"I am. But pump your brakes. You want me to throw the fight?"

"I don't want a fight."

Jarrod chewed at him for a moment. "Yeah, I can believe that."

"Fighting is not my style. What I am saying, is take what you've been offered, and do your best to lie low. Your life will be considerably easier. And longer."

Jarrod laughed under his breath. "If you're asking me to take a dive, you'd better consult your Evil Sorcerer's Manual. You're doing great so far with the whole thing, by the way. You've got the robe, the mannerisms, that voice thing. This little intimidation speech. It works for you. Me, I couldn't pull that off."

"This is who I am."

"Sure," said Jarrod.

"I am not saying—" he hunted for the word, and then settled on Jarrod's term, "—take a dive, Jarrod. I'm saying, let us not rush into anything that would make us," again, he searched for a word, "uncomfortable."

Jarrod swabbed another sausage in mustard. "I'm a soldier. Comfort is not one of my concerns. Your comfort, much less so.

No offense."

"You're not going to give me a lecture about how avoiding a fight isn't in your character."

"Funny, I've had this talk a lot, recently."

"I'm sure. I was there when you took down Loth."

Jarrod's eyes hardened as he locked them with Ulo's. "Then let's talk ignoble ends. If you fuck with me, I'll take whatever pieces of you are left when I'm done, and I'll load them into a catapult, and launch them in the general direction of your homeland."

"So, you *are* going to kill me."

"You decide."

"Were you raised a wrathful jingoist, or is it more of a birth defect?"

Jarrod cleared a fennel seed from his incisor with a fingernail as his wine was refilled. "Do you want an ass-kicking? I'm free after this."

"Atta boy."

"Do me a favor," said Jarrod, "Piss me off."

"Every man has his price. Consider yours."

Drums and dancing girls began. Jarrod picked up his wine and stood. "I didn't come here to sell my soul," he said. "I came here to buy it back."

"We'll talk again," said the sorcerer.

"Only when I negotiate your surrender."

V

SCHERZO

"Never interrupt an enemy when he's making a mistake."

- Napoleon Bonaparte

"**O**h, my sister's name is Tilly, she's a whore in Piccadilly, and my mother is another in the Stra-a-and . . ."

Jarrod sang loudly astride Perseus as they slammed through the king's hunting trails on Javal's tail. The crash of his armor, and the horse's barding and steeled hooves, clamored in time.

". . . and my brother sells his asshole at the Elephant and Castle, we're the finest fucking family in the la-a-and . . ."

Jarrod was trying to remember verse two when Perseus skidded to a stop and he slammed against the beast's neck.

Four ogrish things appeared ahead of him in the road. *"Javal!!"* he yelled, drawing his arming sword and flipping his shield into his hand. *"Ambush!"*

When they charged, they were unlike anything he had ever seen.

Incredibly, impossibly fast, they moved in leaps and were at him, clubs and claws flailing, nearly as tall as Jarrod was, seated.

Perseus was trained to fight but Jarrod hadn't yet learned to direct him; without orders, the huge roan fought only reflexively, turning and biting and kicking at each blow hurled into the barding. He caught one with both rear hooves and flung it off the road into the trees.

Jarrod couldn't get a clear swing with the horse's haphazard movements, and in seconds one of the gargantuan creatures had yanked him from his saddle. He landed on his back and rolled over his head, springing up to his feet—between a career as a stuntman and a black belt in Judo he could fall on his ass from six feet in the air and walk away whistling—and he barely managed to duck a haymaker from a giant club which would've brained him.

He was now on his own turf—sort of. They were *huge!* Eight feet tall? Taller? Black claws and red skins and tusks.

And armor.

One grabbed his shield and pulled; Jarrod took off a hand with the arming sword and on the return he swatted its sword aside and delivered a thrust under the eye through the open face of its helmet.

He yanked the blade free, at which point one of them bowled him over.

He rolled sideways as a club scattered the gravel right where his head had been, and as he found his feet, Perseus charged in and smashed the sheth over sideways.

Jarrod put his back to the saddle. Perseus stayed behind him.

The sheth climbed to its feet, snarling, "I'm a'kill you, human. We eat horse tonight!"

"Not this horse," said Jarrod. As he rushed at the sheth, it ran back, frantic. He broke the attack and backed up to Perseus, again.

He had the wrong sword.

Late nights with a diamond-honing kit had made the arming sword's edge long past sharp; an edge that would take a head the way the best *katanas* could. But that same edge, microscopically thin, the Martensitic needles molecularly aligned, would fold over and self-destruct against a coat of plates.

That's why you have two swords, dumbass.

It sure took that hand off, though. Damn. Nice edge.

The *gran espée de guerre*, conversely, was not sharp by conventional definition—you'd have to punch the sword to cut yourself on it. It was, however, a masterpiece of edge geometry and blade harmonics, with a fat trick bevel that made it function less like a kitchen knife and more like a splitting maul, specifically designed to wreck mail and collapse a helmet or pauldron without suffering much damage.

But it was on the far side of the saddle, beside his hammer. Which would also work here.

His knees were shaking so hard his armor rattled.

He was going to die.

After all this, he would die for grabbing the wrong sword.

At the very least, he knew, he was about to ruin the arming sword irreparably, and possibly break it, which would lessen his chances of getting through any further court intrigues with all his extremities still attached.

Think, think, think, think.

Your answer is four feet away. Figure this out.

The sheth moved apart until they were at the edges of his vision. Jarrod kept his back to Perseus, swiveling his head with a monster on either side.

One would charge as soon as he focused on the other. If he took the time to get into the saddle, both would charge, and take Perseus down, and if he got injured when the big horse fell, he was done.

Four feet might as well have been an ocean.

He wondered if he could duck under Perseus. If he could get to the *gran espée de guerre*, things would seriously start going his way.

He'd never ducked under Perseus before. He wasn't sure how he'd react, but one thing he did know about the big horse was that he didn't like surprises.

God, please, get that fucking weapon in my hands and I'll always grab it first from now on, I swear.

I've learned my lesson. Really. Got it. Thanks.

He tried to move around Perseus to the front.

As he moved, they both approached. He struck a guard and took a step forward, menacing, then turned to the other. They each backed up.

Huh. They're sure scared of you.

It took him a moment.

They don't know you have the wrong sword.

They didn't see that you hit the unarmored parts of their pal back there. They just saw meat flying and blood spurting. And no way in hell do they want a piece of you right now.

He heard the approach of an armored horse, the sound of a subway.

The head of the beast to his right exploded, the end of Javal's spear smashing through it. As the monster crumbled into the road, Javal spun his horse beside Jarrod.

What had seemed to Jarrod an eternity had been only the minute it had taken Javal to don his helm and gauntlets. "Get on your horse!" His voice was louder than any Jarrod had ever heard, an operatic baritone that exploded through the forest.

Jarrod sheathed his sword, slung his shield onto his back, then grabbed the mounting braid and swung up into the saddle.

"Stay close!" Javal's voice was adamant, possibly even angry.

Faced with the two knights, out-armored, outgunned and with no flanking support, the last sheth made a retreat, scuttling sideways into the trees.

"Do we give chase?" Jarrod asked.

"Hell, no." Javal kicked his horse around and jumped down next to the dead sheth. "Help me get his armor off. Helmet, too. Hurry."

Jarrod and Javal dumped the armor and helmet onto the table in the Chambers On Nine. The stink was a thing alive. Sheth had a graywater smell, not quite sewage, but green meat with a faint patina of old onions and dog shit.

Jarrod threw up out the window. His voice was a leather-lunged shout as he yelled an apology down at the hillside.

"Anyone out there?" asked Javal.

Jarrod wiped his mouth with his hand. "Better safe than sorry."

"Good man."

"So, who's going to go get Prince Skippy the Wonder Soldier?" asked Jarrod.

"I guess that's me," Javal grumbled. "I'll be right back. Your turn to watch the gear. You want a drink?"

"Something strong," said Jarrod.

Sir Dahl was in the room a moment after Javal left, in warrior blacks with a sword belt. "Is this it?" he asked.

"That was fast. And yes." Jarrod spread the armor out on the table and the knight began picking through it.

"Mail, coat of scales . . ." he shook his head. "Gavrian armor. Pretty amazing."

"Yes," said Jarrod. "It is."

"How'd you take him down?"

"Took a hand, and then stabbed him in the eye."

"With what?"

Jarrod tapped the handle of his arming sword.

"May I see that?" said Sir Dahl.

Jarrod drew it. Blood and brains had caked it into the scabbard and it came free with some effort. Gore coated the fuller.

"Wow," he said. "I need to clean this."

"No worry," said Sir Dahl.

"Careful," said Jarrod. "It's sharp."

Sir Dahl pointed it at him. "Good."

Jarrod looked down the blade of his own sword.

That was really stupid.

"I can't believe you fell for that!" Dahl laughed. "You're an idiot! After all that, you're just an idiot."

"You're gonna die," he told Sir Dahl.

"I doubt that," said Sir Dahl. "My men will be here in just a moment, and they'll dispose of this. And of you."

Jarrod stepped back. "You know, you better get rid of everything, then." He reached into his pocket and pulled out a set of brass knuckles. "We also found these."

Jarrod flicked his wrist and the knuckles hit Dahl in the face, causing just enough of a startled response that Jarrod could knock the sword away with one hand and smash Dahl in the eye with a savate *fouétte,* whipping his foot into a wrecking ball. Sir Dahl collapsed, squirming and holding his face.

"Sorry, man," said Jarrod. He toed the sword into his hand and bent to pick up the knuckles. "I hated to do that. But, you know. You were kind of being a dick." He'd gashed his hand on the blade and blood dripped from the pommel and ran down his arm.

Two more men with swords, men Jarrod hadn't met, charged through the door. Jarrod had them at swordpoint as they entered, working his right hand into the brass knuckles. "I will kill every one of you. Lie down on the floor, with your hands on your heads."

"Can we attend to him?" asked one.

"No."

Albar came into the room just as they got into the prone. "What the hell is going on?" he demanded.

"Yeah, about that," said Jarrod.

"You're under arrest!" Albar screamed.

"Draw, you fucker," Jarrod suggested. "Let's go."

Javal appeared behind Albar. "Jarrod, don't kill the heir presumptive."

"You keep saying that," said Jarrod. "But I don't think you mean it."

"What the hell just happened?" asked Javal.

"Sir Dahl pulled my own sword on me. So I kicked him."

Sir Dahl was unconscious and blood was spreading near his head; Jarrod was pretty sure he'd blown apart his eye socket.

"How the hell—" Albar began, looking at Jarrod's sword. "If he had your sword, how did you—"

"Shut up," Javal said, and yelled out the door for a healer. Jarrod knelt next to Dahl and checked his pulse at the throat. Dahl grunted.

"He's alive," said Jarrod, "but he's going to lose the eye."

Albar was incredulous. "From a kick? How is that possible?"

"Come over here," growled Jarrod, "I'll show you." He felt like throwing up again.

"Jarrod, tell me again. From the beginning," said Javal.

Jarrod stood. "Sir Dahl came in right after you left. He looked at the armor. He asked me what we killed the sheth with. I told him I killed it with my sword. He asked to see my sword. I gave it to him."

"You're an idiot," said Javal.

"Yes, sir, we covered that. He pointed my sword at me and said his guys were coming to take this stuff away, and me with it. So I kicked him."

"In the eye."

"Really hard," Jarrod added.

"Apparently," said Javal. "Any witnesses?"

"No."

"And these two?"

"Sir Dahl said his guys were coming. I figured these two were them."

Albar looked at the armor on the table. "What is this? It stinks!"

"That was on the sheth we killed," Javal said. "So it seems you have a problem, Albar."

A knot of people had gathered around the door.

"All of you!" Albar shouted. "Out!"

Durvin pushed his way through the crowd and knelt beside Jarrod and Sir Dahl. "He might die, sir, if I don't get him into my chambers immediately," Durvin told Albar.

Durvin brought in two fairly big guys to carry Sir Dahl. Javal ushered them out, closing the door. Dahl's seconds were still on the floor.

"You might have just killed a knight," said Albar, pointing at Jarrod.

"Yes," Javal said, turning on Albar. "He might have. A knight from a border castle, who threatened to kill a rider who's here on special orders from the king."

"What orders?" Albar accused.

"If it was your business," said Javal, "you'd know."

"You will tell me," Albar pointed at Jarrod, "who you are, and what you're doing here."

"Sure," said Jarrod. "You want to discuss it closer to the window?"

"Jarrod," Javal warned. He turned back to Albar, continuing, "Sir Dahl threatened to kill Jarrod in order to destroy evidence of what amounts to a Gavrian act of war. That makes Sir Dahl a traitor, and that still leaves the question of these two." He nodded to the two prone knights, who still had their hands on their heads. "If anybody is to be arrested and interrogated, I'd suggest we start with them."

"I don't know these men," said Albar.

"Neither do I," said Javal. "But I'm sure we will."

"We need to get a message to Gateskeep," Jarrod suggested. "They need to know what's going on."

Javal looked at Albar, then at Jarrod. "I'll see that it's done."

VI

MOLTO ALLEGRO

"In truth the science of arms is merely the science of deceiving your enemy with skill."

— Salvator Fabris, 1606

"**Y**ou built *Gavrian armor?!*" Loth threw his chalice off the table and two warlords restrained him as he pulled for Ulo.

Ulo addressed the War Table. "Come spring, we move north."

Loth shook them off. "We have to," he said. "We're lucky they haven't declared war, yet. Gbatu, in our armor. That's war."

"They won't move on us," said Ulo. "They can't. Their troops are going to be tied up, chasing down the gbatu. We mass our troops now. *Right now.* And we start moving them through Ulorak, and into the Shieldlands from the east, at the end of winter."

"That puts our attack out for at least two moons," challenged Commander Gar, who headed a large mercenary company out of Axe Valley. Gar was large and enormously fat with a heavy beard.

His scarred, powerful hands still spoke of years on the battlefield behind an axe.

Loth said, "Two moons during which your boys can pick up a fine coin or two running weapons and armor through the canyons of Falconsrealm. You should be the last one complaining."

"Why should we move north?" asked Hanmin. "If Albar comes around to our way, we can sit back and watch the civil war unfold. Let him do the fighting."

"The Hillwhites will not rise against Riongoran-Thurdin," said Ulo. "Why do you think I did it this way?"

"Because you're an idiot," said Rute.

"No," said Ulo. "This is sound."

"To what end?"

"We continue to arm the gbatu," Ulo repeated calmly. "When we get there, we enlist them as an auxiliary force."

The room erupted again.

Mukul lit a pipe at the window. He was tapping out the bowl over the sill before everyone had finished yelling at each other.

"Soldiering is a calling," Loth snarled from the far window. He was so infuriated he wouldn't even sit at the table. "Those animals have no business on the field beside us."

"Their business," Ulo insisted, "is to harass and attrit. My word, gentlemen—if ten armed sheth can tie up ten knights—"

"What's to keep them from attacking us with the weapons we've given them?"

"The promise of more," said Ulo. "If they attack Gavrian forces, we start arming their tribal enemies instead."

"You've worked this all out," growled Loth.

"Of course."

There was silence for a long minute.

"Assuming we adopt this plan."

"Oh, it's adopted," said Ulo. "It can't be undone. We must go forward."

"Must we," said Loth.

"Yes," said Ulo. "Because they'll solve their gbatu problem—eventually—and once they do, they'll be coming for us with everything they've got."

"You're mad," said Marghan. "This is insanity. You've started a war."

"*You wanted a war,*" said Ulo. "You wanted Falconsrealm. It's hanging, ready to be plucked. But you must commit. You must strike. Now. You will never have another chance."

"What of strategy?"

Ulo shrugged. "Move into the Shieldlands and take Falconsrealm."

This brought a spiteful laugh. "It's that easy, is it?"

"You said you could take Falconsrealm if you had the manpower. I delivered. Now you deliver. Because if you don't hit them, and hit them hard, next summer they'll turn Gavria into Gateskeep South."

Grunts and shaking of heads.

"Is there another difficulty?" growled Ulo.

A warlord admitted, "Only that High River Keep is one of the best-defended castles in the world. Once we get there, how do we take it?"

Ulo and Mukul had thought that one out weeks ago. "From within," said Ulo. "With spies, and bribes, and assassins, and by sneaking our finest warriors in on scutage, and offering commissions in our armies for all the Falconsrealm chivalrics who cooperate."

"There's still the question of Albar."

"He's an ore baron," said Ulo. "We have something he needs; he has something we want. The Hillwhites want Falconsrealm. They wouldn't be marrying into royalty otherwise. I say let's give it to them. They side with us, and we roll them into Gavria the way you did to Ulorak, and then we tax them. What's the difference if the Hillwhites run Falconsrealm or we run it? The morning of the siege, he'll open the gates for us himself."

All agreed, though there was much chin-rubbing and grunting.

Ulo stood. "First, though, we use the gbatu to draw out troops from the castles and forts along the main road to High River. The local lords will have to side with us."

"They could make us starve them out. It could take moons."

"If they hole up," said Ulo, "we massacre the town."

There was swearing around the table.

Rute stood up. "I will have no part of this!"

"Do you want to know how I defeated the Eastern Freehold?" Ulo asked. "This. The willingness to wage absolute, comprehensive warfare. This is why I have the foundations of an empire if I so choose, and you do not."

Marghan's words were deliberate. "Choose your next words carefully, wizard."

"I *chose* to ally myself with Gavria," said Ulo. "Make no mistake. You saw what I'd done, and you wanted my expertise. This is what I bring you."

"You've brought us a war."

"Yes. And I'll win it for you. But we win it my way. Surround them. Starve them. Hit them with what they fear—armed hordes of gbatu—and then if they don't cooperate, burn the villages to the ground. Leave the limbs and heads of their children in piles outside the front gates."

"You'll never find a Gavrian warrior who'd do it," said Loth.

"If they won't, I've got men in my own army who will. Men who make Lord Elgast of Skullsmortar look like a generous and kindly benefactor."

"He's insane," someone said. "We've brought a madman to the War Table."

Ulo bristled at him. "I would think you'd rather have a man like me on your side."

Gar stepped in. "Once we've manned the other strategic points along the mountains, we launch one massive assault. When we get to High River, we make them the same offer."

"What's to keep Gateskeep from coming in behind us?" offered someone.

"Look at those mountains," Gar stabbed his finger down on the map. "There are only two roads out. Long Valley and Axe Valley. If the western side of Gateskeep was passable we'd have taken Gateskeep eons ago. No one travels there. When they come around the mountains, we'll see them. And we'll hold the Princess as our insurance against a coup, or a full-on assault."

"Albar will never go for that," said Loth.

Gar's voice was low and cold. "Please, let him argue."

Ulo was quiet for a moment. "Fine," he decided.

Loth spoke. "Once we've taken High River Keep—which, as you say, Albar may do for us—we'll have our new base of operations. So let's get some men inside working for us—Commander Gar is on that, already—and then let's get there. The minor details will sort themselves out as we go. Right?"

"You know that if we start leveling towns, Gateskeep will fight an all-out war."

Ulo smiled a slow, wicked smile. "That's coming, regardless. This way, they fight us on our terms."

Gar's smile mirrored his. "Now, he's thinking like a warrior," he commended to the rest of the table.

Loth grumbled, "And not a moment too soon."

Two days later, Jarrod rode beneath the barbican into the

village of Horlech. It was noon, and they'd been riding since early morning.

Both knights of the Stallion assigned to Edwin's Keep had vanished.

To be fair, people vanished all the time around here, Jarrod found. It unnerved him. It wasn't like anyone traveled the countryside with a GPS tracking system in their phone. However, with the disappearance of the two knights, the joke circulated in High River that there had been another pitchfork accident.

The issue, Jarrod had learned, was that the knights had been assigned to Edwin's Tower to curb Edwin's predilection for procuring bedmates from the townsfolk, something that wouldn't have been a big deal in sex-positive Falconsrealm except that Edwin preferred to have his men bring him prospective bed bunnies at swordpoint.

In a culture so awesomely sexually empowered that getting your sword waxed was practically the national sport, Jarrod figured it would take a special kind of illness to resort to rape.

It wasn't unthinkable that these guys had been offed for getting in the way of the duke's recreational activities. They'd specifically been tasked with cramping his style at every turn. And not just to fuck with him, but to prevent an insurrection in the town, which consisted of a large garrison of Gateskeep and Falconsrealm soldiers.

He cracked his knuckles again. He'd been cracking them a lot as they rode. He looked forward to meeting this guy.

Javal was ahead of him, on a black mare with a white blaze that Jarrod had heard was one of the most expensive horses in Falconsrealm. These were well-patrolled roads, so they wore simple clothes and led a single pony with their armor.

This was Jarrod's new riding horse, a sleek black mare like Javal's that he'd named Lilith. She was light-footed and fast and had a smooth, rolling single-foot gait that took little effort from him to ride; he'd fallen asleep in the saddle just this afternoon. And best of all, she was small enough that he could backflip into the saddle, even in his light shirt of mail. That had impressed the living shit out of everyone who'd watched him struggling with Perseus for the past quarter moon.

His helmet hung from his saddle beside the *gran espée de guerre*.

He was hungry.

At the top of the hill ahead of them slouched Edwin's Keep, the nearly-fallen tower on the Gateskeep border.

Jarrod had gotten the skinny on Edwin during the ride. Edwin was Albar's eldest brother, a patrician and ridiculously rich. His title of duke was honorary and for all intents and purposes, bought.

Jarrod was beginning to loathe politics the way Javal did.

Most of the nobility contributed in a measurable capacity— hunting, breeding horses, negotiating trade, managing the affairs of the castle, mediating affairs and disputes—which is where the local feudal model broke down from its Earth counterpart. Everyone worked, it seemed. Except guys like Edwin. Tall, handsome, moneyed, and thoroughly superfluous. He'd been given a sagging tower on the Gateskeep-Falconsrealm border mostly to keep him occupied. Plus, he had the money to keep fixing it.

With no real power or position, Jarrod had pointed out to Javal—and correctly—that Edwin would have a tremendous amount to gain by siding with Gavria. The fact that the Hillwhites had made their fortunes in the ore trade amplified this. If there was a war, they stood to gain tremendously.

They stopped for lunch at a tavern whose door opened onto the road between Horlech and the great tower. It was a soldiers' hangout, and Javal was on good terms with the owner and a couple of the servers. Lunch was fried turnips with yellow tomatoes and bacon, and quart-sized steins of beer. Lots of steely-eyed guys lounging around and drinking. Quite a few offered them salutes with their steins. Jarrod felt better. These were his people.

They armored up outside, Jarrod in his heaviest mail—he'd brought three shirts of it from Earth in varying weights and this one was heavy-gauge wire from welded, case-hardened steel— his coat of plates, and a Damascus steel gorget and mantle with matching grand pauldrons, the metal rippled in a spectacular tree-ring design. Over this he threw his black titanium coif and donned his huge steel Barbute, clipping his custom bite guard to a tether around a small bar inside the locking visor.

He adjusted his swordbelt around the coat of plates, slipped a large spiked warhammer into its frog beside a Ka-Bar, and strapped the *gran espée de guerre* around his waist, the handle jutting nearly to his collarbone. The baseball-glove smell of his coat of plates was comforting. And empowering.

Most of the soldiers who wandered past, whether stumbling out or drifting in, gave them a long look. It had been a long time since they'd seen knights in full armor, and Jarrod's armor clearly identified him as being from out of town.

"I don't think your sword is big enough," Javal joked. Javal wore an ornate suit of *cuir bouilli* over his mail, dyed black and mossy green and articulated like a full field harness with the order's coat of arms inlaid in silver on his chest.

Jarrod needled him back. "I'll need it if they're wearing as much armor as you are."

He was well familiar with the physics involved in Javal's armor, even if Javal wasn't; *cuir bouilli* was medieval plastic. Left in hot water, the tannin aggregates in the leather create a resin, effectively a polymer, that cools to the hardness of oak.

Jarrod's own bazubands and shovel-knee greaves were made from the same process, only glued and riveted over high-density polyethylene for extra protection. He'd done backyard destructive testing on *cuir bouilli* with axes and swords. *Cuir bouilli* over riveted mail and an arming jacket was astonishingly effective.

The articulations in Javal's armor further proved to Jarrod that the only reason these guys didn't have full-body steel harnesses was the lack of blast furnaces to produce large plates of slag-free steel. If an armorer could work out the angles and joints to articulate a suit like Javal was wearing—which obviously he could—then the only thing stopping the same armorer from knocking together a rig of full-blown Maximillian plate armor was a lack of materials.

It also occurred to Jarrod that if they could build articulated armor, then they had to have been fighting in armor for a very, very long time, here. Articulated *cuir bouilli* like Javal's had been mentioned by Chaucer in the Fourteenth Century, which put it a good five hundred years ahead of their metallurgy and two thousand years ahead of the advent of riveted mail. Probably more than that, since on Earth everyone seemed to figure things out a lot faster than these guys did.

They were on the cusp of a major arms advancement. They just didn't see it yet.

If you could import sheets of ten-gauge mild steel to this planet, you could buy and sell the Hillwhites.

He pushed the thought aside.

Jarrod knew, the moment that they arrived at the main gate to the keep, that things weren't quite right. He'd had time to get used to the cheery nature with which Gateskeepers and Falconsrealmers greeted guests, and he was fairly sure that this time they weren't welcome.

This was a small castle, really just a well-placed tower with an attached manor and some walls. At sight of the sagging tower, Jarrod muttered, "Hey, look at that. It's my television career."

"What?" said Javal.

"Nothing," said Jarrod, and they rode directly up to the front door.

Javal grabbed the sergeant of the guard, a knight of the Order of the Swan named Orvyn, and steered him inside. Jarrod followed at Javal's behest.

"We're here to see the duke," said Javal.

"No one sees the duke," said the sergeant.

"That's not what I hear," said Javal. "I heard he had visitors. Very recently. We need to discuss a few things with him."

"Sir, if I let you up there, he'll kill me as soon as you leave," Orvyn said.

"Talk," suggested Javal.

"Gladly. They've been gone five days," said Orvyn. He looked to Jarrod, who said nothing, his visor still closed.

"Gone?" said Javal. "We heard their mounts are still here."

"All their mounts. And their armor," the sergeant admitted. "We don't know where they went. We figured maybe they'd left for High River."

"No one from this keep comes to High River," said Javal. "Least of all, should I add, Duke Edwin."

"Well, the duke has been a little busy."

"He gets that way," said Javal. "Or so we hear."

"Got himself a little trophy up there. An elf. Says his boys caught her at one of the mines near the Stronghold."

"That's an act of war," Javal told Jarrod.

"Only if he gets caught," said Orvyn.

Javal shook his head and swore silently. "We'll have a word with the man," he said to Orvyn. "Anything out of the ordinary around here?" he asked. "Besides that?"

"Commander Gar of House Fletcher was here the night they vanished. He was meeting with the duke."

"Interesting that he wouldn't drop by the royal seat to pay

his respects, being a half day's ride away."

"He didn't ride. A wizard gated him here."

Javal looked impressed. "That's some big magic."

"Indeed," said Orvyn." I didn't know he had a wizard that strong out there."

Javal turned to Jarrod. "Gar is a well-known, and very well-fed, commander from the southern borderlands. He runs a small, for-hire outfit," Javal's voice trailed off. "Son of a toothless whore."

"Let me guess," said Jarrod. "They hire themselves in on scutage for border lords."

Javal swore quietly. "Among other things." He spoke to the sergeant. "Anyone you have here, on scutage, they come talk to us."

"That's every damned soldier in this place," said the sergeant.

"Every soldier?"

"Except me, sir. And the two knights of your order, the two we're missing."

"How many total?"

"Seven, plus me. Now five plus me. Look, I can't let you up there. They'll kill me once you leave."

"Jarrod?" asked Javal.

"Sorry about this," Jarrod said. A moment later, with the sergeant on his shoulder blades and one foot up near his ear, Jarrod said, "I overpowered you, right?"

"I'd say," the sergeant groaned. "Damn."

"Just stay there and pretend you're unconscious," Jarrod suggested.

"Will do," the sergeant groaned. "Have fun."

"You've got to show me that," Javal said, as they double-timed up the stairs.

"I did," said Jarrod.

"Not that one."

The manor house was only two floors, and the grand entrance to the tower was a large stone arch, unguarded. "Through there."

"Right."

A winding staircase with doors every so often. "Any idea which one of these?"

"The top."

"Why am I in this much armor?" Jarrod griped, three floors later.

"Because getting out of here might be harder than getting in."

They stopped at a massive door at the end of the stairwell. Javal slammed his fist against it three times. "Duke Edwin! Open this door!"

"They're coming," said Jarrod, listening behind.

Javal had his ear against the door. "They're not the only ones." He knocked again. "Duke Edwin!"

Jarrod stepped forward and drove his heel against the door right above the handle. The echo rocked the entire tower.

He was reaching back to do it again when the door opened.

Edwin was tall, dark-haired, and had the same narrow eyes as Albar, but a broader jaw and a calmer demeanor.

He was also, Jarrod couldn't help but notice, stark naked. And exceptionally endowed.

"Sir Javal," said Edwin. "To what do I owe the privilege? And who let you in here?"

"We cold-cocked your sergeant," Javal admitted. "He was being uncooperative."

"Good for him," said Edwin. "Who's this?"

"My sergeant," Javal said. "We heard you have an elf in there. Is that true?"

"You boys want a turn?" asked Edwin. "I'm almost done."

Jarrod hit him with a steel-shod left to the liver like a cannonball and swatted him in the head with his palm as he doubled. Javal shoved Jarrod back.

"That was foolish," Edwin growled, straightening and coughing. "I'll have your hand for that."

"Try it," said Javal. "We're here on orders of the king. Come against us, you come against him."

"Your order needs to mind its own business," Edwin spat.

"Sir Aidan and Sir Rohn are my business. You, committing an act of war with your prick, is my business."

Five soldiers were now behind them on the stairs, armed to the eyeballs in mail and helmets. Two had spears. Three had axes.

Edwin spoke to the soldiers on the stairs. "Gentlemen? Show the captain, and his sergeant, here, the way out."

At the front door, Jarrod and Javal found themselves facing the five soldiers, who had begun to break up and form a semicircle.

Jarrod raised a palm for them to be patient, and took a moment on the last stair to lock his visor, seat his mouthguard, and snug up his gloves. Then he cleared the *gran espée de guerre* from its scabbard in a sweeping and grandiose movement that focused attention on the alarming scale of the sword. He raised it in both hands and everyone backed up.

Javal slapped his visor shut, his sword and dagger practically leaped into his hands, and it began.

Jarrod caught a speartip with the end of the big sword, rode it down in a *coulé,* and took off most of the soldier's hand right through his glove. Jarrod shoved him down with a heel on his thigh, then spun and drove the balance of the blade into another's helmet with both hands. The soldier went over and lay in the mud with his legs kicking, his helm split and creased as if he'd been hit with a crowbar.

Another stepped back, swearing, fending with his spear but clearly not wanting to engage.

The last came at Jarrod swinging his axe from over his shoulder, and Jarrod drove his elbow into the haft and the axe banged against his shoulder flare and skipped off the heavy Damascus steel. Jarrod trapped the arm, twisted, and hip-threw him into the mud, dented the spectacles on his helm with a heel-stomp, then toed the axe up and kicked it a few yards away.

Jarrod turned and faced the last, who fell to his knees and threw his spear away. "Please don't kill me, sire."

"Fine," said Jarrod. "Tend to him," he motioned to the knight with the bashed-in helm, whose legs had ceased spasming.

"I think he's dead, sire."

"Well, check, damn you!" Jarrod snapped. At that point, the soldier he'd face-stomped plowed him over from behind.

Jarrod's vision cleared to see that the guy had a sword, one of the local heavy bastards, and it was coming down, two-handed, as he was getting up. He slipped left and the impact on his shoulder was terrific; his back wrenched and his hand went numb.

The soldier fell back, holding the handle of his sword and nothing else.

Jarrod wiggled his fingers, stood, and stepped forward, brandishing the greatsword.

In the Gateskeep language, telling someone "you're fucked," is not pejorative. They do, however, have a colorful idiom that loosely translates to *ass in the air and waiting*. Jarrod used it here to illustrate the soldier's situation for him.

Javal, done dispatching his opponent, moved in from Jarrod's three-o'clock. "Give up, sir," he suggested.

The soldier drew a slender knife from his belt.

"Don't do that," Jarrod begged. "I don't want to kill you."

"I wish I felt the same," the soldier said, and tackled him. A moment later he was face down in the mud, with Jarrod kneeling on his back and drowning him.

Javal stepped on his hand, removed the knife from his grip, and ordered Jarrod to get up. Jarrod did, and stomped on the soldier's crotch.

Sergeant Orvyn stood at the doorway. "You gentlemen about done?"

"Come here, sergeant," Jarrod knelt by the fighter whose hand he'd injured, and pulled off the man's glove—not much more than a welder's glove—as the man held his arm at the wrist, weeping. The big sword had done its job; the hand had been severed across the distal transverse arch and pumped blood into the mud.

"Hold him," Jarrod ordered. "Hold his arms." He unbuckled his blowout kit from his swordbelt and slipped a tourniquet over the hand above the wrist. "This is going to hurt," he told the soldier, "but it'll save your life. Do you understand?"

"Yes."

"Don't fight me." He twisted the windlass until the man screamed. The sergeant held him from behind, with his good arm up in a hammer lock.

"Jarrod!" shouted Javal.

The bleeding slowed to a trickle almost immediately. Jarrod tore open a packet of Quik-Clot gauze and stuffed it into the wound. The man screamed even louder as the caustic induced, and then passed out.

Jarrod packed the wound with Quik-Clot and Javal watched, eyes wide, as the bleeding stopped almost immediately.

"This material cauterizes when it reacts with blood," Jarrod explained, securing it with duct tape around the hand. "He lost the hand but he's not going to die. You got a good healer?" he asked the sergeant, who nodded.

Jarrod picked up his sword from the mud. "Go get him. I need to talk to him. You," he said to the soldier who'd surrendered, "Fetch some rags and some grease. You can clean my sword."

Javal, Jarrod, and Orvyn went through the apartment that the two missing knights had shared. Their armor trunk, though it felt full, was locked.

"And you're sure there's no way we can go back in there to get her?" asked Jarrod, for the third time.

"And then what?" asked Javal. "Beat down his door, steal her, and then what? Tell me the next part of that, and I'll consider it. What happens two iterations later? Three?"

"Get her . . . I don't know. Somewhere safe. Home. Out of there."

"Here are your next three iterations," said Javal, "Based on the fact that he's a duke.

"One: he'd consider it theft. So, two: you'll hang. Then, three: he'll send out every soldier in this town to recapture her, because if she gets back to the Stronghold and tells the Faerie what he did to her, we'll be at war with them until the next Cataclysm. So, no. She stays. Our mission is here," he thumped the armor trunk.

"I'm taking possession of this," Javal told Orvyn. "We'll get it open and return whatever's inside to their families. It's the least we can do."

A knock at the door, and an older man asked for Jarrod. He was Hul, the duke's sorcerer and healer. "I wanted to thank you," he said.

Jarrod bowed. He'd explained to Hul about releasing the tourniquet slowly, and then loosening the Quik-Clot by soaking with salt water.

"Did it work?" Jarrod asked.

"You saved his life," Hul said, handing Jarrod back his tourniquet. "Would it be an imposition on your magic if I borrowed that technique?"

"By all means, you should," Jarrod said.

While Javal and Orvyn went through the room, Jarrod showed Hul how to fashion a tourniquet with a windlass, how to apply it above the wound and never on a joint.

Hul thanked Jarrod, bowed, and showed himself out. Javal asked to see the tourniquet. Jarrod showed him how it worked.

"In my homeland," Jarrod said, "every soldier carries one of these. Some carry two. They train to put it on in the heat of battle, and once this became standard procedure in our army, our casualties halved immediately. There's no reason to ever lose a man because of bleeding from an extremity. Hell, our best soldiers have been known to put this on and keep fighting."

"So you killed one," Javal said, "Then you granted mercy to the second, spared the third, and healed the fourth. Do you not remember the conversation that we had?"

Jarrod looked him in the eye for a long moment. "Killing's not always the answer."

Javal rifled through the dead knights' trunk. "In this case," he said, "you killed just enough people to make your point and stop the fight. That's better, I guess."

Jarrod shrugged. "I'm pacing myself."

Javal shook his head, chuckling. "That was some amazing fighting. That sword of yours is really something."

"Thanks. So, what did you learn while I was off being a wimp?"

Javal clapped him on the shoulder. "While you were talking

with Hul, I got some intelligence out of Sergeant Orvyn. There's been an assassination at the Gavrian Parliament. Their Lord High Inquisitor, Lord Marghan, is dead."

"Inquisitor?" asked Jarrod. "Could there possibly be a more evil-sounding name for anyone?"

"He's the head of their intelligence network. Or was," Javal corrected. Jarrod was staring at the outside of the trunk. "We have our own, of course," said Javal. "You haven't met Lord Gristavius?"

Jarrod was staring closely at the outside of the trunk.

"'Lord High Inquisitor Gristavius?'" Jarrod repeated. He looked inside again. "No," he said. "And sweet Jesus, I'm okay with that."

The trunk held the detritus of a military man's life: socks, a dagger, spare boots, various clothes, and some letters. He opened up the letters and skimmed through one, then another. He still didn't read the Gateskeep language well, but he grasped enough words to tell that they were letters between one of the knights and his mother. News from home. Hope you enjoyed the socks.

Jarrod stuck his arm inside the trunk again, then measured it against the outside. "So," he said, "someone has to replace the spymaster. Someone Gavria will trust with all their secrets. Any idea who that will be?"

"No. What are you doing?" asked Javal, curious.

Jarrod snapped open his multitool to reveal a pipe reamer, and pried at the bottom of the inside of the trunk. It was snug, but lifted with effort. "Got it," he said. "False bottom."

Underneath was a second batch of letters, bound in twine and still sealed with wax that bore an impression from a signet ring.

"Captain?" he handed them to Javal.

Javal untied the twine and opened the top letter. Jarrod looked over his shoulder. "What is it?" He didn't recognize the language.

Javal did. "We're leaving," he said. "Right now."

Loth swung Ulo's chair around, slammed it against the wall. His lip snarled but his voice was low: "Heed this, you damned fool—"

Ulo boredly tapped Loth's hands and motioned for him to let go.

Loth loosened his grip on Ulo's lapels and stepped back.

"I don't know how you managed this—" Damn, it was hard to stay mad at someone so calm.

"I managed nothing," Ulo insisted. "How could I have done anything? I was several days' ride from here."

"Yes, you and Mukul, building a war."

"You have asked me to."

"Listen to me," Loth stressed. "I don't care what you've built. I don't care what you've done. You are here—you are alive—only at the convenience of Parliament. Take only what you're offered, and no more."

"I will take," said Ulo, very precisely, "what I want."

"You need to be careful with your words," said Loth.

"Marghan wanted me dead."

"*Everyone wants you dead!*" Loth stepped back, and slumped against the wall, rubbing his temples. "As you're about to see."

"Meaning?"

"Marghan has sons. You won't live a week."

Ulo sighed, and then stabbed the air with a finger. A parchment on the desk next to Loth began to smolder and erupted in a small flame.

He pinched his fingers together, and the fire died with a wisp of smoke. "Let them come."

"Oh, they will," Loth assured him. "They are knights, and strong. No magic will save you."

"Not as you know it," Ulo corrected. "Your leaders are afraid that I have my father's magic. Remember, he once flayed a man to his bones beneath his armor. He struck down an entire tower with a wave of his hand, and diseased the army raised against him. Kaslix is afraid that I have a power this world hasn't seen in hundreds of years, which is why I'm here."

"Do you?" asked Loth. "Do you have your father's magic?"

Ulo nodded. "I have more."

Loth sat at a long table in the officers' chambers of the Hold of Gavria, across from Commander Gar. Alone in the huge room, they still spoke in hushed tones.

Gar, commander of the House Fletcher Independents of Falconsrealm, had covertly been appointed as a warlord of what Gavria had deemed the New Falconsrealm Forces—the various unaffiliated troops skulking about Falconsrealm and the Shieldlands awaiting Gavria's orders.

The wad of letters that Javal and Jarrod carried back to High River contained, among other things, a handful of missives between Commander Gar and various mercenary knights with alarmingly specific instructions to accompany weapons and armor coming in from ships on the Border River and instructions to cache them at sympathetic keeps and manors throughout the Shieldlands. Worse, though, was a note from the Lord High Chancellor of Ulorak to Duke Edwin Hillwhite.

Gar was having a tough time remaining calm. His signature was on some of them, as well.

A handful of his hardest troops, under Duke Edwin's direction, had done horrible things to Sir Aidan and Sir Rohn to try to convince them to cough up the missives. Both of the knights of the Stallion had died in tremendous—and, Gar felt, deeply unnecessary—pain, with Edwin standing over them in clinical interest long after Gar had left the room in revulsion time and again. All this because Rohn's last words were a promise to Aidan that if they didn't talk, Edwin's death would be worse than theirs; a statement the duke saw as a personal challenge.

It had been enough, though. Throughout days, neither had said a word except to recite the promise that Edwin would die worse. And now they were dead, and the letters were still missing. And Edwin was getting the way he tended to get, which tended to make men like Gar nervous.

On top of it, he now sat across a table from General Loth, a sworn enemy of many years' standing, and the one man he feared above all others, even Edwin. The Hillwhites, he thought, certainly had a gift for bringing people together.

Gar tossed down a short mug of whiskey in two gulps. "Last I heard, Sir Javal of Ravenhurst was getting involved. Those guys were members of his order."

"That's going to get complicated," Loth admitted.

"I've got a contingent of hard men on scutage at High River. I doubt Javal even realizes what he's gotten himself into. Him and his snot-nosed sergeant. My men will take them out."

"That 'snot-nose' bested me at hand fighting," Loth reminded, his voice that of a man who'd recently eaten a lime. "And if you think you can take Sir Javal in a fight, you're a fool."

"I didn't say me," said Gar. "I've got men who can do the job."

"I'd like to meet them."

"No," said Gar. "You wouldn't."

VII

BOURRÉE

"If you do not have audacity of heart, all else is missing.
Audacity, such virtue is what this art is all about."
— Fiore dei Liberi, c.1409

J arrod would never have believed that he'd one day be so
exhausted. He staggered up the stairs of High River to his
chambers and flopped on his bed, in his armor.

Javal joined him, closing the door behind, some minutes
later.

"You checked for pitchforks," the knight assumed.

Jarrod opened one eye and glared at him.

"And?" Jarrod needed to know.

Javal opened his hands, indicating that he was powerless in
the situation. "There's a formal feast tonight. Ambassadors from
Gateskeep. We can't see *anyone,* until at least tomorrow. Alby, the
genius, says affairs of state can wait."

Jarrod's hands went to his aching forehead. "I can't believe
this."

"For dinner tonight, leave your swordbelt but bring a

Joseph Malik

dagger."

"What, no forks?"

"Wise-ass. They'll be looking for us."

"Who will?"

"Everyone. Be forewarned," he added. "This castle is crawling with southerners. I'm fairly certain a good percentage of them, if not Gavrians, are from Gar's forces."

"Great. What do I wear?"

"Warrior blacks. It's a formal feast. But wear boots you can run in. I'd suggest you bathe. Hurry."

In a chamber one floor below Jarrod and Sir Javal, Carter Sorenson tried again to lace his knee boots. Even in ten tries, he couldn't make them look quite right. There was a method to fold the extra leather neatly underneath and anchor it there while crisscrossing the laces symmetrically up the front. And he didn't remember it.

His legs ached, and his face was windburned around his beard from a long afternoon against a headwind heavy with hail and rain. He understood now why the route between Gateskeep Palace and High River was called Hellweather Pass.

He cursed, took a deep breath, and surveyed the puzzle.

Daorah appeared in the doorway, and watched him tie and untie the garters. She giggled at the sight, and he looked up and flushed.

"I just can't do this," he admitted, adding, "Wow," as his eyes traveled her. She wore a bright red court dress, cut low and cinched tight, a mink cape covering the scars on her shoulders. Her hair was tamed as best it could be, muzzled under a headdress of black and gold beads.

"You look—" Carter hadn't the words.

"Don't say it," she interrupted. "I think I look perfectly ridiculous."

"—ah, harmless," Carter decided.

She commended his choice of words with a stern nod. "Clever man. Here," she bade him give her his foot, and deftly cinched up his boot. Then, from her ankle, she handed him a short infighting dagger in its sheath. "Put that somewhere," she instructed as he gave her his other boot to tie.

Carter looked his garb over. This was his introduction to the Highriver nobility; he had dressed in a green silk brocade tunic with an unlaced V-neck and capped sleeves over his black, gold-embroidered lord's tunic and deerskin trousers. The sleeves of the lord's tunic he'd rolled up, baring his forearms. His gold ambassador's sash crossed his chest and tied near his belt. He looked prouder than Hercules, fiercer than Conan, thrice the hellion of Jon Carter. He was the king's prize tonight, the world's most awesome warrior.

After a moment's thought, he stuck the dagger down the front of his pants, securing the trousers' drawstring through the belt loop of the scabbard. "Ain't no man in the world gonna search me there, huh?"

"You intend to make me fight for you?" she grinned, patting his crotch. "The ladies will be coming for you in droves."

Carter offered her his arm. "My lady knight?"

She accepted it with a coy nod of her chin. "Chancellor."

As he loaded up his plate from the various trays floating around the table, Jarrod grumbled about his hopefully-temporary prohibition. He craved a night of raving debauchery.

However, he'd decided that horny, drunk and loud was not the best thing for a hunted man to be tonight. And with the threat of unknown evildoers looking to make his life complicated, he made a point to not seek out Daelle. He was mildly perturbed that he found this harder than he thought he would.

Since it was a formal feast he wore a black cape with his rider's pin. The molded carbon-fiber shoulders of his jacket exaggerated his taper beneath an oversized set of warrior blacks. With a belt cinched tight around his warrior blacks he appeared to sport a physique that would have Mighty Mouse asking him for workout tips.

Sir Javal seemed to be enjoying himself, laughing and pushing elbows with the noble next to him as the table piled higher and higher with the best food in the land: whole fowl baked with a crust of egg and cracked pepper, sausage and clotted cream pie, ten varieties of root vegetable dishes with twice as many gravies, and tender steaks of venison and lamb. There was coffee—real coffee—from Gavria, a selection of wine from Gateskeep, and cheeses galore.

Jarrod paced himself, not wanting to become too stuffed to fight his way to the door should need arise. He quietly ordered the wine server to fill his mug with coffee in the kitchens rather than pour him a drink from a passing tankard.

Jarrod toyed with a bowl of steaming leek soup and stared lovingly at the sausage pie as it passed him. *When this is over, I'm gonna get so fat,* he promised himself.

Across the table from him, the noble observed, "Here are the ambassadors." The feasting hall din rose to ride a sea of applause.

"Jarrod," Sir Javal pointed toward the door, where a man who had to duck his head through the doorframe made a stunning appearance with a tall, dark-haired woman in red on his arm.

Jarrod set his knife down. *Carter!* "Excuse me, my lord, sire," he begged them both, straightening the front of his black cotehardie as he rose. "Carter!" he yelled uselessly through the noise, raising his arm to signal.

Carter and his lady were weaving their way over to the ambassadors' table, on the right of the vacant seats of prince and princess, and opposite the High Council, where Sir Javal's foster father, the venerable Lord Nor of Ravenhurst, sat quietly, pulling his beard.

Jarrod made his polite way to the far end of the room, catching Carter's arm. "Hey!"

Carter turned in surprise. "Jarrod!!" They embraced briefly.

"What the hell are you wearing?" Carter asked quietly.

"Arming jacket," said Jarrod, adding in English, "Motocross gear." He was glad Carter hadn't embraced him lower; he'd have felt the pistol tucked into his waist beside the carbon-fiber backplate.

"Expecting trouble?" asked Carter under his breath.

"You have no idea," said Jarrod through his teeth. "We gotta talk."

Carter was grinning for show. "I've got your back. Keep smiling. How have you been?" he asked in the Gateskeep language.

"Oh, you know. I'm—" *wanted by half the Court, and holding military secrets that could get us both crucified.* "Ah, training," Jarrod shrugged. "Order of the Stallion. It's difficult. You're the new ambassador to Falconsrealm?" he changed the subject.

Carter puffed out his chest. "No, I'm here as a Chancellor. This is Knight Commander Daorah Uth Alanas, of the Royal Pegasus Guard."

Jarrod accepted her hand and kissed it lightly. "Commander."

Daorah replied, "A pleasure, rider."

"Please, join us at our table," Carter invited. Jarrod shot a furtive glance at Javal, who was watching him intently. *What is he staring at?*

Could Carter be on Albar's side? He was, after all, Albar's guest.

Jarrod doubted it. But then, at the moment, he and Javal were more or less outlaws, largely depending on whom one talked to.

So, now, wait. If Albar knows what's on those missives—which likely prove that he's in league with Gavria, planning to overthrow the whole country—could he somehow have convinced Gateskeep to hunt us down? Is that why Carter's smiling so broadly? And Gar has guys here, somewhere, and surely he has friends on the royal council—he's a commander just like Carter's babe, here.

Geez. I'd hate to fight Carter.

For that matter, I'd hate to fight Carter's date.

Jarrod got the go-ahead from Javal, and Carter motioned the three of them toward the table and ordered the steward to bring another plate and seat for Jarrod.

From the dais, Jarrod could see the entirety of the gala. He sent a server for his plate, which was at a table out on the floor. He saw that Sir Javal had moved to one of the nearer tables, which was full of knights of their order.

"So, you're a King's Rider for the Order of the Stallion?" Daorah spoke around Carter.

Jarrod nodded in affirmation as his new stein was filled with the potent black beer he'd come to love so much. He whistled for the other page, a boy named Hilg, and passed his stein on to Carter.

"Quite impressive," Daorah admitted.

Beside her, Carter raised Jarrod's beer. "May you live so long as you want, and never want so long as you live."

Hilg arrived with Jarrod's coffee, and he returned, "May the halls of your home be blessed with the sounds of running children."

Jarrod didn't miss that Daorah's hand gripped Carter's at this.

"So, are you enjoying yourself, yet?" Jarrod asked, half a joke.

Carter choked, recovered, and answered, "Time of my life. I killed a sheth."

"Yeah, I heard," Jarrod said.

Daorah added, "He's far too modest. He killed three sheth. He fought them naked as a babe, and one was a chieftain. The Chancellor broke its neck with his bare hands."

"The guy in the armor," Jarrod said.

"Yeah, that guy," said Carter. He put his other hand on hers and they smiled a loving smile at one another. "It was a teamwork kinda thing."

"Wow," Jarrod breathed at the thought, double *wow*-ing as a blonde woman in white lace and far too many jewels entered the main doors to the feasting hall, accompanied by four guards and, Jarrod's heart sank at the sight, nearly-Prince Albar. Jarrod's soul shrank to the size of a cinder. *What is it with rat-faced assholes and hot chicks around here?*

The room erupted in applause and cheers as the two (and even as much as he'd have liked to have bashed Albar's teeth out, Jarrod admitted they were a stately couple) stood on the dais at the head of the hall.

"Wow," agreed Carter.

"I would hit that like the fist of a wrathful god," Jarrod admitted in English. Carter spit some of his drink onto the table.

"What did he say?" asked Daorah.

"I'll tell you later," said Carter.

The ambassadors rose one by one, as Albar and his fiancée, whom Jarrod knew was the Princess Adielle, eldest child of the mighty King of Gateskeep, worked their way down the bench side of the table in greeting.

Jarrod had never seen Adielle until now. They locked eyes, a moment as awakening and sweat-inspiring as stepping on a rake. *Ah, Princess,* he sighed wistfully, *you are most definitely worth dying for.*

Adielle enthralled Jarrod, for two distinct reasons: she had azure, trusting eyes and a smile like warm cocoa; and two, she was the first princess Jarrod had ever been within arm's reach of, and so presented with the remotest possibility of saving.

Okay, may the halls of our *home be blessed with the sounds of running children.*

Hell, Jarrod realized. *I have to introduce myself.*

He dropped to one knee before her with his chin on his chest and his fist on his heart. *Say it loud. Let every man here know who to come kill.* "King's Rider Jarrod Torrealday, Son-Lord of Knightsbridge, Order of the Stallion, Highness."

The princess's voice, all projection and patient warmth, had the slow sweetness of caramel. "Ah! King's Rider Jarrod! We're told to expect great things from you! I understand you're quite a swordsman."

Albar's lip curled into something like a snarl. It wasn't quite a threat, but a distasteful sort of glare which Jarrod didn't see but the rest of the room certainly did.

Jarrod smiled at the floor. Ooh, Skippy, that had to hurt.

But how he wanted to tattoo those three words, *Quite A Swordsman,* on his arm, and paint them on his shield in quotation marks with her royal seal below. "Your words, Highness, are too kind," he insisted.

She extended her hand and he took it. "Arise, rider."

He rose, staring into those incredible eyes, and bent to her hand, "And as for my sword, fair princess," he smelled lavender as he kissed the braided ring on her middle finger, "it is forever yours."

Albar's voice was sour and broad with disdain, and it grew

to insult Jarrod before all as he announced loudly, "Enough, sir! There'll be no groveling at my table!" This brought a laugh from the entire room.

Carter gave Jarrod a sly wink, implying that all of Gateskeep knew Albar was an asshole.

Jarrod was still grumbling into his tea about feeding Albar his teeth when Javal stood, as did his table; knights of the Stallion, all.

Across the room another knight of the Stallion stood, urging his table up.

Every knight and rider of the Stallion stood, a dozen men and four women, all in warrior blacks tonight and several with silver and gold officer's braids prominent. Javal pointed to the stage, at Jarrod, and Jarrod looked around, then stood.

"The hell?" asked Carter.

Jarrod shrugged. "I dunno. But when in Rome."

Every knight of the Stallion, one by one, pointed to Jarrod.

"Aw, shit," Jarrod griped. "What'd I do now?"

"I have no idea," said Carter.

Daorah whispered in Carter's ear.

"Oh," said Carter.

Chavis, Lord High Chancellor of Falconsrealm, walked onto the dais. Sir Javal joined him.

Princess Adielle stood and walked down the ambassadors' end of the great table. She put her hand on Jarrod's shoulder as she passed him. "Come with me, rider." He did exactly so, following her around to the front of the dais where all the knights of the Stallion were still pointing at him as he moved.

He couldn't help but notice that Albar, still sitting, was glaring.

Javal and Chavis were walking toward Jarrod. Chavis had Jarrod's swordbelt.

"Sire?" asked Jarrod. Javal said nothing.

The room went completely silent.

Adielle drew Jarrod's arming sword, and the blade exploded in the light from the torches and chandelier. Brighter, though, was the appreciation on her face and the catch in her breath as she saw the weapon.

Javal spoke. Loudly.

"King's Rider Jarrod Torrealday, Son-Lord of Knightsbridge!"

"Present, sire," Jarrod answered.

"Kneel," said Adielle.

Jarrod knelt.

Javal addressed the room.

"This young rider," Javal began, "came to us one moon ago. He is his homeland's armed combat champion, and for that he became a King's Rider."

This received a fair amount of applause. Javal waited for it to die down before raising his voice again.

"Yesterday, he and I found ourselves in a fight with five men, just the two of us. I slew one.

"This young rider, however, slew one as well. He then granted mercy to another. He disarmed and spared a third, whom he could easily have killed. And then he healed the last after defeating him."

This brought low murmurs from the room.

"When I asked him about his actions, he said, and I quote:

"'Killing is not always the answer.'"

More murmurs, louder. Then a smattering of applause that slowly turned into a roar.

Jarrod looked up to find the princess holding the sword by handle and blade in her open hands and looking down at him with a gentle smile; a best-friend-in-the-world smile, not a regal stage smile.

"Do you," she said, "Jarrod, Son-Lord of Knightsbridge,

swear fealty to, and do homage the Crown of Gateskeep?"

Jarrod's eyes burned holes through her. "I do," he said.

"Do you hold that knighthood is a sacred trust? That the obligations of your service to the King of Gateskeep and to the Order of the Stallion will demand your efforts every moment of your life?"

"Unquestioningly."

The room quieted, and she handed him his sword. He accepted it in both hands.

"I pronounce you a knight in the service of the Order of the Stallion of Gateskeep," she said. "Go forth, Sir Jarrod, The Merciful, and continue to be a light and a warmth in the dark and cold corners of the world."

Javal announced, in a parade voice, "Arise! Sir Jarrod, The Merciful! Knight Lieutenant in the King's Order of the Stallion!"

The room went nuts.

Jarrod bent to kiss Adielle's hand again, then saluted Javal, who shook his hand and embraced him. Chavis took Jarrod's sword and returned it to its scabbard, then buckled the swordbelt around his waist. Jarrod, being left-handed, had to help him with it a bit.

A page presented two steel spurs on a velvet pillow along with a silver officer's braid and a knight's mark—a gold horsehead pin about the size of a silver dollar, nearly twice the size of his rider pin. Javal removed Jarrod's rider pin and slipped the braid through his arm, pinning it in place with the knight's mark. Jarrod put the spurs in his pocket and saluted the crowd on Javal's quiet command.

Jarrod shot a look over at Carter, who was beaming and holding Daorah's hand.

The only one in the room who wasn't smiling right then was Albar.

Jarrod stalked quietly down the fourth-floor hallway, returning from a distant water closet which Javal had assured him would be unoccupied. Dangerous as it was to be this far removed from the bustle, after eight cups of coffee he had no desire to wait in line.

And besides, he needed a moment away from the bustle without everyone congratulating him to death.

That was it, pal. The sword, the princess, the whole thing.

But . . . "The Merciful?"

The Merciful.

Christ.

Doesn't exactly strike fear into the hearts of evildoers.

"Sir Jarrod the Merciful."

Ming the Merciless.

Erik the Red.

Krum the Horrible.

Germanicus.

Maximin the Thracian.

Magnus ver Magnussen.

Captain Blood. There's a name.

Darth Vader. Darth Sidius. Darth Maul. Darth Anything, really.

Darth Jarrod.

"The Merciful."

There is just no way to make that sound badass.

"Sir Jarrod, the Inestimably Motherfuckin' Badass."

This length of the hall was candleless.

A glutton for punishment, he reminded himself of the moonlit night he'd spent alone in the most haunted castle in all of Scotland.

Sir Jarrod the Brave.

He remembered, too, that on the way home he'd packed five pounds of artisanal landjaeger sausage in his checked luggage, causing a bomb-sniffing dog to lose its mind. Watching from handcuffs as his luggage was taken to the end of an abandoned runway in Heathrow and detonated.

Sir Jarrod the Injudicious.

Carter's babe, the Knight Commander with the long name that Jarrod couldn't immediately remember, met him halfway upon his return. She moved quickly through the candlelight, shooting glances behind her at short intervals.

Jarrod stopped, took one step back, and eyed her cautiously, as she had a good-sized knife in her hand.

Circumstances being what they were, Jarrod let his pulse elevate a bit. He trusted no one, even as benevolent as she had seemed.

As she approached, she made no threat with the knife, and a good thing, that. Her shoulders were as strong and corded as his own and she was a knight officer, besides. From her scars alone he figured she could plant him, no contest.

"I found him," she whispered.

Jarrod pulled the XD from the small of his back and racked the slide, holding her center mass just over the sights. He indexed his finger along the trigger guard; the Springfield had a grip safety. "Don't move."

She spoke before he could. Her words were a hiss. "What is that?"

"It'll kill you."

"I believe you."

"Good."

"You're a dead man. Tell me everything you know."

"You tell me what *you* know."

"I know you're not going to get out of here alive tonight." Her voice hardly carried past her lips, but the Gateskeep sibilance cracked hard off the ornate wall.

"Let's try this again." He backed it up with a step forward, and she sighed in impatience.

"Fool," she shot another glance behind her. Jarrod squinted over her shoulder, and double-taked as Carter appeared.

"Hey, man," Carter waved. "Whoa, *whoa!* You brought a gun?"

"You didn't?"

"No." He shook his head in self-disgust. "Shit." He reached into his pants and pulled out a knife.

"Is that a knife in your pants, or are you—"

"There's gonna be trouble in a minute. But I'm guessing you knew that."

"What do you know?" Daorah asked. "Why are they after you?"

"How much time have we got?"

"Until they find you," said Daorah.

Jarrod looked around quickly, then beckoned them into a shadowy corner where he could see behind them. "Here's the deal," he said. "That sheth you killed," he nodded to Carter. "We ran into four more, twenty days later, in the same armor. That armor is from Gavria. No doubt."

"Yeah. We got the message."

"So you know about Sir Dahl."

"No."

"That started when we brought back a suit of the armor. Sir Dahl, and then two of his guys, tried to kill me and take the armor before we could show the War Council."

Daorah swore quietly. "Where is Sir Dahl now?"

"Convalescing."

Daorah shook her head. "Wow."

"So who else is trying to kill me?" asked Jarrod.

"House Fletcher," Daorah said, exasperated. "There are five

of them right down this hallway, looking for you."

"That actually makes sense," Jarrod grumbled. "Okay, quickly: I don't have any proof just yet, but what I know is that a wizard gated Commander Gar of House Fletcher into Edwin's Keep about the time that two of our order disappeared from there. Gar was there the night those guys disappeared, by my understanding. Edwin's Keep is completely staffed with House Fletcher, now."

"House Fletcher staffs castles all over Falconsrealm," said Daorah. "That's not unusual."

"Fine. In the trunk that belonged to one of our missing knights, we found a stack of letters bearing the seal of the Chancellor of Ulorak."

"Did you read them?" asked Daorah.

"We didn't open them. We were going to save that for the Gateskeep High Inquisitor. But, we figure the knights who vanished had a lead on who's arming the gbatu. We think it involves either Edwin, or Albar, or both."

"Why would they arm the gbatu?" Carter asked. "That's what we can't figure."

"Force multiplier," said Jarrod. "Tie up our guys while they move a main force body down the highways."

"Jesus," said Carter. "If you're right, we're ass in the air and waiting."

"And not in that good way," said Daorah, shoving Carter playfully. He winked at her.

"You're telling me," agreed Jarrod. "We don't have the manpower. We're gonna get our asses kicked."

Carter ticked off on his fingers. "Okay, so we've got sheth in Gavrian armor. We've got letters from Ulo's Chancellor going to the brother of the guy who could take this country over with Gavrian help."

"Plus, the Hillwhites would make a shit-pile of money

arming us all up to fight the sheth even if we avert this thing. We'll need heavier weapons, heavier armor, armor for the horses."

"The letters get intercepted, and the two guys who intercepted them go missing. You think they stole the letters from Gar?"

"That's what I figure," Jarrod said.

"And now Gar's men are trying to kill you."

"Apparently."

"Because they assume you have the letters."

"That's about it, yeah."

Daorah was looking back and forth between them. "You two are amazing."

"Those letters would probably reveal the supply lines," Carter offered. "They're going to want them back. Do you have them?"

"No."

"Do they know that?"

"No."

"Ooh, that sucks," said Carter in English.

"Yeah," Jarrod agreed. "We need to read those letters," he decided, speaking in the Falconsrealm dialect again. "We need to know what's in them, and if you're right—and I think you are— then we need to go after the supply lines. If we can eliminate the network before the gbatu are armed to the teeth, we can stop this whole war in its tracks."

Daorah shook her head a couple of times. Her mouth was hanging open, and it took her two tries to make the words come out. "You two . . . would risk your lives . . . trying to stop a war in its infancy . . . rather than wait and risk your lives to win it?"

They both stared at her.

"Absolutely," said Jarrod.

"In a heartbeat," said Carter.

"Hell," added Jarrod, "Why go to war and fuck up a perfectly good horse? I say we shut this thing down while we can. Then I can put my feet up. Spend the rest of my days surrounded by enough grateful and adoring maidens fair that I can try them on like hats."

Carter fist-bumped him and added, "Go fishing. There are bass in Rogue's River the size of my leg. Come up, we'll get a couple of them on the line."

"I'm in," said Jarrod.

Daorah shook her head. "Boys."

The thoughts that began to form were torn apart by the sound of running footsteps.

"Go!" whispered Jarrod.

Four gaily-clad men appeared out of the darkness at a run. Jarrod recognized none of them, though all four moved with the robotic, muscular sprint he recognized from a summer of running trails with knights. Very fit, very strong men.

They weren't stopping. Two had daggers drawn. As he heard the words, "That's him!" Jarrod broke and ran.

He ran like hell, down the corridor, around to his right for a hundred steps, boots ticking on the stone floor and then on the stairs, past the water closet, circling up and around, climbing to the next floor—to where, he didn't know.

After three floors, the climb became noticeably steeper, the walls closer. He was in one of the corner towers of the keep.

Up and up and up until his legs were numb and his lungs ached, and there was the door.

Jarrod hit the door, slammed it open, and drew his sword, slamming it shut again.

The door exploded open and a lone man staggered onto the rooftop, wheezing. Jarrod pointed his sword at him.

"House Fletcher, I presume," said Jarrod.

"Come with me," the man gasped. "Right now."

He was tall, and strong, with copper-red skin and a ponytail with the sides of his head shaved. His cheeks were tattooed with what Jarrod could only figure were mazes. The stairs, however, had clobbered him.

He spent too much time lifting heavy things and not enough time running.

"I don't really see that happening," Jarrod admitted. "Where are your buddies?"

"Listen to me," the man said, still breathing hard. "We have your little friend, understand?"

Jarrod menaced him. "What's that?"

"The little sorcerer," he said. "Daelle."

"Keep talking," said Jarrod.

The man took a few deep breaths. "I don't have to tell you a damned thing."

"I beg to differ," said Jarrod, nodding to his sword.

"You don't know where she is," the tattooed man said, "and they're going to do some pretty nasty things to her until you get there. So you can kill me, or not. But if you kill me, you'll never find her, and that's bad for her."

Jarrod let his guard down carefully. "If I go with you, you'll let her go?"

"I can't promise that."

Jarrod put his sword up again and clicked his tongue. "That's a shame."

"Look, hero. The longer we dally, the longer they dally. You understand me? Do both of you a favor and spare her the pain."

"You're not going to give me your name?" Jarrod asked, as the tattooed man buckled Jarrod's swordbelt around his waist. It took him a couple of tries.

"I'm left-handed," Jarrod said, helpfully. "It goes the other way—no, like—yeah. And you're lucky you guys have Daelle, because I could have killed you about six times by now."

"You don't get my name."

"Seven times."

They were outside the keep at the bottom of the stairwell that led out of the tower, and the man prodded him in the back to walk.

They crossed the plain where the fighters trained, heading for the four-story barracks at the far end. At the door to the barracks, they made a quick turn down a flight of stairs that led underground with a door at the bottom. A storeroom, Jarrod guessed.

Soundproof.

Secondary crime scene.

Really bad idea.

"Down there," the man said.

"If they've laid a finger on her," Jarrod threatened as he descended.

"What they do to her is up to you."

Jarrod stopped in front of the door. It was really dark.

The tattooed man shoved Jarrod. "Open it."

Jarrod opened the door. "Honey?" he called. "I'm home."

It was a storeroom, smoky, lit by a fire in a wall and a couple of torches. Stone walls, sacks of things on wooden shelves, shovels hanging from hooks, a well in the center.

"I got him," the tattooed man shoved Jarrod into the center of the room near the well. Daelle was in a corner, rumpled in a torn blue evening dress and either bound or cuffed. Her face was bloodied and her eye swollen shut. She sobbed Jarrod's name.

I am going to do so much more than kill you guys.

Ten men. Nine, plus the tattooed guy.

He thought of war.

Of mayhem.

He thought of hunting every last one of them across wastelands.

All but one in tunics or arming jackets. Nobody in mail. Guardsman's swords.

Gar's goons.

"Impeccable timing," said a fat man in a gray and green doublet, undoubtedly Gar. He wore a long saxe horizontally under his great belly in the manner of Axe Valley mercenaries. "Where are the other two?" he asked the tattooed man. "The big one, and the commander?"

Tattooed Guy said, "Those two are gonna be dead tonight. The rest of my team's working on that."

Jarrod couldn't help but laugh out loud.

Tattooed Guy shoved him. "You think that's funny?"

"Yeah," Jarrod chuckled. "I really do."

The fat man grunted, then addressed Jarrod. "You know me?"

"Yes," said Jarrod. "You're the pig who escaped from the spit for dinner. We missed you."

This brought groans and a few catcalls. Gar looked to his men and motioned for them to quiet down, smiling a bit. "We're going to talk for a while," he said. "And Von, there, he's going to watch the door to make sure you don't leave."

"Von, huh?" Jarrod said, turning to Tattooed Guy. "Was that so hard?"

Von grumbled.

"Here's the deal, Lieutenant," said Gar to Jarrod. "The sooner you tell me what I want to know, the sooner we kill you."

"Wow," said Jarrod, stone-faced. "How can I refuse an offer like that?"

"You can't," said Gar. "Because you're going to die tonight, anyway. But—and here's the catch—we can't kill you until you tell me what you know. So you talk, and then once we kill you, I promise, we'll let her go. If you stop talking, we start cutting pieces off of her."

Jarrod grunted, all business. "Understood. What do you need from me?"

"The letters," Gar said. "Where are they, and who else knows about them?"

"The what?" Jarrod asked.

He heard cloth ripping. Daelle screamed. There was commotion in the corner around her, men cheering and catcalling. He put it out of his head.

"The letters," Gar repeated, louder.

"I don't understand," said Jarrod.

"The *letters!*" Gar screamed, his jowls going red.

Jarrod snapped his fingers. "Oh, the *letters!*" he said, brightening. "Forgive me. I'm still learning your language. She's my translator."

He reached into the small of his back. "I've got your letters, right here."

"Where did he go?" Javal wondered, as the dancing girls did their thing on the dais. "He was heading for the water closet, one floor up."

"That was two songs ago," said Durn. "It's not that far of a walk. Do you think the little guy found himself some company on the way back?"

"He hasn't eaten since yesterday," Javal said. "So I doubt he'd miss this. Besides, he'd be with one of the dancers, anyway. His translator isn't here, either," he said, looking around.

"Come to think of it," said Durn, "The Chancellor and the commander left about the same time."

Javal tapped every knight at the table and stood. "Every one of you who's sober, with me. Right now."

"What the hell is that?" said Gar.

Von's hand went to Jarrod's arming sword, slung on the wrong side; first his right hand, then his left, then both as he struggled to clear it.

It cost him his life.

Jarrod indexed, braced, and as the arming sword came free he emptied two rounds into Von's chest and a third into his forehead, opening his skull across the wall like a melon fired from a cannon. Jarrod's ears disappeared under a landslide of whine.

His hands trembling, his vision cloudy, he pointed the gun at the group.

The commotion in the corner had stopped.

He didn't have a clear shot at Gar.

Time slowed.

"Fuck you," he muttered through gritted teeth, and shot one, knocking him over.

And then another, blowing off his jaw. The man next to him collapsed, hosed in gore.

Gar hit the floor and Jarrod emptied the magazine, fourteen more rounds, tracking diving bodies and shooting for center mass. The pistol roared again and again, impossibly loud, cracking the world in half.

When the gun clicked, blood was spreading fast across the dusty floor from a stack of bodies in the corner. More than a few groaned and sobbed.

There were still two standing—Gar and one other—and one on his knees, retching. Gar's fine doublet dripped with blood.

Jarrod kicked his sword up into his hand and sheathed the pistol.

What he didn't have was a second magazine.

The soldier next to Gar was older, big, and unafraid. He kicked the puking soldier, who got to his feet, saying something Jarrod couldn't hear or understand; possibly in Gavrian, possibly because Jarrod's eardrums felt like they'd been blown clear down to his tonsils.

He saw Gar's lips moving but couldn't make out the words. Gar's eyes traveled towards the door as he spoke.

Jarrod backed up to see the door opening.

He unclipped his cape and wrapped it around his arm.

Javal, Durn, and the knights of the Stallion met Carter and Daorah coming down the stairs.

"Where's Sir Jarrod?" Javal asked.

"He was behind us," Carter said. "We ran into some trouble." It was then that Javal noticed that both Carter and Daorah had greasy black-red blood up their arms to the elbow.

"House Fletcher," said Daorah. "We took two of them down. They're up on four. Two more got away. They were headed this way."

Durn swore under his breath.

"Are you wounded?" Javal asked.

Carter shook his head. "Nothing serious."

"Did anyone get past you?"

"One guy. About your size, with a tattoo on his face."

Javal and Durn headed up the stairs at a run.

Jarrod backed into the center of the room as more and more men came through the door, down the stairs. He quit counting at eight.

Tight quarters. No armor.

Oh, Lord, this is gonna leave a dent.

Sir Jarrod, the One-Handed Since That Whole House Fletcher Incident.

He was acclimating to the ringing in his ears. He heard Gar's gristly voice admonishing them not to kill him.

"Good luck with that," Jarrod grunted, menacing the group with his sword. Four of them had their swords out; short, heavy guardsman's blades. None of them were in armor.

Saber rules. Get the touch and get out. Be the last man standing, get to your medical kit, tourniquet off your stumps. This is where you earn it.

He'd settled into a space in the room with the well on his left, the pile of bodies behind it, and Gar and Big Guy behind the pile and Daelle behind them; and a wall with a rack of shelves on his right at an angle, making a funnel into him wide enough for one man on either side. They'd be reduced mostly to thrusts in the cramped quarters, which gave him a few inches of reach with the arming sword.

Two engaged, one down either side.

Amateurs.

He feinted, cutover, and slashed one across the eye; sidestepped, enveloped, and took half a foot from the second.

Swords clattered and rang on the wooden floor and both collapsed, wailing and writhing. He stabbed the one with the injured foot, below the scapula, into the lung. He slipped the sword out—so, so sharp—and fell back deeper as the next two leaped over them.

You know what we call this?

Jarrod stabbed one in the face, throwing the sword out to grab it by the pommel for the extra inches. The wounded man fell back, shrieking, blood in rivers between his hands.

We call it a "Fatal Funnel."

He adjusted his grip and engaged the other with a heavy parry, whipping the cape down on the blade to entangle it and spearing him low in the belly as he fell backwards.

*Never, never, **never** run straight into someone who's ready for you.*

The sword split a wide hole as he pulled it free. Organs spilled out from beneath the soldier's arming jacket as if Perseus had kicked him.

Never.

The next four, five, six, rushed Jarrod bare-handed, driving him off his feet and pinning him to the floor. His sword clattered away and they began beating him. He saw flashes of light but the padding in the jacket helped. A bit.

"Hold him down!" Gar yelled. "I'm gonna take some pieces off the little bastard!"

They pinned Jarrod's arms and legs, and Gar was standing over him with his saxe. "Gonna take some fight out of you, boy," he said. "Then we're gonna have us that little talk."

Javal and Durn hit the stairwell at the tower.

"They can't be up," said Durn.

"You just don't want to climb those stairs."

"Yes," Durn agreed, "And think about it. Where are Gar's boys? What's the one area that he controls?"

Javal saw the door to the right of the tower. The door, he knew, led to a stairwell exiting to a path long worn across the quad to the barracks; the shortcut for the changing of the tower guard.

Six more knights of the Stallion were heading down the hallway toward them at a run. Javal yelled at them to bring every sworn knight in the castle to the enlisted barracks, immediately.

He and Durn headed down the stairs as knights started yelling out of windows and into hallways, setting the entire castle on alert.

Don't panic.

Jarrod looked up at the point of the long saxe, flickering in the firelight.

Breathe.

It's going to work out.

It's just going to hurt until then, that's all.

Jarrod choked back blood; his nose was broken and he'd had the wind knocked out of him. But with two Golden Gloves bouts and a winning *savate* record under his belt, fighting for air around a busted nose and seeing electric purple Cheetos everywhere was no more a concern than seeing the CHECK ENGINE light come on.

You wanted to buy your soul back. Here's your chance.

Oh, God, this is going to hurt, though.

Gar's face was greasy with sweat, his eyes wide and more than a little crazy. "And before I'm done with you, you're going to teach me to use that lightning stick of yours. I could use me some magic like that."

Someone reached into his waistband and pulled out the little pistol, handing it to Gar, who grinned as it shone in the light. "It needs to recharge, yeah?" asked Gar.

The one who'd taken the gun punched Jarrod in the stomach. He missed the high-impact chest plate and hit the padded kidney belt. It still hurt. "Answer him!"

Wait for it.

Jarrod knew that the more men there were working in concert, the sooner one of them will make a tactical mistake. This was what he had counted on, and capitalized on, taking out the first four on either side of the well so quickly only because they'd never done it before.

He knew these men hadn't drilled at what they were doing right now. They'd been jockeying for position and playing grab-ass trying to hold him down, and if there hadn't been so many of them he'd have been free, already.

And it's not like they practiced holding somebody down while Fat Boy does impromptu surgery, that's for damned sure.

Somebody's gonna flinch, and I'm gonna have his ass.

He waited. The saxe hovered as Gar examined the gun.

Oh, he likes the shiny thing.

The guy on his right leg let up.

It wasn't much; for a fraction of a thought he applied half strength, then let go completely for a quarter of a second to shift his hands. Jarrod's right leg snaked free.

As survivors of the night would later recount, that was when it all went to hell.

The leg leaped up like a thing alive and locked around the man's neck and shoulder, pulling him forward and knocking Gar off-balance.

Gar, by incidence, stabbed the man who was pinning

Jarrod's left hand, long and deep from his eye socket down through the cheek and exiting near his ear.

Jarrod found his left hand free.

He punched Gar in the testicles and nailed him with a palm strike under the chin, knocking him sideways.

The man who'd been holding his right arm—unsettled by the screams of the blinded man beside him and watching his other buddy turning red, and with absolutely zero grasp of what exactly was happening—let go of Jarrod's right hand to try and work Jarrod's leg free from around his friend's neck, figuring that would remedy everything.

Jarrod cranked the leg down tighter and slammed his carbon-fiber-shod elbow into Helpful Guy's skull several times until he collapsed. As the man on his left leg gave up his hold to try to control the arm, Jarrod bucked out of the pin altogether, locking down the triangle choke with his left knee on his right ankle. The soldier in the choke turned dark purple.

Hanging like a spider monkey from a rapidly-asphyxiating guy a hundred pounds heavier than himself, Jarrod considered things to be going pretty well.

It was the other nine men in the room, the alleged professionals, who had no idea what to do next or how to do it. It occurred to more than one of them that they might have awakened some sort of demon inside Jarrod that had caused him to sprout extra arms.

It took a couple of long seconds before someone finally started kicking him, attempting to peel him loose through brute force and ignorance.

Jarrod covered his head with his arms, and felt the blows on the motocross armor. He couldn't help but grin. As long as they kept hitting him with fists and feet he might as well have been wearing the field harness he'd left at home.

Two men helped the soldier in the choke to stand up, with

Jarrod still hanging off him. It was the worst possible thing they could have done; standing up amplified the lock. He collapsed, driving Jarrod into the floor.

The others stomped and beat on Jarrod, but the guy in the choke was limp and Jarrod shoved him back with both legs and rolled away.

On his way up he grabbed a man by the jacket, swept his legs, and the world was targets. Unwinding, his elbow pulverized an orbital bone; an eyeball bulged. Someone drove a heavy fist into his spine, hit the ultralight armor, and yowled, swearing.

Jarrod cracked out teeth with his forehead, collapsed a knee with a heel stomp, a flurry of punches and elbows drove someone back, and then a huge opening led to a *fouétte* upside the head that smashed someone else back into the well, screaming—the same man whose leg he'd just broken. Another flurry and a knife-edge kick splattered someone into Gar, who fell into a wall of shelves and brought the whole world down around him from the sound of it.

Two more jumped him and tried to wrestle him down. He snapped an arm backwards at the elbow and pulled the other one close and rolled, hurling him across the room into the wall with his feet.

Jarrod flipped to his feet and stomped on a hand, then scattered a crawling man's teeth across the floor like kicking a bowl of ice cubes.

Someone big grabbed him from behind, shooting an arm down over Jarrod's chest and locking him in a bear hug as the last stepped over bodies, a sword in his hand. "Hold him!" the one with the sword shouted.

Jarrod twisted into the big guy with a handful of arming jacket and kicked his legs out, cartwheeling him forward over his shoulder into a pool of blood and spraying gore in all directions.

The man with the sword froze, his eyes flicking between

Jarrod and the man he'd thrown. "Are you some kind of god?" he asked.

Jarrod kicked a guardsman's sword into his hand and flipped it around a couple of times. "Find out," he growled.

A feint, an envelopment, and then Jarrod cut the man's throat and left him squirming on the floor, an ocean of black glimmering out into the firelight as he kicked and choked, yet another sputtering voice among the chorus of moans and sobs and the frantic yelling of the guy in the well.

Jarrod looked left and right as he stepped over bodies, stabbing the groaning ones for good measure and stomping on any body parts that moved. The air was thick with blood and smoke and piss and voided bowels.

His right hand was broken and swelling.

The man Gar had stabbed was holding his face together with both hands, his legs squirming in a pool of something Jarrod didn't want to think about. Jarrod let him live, reaching beside him to pick up the gun. He shook it off and holstered it.

He kicked and yanked his way through heavy bodies and weeping, useless men until he found his arming sword. He toed it into his hand, sighting down the length for damage. A few bangs on the edge near the balance but no major splits. He shoved the guardsman's sword into someone trying to crawl for the door, who howled for a long moment and then took to sobbing.

He left it jutting, Excaliburesque.

The guy in the well would not shut up.

The big soldier he'd thrown halfway to hell started to groan. Jarrod took four broad strides and stabbed him through the throat, blood jetting onto the wall nearby as he worked the blade back and forth. It would not do to have any of these guys on their feet and pissed-off. Not now. Not after all that work.

Something caught in the back of his mouth, and he coughed several times until he threw up what felt like a pinecone. When he spat it out, it was a mouthful of frothy blood, pink and foamy in the firelight.

When he thought about it, he could feel a cramping pain in his back, a tension pneumothorax. One of his lungs was collapsing as his chest cavity filled up with air.

He'd either been stabbed and hadn't felt it, or he had a busted rib that had punched a hole in his lung. Every breath was getting tougher.

Whatever the cause, it was going to be a real bitch in a few minutes.

He wondered if he had the balls to self-apply a needle thoracostomy. He had the rig in his blowout kit but he'd never even considered trying it on himself.

He was not looking forward to the adrenaline wearing off.

Gar lurched out of the corner, swearing under his breath, his long saxe in his hand.

Jarrod flipped his sword around a couple of times and came up in *tierce*. Blood and dirt caked him from his boots to his hair, which was plastered to his face and goatee with sweat and gore. "Yeah, come on," he rasped. "Let's fight."

Sir Urlan was in the feasting hall when he saw Daelle. For the first time in over a year, since the annulment, she put herself in his head, as powerful and clear as when they were children.

And dark.

She was in trouble. She was in pain. Her hands were bound.

He couldn't see exactly where she was, but he knew that place, those stairs and that door.

Where the hell was that door? He'd seen that door. He'd never been behind it, but he'd seen it.

Jarrod was in there, too, fighting like hell itself unleashed: throwing people through walls. Blood in geysers. Panicked men screaming.

He saw the path.

He knew which door.

He slammed his beer, stood up, and went and tapped Saril at the next table. "On me. Trouble. It's Daelle. And Jarrod."

Saril grabbed two others from his end of the table, and they all headed for the door, moving fast.

"Gear?" Saril asked.

"No time," said Urlan. "Come on!"

Albar and Adielle wondered where everybody was going.

Rising through the music, faint at first, then multiplying, the watchman's bell began to ring.

"Jarrod," Gar started, his saxe up defensively.

Jarrod circled, out of attacking distance. "*Sir* Jarrod, the Merciful," he corrected, his voice equal parts gravel and leather. "Not that you'd know it here in a moment."

"You wouldn't want to come work for me, would you?" Gar said, gesturing to the destroyed room with the tip of the saxe. "I could use a man like you."

"Not on your life, asshole."

"Whatever they're paying you, I can do much better. Your own castle. Your own lands. Here, or even in Gavria. Either. You'd be rich. You'd never have to work again."

"I *like* this work," Jarrod snarled, menacing him with the arming sword.

"It shows."

"Where are my friends?" Jarrod demanded.

"Your friends are dead," Gar said. "My boys will have killed them by now."

Jarrod's eyes hardened further. "Oh, you'd better hope not."

The door burst open, and Jarrod moved a step closer to Gar, brandishing the sword. "Stay back!" he told whoever was at the door, not looking at them.

He heard bells in the distance; Easter Mass, letting out.

"It's Saril."

"And Sir Urlan, sire."

Jarrod didn't take his eyes off Gar. "Who's with you?"

"Rider Peric," a tough older guy from the north; Sam Elliott with a salt and pepper goatee in braids.

"Bevio, sire." Bevio, the beefy redheaded kid with the name that always made Jarrod think of Shakespeare.

"Well, buddy, I think that's the game," Jarrod growled, gesturing with his sword for Gar to drop the saxe. Gar laid it down and stepped back. "Put your hands on your head," Jarrod said. Gar did. "Stay there."

Urlan made what Jarrod figured was a spiritual gesture of some sort. There was a lot of swearing. Bevio threw up.

"It's okay, sire," said Saril, moving toward Jarrod cautiously. "Just take it easy."

"Saril," Jarrod warned, "brother, I'm a little on edge. So you all just stay the fuck back until I tell you otherwise."

"Sure," said Saril. "Take it easy. I'm on your side. Are you hurt?"

Jarrod kept his eyes on Gar. "No. Yes," he corrected himself. "Not bad."

Urlan went to Daelle, his eyes on Gar. He cut her free and she was in his arms, sobbing and wailing.

Urlan went red, then white, and moved on Gar with his sword out. Gar flinched.

"No!" Jarrod shouted.

And then it occurred to Jarrod: Daelle had put the whammy on Urlan. She had the strongest connection with him. She couldn't read thoughts from a distance, but she could sure as hell send them.

And God bless him, he'd brought the biggest guy in the lists and two others. With swords. And apparently he'd sounded the alarm.

Sometimes, even the shitheads come through.

"The High Inquisitor's going to want a few words with him," said Jarrod.

"I can imagine," said Urlan.

"Saril," said Jarrod, "there's a body near the door missing most of the head. He's wearing my swordbelt. I need my swordbelt. Right now. *Now.*"

Saril found the body and got to work.

"You killed *all* these men?" Peric asked.

Gar nodded, his eyes serious. "He did. I've never seen anything like it."

"I have your belt, sire," said Saril.

"Toss it over here," said Jarrod.

It hit the floor near his foot. Jarrod still held Gar at swordpoint. "Rider Peric. Get to the top of the stairs and contain this area. Healers and officers. No one else."

"Done, sire."

"Sir Urlan, you get Daelle to a healer." Urlan was already pulling off his warrior blacks for her to wear. "Rider Saril, you come over here and relieve me. If he moves, do something to him that hurts."

"Gladly, sire."

"And me?" asked Bevio, still spitting.

Jarrod let his guard down for the first time. "Go find a long rope and get that poor son of a bitch out of the well."

Carter heard the bells overhead and the yelling. It took him a moment to discern that they needed to head for the barracks.

Daorah's knife came out. "Hang on." In a few quick slashes she had cut the dress above her knees. She handed the knife to Carter. "Do the rest."

He grinned at her.

"The back, idiot."

"Can't blame a guy for tryin'," he sighed.

They left the extra scraps of material on the stairs and sprinted across the quad.

"You said you didn't run," Daorah joked.

"I run when it's important," said Carter, outpacing her. But damn, the woman could move.

A knot of knights was gathering at the barracks, unsure of what they were looking for or what the emergency was. Those who had brought fire buckets looked around in confusion.

"Down here!" an older guy with a deep voice and a really cool beard yelled, and pandemonium ensued as thirty people tried to get down the stairwell at the same time.

"Officers and healers only!" Peric ordered. "Officers and healers only!"

Carter shoved his way through. "Chancellor, coming through. Chancellor, coming through. Move."

"What happened?" Carter asked someone at the bottom of the stairs as Daorah ducked under his arm.

"Sir Jarrod the Merciful killed a hundred men in there," someone said.

"A *hundred?*" Carter repeated.

"Carter!" Daorah called from the room, "You better see this."

Carter stuck his head inside.

The stacks of bodies; the broken shelves; the lake of blood, ankle deep in places; the brains on the wall and the odd disembodied organ; and the smell.

The smell, like a punch in the eyes.

They weren't all dead. Carter heard moaning and whimpering from a few points in the wreckage as his eyes adjusted.

A tall young rider had a fat guy at swordpoint in the back of the room. Jarrod's translator was in warrior blacks for some reason and a little rat-faced guy had his arm around her, showing her out of the destroyed storeroom.

"Make a hole!" someone yelled, as Javal pushed past with Durn behind him.

"Commander, Chancellor," he nodded.

"Captain," said Carter, and watched as Javal went white, staring and blinking in the stench.

A moment passed and no one said a word.

"Over here," said Daorah.

Jarrod was sitting against the wall before her, shirtless and gazing into the dark with his knees up and his sword in his hand. Blood caked his entire body, and he had a bandage on his right hand and another high on his left side. Something tiny and bright yellow that Carter couldn't identify was sticking out of Jarrod's chest near the bandage, giving a small hiss as he breathed.

"Jarrod," said Javal gently. "Did you do this?"

"Yes," said Jarrod to the far wall, exhaustedly.

"All of it?"

Jarrod licked his lips. "Yes."

Javal knelt in front of him and looked into each of his eyes. "Are you all right?"

Jarrod thought about it for a moment. "I'm going to say no," he decided.

Carter stood behind Javal. "I'm right here, man."

"Hey," said Jarrod.

"Are you wounded?" Javal asked. Jarrod was sitting in a half-inch of blood and it was impossible to tell whose. "What's that in your chest?"

"Collapsed lung," Jarrod said slowly, "This will fix it. Do me a favor, though."

"Anything," said Javal.

"Arrest Gar," said Jarrod. "I'm pretty tired."

Javal's voice was gentle. "I can do that. Anything else?"

Jarrod was quiet for a couple of breaths. "No. I'm pretty tired," he repeated.

Daorah looked to Carter, who looked to Javal. "Okay," Javal beckoned to Durn. "Durn, you and the Chancellor. Get him up."

Daorah pried Jarrod's sword from his fingertips. "I need that," Jarrod slurred.

"I know," she said. "I'm just going to carry it for you, Lieutenant."

"Thanks," said Jarrod. "I'm pretty tired."

"I'm sure you are."

"Get my jacket, too."

Carter got under Jarrod's arm and lifted his legs. Jarrod snarled and grunted as the lift put pressure on his chest and moved the catheter. "Come on, buddy," said Carter, "I got ya."

"Get him to Durvin," said Javal. "He'll know what to do."

"Done," said Carter.

"These guys need healers," Jarrod slurred.

"Not your problem, pal," Carter grunted. "Sir Durn, you want to clear us a path?"

"Love to," said Durn.

Javal stood by Saril. "Nice arrest, rider."

"I had the easy part," said Saril.

"Nothing here is easy," Javal said.

"I'll accept that, sire."

"In fact," said Javal, "Since you're still functional in the midst of all this, I need to talk to your commander. It might be time for you to take on more responsibility."

"Thank you, sire. Don't hold it against Bevio that he lost his dinner."

"I'm sure I'll do the same later, when no one's looking."

Javal addressed Gar, whose hands were still on his head. "Commander Gar. Missed you at the feast."

"Captain," Gar nodded. "I was a little busy."

"So I see. Are you injured?"

"Not really," said Gar.

"So, all this blood belongs to your men," Javal deduced.

Gar nodded.

"What happened?"

Gar thought for a moment. "There's something evil inside that man."

"Good thing he's on our side," said Javal.

"You can't arrest me," said Gar.

"With all due respect, Commander," said Saril helpfully, "I'm fairly certain Sir Jarrod just arrested the hell out of you."

"He's got a point," said Javal.

"You can't hold me."

"I beg to differ," said Javal. "The Lord High Inquisitor will need a statement from you. We're going to take you someplace where you can hang quietly and think about what you want to say."

VIII

ALLEGRO

"It is well known, and a sad fact, that in no profession is jealousy displayed with more bitterness than among fencing masters."
— Egerton Castle, 1885

J arrod dreamed of Paris.

A smoky bar on Rue Champollion, two weeks before the Fencing World Cup. The stink of those awful brown cigarettes and the peal of French women laughing in his ear. The oily aftertaste of Jasmine Flynn's lipstick as he sipped Bordeaux so gentle and mellow that it went down like rosewater.

Jasmine Flynn. Nickelodeon princess all grown up, Hollywood darling, gracer of teen magazines and red carpets. Astonishingly lovely and Tinsel Town tough, she was his better judgment personified and a bulwark against the rumbling, brake-squealing catastrophe of his life. They were the ideal storybook couple: rogue and princess, bad boy and good girl. The press loved them. The fans loved them.

Everyone loved Jasmine.

A shout—his name—and he turned to see Vittorio DeCarlo

standing in the doorway, his eyes narrowed to slits. Vittorio, the Sicilian Slasher. World-class *sabreur.* World-class temper.

Jasmine pleading with DeCarlo in Italian, Vittorio raging in return, yelling from the door with two men holding him back.

"That guy will *not* leave me alone," she sighed. "I never should have spoken Italian to him."

"I speak Italian. Hang on." Jarrod stood up and set his glass down. *"Hey, Vittorio!"* He made a grand and theatrical masturbatory gesture in Vittorio's direction and the entire bar erupted with laughter. Jarrod sat down again and told Jasmine, "They talk with their hands."

Vittorio pulling at his friends, screaming at Jarrod in Italian, hand gestures and shouts above the music. Jarrod yelling back in pidgin Italian, aping his gestures: *"Prosciutto de Parma, eh? Giuseppe Verdi! Pasta e fagioli!"*

Vittorio's face purple in apoplexy, spit flying with the curses.

"Romano!" Jarrod yelled back, *"Mozzarella!* Get the fuck outta here!"

The Sicilian Slasher slamming the door hard enough to crack the glass should have been his first warning.

Jasmine's voice, more than a little worried. "I don't think I've ever seen a man that mad."

"You haven't hung out with me enough, then."

A giggle. A kiss.

Pacifying the bartender with a fifty-euro note. Stepping out into the stinging Paris rain.

Vittorio was waiting outside with a saber already drawn and a crowd behind him. He tossed Jarrod a sword.

He'd caught it easily, the grip melding with his fingers. Not a saber, he saw, but a rapier. Exquisitely balanced, antique. Breathtaking.

And deadly. No question that it had been sharpened.

The crowd widened, phones came out, Jarrod cursing the

Parisian vultures. Foolish romantic bastards.

"Je ne vous combattrai pas!" He dropped the weapon on the ground, and oh, what a champion-caliber bad idea: Vittorio's blade slashed across his forearm, going for his eye but even drunk, in the dark, in the rain, Jarrod was fast. The blow had laid him open to the bone, though; through the jacket and under the wrist, long and deep, the stuff suicides were made of. He stumbled back as the rain washed his life over his fingertips, swirling into the gutter. Jasmine shrieking.

Vittorio pinked him on the shoulder. Slashed the side of his head. More blood, hot and steaming down his neck in contrast to the chill of the rain.

Backpedaling, the blade flashing at him. Screams from the crowd. *So it ends. You die in a duel in Paris.*

Not even a duel. You chickened out.

Jasmine screaming at him to pick the sword up.

Jerry, he's going to kill you.

Yes. Yes, he is.

He toed the rapier into his hand and stepped into attacking distance, Vittorio's face a mask of indignation and even amusement as he lunged. Jarrod knocked the rapier down and the blades began to sing in the sizzle of the rain as he bulled the big fencer back. "Come on, motherfucker," he snarled.

Another exchange, impossibly long for *sabreurs*, followed by an explosion of ice low in his gut as he missed a parry on the inside line. He jammed his palm hard under Vittorio's nose, snaking a foot behind.

A thunderstrike of white pain was Vittorio letting go of the rapier and slipping on the wet sidewalk. His head hit the pavement, and it was over.

Caught on a dozen phones, the moment would circle the world, replaying in slow-motion from every angle on every news station on the planet and a hundred more times in court. A hundred million YouTube hits for *The Deadliest Man Alive.*

His own voice in his ears, a single screamed obscenity lost in a swirl of European sirens as the streetlights faded.

Months later, drinking Glenmorangie straight from the bottle while staring off a cliff over a cold New England bay, rudderless. Persona non grata in France, outcast in America, barred from competition forever. Jasmine's manager and lawyers coming down hard with a series of no-contact orders, dozens of pages of impenetrable ass-covering boilerplate protecting her career and their investment from any defamation of character that may ensue from associating with a man accused of murder, acquittal or no. Flowers for her birthday returned with a desist order.

The tabloids, the evening news, even a savaging of fencing itself in Sports Illustrated. All of it a drunken blur.

The world didn't—couldn't—understand. He'd saved his own life by taking another; unforgivable behavior in civilized society.

The worst was knowing that if it ever happened again, he'd respond the same.

He was branded. He was a killer.

He threw the empty bottle off the cliff and watched it float out into the breakers.

"He killed everybody?" Ulo asked. "Everybody?"

"To our best knowledge," said Loth. "Twenty men."

"So? I've killed twenty men," bragged a warlord.

"Not in a row," snapped Loth.

He wished he could've been there to see it, though. One lone knight, laying waste to what amounted to an entire phalanx. It was another plane altogether. They were dealing with a god of war incarnate.

And now, with twenty of Gar's best men cut into small pieces, the missives in the hands of the Lord High Inquisitor, Gar himself imprisoned in Falconsrealm, and Gavria expecting a declaration of war, there were words stronger than disaster but no one dared use them.

"Who is this man and why isn't he on our side?" Mukul asked.

"He's a warrior from Ulo's homeland," Loth said.

"He's no warrior," said Ulo. "He's . . ." How to explain a stuntman? ". . . an actor."

Loth was incredulous. "The King of Gateskeep brought an actor to train their knights?"

"He teaches actors how to pretend to fight," said Ulo. "To make it look real."

"For . . . for theatre?" asked Mukul. "Acting?"

"Are you saying Gar's men are pretending to be dead?" asked Loth. "Because I'd say this is pretty damned authentic."

He knew the plan, loosely: lure Jarrod to an underground storeroom and make him talk. Back it up with enough men that he couldn't fight at all, much less fight his way out.

All he could figure was Jarrod must have beaten them there somehow, and arranged the room to his advantage. Maybe he'd stashed a weapon. But what weapon?

Twenty men.

Loth thought back to how Jarrod had pulled the castle out from under him a moon ago. How he'd been beating the hell out of Jarrod until the world had cartwheeled out of control and he'd ended up on his back, helpless, shattered with fear, Jarrod standing over him with eyes like knives.

And that, he knew, was it.

Jarrod may not have thrown them each through the air, but whatever he'd done, the concept was the same. Those boys had gone into the fight knowing precisely what they were doing, until Jarrod showed them that they didn't.

One way or another, he'd gotten ahead of them all.

"He deals in the illusion," said Ulo.

"The hell he does," Loth grumbled.

"So he is a sorcerer," said Mukul.

"No," said Ulo. "He's no sorcerer. Just a fighter with a gift."

"So he's a mercenary," said Mukul. "Then he can be bought."

"No," said Ulo. "He can't."

"You don't understand," Loth said. "The King of Gateskeep brought him here to train their knights."

"Then he can damn well train ours!" Mukul snarled.

Ulo held up his hand for silence. "I'm going to High River tonight, with Mukul," he said. "We'll negotiate for Gar's release."

"And if they refuse?"

Ulo's eyes met Mukul's.

"They won't."

"So, I told you to do something worthy of song," said Javal, "But damn."

Jarrod's cane leaned against the table in the dining hall. "Just following orders," he slurred around the swelling of his face and his broken nose. His beard had been trimmed short and his hair now jutted at wild angles from his ponytail where the clots had been clipped out; his first fighter's cut.

Javal smiled and clapped him on the shoulder gently. "Do you want a slab of bacon?"

"My mouth hurts," said Jarrod, "Oats are fine."

Javal gestured to Jarrod's bowl. "Oats, huh? So you're a horse, now?"

"A common misconception," Jarrod muttered, "when viewed from the waist down."

"At least your sense of humor isn't injured. The final count looks like seventeen," Javal said. "Four lived, including Gar."

"One does what one can," Jarrod grumbled.

"You probably won't ever have to kill anyone again."

Jarrod swallowed. "Meaning?"

"Meaning no man in his right mind will ever cross swords with you."

"You say that," said Jarrod. "Give it a week."

"You'll be laid up more than a week, my friend."

A broken hand, a broken nose, probably a broken sinus bone, a deep cut on his calf that had required stitches, and the puncture wound that had led to the collapsed lung. Plus dozens of contusions, abrasions, and cuts; both knees and his tailbone bruised so black that he could barely walk. The padding in the impact armor was the only reason he hadn't fractured enough bones to effectively paralyze him.

As it was, it hurt to move and he hated every moment of his waking life.

Jarrod was quiet for a while, staring at his oatmeal.

"You're going to be okay," Javal assured him. "You'll grow through this."

"Lines of silver," Jarrod said. "Daelle gave me a cup that had broken."

"That," said Javal. "Very much, my friend, you are that. You are repaired, and you are magnificent."

No one had said a word about the gun. Jarrod chose to leave it that way. He'd stripped it and cleaned it and now wore it at his side under his robe. Because Javal was right: no way in hell was he fighting anybody for another month at least.

"What happens now?" Jarrod asked.

"You heal," Javal said. "From here, it's an affair of state. The missives implicate Edwin. Gar says that Edwin killed Sir Aidan and Sir Rohn. At least, he directed the most interesting parts. I believe him."

Jarrod nodded. "Are we going after him?"

"I am. You're not. Albar doesn't know this, yet."

"What happens to Gar?"

"Ulo Sabbaghian and the Gavrian High Inquisitor are coming tonight to negotiate for his release."

"Here?" Jarrod asked.

"Chancellor Sorenson, Master Gristavius, Albar, myself . . ."

"Son of a bitch," Jarrod swore, grabbing his cane and rising with a series of groans.

"I don't care," Jarrod said to Durvin. "I need to be one hundred percent until tomorrow morning."

They talked in the small study in Durvin's work chambers. A chill blew in from the window. Jarrod smelled snow.

"It doesn't work that way, sire," said Durvin. "Drink this."

Jarrod did. The same black, smoky liqueur he'd had upon arriving at High River. The pain rushed away in a riptide.

"That's the best I can do," said Durvin, sitting on the corner of his desk. "The damage will heal, but I can't heal you any faster than you can heal yourself."

Jarrod closed the door to the study. "A man may try to kill me tonight. A man no one in this castle can stop."

"Then I suggest you find someone outside this castle," Durvin said. "I can't heal you."

Jarrod flexed his hand as best he could.

It wasn't much.

"Who can?"

Two floors below, Carter entered Daorah's chambers in his war gear.

Unlike Jarrod, Carter had brought a full set of field armor.

Also unlike Jarrod, he'd decided screw local technology, and screw blending in. If he was in armor, he was out to put some blood on the walls, and he wanted anyone who saw him to know it.

Some years back, Carter had gone to the best armorer he knew with a few thousand dollars. "Scare the hell out of 'em," he'd told him. "I'm seven freakin' feet tall. I bench press four hundred pounds. Let's do something with it. No costume bullshit, either. I want to be bulletproof." The result was what he was wearing now: a fully-articulated field harness, heat-blued to be almost black, that made him resemble a hellish god of war having a bad day.

The massive black pauldrons were peened and shaped into fanged skulls with overlapping scalloped plates at his upper arms resembling dragon's scales. The black helmet was a demon's skull with evil, slanted eyes and spikes set as gleaming chrome fangs in a mouth that grinned.

The knee cops were skulls to match the shoulders. His gauntlets were steel claws with spiked knuckles.

Daorah's cup of dandy shattered on the floor. She yelped and backed up, going for her axe along the wall.

He snapped the faceplate up. "It's me, it's me."

"Holy hell," she breathed.

He hadn't put it on in months, so he'd been wearing it around the castle to make sure it still fit. Every so often he'd stop to adjust a strap, shake one leg or the other, smack himself about the helmet while he looked up or down, and so forth.

Some men had seen him and screamed.

His two-handed greatsword hung off his shoulder and a spiked, two-handed warhammer dangled from his belt beside a fantasy-style longsword—a serious, high-quality tool-steel blade but as ridiculously historically inaccurate as the rest of his getup.

"I . . ." she was at a loss for words.

Carter shrugged. "If they're coming to kill me, I'm gonna make 'em earn it."

"I'd say," she said. "How did you afford that?" she walked up to him and started knocking on the armor. "This is steel. The whole thing. It's all . . ." she walked around behind him, ". . . steel."

It was the equivalent, in Falconsrealm terms, of having a Lear jet made out of hammered gold.

"Even your mail is steel?"

"Even my mail is steel," Carter said.

"I wouldn't have any idea how to kill you in that. You could . . ." her voice trailed off. "Babe, you could walk through a war."

"Let's hope I don't have to," Carter said.

"How did you afford that?" she asked. "Are you a king? You're a king."

"I'm not a king," he said. "My homeland is wealthy enough that steel is common. This was still very expensive."

Jarrod knocked on the door to Daorah's chambers. "Commander," he announced, "Lieutenant Jarrod Torrealday for Chancellor Carter Sorenson."

"Enter," said Carter.

"Holy shit," said Jarrod, in English. "You brought that? Seriously?"

"No," jibed Carter, "I brought it ironically."

Jarrod shook his head. Daorah could tell that they were ribbing each other.

"You look better," Carter said, switching back to the

Gateskeep dialect.

"Yeah. Durvin fixed me up. It's a temporary thing, though. I'm numb, I'm still busted up. I still can't close my hand all the way. Man, look at you. One-man army."

"You didn't bring your heavy gear?"

"No, I brought a gun."

"A what?" asked Daorah.

"Nothing," said Jarrod. "So, tonight. How does this go?" he asked Daorah.

"Ulo Sabbaghian will be there. Gar will be there. Gar will plead his case. We'll negotiate with Sabbaghian and whoever else he brings. If he gives us a deal we like, we give him Gar."

"No trial?" asked Jarrod.

"We know what he's done," said Daorah. "It's just a matter of seeing what we can get for him. He may be of more use to us as a bargaining chip than as a corpse."

Jarrod looked at Carter, then at Daorah.

"Be careful in there tonight. Both of you."

"Don't you have to be there?" asked Daorah.

"No. I can't get up that many stairs."

"But you can walk," said Daorah.

"For now," said Jarrod. "Javal told me to go to the Sticky Pig and get drunk with Saril. You should come," he told Carter.

"I'm the Chancellor to the King of Gateskeep," said Carter. "I have to be there. There's nobody else who can do my job."

"This has the potential to go bad, real fast," said Jarrod.

"This is a cinch, brother. What's he going to do?" Carter banged his fist against his chest.

Jarrod relented. In his helmet, Carter was nearly eight feet tall and the medieval equivalent of an Abrams tank.

"I'll pick up a barrel of whisky," Jarrod said. "If you're right and I'm wrong, and this thing goes off without a hitch, it's yours."

"First drink is on me," said Carter.

They shook on it.

Crius Lotavaugus knocked on the door to Jarrod's chambers.

At first Jarrod didn't recognize him, as Crius had a hood pulled over his head. He closed the door and took his hood down.

"I appreciate you coming incognito," said Jarrod.

Crius smiled. "'The Deadliest Man Alive,' indeed. They said you killed twenty men."

"Seventeen," Jarrod grumbled. "And this isn't over, yet. I may have to do it again, really soon."

"We are immensely proud of you," said Crius. "You're everything we hoped you'd be."

"Well, the war hasn't started, yet," said Jarrod.

"Have you got this figured out?" asked Crius. "Do you have anything I can take back or send higher?"

"Yes and no," said Jarrod. "I think I have an idea of how this is going to unfold. The problem is, if I tell you what I know, someone will know you were here. Right now, anyone who talks to me is a target. So we can't let anyone know that you healed me."

"I understand."

"You are going to heal me?" Jarrod assumed.

"I'll do my best," said Crius. "I can speed your healing. Can you last a week?"

"Durvin did his thing," said Jarrod. "I can make it."

"I need you to tell me what you know," said Crius. "You may not be as lucky this time."

Jarrod told him what he knew. When he was done, Crius healed him.

Half of the great ringed moon shone over the edge of the world as the sun set. The skies, bitterly clear, were lavender and crimson out the windows of the Chambers On Nine.

Carter leaned against the side of the window, a beer in his hand, dressed for murder with Daorah across from him in a mailshirt and a swordbelt. Gar, freshly scrubbed and not too much the worse for wear, was in a corner, still gnawing at a bacon-wrapped rack of venison while two guards looked on.

Dinner had been magnificent. Carter was sorry Jarrod had missed it.

Javal had been disappointed that Jarrod wasn't present, but he had given him a pass and no one wanted to ask him to climb nine flights of stairs in the shape he was in. Plus, if things did get serious, Jarrod in his current shape would be a liability.

Gristavius, a tall, severe man with a white beard and a shaved head, smoked a pipe against the other window.

Carter wished that he wore a watch. "Guy's a damned wizard," he fumed. "It's not like he's stuck on a road somewhere."

"He said this evening," Daorah shrugged. "It's evening."

Albar, at the long table, poured himself a short glass of whiskey from a decanter, then caught Carter's eye and poured him one as well, rising to take it to him. Carter thanked him, raised the glass in a wordless toast, and pounded it. It was soft, and smoky, and warmed him from the inside like Iron Man's arc reactor. "Is this from the Sticky Pig?" he hoped.

"Indeed," said Albar. "Another?"

"Love one. Thanks."

Albar took his glass. Carter watched a pegasus slowly winging its way across the valley, a lone rider on patrol.

"That's the next thing," Daorah told Carter, nodding out the window. "When this is done, I'm teaching you to fly."

Ulo appeared in a corner of the room, in fine silver and black clothes, a sword in his hand. His hair flowed behind him as a wind kicked up in the chamber, scattering parchments.

With a blow of his sword against the air, he knocked Carter and Daorah out the window from twenty feet away.

Carter caught the ledge with one hand, then two. Daorah grasped at his foot, missed it, and fell, screaming.

A body falls a hundred feet in two point four seconds.

Her screams stopped just about that much later.

Carter heard someone shouting for Jarrod, then what sounded like an explosion; like the world falling in. The tower shook beneath his hands.

The tips of his fingers scrabbled at the sill. His toes found purchase, then his knee, then his toe again, higher, and he threw an elbow over the ledge and heaved.

From here he could see the rest of the room. The stone table was on top of Javal, upended. Gristavius was still in his chair, a waterfall of blood gushing from his mouth. Albar's neck was clearly broken, his face purple, frozen in a terrified gasp. Gar was face-down but not moving. The two knights who'd been standing guard at the door lay askew, rag-dolled and broken in their mail.

The last thing Carter saw as he heaved himself through the window was the impossible sight of Ulo dragging Adielle through the far wall.

Then, as suddenly as it had begun, the room was still.

Jarrod was at the Sticky Pig with Saril. A band played uptempo in the corner with a flute, a drum, and something strummed in cluster chords. A few people danced. Jarrod was eating a slab of stringy roast that the owner claimed was elk, but Jarrod had the feeling it was horse. The bartender pushed a bowl at him, small fried tubers with gravy.

Jarrod threw back his beer and ordered another. "Gavria is arming the gbatu," he said quietly, leaning into Saril. "We're just a few words away from full-blown, three-way war. Us, Gavria, and the gbatu." He was a little drunk. "A great big goddamn war."

"And when it's over, Ulo is King of Gavria?" asked Saril.

Jarrod put his beer down.

The people in this world lived, and thought, in the immediate, and it drove Jarrod nuts. They didn't think in global terms because they didn't see the world as a cycle of larger events that happened outside of their perception. They didn't have CNN. They didn't have college courses in international studies or globalism or sociocultural anthropology.

That global approach, he was sure, was the thing that Ulo brought to the table in Gavria, and it was why Gavria was now so far ahead of Gateskeep, at least as far as this war that was unfolding.

Talking to local people, even people like Saril who were quite bright by Falconsrealm standards, frustrated Jarrod because he saw the world in relationships that were far too large for them to comprehend.

"Saril, I need you to understand this. There are no coincidences. All the things you see, all the things you know and will ever learn, are only glimpsed fragments of relationships far larger. Once you learn to regard them as fragments—"

And then he had it. All of it.

"Holy shit," he said quietly.

"What?" asked Saril.

"He's already a king," said Jarrod. "Or, at least, he was."

"Yes," said Saril. "And?"

"Why give up a kingdom?" asked Jarrod. "What does he get out of the deal?"

Saril blinked. "Well, he became Lord High Sorcerer."

"Yes, but what does he get?"

Saril shook his head and shrugged. "Sorcerer . . . stuff?"

Jarrod stabbed at the bar top with his finger in cadence, "Nothing. Not a damned thing.

"In fact," said Jarrod carefully, as if checking his work while he spoke, "as Lord High Sorcerer, he loses money."

"Then why would he do it?" asked Saril.

"Because he knew Gavria would kick his ass if he didn't. They just rolled his country up, didn't they? I mean, Ulorak wasn't part of Gavria; that's recent, right?"

"Very."

"He has to pay taxes now. He can't be happy about that. But if the Gavrians are fighting both the gbatu and us, they won't have the manpower to fight him if he secedes. Oh, goddammit. Oh, fuck me. We need to get back to the castle. We need to get back there right now."

The door to the tavern blasted open. A knight shouted for Sir Jarrod the Merciful.

The music stopped.

"Do you never rest?" asked Saril.

"Here," Jarrod announced, adding, "More or less. I'm pretty drunk."

"Outside!" the knight shouted.

"That's gonna take some work," Jarrod admitted.

Saril set his beer down, "I'll check it out." Jarrod, slower even with Crius's recent help, hobbled to his feet and grabbed his cane.

He took his beer with him. He figured he'd need it.

A huge posse had gathered, over a dozen knights and soldiers from the castle.

Jarrod opened his cape to show his fourragere. "Lieutenant

Sir Jarrod of Knightsbridge."

"There's been an incident," said one of the knights. "Captain Javal is dead. You need to return immediately."

Jarrod put a hand on Saril's shoulder. "Come on," was all he said. "We have work to do."

Jarrod and Saril pushed their way through the masses.

Carter was still in his armor, at the bottom of the tower, kneeling over Daorah as Durvin worked on her. A few knights and lords milled close, muttering in low tones.

"I'm here," said Jarrod. "Hey, buddy."

Daorah was conscious, and smiling. "Lieutenant," she said. "I bet you didn't know I could fly without my mount."

"Don't speak," said Durvin, as several men rolled her onto a litter.

It is one thing to speak of a man having murder in his eyes, but Jarrod had never seen anything as black and deadly as what flared behind Carter's jaw as they carried her away.

"He has the princess," said Carter. "I'm taking an army down there to get her. You coming?"

Jarrod unlocked the door to his chambers and took a candle from the wall outside.

Saril followed him in. "A war? With whom? Ulorak? We can't fight a war against Ulorak. What about Gavria? We need to fight Gavria."

Jarrod lit candles throughout the apartment. "I don't know

who the hell we need to fight," he said. "Fuck, it's cold in here. What happened to summer?"

"It's gone," said Saril. "This is autumn. Besides, you haven't seen cold until you've seen winter."

"Oh, I can't wait," grumbled Jarrod.

Someone had set a folded note with a broken wax seal under the cup gifted from Daelle. Jarrod picked it up, lining up the edges of the seal, and held it under a candle.

Saril looked over his shoulder. "That's the seal of the Chancellor of Ulorak," he said. "What are you doing with that?"

Jarrod handed it to Saril. "Read it."

Saril unfolded it, his eyes flashing across the script.

"It's from the Lord High Chancellor of Ulorak to Duke Edwin Hillwhite. It's a promissory note," he said after a moment.

"A promise of what?" asked Jarrod.

"My Uloraki is weak," said Saril. "But I believe this says that Ulorak promises him an additional hundred suits of sheth armor."

IX

ETUDE

"It is a great ability to be able to conceal one's ability."
— Francois de La Rochefoucauld

"Edwin's an ore baron," said Carter, lining up his beer stein exactly with a crack in the table. He and Jarrod talked in Carter's guest chamber. "He sells iron. He doesn't buy armor. Why is he buying Uloraki armor?"

Jarrod swore and softly pounded his hand against the windowsill. "And only a hundred suits. It doesn't make any sense."

"You know for a fact that this is the sheth armor," said Carter.

"Why else would he be buying it?"

"Why wouldn't he just make it himself?"

"Because people would talk," said Jarrod. "Some smith, someplace, would say something about making suits of giant-sized armor. He needs to be insulated from this."

"It's a loss leader," Carter said, half a beer later. "Check it out. When I opened my gym, I needed customers, right? I gave out half-price memberships for the first month. I lost my ass at first, but made it up in the long run."

"Okay."

"Edwin fronts the money, the gbatu get this armor. Ed knows that we'll beef up our forces to counter the new threat. We quadruple our iron requisitions; he makes a mint. And if—if—Gavria marches on us, he can fund both sides. Hell, he's a war profiteer."

"Who isn't?" asked Jarrod. "Javal knew this was coming. He left this for me. We boosted this letter and several others from Edwin's Keep four days ago. Goddammit. This is what Gar was trying to kill me over."

"This is what everybody is trying to kill you over," said Carter. "We're talking fortunes, here. This is immense."

Jarrod let out a long breath. "I need to think," he said. "We are about to enter a point in this war—and this is now a war, make no mistake—where we can actually make a difference. You and me. If we do this right."

Carter blinked. "What do you need from me?"

"Javal's funeral is tomorrow. And Albar's, the day after that. I need you to render my apologies to the royal family," said Jarrod. "But I have other business, for the order."

"You're not going?"

"Hell, no. I'm not going to show up anyplace I'm expected for quite some time. I was supposed to be in that room, you know."

"I was in that room, you know."

They stared at each other.

"Is she going to be okay?" Jarrod asked.

"She's fine," Carter said. "It looked like she broke her collarbone. Maybe her shoulder. She'll be fine."

"Okay," said Jarrod.

"So you go do a thing. Then what?" asked Carter. "There's

more. I know you. What else?"

"I need you to go to the king and ask permission to attack Ulorak," said Jarrod. "With everything you've got. Not Gavria; Ulorak. And you take every motherfucker who can carry a sharp stick."

"I was hoping you'd say that."

"I need a week to heal up," said Jarrod. "And when I do, I'm going to take care of Edwin. But I need to disappear for a while, so if anybody asks, you haven't seen me."

The royal stables were quiet in the evening.

Jarrod made his way to the back, finding Perseus calm and patient in his huge stall.

"You can't be here," said a voice. A young voice. Jarrod knew the guy; he was one of Perseus's handlers, a kid named Iaxol, whom Jarrod called Jack. "That horse belongs to Lieutenant Jarrod." Jack loved Jarrod, and was always trying to help him with the finer points of horsemanship.

Jarrod turned on him. "Hey, Jack."

"Sir!" Jack saluted, beaming. "They said you were dead, sir!"

"I need you to shut up, right now," said Jarrod.

"Yes, sir."

"I need all the tack, riding gear, barding, and saddlery for Perseus. Immediately. And extra blankets. Ready the horses and put Perseus's gear on the cart, along with as much food as they can pull. Brush down Lilith and get her ready to travel. You do this and you, alone. Don't tell anyone what you're doing."

"You're taking them out, sir? Right now?"

Jarrod looked left, and then right. "No," he said. "You are."

Jack was tying Lilith off to the back of the loaded cart when Saril showed up with Bevio and Rider Peric. All three were in shirts of mail, all three had brought riding horses. Saril's mount led a small, sturdy pack horse with bivouac gear on one side and a whole shitload of shields and weapons on the other. Peric had a warhorse on a tether, a big, powerful black mare that rippled with muscle. Not as big as Perseus, but big.

One of the massive square-headed dogs from the castle, brindle with a black face, trotted beside Peric's riding horse, his tongue lolling in joy. "Yeah, why not," Jarrod grumbled. He was not a dog person.

"Figured we might need security, sire," said Peric, swinging down. "He's a good dog." He clapped Jarrod's hand in both his. "Good to see you, sir. We feared the worst."

"It is the worst," said Jarrod. "I'm glad you two are coming," he said as Bevio joined them.

"What about Javal's funeral?" asked Bevio. "And Albar's?"

"We're going to skip that," said Jarrod. "The people who killed them are looking for me. They figure I'll be there. I've come too far to go walking into swords on purpose at this point."

"Okay," said Bevio.

"Just so we're clear," he said to Bevio and Peric, "the three of you are temporarily detached from your orders and attached to the Order of the Stallion, under me, as my sergeants. My loyalty is to the King of Gateskeep and the Princess Adielle. Your loyalty is to me. Are there any questions on that matter?"

"Are we going to get the princess, sir?" asked Peric.

Jarrod was quiet for a moment. "No."

"What's the mission, sir?" asked Bevio.

"He didn't tell you?" said Jarrod, looking to Saril.

"He said to follow him, and whatever you asked us to do, to say, 'yes.'"

"That makes it easy," said Jarrod. "We need to do some dirty work. There's a war brewing, and we need to stop it. There are actually two wars about to happen, and possibly three. We need to stop at least one of them. Ideally, all of them."

"And how do we do that?" asked Peric. "Respectfully, sir."

"It's complicated," Jarrod said. "And we can't do it from here."

Jack was standing next to them. "Jack, how old are you?" Jarrod asked.

"I don't know, sire."

It didn't surprise Jarrod; a lot of Falconsrealmers didn't keep track of their age. Jarrod guessed him to be fourteen or fifteen.

"Here's the deal," he told Jack. "The four of us need to disappear. There are traitors who will hunt us down if they learn where we've gone. Do you understand that?"

"Yes, sire."

"The problem, Jack, is that you just helped us out. And if, in the morning, our horses are missing and you're still here, you're going to hang for thieving, or at least get fired and probably horsewhipped, if I know your boss."

"I can take a whipping, sir."

"I'm sure you can," said Jarrod. "But if you tell anyone you helped us, we all die. But first, someone is going to cut pieces off of you until they're convinced you've told them everything. These are evil men."

"Yes, sire. What should I do?"

Jarrod looked to the others. "I need a valet, and we could use a horse master," he told Jack. "So you have a choice. You can go back in there and get your tools and drive the cart for us, or you can stay here and take your lumps."

"I'll do it," blurted Jack. "I'll go with you, sir."

"You'll have, what, nine horses to take care of—expensive horses—plus that damned dog, plus whatever else we need done around camp. Scullery, firewood, security, whatever. It's shit work and all I can pay you right now is adventure and glory and stories to tell, but I'll make sure you don't freeze and you don't starve. And if you do well, and if you and I survive this, you can run my stables and breed my horses when I get my own castle. You'll be rich. And you'll have some fun along the way. How does that sound?"

"I'll be right back."

Jack disappeared. Jarrod turned to the others. "There's going to be a lot of riding, a lot of hiding, and a lot of people are going to die and we may, too, before this is all over. But so help me, we're going to break the hearts of some very bad people. We're going stop this war before we need to win it. Are you with me?"

Saril said, "You couldn't stop me."

While Jack was gone, Jarrod dug through the duffle bag and came up with a dagger, a multitool in a leather holster, a black cashmere sweater, a woolen watchcap, a thick fur cape, wool mittens, and a spare swordbelt.

Jack showed up about then, lugging a huge wooden toolbox that Bevio took from him and set on the cart with one hand. Bevio, though round-faced and soft-looking, was immensely strong.

Jack was beaming as he buckled on the dagger and multitool. He looked dangerous and wily once he'd donned the watchcap and cape. Bevio and Peric climbed into their saddles and Jack climbed into the cart.

Jarrod took Lilith's reins from the cart, saying, "The kid belongs to me, guys. Don't give him any shit." He grabbed the saddle and mounted with a backflip. The dog wuffed distrustfully at him.

"And to think," said Peric, "I saw you nearly dead

yesterday."

"A lot of people did," Jarrod growled. "Let's go ruin some expectations."

He snapped the reins and settled back in the saddle as the procession, at this point pretty much a circus, muscled up and moved out. The cart horses strained, the leather harness creaked, and then the wheels broke free from the mud and with a lurch they were rolling.

Loth looked across the table at Kaslix, Lord High Chancellor of Gavria. He folded his hands on the table and shrugged. "He said he was going to High River. He and Mukul, to negotiate for Gar."

It was morning. Coffee steamed from ceramic mugs, and a serving girl set a plate of sausages blistered with fat in front of Loth. She left in a whiff of perfume and a flash of jewels.

Without his signature dark robe and hood, Kaslix was bald, deeply tanned, whip-thin, and nearly a hundred years old though he looked half that. Rumors abounded that he was part Faerie, that he was part demon, that he was both, that he had made a pact with dark forces.

Word had already reached Kaslix, through a telepath at High River on Gavrian retainer, of the night's affairs.

"You believe they never arrived?"

"I find it convenient," said Loth, "that the moment that the most powerful sorcerer in the world has his every enemy in one room, he kills them all and disappears."

"Maybe the gods finally smote the bastard," said Kaslix.

"I would bet my life that he and Mukul are in Ulorak right now, toasting their victory," said Loth.

"Good," said Kaslix. "Because I'm asking you to do exactly that."

"Toast their victory?" Loth's tone was puzzled.

"Bet your life."

"What do you need from me?" Loth asked.

"Sabbaghian's head," hissed Kaslix. "I need you to find him. And if he's alive, I need you to plan a war."

Jarrod shook four ibuprofen capsules out of the bottle and washed them back with a swig of bourbon.

This was going to be unpleasant.

They were taking a midday break. The horses drank from a shallow spot in the river just off the road as Jack checked them over, brushed them down, and tightened and adjusted various things. Perseus had his feed bag on. It was another Falconsrealm day, gray and cool and spitting rain off and on. They had all shucked their armor.

Jarrod sat on the cart. Crius's magic had done the opposite of Durvin's; Jarrod was healing up but he was sore as hell. Oh, God, it hurt.

He applied a coat of neatsfoot oil to his leather motorcycle jacket. His fingers hurt, his face hurt, his neck hurt, his ass hurt.

The rain started again as Bevio brought him a pile of berries. The dog, named Dog, rolled in the wet grass and flopped his jowls around in rapture.

The break in the mountains loomed to the east.

"Due east from here," said Peric. "Wide, flat, a river to water the horses, plenty of grass. Best of all, nothing but subsistence farmers. No mines, no trade, no villages. No one goes through there. It's called the Dragon's Trail."

"Are there dragons there?" asked Jack.

"Maybe," said Peric. "If they're anywhere, they'd be there. I do know it leads to the Silver Gate and the Faerie Stronghold if you follow it long enough. Not that anyone ever does. That whole road? Nobody on it. By this time tomorrow, we'll be exactly nowhere."

Jarrod let out a long, slow breath. "That's where we need to be."

A week's ride south, four large Uloraki soldiers in heavy armor pushed Adielle in front of Ulo, King of Ulorak.

Ulo sat on his great black throne in his silver and black clothes, smiling for the first time in a long time. She was still in her evening dress, rumpled, dirty, shackled hand to foot.

Beautiful, even in her filth; statuesque in her defiance.

"This is the part where I beg you for mercy?" she assumed, shaking off one of the soldiers' hands.

"That won't be necessary," said Ulo.

"Who are you?" she asked.

"I am King Sabbaghian of Ulorak. Until recently, Lord High Sorcerer of Gavria."

"You can't keep me here," Adielle's voice was stern. "And if you lay so much as a hand on me, they'll kill you a thousand times over," she warned.

"Albar is dead," said Ulo. Adielle fell over, wailing.

"Javal with him," Ulo continued, "and Gristavius. And a few others. That giant Chancellor your king no doubt sent to kill me." Ulo motioned, and a dark-skinned woman in jewelry and little else brought him a goblet formed from an upturned human skull set with a golden inset bowl and stem, bowing as she presented it. He sent her away and watched until Adielle finally straightened, threw her hair back, and wiped her nose with her hand.

"What happens now?" she asked.

Ulo sipped at his drink. "For starters," he said with a smile, "You can refer to me as King Ulo."

"You're not my king," she said.

One of the soldiers shoved her to her knees, and she stood right up again.

Ulo raised a hand to wave the soldier off. "I have no plans to harm you," said Ulo. "In fact, it's in my interest to keep you well. But make no mistake. Your life is mine to do with as I choose. You'd be wise to remember that."

"Is that so," she muttered.

"Yes. You idiots put everyone who had any chance of countering me in the same place at the same time. They are all dead, and you are my shield," he continued. "I'd imagine that Gavria will take Falconsrealm at this point, and fairly quickly. I give good odds they're going to hand it over to the Hillwhites. Once they do, I'll send you back to Gateskeep, and you can fight a war with Gavria if you like. Win your throne back." He sipped at the skull goblet again. "I did it once. I recommend it.

"But I am done fighting," Ulo said. "Ulorak stands sovereign."

By the second day riding northeast, Jarrod was throwing up from the pain. He was now riding in the back of the cart, but still stopping every couple of hours to rest. His tailbone and knees were so bruised that every rock and bump felt like a new broken bone.

The team had discussed not going on, but food was running low and they needed to get to some sort of homestead, or an area where they could safely rest and either hunt, gather, or fish until Jarrod had recovered.

By evening of the second day they crossed the crest of a foothill leading to the Falconsrealm Mountains and saw smoke spires. Nestled in the valley below, lights gleamed in the windows of five neat houses around a gabled firepit. Not quite a village; a small farming cooperative.

They couldn't get there fast enough.

Saril swung down from his horse to greet the young men who came out to meet them. One had a bow, another had an axe. It didn't take but a moment to explain that they had an injured knight and needed to put him up for a few days. The young men met them with smiles and claps on the back and arranged Jarrod in a bed in one of the men's houses.

He slept for three days.

Jarrod awoke to the smell of pot roast and woodsmoke. He was hungrier than he'd ever been in his life.

He was on what amounted to a covered straw bale, in a small room with a low ceiling. A candle burned next to him.

He rolled to a sit and let out a groan. He was still sore. Not as sore as he had been, though, and even by the candlelight he could see that his bruises had faded.

A red-haired girl not much younger than Daelle, boyish, unformed, and adorable in a simple night dress, appeared at the door. "Sire?" she asked. "Are you well?"

"No," Jarrod said. "But I will be. Thank you for your hospitality. I assume this is your house."

"Your men are staying in other houses," she said, coming inside. "We don't have a water closet, so you'll have to go use the stream."

Jarrod nodded. "I need food. I can pay you."

"You don't pay us, milord," she said. "You've never stayed at a farm before?"

"I haven't had the pleasure," Jarrod said.

She giggled. "When you arrived, Uncle Arvald went out and killed a doe for you. He's an excellent hunter. You should meet him . . ."

It occurred to Jarrod, from the way that she began to ramble, that these people didn't get many visitors. The girl was obviously eager just to talk to anyone.

". . . tough but Mother cooks it in pork fat with vegetables for a full day until it falls apart. You'll like it," she said.

"I can smell it from here. I will eat as much as you can carry," said Jarrod.

The girl disappeared, and the curtain to the room opened to allow a strongly-built man with a long braid and beard, in simple clothing straight out of Migration-Era Northern Europe, to enter. "Uncle Arvald," Jarrod assumed.

"I'm Arvald's brother," the man said. "I'm Brac."

"Greetings, Brac. I'm Sir Jarrod, The Merciful, Knight Lieutenant in the King's Order of the Stallion."

"It's a pleasure to meet you, sire. We weren't sure if you were going to make it. How do you feel?"

"I had my ass kicked," Jarrod admitted. "We may be here a few days yet. I apologize for the inconvenience."

Brac waved a hand. "No. We're glad to help. Your horse master says you killed a hundred men in a fight. Is that true?"

"He's a boy," said Jarrod. "He loves me and he tells stories."

"May I ask how many men you did kill?"

The girl arrived with a tray bearing several pears, a thick

candle, a mug of something alcoholic, and a large wooden bowl of sliced pot roast and vegetables. Jarrod felt like crying. The food looked marvelous.

"Seventeen," said Jarrod, as she set it before him. "But they had it coming."

"Traitors?" the man asked.

"In so many ways," said Jarrod. He found that he could work a fork with his previously-broken hand. Crius hadn't been fucking around. The magic was working.

The mug was beer.

Really good, malty, thick beer.

"How do I repay you for this?" asked Jarrod.

"Your men are helping us with some of the upkeep around here. That's plenty. It's good to have you here. That Bevio is like having an extra ox."

"He's a good man."

"Your man Peric is letting me breed your dog to one of mine. I've got a red-nosed bitch in heat right now. She's not a war dog, of course, but she's given us some good watchers for our livestock. That dog will strengthen the line and the pups will be worth some good trades."

"Good to hear."

"In the morning, can you give us the news from the capital?"

"Absolutely," said Jarrod. He'd already eaten everything from the bowl, and started on the pears. "I'm going to eat all this and then pass out. Please be so kind as to wake me for breakfast."

Jarrod was able to stand and walk to breakfast, and better still, he was able to walk to the stream out back and bathe himself first. His clothes had been scrubbed and dried, and during his bath he caught up with Saril, who was on the shore giving him the latest.

Bevio and Saril had been helping with the chores, Jack had been great with the horses—both theirs and those of the farm—and Peric had spent most of his time hunting with Uncle Arvald. They were the two oldest men on the farm, and enjoyed a special place among the family.

It shocked Jarrod that he had been asleep for three days.

Saril helped him into his clothes and boots, and handed him his swordbelt. Jarrod flossed, rinsed his mouth with a handful of water and a couple of drops of mint oil, tied his ponytail back, and shrugged into a cashmere turtleneck and a cable-knit sweater. The wind from the mountains was cold and powerful, and lent a sense of purpose to the day.

Breakfast was served outside. The central gazebo had a firepit and a smoke-hole in the center. Inside the gazebo were five long tables, and the sense of community was overwhelming as everyone filed out of their houses, hugged hellos, and began making breakfast: sliced apples, boiled eggs, seared slabs of pork, root-vegetable nests fried in the pork fat and dunked in powerful homemade wine, and gallons of roasted dandelion-root coffee with honey.

"If we didn't have other business," said Jarrod as his plate was filled for the second time, and this time someone had placed a smoked trout crusted in rock salt on it beside the vegetable nests, "I would never leave."

"On that, when are we leaving, sir?" asked Saril.

"I want you gentlemen to help these men for one more day. Whatever they need. We will do a full equipment layout today before it gets dark. Then I want an inspection of the animals and the cart. Peric, you still got that damned dog, I hear."

"He's got the best job, here," said Peric.

"I'm loving that dog," said Brac, shaking Peric's hand with a deferential nod to Jarrod. "Good morning, milord."

"Please tell me you do this every morning?" said Jarrod to Brac. "That this," he gestured around him with his fork, "is a typical day, here. Tell me, truthfully, your life is this good."

"We don't always have as much luck hunting," said Brac. "Your man Lord Peric is quite a tracker. But generally, milord, yes. This is what we do. We eat. We work. We sing. We hunt. We fuck. We do it all again the next day."

"Men?" said Jarrod. "I quit. I'm staying with these good people. You can go fight the war yourselves."

As the laughter subsided, Jarrod asked Brac to walk with him.

"You'd asked me for news from the capital," said Jarrod.

"Yes," said Brac.

"The King of Ulorak, near the Eastern Freehold, kidnapped the princess four nights ago."

"You're jesting."

"No. He killed the heir presumptive, and a delegation from Gateskeep."

"How?" asked Brac.

"We don't know," said Jarrod. "He's a wizard, but he can use his powers for bad things."

"You'd said something about traitors, last night," said Brac.

"I did," said Jarrod. "That's something else. There may be men looking for us."

"Are you in danger?"

"No," said Jarrod. "And neither are you. You never saw us. We were never here. I don't know you."

Brac toed the dirt and looked south to the mountains. "I fought in the last big one," he said. "We pushed back the Eastern Freehold at the Border River ten years ago. I'm no knight," he admitted quickly, "I volunteered."

"Thank you," said Jarrod. "We can't do it without you."

Brac chuckled to himself. "Marched for fifteen days to get to the fight, killed two dozen men, turned around and walked back. I was glad to do it. Walking through that door after that," he nodded to his house, "Proudest day of my life."

"Princess Adielle was my daughter's age," he looked back at the girl who'd brought Jarrod his food the night before. "She rode down there, to the front. She stayed in our camp, helped the wounded, comforted the frightened. She was a girl, and still twice the man of some men I've met."

Jarrod sighed. "She knighted me," he said. "She's the one who dubbed me 'The Merciful.' I gave my vows to her."

"I'd die for her," said Brac. "Say the word."

"You may get your chance," he said. "If we march on Ulorak, word will come."

"She deserves better," said Brac. "Some things are too perfect for the world they live in."

"That, they are," agreed Jarrod.

"Tell the family. We'll send men when you need them."

Jarrod looked over the equipment layout.

They were well-armed. Their mail was heavy and strong, their packs were full of sturdy and warm clothes. Everyone had a sword, a shield—or two—and an axe, except Jack. Jarrod had his great sword in addition to his hammer, arming sword, and a tomahawk.

He wished there was a place to buy another horse. What he was planning would require one more horse to really pull off with style.

He stopped by a suit of what he swore was miniature horse barding at Peric's layout. "Is that. . .?"

"For the dog," said Peric. "Mail, backplates, helmet."

The plates were black cuir bouilli, but holy shit, Jarrod thought. The dog weighed a hundred and twenty pounds and had a head like a bowling ball with two-inch teeth. "Has he been trained to fight in that?" asked Jarrod.

"Oh, he loves it, sir," said Peric. "Put this on him, he's all business."

"Okay," Jarrod said. "Score one for the dog. Worst case, Jack can ride him into battle."

He gifted his plastic training armor to Jack, along with the bull-rider's vest and arming jack that he usually wore under it, and also gave him his great sugarloaf helm and a tomahawk.

The guys had been working with Jack daily, going over basic knife and wrestling drills. He still sucked, and showed little promise—he was young and small and not terribly confident— but the way most people fought around here, adrenaline and ignorance could carry a well-armored guy a long way.

Jack gave him the report on the horses. One of Perseus's front feet had begun to founder but Jack said it was probably a combination of too much grain and his habit of pawing when he wasn't exercised enough. It wasn't nearly severe enough to restrict travel and in fact, Jack theorized, he should improve once they hit the road again.

The dog, of course, had never been better in his life. He sat beside Bevio in moronic contentment, sporting a massive erection with tendrils of drool from each side of his mouth.

The cart was strong and all the joints were tight.

"Aches? Pains? Blisters?" Jarrod asked the team. "Anybody have anything wrong at all? A weird rash, hemorrhoids, a broken boot heel? We're going to war, guys. Let's get your shit fixed, now."

Everyone looked at each other.

"I'm scared," Jack admitted quietly.

"That don't count," Peric growled.

Jarrod took them to the gazebo, where he unrolled a map from its case on one of the tables and set a rock on each corner.

"Okay," he said. "You've been asking. I've been thinking. Here's how we win this thing."

X

BRUSCAMENTE

"He who draws his sword against the prince must throw the scabbard away."
— 17th-Century proverb

F ive days later, Jarrod and his small circus rolled into Horlech and stopped at the tavern where he and Javal had eaten, before. The beer was still magnificent and served in massive steins, the food the same as it had been. The owner even remembered Jarrod, and upon hearing of Javal's demise, had fed the team free of charge.

They used the space outside to armor up. Jack helped Jarrod with Perseus's armor, which took the better part of half an hour, two hundred pounds of mail and plates dyed Gateskeep green and black.

Jack had been practicing putting on his armor, and looked more or less professional donning it and absolutely fearsome once he seated his helmet.

Bevio cinched down the straps on Dog's armor and smacked him around a little. Muscles rippled under brindle fur everywhere the armor wasn't.

Okay, yeah, thought Jarrod. I wouldn't screw with that thing.

Jack would head to the stables with the cart and secure an extra horse and ten days' feed for the lot. Dog, who had bonded with Jack, would ensure Jack got his way.

Jarrod swung up onto Perseus, towering above the others on the big blue horse. He was in every bit of armor he could manage, same as he'd shown up before: coat of plates, grand pauldrons, Barbute, *gran espée de guerre* at his hip.

They passed through the barbican without a word, and rode up to the front doors, which were open. Jarrod had to duck his head as he kicked Perseus into the main antechamber with the others on his tail.

Horlech had two functional knights left including Orvyn, relying instead on a handful of local rented mooks. Jarrod could tell that they had absolutely no idea what to do when four knights in full dress rode through the front doors into the grand hall and stood there, horses stamping and snorting.

One tried to approach Perseus, who stepped forward at him and let out a noise that was a cross between a mule, a bear, and fingernails on slate.

"He doesn't like you," Jarrod said. "I'd stay back."

Orvyn came down the stairs. He saw Jarrod atop Perseus and sagged. "They made you an officer?"

"Go get him," Jarrod ordered. "Or I will."

"He'll never come down for you," said Orvyn. "You know how this is going to go, sir."

"Do I ever," said Jarrod. "Peric, with me. Saril? Bevio?"

All four swung down from their mounts. Swords rang from scabbards and spears pointed. Orvyn begged his men to put their weapons down, explaining that this was Sir Jarrod, the knight who'd killed all those men in that fight at the palace.

His men laid down their spears.

Jarrod had shown Saril and Bevio how to take prisoners: in moments the guards and knights were lying face down, legs spread, hands on heads, as Saril and Bevio kicked the weapons away.

Jarrod heard the all clear as he reached the top of the stairs.

Peric stood away as Jarrod cocked his foot back and drove it against the door near the latch. The boom echoed through the tower.

Dust floated down from the rafters.

In a moment, locks rattled and Edwin flung the door open, naked and enraged. "What the hell?" he demanded, at which point Jarrod grabbed him by the throat, kicked him in both shins, and threw him back into the room. Edwin buckled, weeping and holding his legs. Jarrod kicked him in the stomach.

"Cut her free," said Jarrod. Peric unlocked the leather manacles holding the elf girl to the headboard while Jarrod dropped to one knee and continued to beat the crap out of Edwin. With astonishing strength, she bowled Jarrod out of the way and lifted Edwin by the testicles with both hands, slamming him against the wall. She leaned her face within an inch of his and revealed a set of catlike fangs. "Now you die," she hissed.

Jarrod locked a hand around her arm to pull her off, and it was as if he'd grabbed a rattlesnake. She was all over him, knocking him to the floor and wrestling him across the room, ridiculously strong and with an arsenal of moves he'd never seen.

He rose to his knees and threw her over his shoulder onto the floorboards. Hard.

"We need him alive!" Jarrod shouted as they came to their feet. She hissed and snarled at him, swaying in a low crouch. "You can kill him later," he said. "I promise."

She was small, under five feet. Her skin was island-girl tan in contrast to her hair, which was white-blonde with brown streaks like a predator's stripes. Thunderstorms lurked behind her violet eyes. Jarrod knew Slavic models who would have murdered her for her cheekbones.

Peric offered her a sheet, and she moved back from Jarrod and tucked it around her. "You will let me kill him?"

"Yes," said Jarrod, "but not now. I'm Sir Jarrod, The Merciful, Knight Lieutenant in the King's Order of the Stallion. I'm taking you back to the Stronghold. Once we're there, we'll render him to your people for justice. We'll get you home or die trying. You will not be harmed again. I will die first."

Edwin tried to shout for his guards, but only creaking noises came out.

"I did not know you could lift a man by his balls," said Peric, his voice round with appreciation.

"I'm going to have you killed!" Edwin rasped.

"I doubt that," said Jarrod.

"You want him dressed?" Peric asked.

"Socks and boots," said Jarrod. "But put those manacles on him and stuff something in his mouth."

Saril and Bevio had loaded the soldiers' weapons onto the cart while Jack and Dog stood over the prisoners, looking fierce.

The castle was in an uproar, with dozens gathered in the antechamber, but no one approached as Jarrod and Peric led the elf woman, in a set of oversized clothes from Edwin's chambers, down the stairs and through the main antechamber with the very nude, bruised, hobbling Edwin behind. Jarrod offered Lilith to the elf, and she looked back at him, crouched, and leaped onto the horse's back from the side, swinging a leg over and landing weightlessly.

Jarrod stared. It was like watching a cat leap to the top of a bookshelf.

The team swung up. Peric led Edwin behind him, Dog trotting beside the duke as they left the castle. Jack climbed into the cart and snapped the reins, Jarrod saluted Orvyn, and they had done it.

XI

GAVOTTE

"There are two rules for success in war.
"Rule One: Never tell anyone everything you know."
— Unknown

"Y ou kick that dog again, and I'll bind your legs and drag you," said Peric.

"You'll die for this!" Edwin threatened for the hundredth time, gasping as he half-ran behind Peric's horse.

"Bullshit," said Jarrod. "Save your breath. It's a long run to the Stronghold."

Edwin screamed and pulled at the manacles. "They'll kill me!"

"Not right away," Jarrod assured him.

"When do you want to shuck this armor?" asked Saril.

"When we make camp," said Jarrod. "I want to be good and sure that nobody's behind us with delusions of grandeur."

"Every man in the kingdom will be looking for me!" Edwin shouted.

"They saw the Order of the Stallion arresting you," said Peric. "What are they going to do? Raise their hands against the king's personal order?"

"Is that what this is about?" Edwin gasped. "About your knights?"

"Oh, no," said Jarrod, turning to him. "We're way past that. This is about high treason. It's about a deal you made with Ulorak to arm the gbatu. It's about you helping Ulo kill your brother. It's about the kidnapping of the princess. It's about war profiteering. And it's got more than a little bit to do with the lady here. How are you doing, my lady?" Jarrod asked.

She nodded, tight-lipped. "Let me kill him," she repeated.

"When we get there, my lady, we're turning him over to your people. You can administer whatever punishment you think is just," said Jarrod.

She smiled, and Jarrod saw the fangs. There was a calculating awfulness behind her eyes, a murderous seething patience that ached from its own chill.

"I knew you would return," she said. "I saw it in you."

"If I had rescued you earlier," said Jarrod, "we'd both be dead, now. I had to wait. It was one of the hardest decisions I've ever had to make. I'm sorry for what happened to you. I will get you home or die trying."

"I understand," she said. "I would rather you'd not killed us both."

"May I ask your name?" said Jarrod.

"Call me Kaeili." There were more vowel syllables in there, but Kaeili was as close as Jarrod could keep straight. He had always seen words in his head before he spoke them, even in English. He had been envisioning the Falconsrealm dialect of the Gateskeep language in English syllables, at least phonetically, but the sounds in her name would require a whole other level of turning his brain inside out.

"Kylie?" he truncated, hoping she wouldn't notice.

"If you can get no closer than that."

Jarrod had once had a long conversation at a party with a girl from Humboldt State named Marie who'd just returned to finish her undergrad after spending three years as a Tibetan nun. She could have taken serenity lessons from Kaeili, who had a stern, formal, yet yogi-swami-hippie vibe that made him actually afraid for what they'd do to Edwin. Not that the prick didn't have it coming, but every now and again she'd turn to stare at her tormentor with the interested coldness of a cat watching a wounded bird flap around the yard. He made a mental checkbox to never piss off an elf.

"I can't undo what he has done, as much as I'd like to," she continued. There were long pauses between her sentences, as if forming each phrase perfectly. "But he'll suffer justice. That will please me."

"You hear that, asshole?" said Jarrod. "It will please her."

Edwin screamed in rage and stumbled on.

"I'm rich," Edwin said as they pulled the gag from his mouth.

Bevio offered him a squab on a spit. He accepted it. They hadn't taken the manacles off.

"I know," Bevio said. "You're a Hillwhite."

"I can make you a lord," Edwin said. "I can give you your own manor and lands."

Bevio shrugged.

"Is this about a reward for her?" Edwin assumed. "Because whatever they're paying you, I can double it."

Jarrod put a blanket around Edwin's shoulders. "You trying

to bribe my men?"

"I'm trying to make him understand," said Edwin around a mouthful of roasted bird, "That loyalties exist for a reason. What good is loyalty if it doesn't bring you anything? What good is an oath that leaves you destitute? Or worse, dead?"

Jarrod shrugged. "Technically," he said, "I am destitute. I left my home and my lands to come here and fight for the king. I own nothing but what I carry with me."

"What about your life?" asked Edwin. "What's that worth? My family will raise an army to come look for me."

"My money's on him," Bevio nodded to Jarrod.

"I can make you so rich," said Edwin. "Let me go, and you can return the girl, and I'll give you your own mine. There's a mountain between Wild River and Ice Isle, with a silver mine. The silver mine. All the money for the kingdom comes from there. A great castle on the sea, majestic views, hunting, it's three days' ride across it. There's a city behind the castle that can provide a string of maidens for each of you that would take an afternoon to walk down. You'd be lords of the Wild River Reach."

"Now, that does sound nice," Bevio admitted.

"Do you know how hollow my life would be, in a place like that?" Jarrod clapped Edwin on the shoulder. "I enjoy this line of work. It makes me feel important. Make sure he gets enough to eat," he told Bevio. "And wash his socks and dress those blisters. He has a long way to run tomorrow."

"You can't kill me," said Edwin.

"I have no intention of killing you," said Jarrod. "But I make no promises for the elves."

It was Carter's first time in the royal audience chamber, and he was blown away that he was invited to sit at the table directly across from the king.

Ravaroth Anganor coughed. "As best we can gather, Lieutenant Jarrod broke into Edwin's keep with a small force of knights, stole Edwin's concubine, and kidnapped Duke Edwin. Ran him out of there in manacles, stark naked, behind his horse."

"Well, points for style," Carter muttered.

"Indeed," said Lord Rav. "The Hillwhites are raising a militia to go after him."

"Do we know where he's going?" asked Prince Damon, on his father's right, down from Ice Isle for the emergency.

"No one knows," said Rav.

King Rorthos Riongoran-Thurdin had once been a broad-shouldered and powerful knight of the Stallion, but years as a figurehead had softened him. His beard was nearly white, his belly large beneath a green jacket threaded with gold, but he had a grace and poise that made no small light of the fact that he had once been a commander.

He spoke. "The Hillwhites are throwing enough money at this that it won't matter. In a week they'll have raised a militia large enough to link arms and walk across Falconsrealm. They will find Edwin and kill those knights."

Carter interrupted the murmuring that broke out. "I know where he's going," he said.

The table shut up.

Carter stood. "She wasn't a concubine. She was a slave, and she's an elf," he said. "A Faerie. That's what the Hillwhites aren't saying. Edwin's men captured her near the mine. Jarrod's returning her to the Stronghold, and he's going to turn Edwin over to the Faerie, where they're probably going to kill him for slaving."

The room erupted. King Rorthos held up his hands, and everyone quieted. "You know this how?" he asked.

"He told me about the elf, Majesty. He didn't tell me what he was going to do."

"Continue," he told Carter.

"Jarrod figures we don't need a third or fourth war going on, which is what Edwin is toying with by keeping an elf as a slave. If Jarrod does this right, he might get the elves watching our flank; they won't take kindly to Ulorak and Gavria arming the gbatu. They'd be valuable allies. This is a goodwill mission, and respectfully, Majesty, we need it."

"He's been a lieutenant for ten days," said the king. "He's already taking on affairs of state, launching covert missions, and now he's appointing himself an ambassador." He laughed. "That's initiative, damn it. Fine initiative. The rest of you could learn a thing or two from the boy."

"That's what you're paying him for, Majesty," said Carter.

"They'll never help us," said the king. "But the Hillwhites have a hand in this, so I don't care if the Faerie flay Edwin alive and fly his skin over the Stronghold like a flag. Maybe it will pacify them for a while, and maybe the Hillwhites will learn something."

The table broke into conversation. The king spoke loudly. "King Ulo holds my daughter, and that's the priority here."

"General Rav," said the king after a moment of thought, "issue a decree. An instant call-up for a yeomanry. Make it a crime to sign up with a professional militia doing anything other than fighting for the crown. This way we break the Hillwhites' backs and buy Lieutenant Jarrod and his team some time."

"Done, Your Grace," said Daral.

The king stood. "As of this moment," he said, "we're at war with Ulorak. Someone might want to let them know."

The keep at Ulorak had been carved into the spire of a black mountain by skilled miners long ago, the pinnacle augmented by the lone mighty tower, once ripped down and now rebuilt. Adielle's room looked out over the valley and the view was stunning, the drop below her window mind-numbingly sheer.

The food was excellent. The room was clean, and there were no rats or bugs. Quiet men in silver robes brought her clothes that were nice enough, coal for her fireplace, and some books every day, straightening the room, cleaning quickly and silently, removing linens. As prisons went, she had envisioned worse.

The door opened with no one knocking.

Ulo's blue eyes flared as he stormed across the room. Behind him, two more silent men in silver robes brought a book and a set of quill pens and ink.

Ulo ground his jaw as they handed her the book and quills.

"Your father is building an army. I guess he doesn't understand that I own you."

"He's coming for me," she said. "He'll kill you."

"You will write a letter," he told her. "You will address it to your father."

She took the quill, and dipped it in the ink, addressing the letter. Her hand shook.

"Let him know that you are unharmed, and in good care."

She scribbled.

"Tell him what you had for dinner." He ticked off his fingers, "Roast fowl, honeyed trout, cakes. Tell him your room is nice, you have a view, your bed is warm, and it is yours, alone."

She wrote.

"A missive carried by fast riders can reach the City of the Gate in nine days," said Ulo. "He has ten days from the time he receives this—and you will tell him this exactly—for him to send me a disavowal of this declaration of war, and a signed proclamation that he has disbanded his yeomanry, or I will take this all away. Your next accommodations will not be as generous."

"I can imagine," she said.

"I assure you, you have no idea."

"They call it Returning to the River," said Saril. "They lay out a slaver on a raft in a quiet part of the river. An estuary. Someplace stagnant. Except there's a hole in the raft, see, so his ass is hanging into the water. Then they force feed him milk and honey so he shits himself. They do this, day in and day out. After a few days of swimming in his own shit, the bugs come. They sting him, and bite him, starting on his cock and balls, usually. Then in a few days, they crawl right up his ass and lay eggs in his guts. Then they eat him from the inside out. Eventually, his guts will pop open and the bugs will spill out and eat the rest."

They were far up the Dragon's Trail, a day away from the Silver Gate, if their maps were right. The team was haggard, thin, and dirty. There had been no chase, and not a sign of habitation once they'd made it through the valleys into the thick of the Falconsrealm Mountains.

The Dragon's Trail meanders between two towering mountain ranges northeast of High River, and they'd been able to make fantastic time once they'd weaved through the Falconsrealm Mountains. The sky-torn peaks of this place, as jagged as a spear wall, were impassable. They had only to keep looking behind them. No one would come from the front, and no one could come from the sides.

The rivers that snaked through the mountains had kept the horses slaked, they lived on fish and berries and the occasional animal that Peric could bring down from his saddle with a small bow. They weren't starving but they weren't doing well, either.

"If they keep giving you water," Saril continued, "it can last for twenty days or more. The elves will make you into a bug factory. Eventually there's nothing left, which is why they call it Returning to the River. They say you go insane long before you die. And the spirits of those who died that way haunt the river banks at night, because they're too crazy to ever make it to hell."

Behind them on a rock, still manacled and still nude, Edwin rolled his eyes. "Will you shut up?"

Saril grinned. "No."

"You know this smoke is like a beacon." Edwin nodded at the rack over the smoldering fire, where Peric was curing large strips of a small bear. "When they find you, I am going to have every one of you castrated," he swore. "I'll blind you and chain you in a dark hole—"

"—until everyone forgets about us?" asked Jarrod. "Funny, I heard someone threatening me with that not long ago. You know a guy named Ulo?" Jarrod clapped him on the shoulder and Edwin growled deep in his throat. "Of course you do," Jarrod said. "You're probably the asshole who was going to do that for him. Or die trying."

"You'd fucking better hope that Ulo's people find you before my family does. We have an army."

"We have him," said Saril, jerking a thumb toward Jarrod, who went off to see about Jack.

"You said that before," said Edwin. "What's so special about him?"

"He whipped every knight in your castle at the same time," said Saril. "Don't you remember? Then he killed seventeen of Gar's best at High River the next day, single-handed. He kicked General Loth's ass at hand-fighting a moon ago. And he fed your little brother his own teeth. If you say you've got a man in this kingdom who can take him, you're a liar."

"I've heard of this man," said Edwin, in a tone that suggested he was putting it all together. "He's a demon."

"I've heard him called worse," said Saril.

"You don't understand," said Edwin. "I was there, at the meeting."

Saril gave him his full attention. "What meeting?"

"When they dispatched Crius Lotavaugus to the demon world. He was to bring back demon advisors for a war. This is one of them."

Saril stood. "Lieutenant!" he shouted. Jarrod came running.

"Tell him what you told me," Saril said to Edwin.

"You're the demon," Edwin said proudly to Jarrod.

Jarrod looked at Saril, who ground his jaw.

"You're the one from Sabbaghian's world," Edwin continued. "Master Crius summoned you from the demon realm. You're not human. You're unnatural."

"Explains a lot," Saril grumbled.

"Crius," said Jarrod, looking at Saril directly, "did not summon me. He came to my house and had a drink, and asked me if I'd come fight for Gateskeep to kick Ulo's ass. I said sure, it sounded fun."

"Now that, I believe," said Saril, after a moment of thought.

"But you're a demon," said Edwin.

Saril, and now Bevio, looked at Jarrod.

"For lack of a more convenient term," said Jarrod. "Yes."

Jarrod's makeshift circus took a breather in a meadow looking across to the Silver Gate, a waterfall the size of a mountain that formed the headwaters of a mighty river and marked the entrance to The Stronghold. Beneath it, the Bridge Between the Worlds thumbed its nose at imagination; impossibly long, impossibly high above the river, and shrouded in mist with the waterfall thundering over it. The sun broke between gathering clouds every so often on this side of the bridge—across the river the clouds swirled, blacker and more violent than he'd ever seen, as if the storm front stopped right at the border—and every so often the bridge would explode into rainbows as a sunbeam passed through the spray.

His men hadn't said much to him in the past few days. He knew that they'd heard rumors of Sabbaghian being a demon. Everyone had.

But the idea that Jarrod was brought here to fight a demon, being one himself, was a bit of a shock.

Saril flopped down in the grass beside him. "We've been talking," he said.

"Uh-oh," said Jarrod.

"If you're a demon, and Sabbaghian is a demon, and if you were brought here to kill him—"

"I wasn't brought here to kill him," interrupted Jarrod. "I was brought here to play a great game against him. With your armies, against Gavria's armies. Sabbaghian on one side, me on the other. That's an important distinction. I am not an assassin."

"Whatever," said Saril. "You're on our side. You're my friend. This doesn't change that. You're our leader, and this doesn't change that either. You're a Lieutenant in the Order of the Stallion and the smartest, toughest man I've ever met, and this changes none of that. I don't care if you come from the moon, Jarrod. I'll follow you." He looked over at the others. "We all will."

There was a new and granitic sternness to Saril; something slower, older, a stoicism that made him seem twenty years his own senior and ready to kick the world in the balls. Where had this guy come from and where had he been ten days ago? This was the man Jarrod needed right now.

Jack perked, looking down the road ahead of them. "Sire?" he said to Jarrod.

Jarrod shook from his reverie. "What's up?"

"Banners," Jack said. "Gateskeep banners. Your order."

"At the gate?" asked Saril.

"On foot, sire," said Jack.

"Everybody saddle up," Jarrod said. "Break's over. Let's go do this thing."

Jarrod knew it was Carter from three hundred yards away. There were no other seven-footers on this planet.

Carter, in warm clothes and a black fur cape, met him with open arms. Jarrod swung down from Perseus, crouching with an oomph as he landed. "I didn't think you'd figure it out," he said.

"The trick was the timing," Carter admitted. "We've been here since this morning. God, that's a big horse."

"Do you have any food?" Jarrod asked.

Behind Carter were two knights of the Stallion in black mail and many weapons. They saluted Jarrod. Behind them all, in his usual shambling clothes, was Crius. "I wouldn't figure you'd miss this," Jarrod said to Crius.

"I like elves," Crius admitted. He offered a greeting in Elvish to Kaeili, who returned it.

"This is truly inspired, Sir Jarrod," said Crius. "Absolutely brilliant thinking. The king is impressed."

"Send him my fuckin' regards," griped Edwin. "You're gonna let me hang, Crius? For this pointy-eared little piece of tail? You're a bag of shit, you know that?"

"Oh, can I please beat him up?" asked Carter, his eyes merry.

"You'd have to stand in line, Chancellor," suggested Crius.

Kaeili conversed with Crius at some length.

Crius became animated toward the last bit of his conversation with Kaeili, and then closed his eyes for what Jarrod figured was a minute and seemed to go to sleep standing up.

"We are in for a treat," said Crius, shaking himself awake.

A knot of figures had appeared on the far side of the bridge, and slowly grew larger. They were, Jarrod saw as they approached, multicolored. To say the least.

"What," said Carter, "the hell. . ."

Nine small, slender men in the most fantastic armor Carter and Jarrod had ever seen—Gothic, fluted armor in explosions of colors mimicking flowers on a spring morning and detailed with silver and gold—waved and called out in bubbling voices that Jarrod couldn't understand: a cross between Gaelic and gargling.

They were on foot, and moving unbelievably fast for being in so much armor.

As they crossed the bridge and spilled out onto land, Jarrod could see that their armor was brightly-dyed, embossed leather, fluted and molded into scales and horns. Even their helmets were leather, and each was shaped and carved into a gargoyle-like visage, some with wings, some with horns, all with fangs.

They approached, and Kaeili greeted them, as did Crius.

Each of the Faerie knights shook hands with each of the humans. They were small and slender, and beyond graceful in their movements. Under the visors, Jarrod could see nothing but huge violet eyes.

A knight in orange and cornflower armor shed his helmet. He could have been Kaeili's brother, as his skin was tan, and his hair was rockstar long and blond with brown streaks, and his eyes had the same sad turn to the corners.

"Akiel of Corimann," Crius introduced. "A prince of the Faerie."

Akiel shook Jarrod's hand. His hand was warm and firm.

"You brought her?" he asked. Like Kaeili, he had pointed, cat-like canines. Jarrod wondered if all elves did.

"Sir Jarrod the Merciful, Knight Lieutenant in the King's Order of the Stallion, Your Grace," said Jarrod. "Yes. This man," he motioned to Edwin, "we render to you for justice."

"For slaving?" said Akiel, looking Edwin over. "They must really not like you."

"We have our reasons, Your Grace," said Jarrod.

"So I would think," said the elf. "But explain to me these reasons, lest I puzzle over this for the rest of my days."

Jarrod looked back at Carter, who nodded.

"Gavria and Ulorak are arming the gbatu," said Jarrod. And it was that simple. "This man is helping."

The prince's demeanor shifted into something that made Jarrod uneasy. "What kind of arms?"

"Mail for the sheth. Good swords. Steel axes."

"To what end?" the prince demanded, turning to Edwin.

Edwin wasn't talking.

"A misguided attempt to distract Falconsrealm's forces, Your Grace," Carter stepped in. "We think—we believe—that this actually bodes worse for your people than for ours. Sir Jarrod, here, believed that this act of benevolence would gain audience with someone from your people who could carry the message. We had no idea you, yourself, would come. We're honored by your presence."

"They have hundreds of princes," spat Edwin. "Every third elf is a prince or a princess. Hell, that little hole of mine was technically a princess."

Jarrod shoved him off his saddle. Edwin hit, rolled, then jumped up and ran for it, up the hill.

"Fuck!" said Jarrod. He'd never catch him in armor.

"I got this," said Carter. He unpinned his cape, took a deep breath, and exploded after Edwin in a linebacker's sprint. His boots left divots.

"Dog! Go!" said Peric, pointing at Edwin. Carter caught Edwin, wrapped him up in both arms, and rolled, body-slamming him hard enough that grass and petals flew.

Dog was there a moment later. He observed the tussle, which was brief, and as Carter trapped Edwin's arm in a figure-4, Dog latched his mouth around Edwin's entire forehead and applied light pressure.

Edwin stopped struggling.

Carter marched him back to the group. Dog nipped at Edwin's heels. Edwin kicked at Dog, and Carter elbowed him in the head. "That dog's a better man than you are," said Carter.

Akiel turned to Jarrod, the show over, and continued. "I appreciate what you've done. It will not go unmentioned." He looked behind Jarrod. "You spent all your provisions getting up here. Did you intend to starve to death on your return?"

"I was hoping we could bag a deer," said Jarrod. "But otherwise, you're correct, Your Grace."

"Our wizards can send you home," said Akiel.

"Could your wizards just send me a sandwich and a beer?" asked Jarrod. "I've still got a lot of work to do."

Akiel laughed.

"If you can ride till nightfall, Lieutenant, we can provide much more than a sandwich and a beer."

Carter, Crius, and the knights hadn't brought horses. Neither had the elves. Jarrod and his team moved at a crawl so as not to outstrip them.

"I thought you had a pegasus," said Jarrod, in English.

"Would you ride a horse half a mile up in the air?"

"Jesus, no," said Jarrod.

"Right? It's been horsemanship, nonstop, for the past few months. I'm getting there."

"We had to disband the yeomanry this morning," Carter told Jarrod, returning to the local language. "And it looks like we have to rescind the declaration of war."

Jarrod asked Carter, "Why don't we just have Crius zap us into Ulo's nest from here? We'll kill the fucker, grab the princess, zap back, and call it a day."

"Yeah, we talked about that," said Carter. "It doesn't work that way. He can only make a doorway to someplace he's been before. Like, he'd never been to the Silver Gate itself, but he'd seen it, so he could get as far as the place where he'd been standing when he'd seen it."

"Bullshit," said Jarrod. "He appeared on my doorstep."

"Yeah," said Carter. "He took me home, too. How did he do that?"

Jarrod thought for a minute. "Wait, no. He reads minds. That's how he was able to talk with us on Earth, remember? He was reading my mind when he sent me home to get my gear."

"He showed up on Earth before that, though," said Carter. "He'd never been there before."

"He showed up at a Renaissance Faire," said Jarrod. "He was probably guessing what it would look like."

"So, we find somebody who's been to The Silver Palace," said Carter, "and then Crius can read his mind. How hard can that be?"

Edwin, on horseback, shouted for Jarrod's attention.

"What?" Jarrod snapped.

Edwin leaned back in his saddle, as smug as Jarrod had ever seen a man. "I've been there," said Edwin. "I've been to the throne room at The Silver Palace."

Crius looked at Jarrod, who looked at Carter. Everyone

looked to Akiel, who looked back to Edwin, who was looking pretty damned pleased with himself.

"Spare my life," said Edwin with a shrug and a roll of his eyes, "And maybe, maybe, I'll let the wizard, here—"

"I've got it," acknowledged Crius. "Very clear. You guys want to go now, or wait until after dinner?"

"Son of a bitch!" Edwin shouted.

"Were you not listening? Or do you not understand how telepathy works?" asked Jarrod.

"We're going to have to get in there," said Carter, "find her, kill him, and make a break for it, which means either fleeing into Gavria—not the best idea—or scaling the Teeth of the World and then tear-assing across the Shieldlands with an army chasing us and the princess over my shoulder."

"We're probably gonna die," Jarrod admitted.

"But you'll do it anyway," said Akiel. "I can tell."

"Oh, without a doubt," said Jarrod. "But we're going out in style. Crius, you'd mentioned at the outset that I could go back home and re-equip. How big of a deal is that for you?"

Crius groaned. "I'd have to rest, fully rest, for a day on either side of your journey."

"Send word to the king to stand the forces down," said Jarrod. "Tell him his Special Operations detachment will have Adielle home in twenty-three days, and if we don't, there'll be nothing left to risk so start the war anyway."

"You're telling the king what to do?" asked Edwin. "Who the hell do you think you are?"

"I'm an officer in the Order of the Stallion," said Jarrod. "I rescue princesses for a living. Do you have any dragons around for me to kill? Because I do that, too."

The elves called it Sanctuary.

The meadow on the far side of the Silver Gate was one of the most perfect places Jarrod had ever seen. Manicured in the devil-may-care-yet-how-did-you-manage-that manner of a Japanese garden, every flower and berry seemed both ideally placed and yet carefree. Roots grew out of the spongy turf in the shadows of fruit trees, shaped through what must have been eons into benches, armchairs, and even soft moss beds under woven lean-tos. Fires crackled in pits and stone fireplaces and several dozen elves lounged, most of them surrounded by gear for excursion: packs, walking sticks, bows. Jarrod half-expected to see Clannad shooting a video.

The elves, alien and balletic, rose to come meet the humans. They left their weapons.

Jarrod shook many hands and forgot most of their names when a young Faerie woman, mind-shatteringly beautiful and smelling for all the world like fruit punch Jolly Ranchers, hugged him to her and kissed his cheek.

"Welcome," she said. "Call me Karra."

Her eyes were mostly blue and her hair was mostly blonde, because she had braided the dark stripes into wiry dreadlocks with feathers tied at the ends. The result was both wild and delicate, a dangerous feral creature suspended in that moment where young women are softly, breathtakingly beautiful.

Some things are too perfect for the world they live in.

She kissed him on the other cheek. "Welcome," she said again.

"Can we stay here?" asked Jarrod.

"No, it's too perilous," quipped Carter as two Faerie women wearing spectacularly little led him to a mossy bench and put a wooden cup of something in his hand.

Akiel gestured around the glen. "You may not cross the next mountains into the Stronghold, but you may stay here as long as you like. We'll provide you food, we'll see to your animals," here, he looked at Edwin, then nodded to the Faerie knights. "And we will return this one to the river."

Four of the brightly-armored knights pulled Edwin from his horse and dragged him out of sight. In moments, his screams were indiscernible from the birdsong.

Carter whistled a few bars of the Oompa Loompa theme. "Couldn't happen to a sweeter guy," he said, taking a drink. "Sangria?" he asked the girl who'd handed it to him. "For me?"

"Wine and juice," she said. "It refreshes."

"Yes," Carter agreed. "Yes, it does."

Karra let go of Jarrod's hand as Kaeili came to them and hugged him close. "I must go," she said. "I have much healing to do, and I can't do it here. I will never forget you."

"This will fade," said Jarrod.

"You will never fade from me," she said, and in five steps she had entered the tree line and was gone.

Karra brought Jarrod a wooden plate heaped with chunks of rare meat and some sort of aggregate berries, and a huge stone cup of wine, and begged him to sit by the fire and talk. "I never get to speak your language," she said. Her Falconsrealm dialect was excellent though the consonants were hard and overpronounced. "And your people tell the best stories."

She ate a piece of the meat, then fed one to him. It was soft and hot and lightly flavored, charred rare with lavender and salt.

"Don't let 'em kill me yet, buddy," Jarrod told the skies. "Give me a couple of days, right here, to plan this thing. Then they can bring it heavy. I swear."

She handed him the wine. "To whom do you speak?"

"An old friend," said Jarrod.

The sangria was amazing. Chunks of berries floated in it.

She wrapped her hands around his on the cup, and his pulse sprinted at her touch. Holding his hands, she pulled the cup to her lips and took a long drink, then put it back to his with a smile and a flash of incisors. "Shed your armor, sire," she suggested. "Nothing here will harm you."

3-6-9-8-7-4.

Jarrod had intentionally chosen his alarm sequence so that he could punch it in drunk. On the keypad, it drew a J.

He held his breath for a moment, counted to five.

No alarm.

Crius was behind him, as was Saril. He waved them inside.

It took him a moment with his flashlight to kick on the generator in the garage.

Lights flickered to life throughout the house. The fridge thrummed and heaters whirred. He hadn't realized how acclimated he'd become to the silence of a world made by hand.

He had no urge to check Facebook.

Saril headed directly for the man-at-arms harness. "Holy hell," he said.

"Yeah," said Jarrod. "That's coming." He opened his arms locker, and tossed Saril a bastardsword with a green wooden handle in a beautiful leather scabbard. "Keep it." He gave Crius a riding sword that was close to what the Gateskeep soldiers used, only made of immensely finer steel with an edge they would never be able to accomplish. "For you, my friend."

He cleaned out his entire locker, packing six swords into two rifle cases.

"You're going to fight the war yourself?" asked Saril.

"Oh, you're gonna help," said Jarrod. "But this stuff will ensure that we win it."

He opened his safe, taking out a pair of one-ounce gold bars and a box of hollowpoint ammo.

He wished he had another gun.

He wished he hadn't drained the fluids from the Audi. He wished his phone worked. He could pop up to Vermont and totally stack this thing in his favor, roll into Ulorak with FN-FAL's and Mossbergs and fuck Ulo over on a Biblical scale.

But time was ticking.

Out to his garage, where he had his serious hardware. A rack of rock-climbing gear; three hundred feet of ten-millimeter rope, a harness, a figure-8 device. He threw it all into an ultralight technical pack and tossed it to Saril, who was staring at the charcoal Audi the way Jarrod had stared at Karra.

"What is it?" Saril asked.

"Horseless cart," said Jarrod. "It's broken right now."

What he was looking for took some digging. He found it in his rafters: a streamlined backpack, black ballistic nylon. He opened a couple of pouches and flaps and closed them again.

"Hell, yeah," he told Saril. "Got it."

He grabbed a second backpack, a towering thing in Multicam, and before they left he emptied his liquor cabinet into it.

Crius built the portal directly in the doorway. Jarrod set the alarm again, and dragging bags and laden with packs and cases, they stepped through to Sanctuary.

Crius gave Jarrod the sketches he'd made; as best he could draw them from what he'd seen inside Edwin's mind. Then he fell over, unconscious.

Jarrod and Carter arranged him on a moss bed near the fire, and looked the sketches over.

It wasn't much to go on.

Ulorak was built into a mountain, mostly caves with one tower on top. Crius could land them in the road just outside, in the throne room, in a water closet someplace inside, in an apartment high in one of the towers, at the boat launch at the very base of the castle down by the pantry and cellars, or in some sort of meeting room that appeared to double as a formal banquet area.

"I wish I knew where she was," said Jarrod, so often that Carter lost count.

"We kill him," said Carter, "She dies. He catches us, she dies. He finds out we're there, she dies. We need to find her, absolute first thing."

"We're going to need to take Crius," Jarrod decided.

"They will never go for that," said Carter. "He's basically the queen on the chessboard. They're not going to risk him."

"What risk?" asked Jarrod. "He can just teleport right out of there if things get hairy."

"Look how wiped out he is," said Carter. Crius was beyond unconscious, twitching in REM. "We'd have to carry him out of there. There's no way he can get us in there and then get us out again."

Jarrod lay back in the glow of the fire, with Karra rubbing his shoulders and kissing the top of his forehead. "I hope he's keeping her well."

"She said she wasn't being mistreated," said Carter. "In fact, the note she sent—wait a minute," he picked up Jarrod's big map, and plunked his finger down. "She said something about her view. She could see the Teeth of the World."

"Northwest," said Jarrod, looking at Carter's finger. He pulled out a lensatic compass and oriented the map.

"How do you know that north is north here?" asked Carter. "You're on another planet, brother."

"Physics is physics," said Jarrod. "We're still standing on a dirt clod with an iron core. As long as this rock has a stable bipolar magnetic field—which it does, or they wouldn't know directions at all—we're good. For that matter, Earth's magnetosphere is pretty jacked up. You can be off by twenty degrees depending where you stand."

"I'm going to have to guess that the guest apartments are somewhat close together," said Carter. "And that she's in one of them. On the northwest side. Our best bet to get out of there, though, is the boat launch. The apartments are way the hell up in the towers. If this pic is right, that's got to be a quarter-mile high. That's the freakin' Burj Khalifa. How are we going to get all the way down to the dock without getting lost?"

"It's a straight shot," said Jarrod.

"The hell it is," said Carter. "That place was built by miners. It's going to be tunnels every which way the further into the mountain you go."

Jarrod rose, went to the pile of gear, and tossed the small backpack at Carter, who caught it and looked it over. "It's a straight shot," Jarrod repeated.

"Is this what I think this is?" asked Carter.

"God, I really hope so."

Carter handed it back to him. "Me, too."

Jarrod lay back in Karra's arms. Carter had a long slug of Johnnie Walker and then stretched out near the fire. In moments, he was snoring.

With a tug at his hands, Karra led Jarrod to his feet, and down a path to a burbling waterfall and a pool glowing heliotrope in the light of the moon. There, she slipped out of what little she wore and pulled him down in a smear of power that tore through the glen like a ghost on fire.

Much later they lay together among the rubble of armor and clothing, utterly drunk with each other. She played with a lock of his hair.

"Come back to me when you've done this brave thing," she said. "I'll wait for you here."

Carter was the first one through the portal. It had taken him a half-hour to get into his full field harness, and he had his greatsword in his spike-gauntleted hand, unsheathed.

He stepped directly through to Ulo's throne room. There was a momentary step down that he didn't expect, and he stumbled and crashed to the floor.

The room was black. The stones were dull black. The torchlight flickered off black rock; the throne, empty, was also black.

Carter climbed to his feet, knowing full well the noise would bring the entire castle. He reached through his eye-slit to adjust his Oakleys.

The noise brought one man, in a gray robe over fine mail and a steel skullcap. "Can I help you?"

He stepped back at the sight of Carter.

"I have an audience with the king," said Carter. "I'm expected."

"Carrying that sword in your hand?" the man said, drawing his own, which was long, delicate, and had a D-shaped bar for a handguard. "I think not."

Jarrod opened his eyes, waiting to have fucked this up. Expecting to see Ulo beside him, expecting to materialize inside solid rock. What if Edwin had been bullshitting, and had only imagined Ulo's palace? Where would he be then?

It was an apartment, lit by a single candle. A small bed with a plush throw. A glowing fireplace with bricks of coal.

His eyes adjusted and he checked his compass. He straightened his sword and checked his belt: pistol, arming sword, med kit. He'd left his armor, and wore his heaviest motocross jacket and a pair of black cargo pants under a black backpack.

The hallway was wide, carved from black stone, and led to a balcony overlooking a sheer drop at one end, and a stairwell at the other.

So much for The Silver Palace. Orwellian, much?

There were four other doors. One of the doors had two guards on it, in plumed, slitted helmets and heavy lamellar armor that hung in skirts to their knees, vaguely Mongol. He checked his compass again. The room they were guarding would not have a window facing northwest-ish. Or at least what his compass said was northwest.

They turned to him and muttered something he couldn't make out.

And then it hit him: he didn't speak Uloraki.

He laughed. There was nothing to do but laugh.

"I'm looking for the princess," he said.

One of the guards looked at the other, and said something else but it sounded affirmative. "Who are you?" he asked. His accent was Gavrian, far back in the throat, thick-tongued and musical.

Jarrod put the compass in his pocket and walked up to them, as if it was the most normal thing in the world. "King Ulo sent me. I'm to talk to her."

He kicked one's legs out, threw the other against the wall, kicked them both a few times and stomped on them for good measure.

Christ, that was a lot of armor.

He drew the pistol, racked the slide, and tried the door.

It was unlocked.

"You have got to be shitting me," he said, and turned the knob. "Worst evil sorcerer, ever."

Jarrod pushed the door open. Adielle was inside sitting on the edge of the bed, brushing her hair and looking up from something she was reading. She stood as he came in. Jarrod holstered the gun. "Highness?"

It took her a moment. "Sir—Sir Jarrod?"

"The Merciful," Jarrod said as she threw her arms around him.

Carter fought the man back, using the greatsword's ricossa as a close grip and fencing with the point.

His opponent was good, but Carter had armor and a lot of it. Several times the smaller sword had skipped harmlessly off his gauntlet or pauldron, completely unable to deliver the necessary momentum to do any sort of damage. The sword had good steel edges that would pierce iron mail or bite iron plate, but against case-hardened steel, it skipped without leaving a scratch. What the guy needed was a pickaxe; what he had was effectively a rolled newspaper.

There was just no way, no way at all, for the little sword to hurt him unless his opponent stabbed him in the face through the grinning mouth of his helmet. And they both knew it. The man kept trying for the face shot, overextending his lunges, feinting and then lunging for the visor. It wasn't a bad idea, but it quickly became clear to Carter that it was the man's only idea.

Carter kind of felt bad for the guy. He let the next feint smack off his vambrace, beat the smallsword down, shifted his feet, and thrust the greatsword out with one hand by the pommel. The Martensitic edge of the tip punched through the man's mail, low on the shoulder beneath the collarbone, and sank nearly three feet into his body. The swordsman fell to his knees with the sound of a tire deflating, and Carter kicked the body off his sword.

"Where's the king?" he asked the man, who was clearly on his way out.

"He's not here," the man groaned. "Skullsmortar."

Carter stomped his foot. "You stupid motherfucker! You make me kill you, and he's not even here? I didn't want to kill you!"

He was talking to no one; the man was dead.

Carter sagged.

"I didn't want to kill you," Carter repeated quietly. He cleaned his sword on a tapestry, sheathed it, and slung it over one shoulder, then opened the doors to the throne room and hauled ass down the stairwell.

Jarrod checked the window. It was far too small. He'd never get a good enough launch and sure as hell not jumping tandem.

"Fuck," he said.

Ahead of them lay a wide plain, dusty and black. There were mountains, but they were miles away. And not to the northwest. She hadn't been looking at the Teeth of the World; she'd been looking at a range of mountains running to the northeast and ending at the Eastern Freehold. Right area, wrong direction. Easy mistake, he was sure, if you'd never been there before.

And worse, he realized, looking down, he was short.

He had been counting on a much longer drop. A thousand feet would have been better. A quarter mile — what he'd judged from the drawings, and damn Edwin's eyes — better still.

He could see the dock, and rowboats, and if he squinted, a couple of people – Saril and Bevio, he hoped. He judged it to be four hundred feet. A small skyscraper; a five-second fall.

He led Adielle by the hand, over the moaning soldiers and out to the balcony to the south, where the wind tore at them.

The gusts on this side had to be nearing thirty miles per hour, beating the shit out of the side of the castle. And here, the mountain sloped away. Maybe eighty feet of free-fall. Not enough for the chute to open.

The rig on his back was an ultra-low-opening custom job with short lines and an oversized chordwise vent for pressurization at low speeds; a true stuntman's special built to survive jumps from 300 feet — and even below, if you had the stones for that kind of work.

The problem was that such a specialized canopy had no sense of humor for adverse conditions.

"Fuck," he said again.

High falls are done in zero wind. Period. When the winds kick up, guys who jump off buildings for a living head to the nearest bar.

With winds like this, and only four hundred feet of drop, he'd have no time to adjust. An off-heading opening would leave a long smear across the side of the mountain.

There would be less wind on the northeast side. He didn't know how much less, but anything less was acceptable. It would have to be.

He looked up.

They were near the top of the tower. The stairs at the end of the hallway probably led to the roof. He was sure there was a roof. And it would give him another fifty feet.

He grabbed her hand and they ran to the stairwell. She started down, and he pulled her up.

"What are you doing?" she asked.

"The roof," he said.

"There's nothing up there," she said.

"I know. Trust me, Highness."

He strained to keep his voice professional, but he had to bite down hard on the rise in his throat.

A dozen soldiers in heavy lamellar armor pushed past Carter, running up the long stairs. No one gave him a second look.

How do you not notice a guy my size in this kind of armor? Carter had to wonder.

He remembered, then, that Ulorak was a trade crossroads, and a lot of men made their fortunes as guards for trade caravans in and out of the area. Big guys in outlandish armor probably weren't a unique sight.

What was unique, though, he figured after a moment, was how nice this place was. The stairs were clean, cross-ventilation carried the smoke from the torches and removed the smells of people and must, and he hadn't seen a single mouse or bug. The castle, although monstrous, was immaculate, as if Ulo had teams of Moonies scrubbing it down in shifts.

And damn, the guards were on it, he noted. Lots of guys, going upstairs really fast, now.

Lamellar. Small overlapping plates sewn onto overlapping sheets of leather. Heavy, tough stuff. And spectacled helmets with cheekplates over aventails. He thought he saw flashes of mail beneath the lamellar. Were he their size, their armor would have outweighed his.

He hadn't seen lamellar here until now.

A few more rushes of men up the stairs and he found himself on a landing above the great anteroom, fifty feet high and a hundred yards across, lit by oil lamps set in great chandeliers. The main doors stood open, looking out onto the great southeastern plain that led to more mountains, then Gavria and eventually the Eastern Wilds.

Bevio, Saril, and Peric were down at the docks on the far side, preparing boats for the getaway.

The problem was, Carter wasn't sure how to get down there. The place was a snakes' nest of tunnels.

He skipped down the stairs and stood at the great doors. The wind was gusting from the southwest, right along the mountains. Assuming Jarrod made it out of the building in one piece, the winds would carry him northeast, and probably pretty far.

He wasn't going to the docks.

This is where you pull out your radio and say something cool, like, "Primary extraction zone is a no-go. Switching to secondary." But, lacking a radio, he hoped they'd figure it out.

Ulorak didn't have a barbican or a gatehouse. The massive stone doors opened directly onto the plain.

Fifty great steps led down to the gritty black soil, and that was it. He looked behind him to see the enormous tower built into the rock face, matte black engraved with yard-wide silver tooling vanishing into the sky. "Wow."

He straightened his sword on his back and strolled down the mighty front steps, nodding to the guards. They nodded back. One waved.

Dozens of people were coming and going. Many smiled and nodded.

"What a nice place," Carter said quietly to himself. Humming to himself, he struck out to the northeast, moving with a purpose.

Up two flights, and there was a ladder built into the rocks, disappearing into a vertical tunnel. Jarrod clicked his flashlight upwards, saw a trapdoor at the top, and two minutes later the pale pewter skies were right above them, the winds hammering off the plain.

This place, he had to admit, was gorgeous. A lovely, acre-wide rooftop garden sported statues and benches and ivy and small fruit-bearing bushes in pots. A couple of elevated observation points looked out over the valley at each end. The ringed moon braced two mountains, spectacular as hell. The clouds tore by overhead.

He had brought an extra carabiner in case he'd needed a static line hookup; he used it now to secure the hatch. With a knurled locking ring on the haft, he hoped it would take anyone quite a while to figure out how to open it.

He was locking it when he saw two soldiers at the far observation point, looking southeast.

One saw him, nudged the other, and they started coming his way, down the stairs to the roof.

Jarrod waved in a friendly manner. They waved back. Jarrod pointed behind them. They waved again and turned back around to whatever they'd been doing.

"Wow, are those guys gonna lose their jobs," Jarrod told Adielle. He led her to the northeast observation deck, within about ten feet of the lee-side ledge. "Stay here." He scooted to the edge and looked over.

It was absolutely sheer, from the observation point straight down the face.

The river was a ribbon of onyx that seemed not nearly far enough below. A mountain, equally sheer, flat black, spanned the world across from them. There were no trees to judge the distance, no rooftops on this side, no people below, of course no cars or streets or any kind of familiar landmarks.

His gut told him it was four hundred feet. It felt like four hundred feet.

But it could have been a thousand feet. It could have been fifty.

He pulled a contraption made mostly from black loops of heavy webbing from a bellows pocket on his pants, clipping them through rings on his packstraps. "Turn around," he told her.

"What are you doing?"

"Trust me. Step into this," he held out a loop of webbing, then another. "Arms through here, and here," he said.

He'd be working at the load limit of the canopy; they were essentially jumping tandem on a reserve chute. He'd run the math ten times. It would technically work as long as the seams held, but it was going to be a fast ride.

"Hurry," Jarrod said. He clipped rings on her webbing to rings on his, pulled on lengths of straps to snug it all down, then clipped another piece around her chest—which was spectacular, he had to admit—and spun the locking ring.

"Are the pegasi coming?" she asked.

Jarrod pulled at the straps on her legs and shoulders. "We don't need them."

Now the soldiers were coming over. Waving and yelling as they descended the stairs.

"What do you mean, 'We don't need them?'" she said. "We can't fly."

He unzipped the top of the pack and grabbed the pilot chute, shaking loose several feet of cord. "Oh, don't be so sure."

A particularly heavy gust nearly knocked them over the edge, and vertigo bludgeoned him as she squirmed. "Stand still," he snapped, and wrapped one arm around her.

The soldiers had stopped to examine the carabiner. They were still yelling at Jarrod as they worked to unlock it, the words lost in the wind and in Uloraki, anyway.

Jarrod shifted his feet, took another step toward the ledge. Her toes were at the very edge of the wall. "We're going to die!" she shouted.

"Yes," he shouted above the wind. "But not today. Close your eyes."

The soldiers got the hatch unlatched and looked up just in time to see them leap off the edge.

The slam of the canopy opening was mind-rattling. He was jumping at nearly double his normal weight, and the stunt chute hit like a son of a bitch to begin with. Adielle's head cracked him in the nose. His eyes watered over and he blinked furiously to clear them.

He looked up, checked his risers through the fog of his vision, and saw the purple wing carving the sky, textbook, beautiful. He spilled some air from the front edge to get them the hell away from the mountainside.

Adielle must have opened her eyes, because she said, "You really can fly."

This was supposed to be the great part. Whenever the chute opened correctly, the rest was an easy stroll. Enjoy the view.

This time, however, it was where the work started. The wind was convection on this side of the mountain; not nearly as strong as the gusts on the west face, but the canyon was channeling the wind right down it, tumbling along the sides making crosswinds in every which way, even straight down.

He felt his risers take a hit, bicycled his legs, spilled some more air, and recovered.

Goddamn, they were heavy.

He blinked a few more times, really hard.

The least amount of buffeting was directly over the water. However, with the princess in front of him he didn't know if he could reach the Capewells to release the chute before he drowned them both.

Conversely, landing on the shore, if he hit a shear or a one of these squirrelly crosswind gusts, could kill them, or worse, break one of their legs and make for a long hike back to Gateskeep.

They'd be down in thirty seconds.

"Um," he grumbled.

"What?"

"Nothing."

At the dock, Bevio, Saril, and Peric had filled two boats with Jarrod's field armor, all their gear, and a few hundred pounds of food from the cellars. They had then pulled the drain bungs on the other two boats and tossed them into the river along with the oars, all of which now floated toward the Shieldlands.

"What is that?" asked Saril, a small keg of whisky on his shoulder. He was pointing up at a giant purple feather gliding across the sky.

"That's Jarrod and the princess," said Bevio after a second. "He's flying. Son of a bitch, he's flying!"

Saril set the keg in the boat and cast off, rowing after him.

"We're leaving," Peric told Bevio, casting off. Bevio grabbed the oars and laid to.

"But the Chancellor?" said Bevio.

"He knows what to do. He'll meet us."

Carter saw the canopy open up out of the corner of his eye, an explosion of purple accompanied by a pop a moment later as the sound reached his ears.

"Holy shit," he swore.

Jarrod was a hundred yards up and moving like a paper airplane, absolutely screaming with the wind at his back. Carter could see the princess in a tandem harness, and he was able to figure from the angle where they were going to land. From here it was a downhill jog to the riverbank.

He was glad he had worn logging boots and not sabatons. He picked up his feet and made time.

"Legs up!" Jarrod shouted as they skimmed the river. He banked into the wind, aiming for what he hoped was soft dirt on the far side. "Legs up!" he repeated.

His heels skimmed the river over the last ten yards, and they landed in a foot of water with a terrific splash and tumbled onto the bank atop each other in the thick mud.

He popped the Capewells as the chute filled up and threatened to drag him back into the river, then unhooked her from the harness, at which point Adielle turned around, painted with mud, and threw her arms around him and kissed him deeply.

"Wow," he said when she was done.

"That—was—amazing," she trembled. "Can we do that again?"

"Let's try not to." He started pulling the chute to him as fast as he could. He wadded it to a manageable size and sloshed to the bank.

He saw what had to be Carter, moving like a locomotive down the slope to the far bank a hundred yards away. Jarrod waved his arms. "Carter!"

Carter was flying down the slope like he'd just recovered a fumble. Jarrod noted that he was moving at an astonishing speed, considering he was probably wearing fifty pounds of armor.

Jarrod waved to the boats and whistled, motioning for them to go get Carter, but Saril was already on it.

Carter planted and cut left, and sprinted down the bank as Saril rowed into the shallows and then braked the boat with the oars.

Carter sloshed out to knee-depth and rolled in. "Go! Go! Go!" he yelled.

Saril heaved on the oars, the current grabbing the boat and flinging it away.

Bevio and Peric picked up Jarrod and Adielle on the far side, and then Bevio, rowing furiously, worked to catch up with Saril and Carter.

"Did you get him?" Jarrod asked Carter as they neared.

"He wasn't home," said Carter, still gasping for breath. He lay back in the boat with his wrist on his forehead. "We missed him."

"Dammit," said Jarrod.

"I'm too old for this," Carter decided.

"I'm feeling that way myself."

"That was pretty awesome, though," said Carter. "That was really cool."

"Yeah," Jarrod agreed. "That was fun."

"So, now what?" Carter asked, not moving.

"Second star on the right, and straight on till morning," said Jarrod.

"We sank the other boats," Peric assured him.

"They won't have horses?" asked Adielle.

"They have horses," said Jarrod. "But the banks are too soft to ride at speed. They can't get down here on horseback, and they can't keep pace with us on foot. The roads are a few hundred meters off, above the river. They'd have to give chase in boats, and now they don't have those, either. The best they could do is try to shoot at us, and if we stay in the middle of this river," he gestured to the dark-green water several hundred yards wide, with hillsides rising quickly on either side, "we're a moving target at the edge of their range."

"If we stay out here, what are we going to eat?" she asked, and then noticed the pile of goods in the front of the boat—hams, strings of onions, a crate of apples, casks of whisky and wine, fresh breads, and a wheel of cheese the size of a small shield.

"You really thought this through," she said.

"We're not there, yet," said Jarrod, as Peric poured a wooden cup of wine from a cask and offered it to the princess, who accepted with a smile. Peric handed a second cup to Jarrod.

"A whole lot of things can still go wrong with this," Jarrod said.

"You know," the soldier told Mukul, "doing something to scare her. Interrogating her. We didn't even know that it was the princess."

"We didn't even know that the princess was here," said the other. "How could we know that?"

"We went over to see what he was doing, because it looked dangerous. And then, well, they just jumped."

Mukul ground his teeth and sighed through his nose. He

turned the carabiner over in his hands and clicked the gate a couple of times. The material was amazing; the workmanship, gorgeous; steel ultralight and bejeweled. Some sort of locking device, but he had no idea what its function was.

"And he flew," Mukul growled. "You're telling me this man flew away with the princess."

"On my ancestors," the soldier said. "He sprouted purple wings and flew away."

"Purple," repeated Mukul. "Damn you, I am not going to tell the king that a man snuck in here, seen by no one, defeated two knights with his bare hands, killed a member of the royal guard in the throne room, and then flew away with the Princess of Gateskeep on purple wings!"

"Sir, it's what happened."

Mukul clenched his fist. "Well, I'm not telling him. You are."

So we are now looking for a master swordsman armed with ultralight steel who can not only fly, but apparently turn invisible at will, Mukul thought. *Either a wizard, an elf, or something new entirely.*

Or, he realized with a stone in his throat, all of the above.

"You two will fix this," he announced. "You will ride hard to Skullsmortar, tell the king what happened, and accompany Lord Elgast, who I imagine will set this matter straight."

XII

ALLEGRO ASSAI

"I have a high art; I hurt with cruelty those who would damage me."
— Archilochus, 650 B.C.

L ord Elgast of Skullsmortar thundered down the black roads on his fine buckskin horse, moving at a pace just past a trot. He had a hundred soldiers behind him, heavily armored in Uloraki mail, including the two idiots sent from the palace. Far behind the horses rumbled carts full of grain and hay.

He was hunting a man with purple wings.

A possibly invisible man, who flew on purple wings.

A possibly invisible man who flew on purple wings, and was traveling with the princess.

There was one road into Gateskeep, and one narrow pass where the road crossed the river at a falls. All the boats had been sunk at Ulorak, which meant the purple-winged man and the princess were either following the road, or following the river. If they were headed for Gateskeep, they'd turn north into the eastern pocket of the Shieldlands. If they were headed for the

Eastern Freehold, they'd ride the river through the Ulorak Gap and clear to the Salt Sea. And then. . .

He didn't want to think about "and then."

He would overtake them at this pace, run them down on the road if they were on the road. If he didn't see them on the road, he would wait in the hills, deploy his scouts, and attack from an elevation as the purple-winged man and the princess crossed the great bridge and started the trek through the northern pass into the eastern end of the Shieldlands.

He watched the skies. The purple-winged man might attack from above.

There were no wings.

If the purple-winged man was King Ulo's compatriot, the swordsman who'd killed twenty men in Falconsrealm, no worry; he'd hit him with a hundred men this time. Then he'd bring the purple-winged man's head back to Ulorak in a bag.

High above the bridge, near a rock shelter, Jarrod and Carter wrestled their way into their harnesses, belting, buckling, and locking each other in.

They kept the fire small, the smoke minimal, but they'd been eating since morning. They all had. Potatoes, mostly. And lots of water. Both at Jarrod's insistence.

"He's going to send an army," said the princess. "I know you're a great fighter, Sir Jarrod. I know you killed twenty men —"

"Seventeen," said Jarrod, stamping his feet. His right boot was laced too tight across the arch, goddammit. Impossible to get to under the steel leggings and half-sabatons and it was already going numb.

"—Seventeen," she continued. "But King Ulo is going to hit you with everything he's got."

"Then he'll have nothing left when we're done," said Carter, ramming his shoulder against a tree and shrugging a few times to seat his breastplate and pauldrons.

"You're not going to kill an army, Chancellor," she said.

Carter looked at Jarrod and grinned. "Not alone."

"We do this here," said Jarrod, shaking his foot. "We end this."

Peric, looking down to the river from the outcropping above, let out a pheasant's call, repeated three times.

Jarrod and Carter came running, with Bevio and Saril behind.

"That's quite a few more than I was expecting," Jarrod admitted, at sight of Elgast's forces. "Shit."

"That's a hundred men," said Bevio.

"They're going to come this way," said Peric. "They're probably going to want this high ground."

"Not yet," said Jarrod. "See how they're fanning out, flanking the river? They think they're ahead of us. They'll watch the river for a while. When we don't show, they'll come for the high ground to try and spot us at a distance. Then we'll take them a few at a time."

"Five of us?" said Saril. "Against a hundred? I'm good, sir, but I'm not that good."

"They have to come up this hill," said Jarrod. "In all that armor. It took us all night to climb it, remember? They won't be able to lift a finger when they get here. They'll be tired, they'll be thirsty, their legs will be too worn out to fight, they'll be moving in small groups. The most tired guys will be at the back, so it'll get easier as we go. We're full of high-energy food, we're rested, we've got plenty of water. We get through the first dozen and we'll take 'em."

They all heard it: horses, behind them, and something moving fast and growling.

Jarrod and Carter turned to see Dog, in his war gear, charging pell-mell for Peric, who grinned and slapped the beast on his armor as Dog rowled with delight.

Jack, grinning in Jarrod's black plastic armor, was leading a menagerie; half a dozen horses, including Perseus and a huge black charger, both decked out for war in full barding.

Jack handed Perseus to Jarrod and the other charger to Carter, who shrugged out of his greatsword and hung it on the saddle.

Perseus nosed Jarrod's shoulder with an affectionate clank.

"That is a big horse," Adielle admitted. "That is a really big horse."

"He's half moose," said Jarrod. "Say hello, Perseus."

Behind Jack were a dozen elven knights in their multicolored armor, riding horse-sized elk with sharpened racks of antlers, and half that many knights of the Stallion on horseback.

"I don't even want to know how he did this," said Peric to Saril. Jarrod was exchanging greetings with a handful of elves who had arrived on foot.

"Prince Akiel of the Faerie Stronghold," said Jarrod, "may I introduce Her Highness Adielle Riongoran-Thurdin of Gateskeep, Princess of Falconsrealm."

"At your service," said the prince, extending his hand. Jarrod couldn't help but note that Akiel was carrying one of his swords, a blue-handled tool-steel warsword that someone Akiel's size would be able to wield like a Claymore.

"Much better odds than I was expecting," Jarrod admitted. "Thank you for coming."

"I wouldn't want to miss it," said Akiel. "We would have arrived earlier but our wizards could only get us so close."

"Are you on foot, Highness?" said Jarrod.

"Momentarily," the elf admitted.

"Well, your timing is impeccable," said Jarrod. "Our guests just arrived."

"I do see you have dressed for a party," said the elf. "You look nice."

"Thank you, Highness. I lack your fashion sense."

"Your people do," said Akiel. "Mind if we survey the ballroom?"

"Please," said Jarrod. "And let me say, I'm open to suggestions."

"Thank you, Lieutenant, but the day belongs to you."

Peric offered to take them to the lookout, which was a lightly-wooded point on the promontory above the rock shelter.

Akiel and several of his knights crept to the edge of the woodline and looked out onto the bridge, where Lord Elgast had hung his banners and deployed his men to either side. Elgast stood in the center of the bridge, arms akimbo, the sun gleaming from his polished helmet, clearly in command of the day.

Peric was concerned that the brilliant hues of the elves' armor would give them away, but what he didn't know was that from a distance, the elves would appear like a field of wildflowers up on the wooded rock.

Akiel looked back at Peric, his eyes flashing behind his visor. "How I love a surprise party."

Elgast couldn't believe what he was seeing. Atop the northern promontory, a huge purple banner unfurled along the cliff face. In a moment, the breeze caught it and it blew in the wind like a streamer.

"There!" he shouted, at sight of two figures above the banner.

Something impacted in the dirt on the near side of the bridge. An arrow.

"One arrow?" said Elgast. He laughed.

One of his officers, on horseback, brought it over to him.

It had a note attached, which he unrolled.

The first thing he noted was the handwriting. The script was gorgeous, literate, definitely highborn.

The elegant lettering went on to lay out an accusation of questionable parentage involving his mother's fondness for whiskey, her poor impulse control, and a pack of warthogs with nothing better to do that night.

"Is this a joke?!" Elgast boomed at the cliff.

He could clearly see one of the figures pantomiming an obscene gesture against the cliff face.

"Go get him!" he yelled. "Bring them to me so that I can kill him right before her eyes!"

"God bless those guys," said Jarrod to no one as Elgast's men scrambled up the mountainside. They quickly had to ditch their horses and proceed on foot. He could see them slowing down, even from here, where they were just specks struggling up the hill. That far slope was steep as hell.

He envisioned the two elves who'd pulled off the ruse, no doubt laughing their asses off. They'd have a story to tell for a hundred years.

He gave Elgast's men another ten minutes or so to get good and tired. Lamellar armor, over mail, was like wearing a thirty-pound pack on your back, and a second one on your chest. It was exhausting. It was solid protection but it was hell on the shoulders, quads, and lower back. Jarrod couldn't imagine running up a hill in it. He couldn't imagine crawling up a hill in it.

He let them suffer until it wasn't funny anymore, until the first specks were about halfway up the hillside and the ones behind had slowed to a crawl. He could feel their legs aching and if he squinted he swore he could see them gasping and stooping over for breath.

Jarrod stepped to the edge of the southern promontory, fully exposed, his breastplate gleaming in the sun.

He whistled as hard as he could, waving his arms.

"Hey!" he shouted. "Up here, assholes!"

"Bastard!" Elgast exploded. "What is he, a sorcerer?" he grumbled.

"You want us to go kill him, sir?" asked one of the knights.

"No," said Elgast. "I'm going to do it myself but I'll let you watch. You," he pointed to two officers, "Go and bring half the others back, and form a second echelon behind us. Leave the rest in chase, in case this is some kind of trick." The officers saluted and rode off in a tangle of dust and vulgarities.

"On me," said Elgast to the others. "Watch and learn."

Jarrod stood at the top of the bald knob, watching Elgast and his team abandon their horses not halfway up and take to leading them on foot.

He counted eleven knights, scrambling and panting up the hill, resting every few steps with their hands on their knees. There were probably more that he couldn't see.

He waved again. "I haven't got all day! Hurry up, fat ass!" he yelled.

"Come down here!" Elgast boomed. His voice was ragged; he was clearly out of breath.

"Why would I come down there?" shouted Jarrod. "Your mother's up here! We've been at it all morning! Gonna give you a baby brother!"

Elgast turned to his second in command. "I am not going to stop at killing that man."

Elgast's first tranche of men, haggard and worn, had found the rock shelter. The fire was still going. Most pulled off their helmets. A few sat down, gasping. One retched.

Jarrod, Saril, Bevio, and Peric galloped down to the edge of the campsite, thundering like gods. In his plate harness, with the fully-visored helmet and his massive greatsword, and atop the leviathan blue Perseus draped in mail and plates and Gateskeep green, Jarrod was the military might of the mountains, personified.

Elgast's knights scrambled for weapons and helmets. Those on foot swung onto their horses, putting themselves together and trying to look organized and dangerous as they did so.

Even their horses looked tired, Jarrod noted.

"I am Sir Jarrod, The Merciful, Knight Lieutenant in the King's Order of the Stallion of Gateskeep," said Jarrod as his men's destriers stamped and snorted. His greatsword gleamed in the sunlight. "I will accept your surrender."

"Thirteen," said Saril to Jarrod, quietly.

One, broad-shouldered and beefy in lamellar armor with a

long, single-bladed axe, stood by his horse. "I am General Elgast, Lord of Skullsmortar," he said, swinging up with an ease that surprised Jarrod, considering his size. His horse was sturdy but small. "I'll kill you now."

"I doubt that," said Jarrod. "Is your king here?"

"You're lucky he's not," said Elgast.

"Says you," said Jarrod. "Let's do this."

With a yell, Elgast and five of his knights charged Jarrod's team, who spurred their armored horses into the onslaught.

Elgast had a lot of men with him, but there wasn't much room in the clearing for everyone to fight on horseback.

There was a lot of yelling, screaming, clashing, and horse noise.

Elgast outweighed Jarrod by fifty pounds, but Jarrod sat higher. Elgast's axe smashed off Jarrod's big teardrop shield, his tassets, and then his shoulder, but Jarrod got the crossbar of his *gran espée de guerre* in the way of the last one to take some of the force out of it.

The axe skipped off Perseus's crinet, at which point Perseus drove his head into Elgast and Jarrod smashed him in his face with the pommel of his greatsword, then punched him with his gauntleted fist, scarring the cheekplate with both blows. Elgast spat blood and Jarrod hit him in the face with the edge of his shield and drove his pommel onto Elgast's gloved hand. Elgast dropped the axe and Jarrod hit him across the ear with the greatsword, leaving a crease in his helmet.

Elgast cursed and disengaged.

Two more tackled Jarrod from their saddles, not unhorsing him but holding him and stabbing at him with small, heavy swords. Jarrod kicked Perseus in a circle, then delivered a thrust of the greatsword through one's lamellar, center mass. The sword sank several inches and he yanked it out again as the knight fell back.

Elgast, a sword in his hand now, urged his horse forward with a yell. Jarrod kicked Perseus, who knew this game. As the spurs dug, the roan launched hard enough to snap Jarrod's head back.

The impact was terrific. Jarrod and Perseus wrecked Elgast and his little steed the way a freight train demolishes a stalled bus, buckling them in half, rolling them underfoot, and then continuing right over the top of them both.

Jarrod turned at the edge of the fray and surveyed the scene. Peric was down, his magnificent mare was down, and three knights were on their feet, hacking at him. Jarrod ran them down from behind, bowling one into a tree and splitting another's helmet with the *gran espée de guerre*. The helmet came apart at the riveted seam and the knight collapsed. Peric kicked the last knight's legs out from under him and as he fell Peric went to his knees and drove his axe into the knight with both hands.

And that was that.

Jarrod spurred Perseus around. Bevio and Saril were shoulder to shoulder, and several of Elgast's men, horsebound, faced them but wouldn't engage. "Behind me!" Jarrod yelled at Peric. He pulled a warhammer with a long pick on the balance from its frog and handed it to Peric, who holstered his axe.

Elgast stumbled to his feet, dirty, bloody, and dazed. He had found his axe again, or one very like it. He rallied his men around him and called for his horse, but his horse had apparently decided that this whole thing was bullshit because he was long gone.

"Smart horse," Jarrod muttered under his breath, patting Perseus's crinet. "You, buddy, not so much. And I love you for it."

One of Elgast's men swung down from his horse, and Elgast swung up. "I've got fifty men behind me!" Elgast shouted at Jarrod.

"Not quite," boomed Carter, riding into the clearing astride a horse nearly as big as Perseus with six knights of the Stallion behind him. He brandished his two-handed sword in one hand, monolithic in his demonic armor. "But it's gonna feel like it in a minute."

Elgast's men spun as Carter's troops rode up behind them.

"We still have the numbers," said Elgast. "Give up now. Give us the princess."

"I don't see that happening," Carter admitted.

Jarrod looked around. Three of Elgast's men were dead, and a handful injured but still in the fight. They were certainly taking the worst of it, though. The bigger horses and heavier weapons of the Gateskeep forces were doing a number on the Uloraki, who were fighting like they were used to being the biggest dogs in the yard and now had no idea what to do.

Peric was on foot, which worried Jarrod, but the old guy was tough as hell and now he had a hammer specifically built to demolish the kind of armor the Uloraki wore.

Gateskeep had eleven men, with ten on horseback; Elgast's forces had sixteen and fourteen, by Jarrod's quick math, respectively. A few more had found their way up the hill, but all of Elgast's men were in shreds. They heaved for breath, they sagged in their saddles, their horses foamed.

Jarrod wanted to keep them tired.

He kicked Perseus forward, and Elgast and five of his knights crashed into Jarrod, Saril, and Bevio.

Jarrod could tell that Elgast was exhausted; he wrestled him back and forth with both hands, then wrapped him up and bent him forward, setting all his weight on Elgast's back, which had to already be searing from the climb. He felt the bigger man sink, and beat on his low back a few times with his pommel before shoving him completely out of his saddle.

Uloraki knights scattered and Elgast's new horse again took off as he rumbled to his feet. Jarrod backed Perseus up and took stock since no one was attacking him. He figured Elgast had given one of those idiotic, "No one kills him but me," edicts. *Have it your way, bozo.*

Saril killed one, jamming the big bastardsword right through the lamellar, getting a bite, and working it back and forth in a clinch as the others beat on him. He yanked it out, and turned to fight the others and drove them off, screaming.

Peric used the long backspike of the hammer to pull an Uloraki out of his saddle, and flipped it around, driving the hammer into his helmet as he lay stunned. Gore sprayed through the soldier's visor.

Jarrod felt Perseus hunch up and kick, looked behind him, and saw an Uloraki footman skidding through the dirt. He didn't get up.

The groups broke again, riding to different sides of the clearing.

Carter's greatsword was sheathed in blood. There were parts of Uloraki soldiers in the dirt, and wounded men screaming and sobbing and thrashing their way to the edges of the arena. Several horses were dead. One of the Uloraki knights' shirts of lamellar was hanging open, cleaved at the shoulder.

Looking out over the Uloraki, Jarrod remembered how he and Carter had argued for hours one night, over pitchers of beer, plates of hot wings, and bar napkins full of scribbles, in regards to the merits of heat treatment versus materials for title of "best" swordmaking technology. Carter stood fascistically loyal to L6, his steel of choice, while Jarrod argued till his last breath that night that it was confirmation bias because Carter had thrown down a ridiculous five thousand dollars for his sword. Jarrod had maintained that there was no difference between tool steel and L6 if the material was properly heat-treated.

Now, though, Jarrod had to admit that Carter's exorbitant purchase had been money well spent. Jarrod's big sword could punch holes and crack helmets, but Carter was literally hacking the Uloraki to pieces right through their scales. Wielded from horseback, with eight feet of moment arm and a ton of mass behind it, the immaculately-forged greatsword was Death's own scythe.

Elgast's forces were now outnumbered.

One of Elgast's men gave the general his horse and Elgast swung up.

"We can do this all day!" shouted Jarrod to Elgast.

Beside Jarrod, Peric straightened his helmet and hefted the hammer.

"I am General Elgast of Ulorak, Lord of Skullsmortar!" Elgast yelled.

"And you're getting your ass kicked," said Jarrod, "in case you didn't notice."

"I have fifty more men coming up this hill!" Elgast nearly screamed. "You are all going to die! You can give up now," he said, addressing the Gateskeep forces, "and I'll take the princess and let your men go. Except you," he pointed at Jarrod with his axe. "You, I kill."

"No deal," said Jarrod, reining Perseus closer to Saril's horse. "You wanna do this again?"

Elgast pointed at the trail leading from the bridge, exasperated.

"I have HALF AN ARMY coming up the damned—"

His insistence was interrupted by the sound of worlds ending as Akiel and several more Faerie knights crested the path in floral-patterned armor that exploded and shimmered in twenty colors. The armor, however, wasn't nearly as impressive as the grizzly bears they rode, foaming from their mouths and matted with gore.

"Holy fuck," said Elgast, reining his horse back a step as one of the bears *broaaared* at them.

Dog charged across the clearing to Peric, his armor smeared in blood, and struck a threatening stance at the Uloraki, heaving and panting. Fighting beside Big Brother Bears had been the best day of his doggie life.

Jarrod wondered if the Faerie chivalry were broken down by genus. Gladiola Cavalry. Freesia Infantry. The Tulip Brigade.

And yet, insanely, they pulled it off. They looked murderous. Terrifying.

The bears really helped with the murderous part.

Perseus took a step sideways as one of the bears lit up again, and then the horse roared back, nails on slate. Jarrod patted the brave son of a bitch.

"Your forces have dispersed, sir," said Akiel, pointing to Elgast. "You should surrender."

"Who—the HELL—are you?!" Elgast stammered.

"I'd rather you not know," Akiel said after a moment's thought. "I will tell you, though, that my forces give chase and I don't give your men good odds." His bear wuffed in agreement. "Lieutenant, I relinquish our heavy cavalry to your command."

Jarrod looked at Elgast. "You can leave now, General," he said. "Walk away from this while you can. It's gonna get real ugly from here."

Elgast surveyed his battered troops. "We'll leave," he said, "but on one condition."

"You're not really in a position to make demands," Carter pointed out.

Jarrod sheathed the *gran espée de guerre* on the saddle, hung his shield beside, and was already getting off Perseus. "I know what you want," he said. "I thought you'd never ask."

Elgast leaped off his horse and handed the reins to one of his men, then swung his axe in a couple of loops to limber up as he strode forward.

Jarrod stopped well out of long attacking distance. "Win or lose," he said, "your men leave after this. The princess comes with us."

"You have my word," said Elgast, loud enough for his men to hear. He choked up on his axe a bit. "I'd suggest you draw a weapon, sir."

"Good idea," said Jarrod. He unsnapped the Springfield from its holster on his swordbelt, punched it out in a textbook Weaver, and put a round through Elgast's helmet.

The horses and bears jumped at the noise and the general went down in a crash of armor and dust, flat on his back.

Jarrod holstered the gun and whistled for Perseus while the knights on both sides steadied their mounts.

The glen fell quiet as he grabbed the knots of the saddle assist, swung up, and opened his visor.

"Tell King Ulo this!" he announced. "I am Sir Jarrod, The Merciful, Knight Lieutenant of the Order of the Stallion of Gateskeep. This," he pointed, "is Lord Carter Sorenson, Chancellor of Gateskeep and chief military advisor to King Rorthos Riongoran-Thurdin. Tell your king: *this stops here.* If he continues to antagonize Gateskeep, we—" he pointed between himself and Carter, "— will return with an army, and this afternoon will seem like a happy memory."

"It wouldn't hurt to tell Gavria the same thing," Carter added. "Don't make us come back here."

The Uloraki spent the next several minutes gathering up their wounded and slinging Elgast of Skullsmortar over the front of a horse. They muttered vulgarities as they rode past the Gateskeep knights and gave a wide berth to the Faerie on the bears.

"Sir Jarrod, The Merciful," Jarrod told them each as they rode past. "Tell your friends."

"I still can't believe you brought a gun," Carter said to Jarrod as the last of them rode away.

"I still can't believe you didn't," said Jarrod. "Come on. Let's go home."

Carter looked out at the valley, the sunset, and the retreating soldiers. "I am home."

Jarrod watched them go.

"Me, too," he said.

XIII

CODA

"Only a warrior chooses pacifism; all others are condemned to it."
— Unknown

J arrod stood with his back to Wild River Reach, enraptured by the sea.

It had been sixteen days.

Thunderous breakers pummeled the rocks in slow motion far below, smashing and whirling gray and white against a dozen jagged islands in the bay. Across the water, the sun hurled the last of its colors against the far side of the mountainous backbone of Ice Isle as the great ringed moon, half-hidden by the sea, prepared to shoulder its burden in the final gasp of the day.

Every now and again a breaker would hit the rocks just right, fluming spray like scattered jewels in the sunset.

"Not bad," Jarrod said. "Not bad at all."

There were issues. The Reach was the size of Long Island, bordered by the Wilds to the north, with a dozen isolated villages and two small towns, plus the City of the Reach itself. From what he'd seen, it was a land as rugged and sheer as Patagonia: jagged sheer mountains, sparse forests, swaths of tundra. Not that he'd have much time for exploring. As Lord of Wild River Reach he was in for endless afternoons of listening to squabbles and disputes from every corner when he was here, and long days saving the rest of the world when he wasn't.

Saril, Bevio, and Peric, newly knighted, would be here in a couple of weeks, with Saril as Lord's Chancellor and Peric as captain of the guard. They would be bringing a contingent of knights and Gateskeep soldiers to oversee the shift in management as the Hillwhites and their mercenaries left the Reach. The three would carry the load when Jarrod was away at court.

The mine was the central source for Gateskeep's silver coinage. Security couldn't be overstressed. Theft was a problem. Smuggling was a problem. Taxes were a problem. One corner or another of the castle was always in disrepair from the constant jarring of the surf, which Jarrod could feel through his boots even up here. It was four days' hard ride to the City of the Gate, where he now had a High Council seat and the title of Lord Protector. He'd be spending half his time at the palace at Gateskeep, and the commute was going to be a bitch.

It was an easy ride to Regoth Ur, though, where Carter and Daorah had taken over the breeding operation for the king's pegasi; another Hillwhite project left orphaned. Of course they'd jumped on it.

Carter promised to visit The Reach regularly. His schedule, when not at court, would be considerably less hectic.

Nothing was perfect.

The view from this balcony, though, was pretty damned close.

Jarrod's hand rested on the hilt of his rapier, his other arm around Karra's waist. The chill and the damp didn't seem to bother her.

Brandt Buxton would get all his students, for good. He'd miss some of them.

He could travel home, but he'd never have the chance to stage a great comeback, to crawl out of the hole he'd dug for himself after Paris.

He'd miss that, too.

Karra's hand tightened on his arm as the last of the sunlight fell behind Ice Isle.

"Are there enough trees here for you?" he asked her.

"No," she said, and kissed him, tugging his lower lip gently between her fangs. "But the forests will wait."

He was eager to see the night.

FINÉ

ACKNOWLEDGMENTS

This book would not have been possible without a great many people.

First and foremost, I want to thank whatever gods are responsible for giving me one of the world's greatest living swordsmiths as my brother and long-time sparring partner: Michael "Tinker" Pearce.

I owe an immense debt of gratitude to SGM (ret.) Michael Jarnevic, whose ruthless and inexhaustible red pen—immortalized in the sleeve of his service uniform at the Indiana Military Museum—did more for my writing mechanics than anything in the 10 years prior. It was SGM Mike who kicked me in the ass to put my stuff out there: "There's no shame in being a failed writer, Joe."

Monique Fischer, my editor, put her fist out and tagged in as my composition coach and stylistic sparring partner, taking up where SGM Mike left off. Monique has a unique gift for calling me on my bullshit without screwing with my voice, and this book would not be what it is without her.

My graphics team, West Coast Design for the original e-book cover, and Lynn Stevenson for adapting it to print.

I'd like to thank the incomparable Tiana Warner for her encouragement and for writing one hell of a book on self-publishing. Get it.

Thank you to my beta readers, too numerous to mention.

Thank you to Badger, the Keeper of Stories.

This book wouldn't be here at all, and neither would I, if not for one of the finest professional soldiers I've ever known, who fought to keep me alive long after he could have quit with no one thinking the less of him for it. I won't embarrass him by naming him here; he'd tell you he was just doing his job. I found an old manuscript of *Dragon's Trail* on a hard drive when I was in the hospital, so in a way, he's responsible for this.

I wrote the final version of *Dragon's Trail* on a steady diet of Bulleit Rye, cheap Chinese food, late 50's hard bop, and both volumes of Tom Waits' *The Early Years*.

If you enjoyed *Dragon's Trail,* please leave a review on Goodreads or your preferred retailer.

Sign up at www.josephmalik.com to receive updates about the release of The Outworlders Book II, *THE NEW MAGIC*.

Coming Soon

BOOK II OF *THE OUTWORLDERS*

THE NEW MAGIC

JOSEPH MALIK

SIGN UP FOR RELEASE NEWS AT
WWW.JOSEPHMALIK.COM

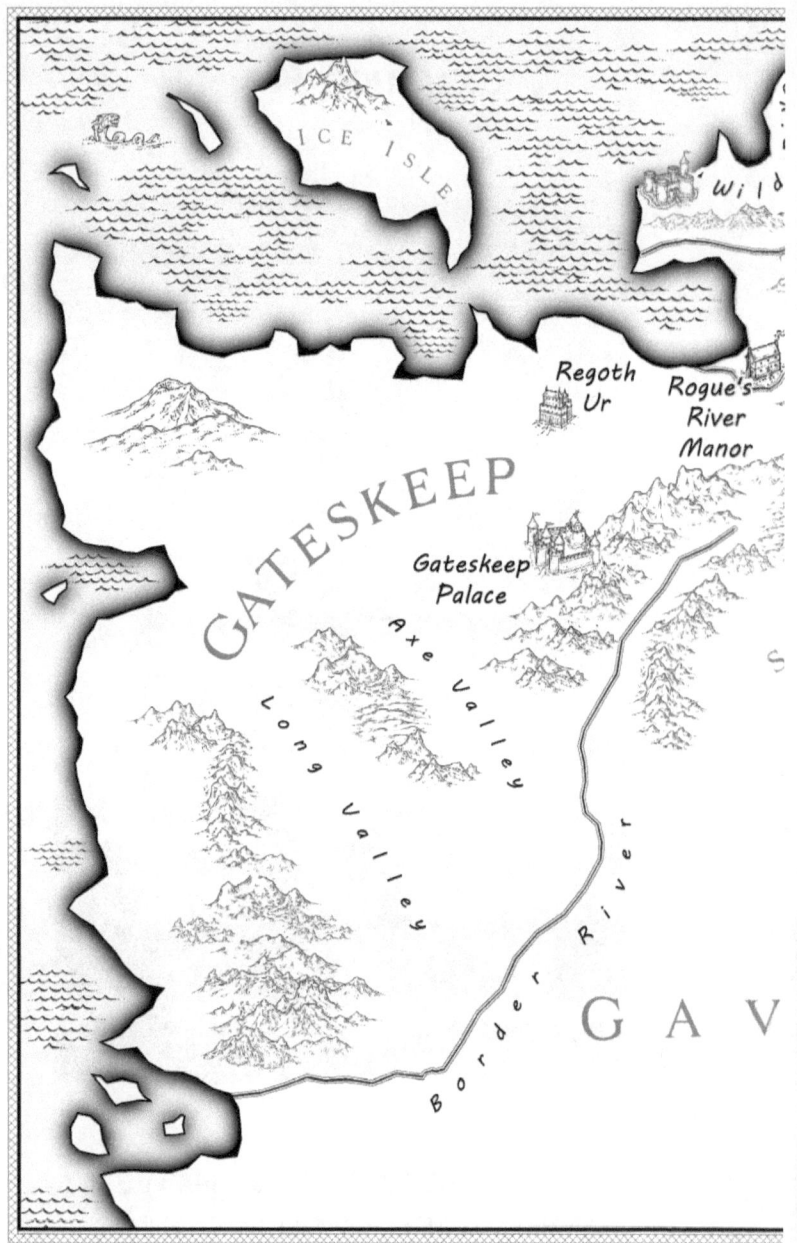

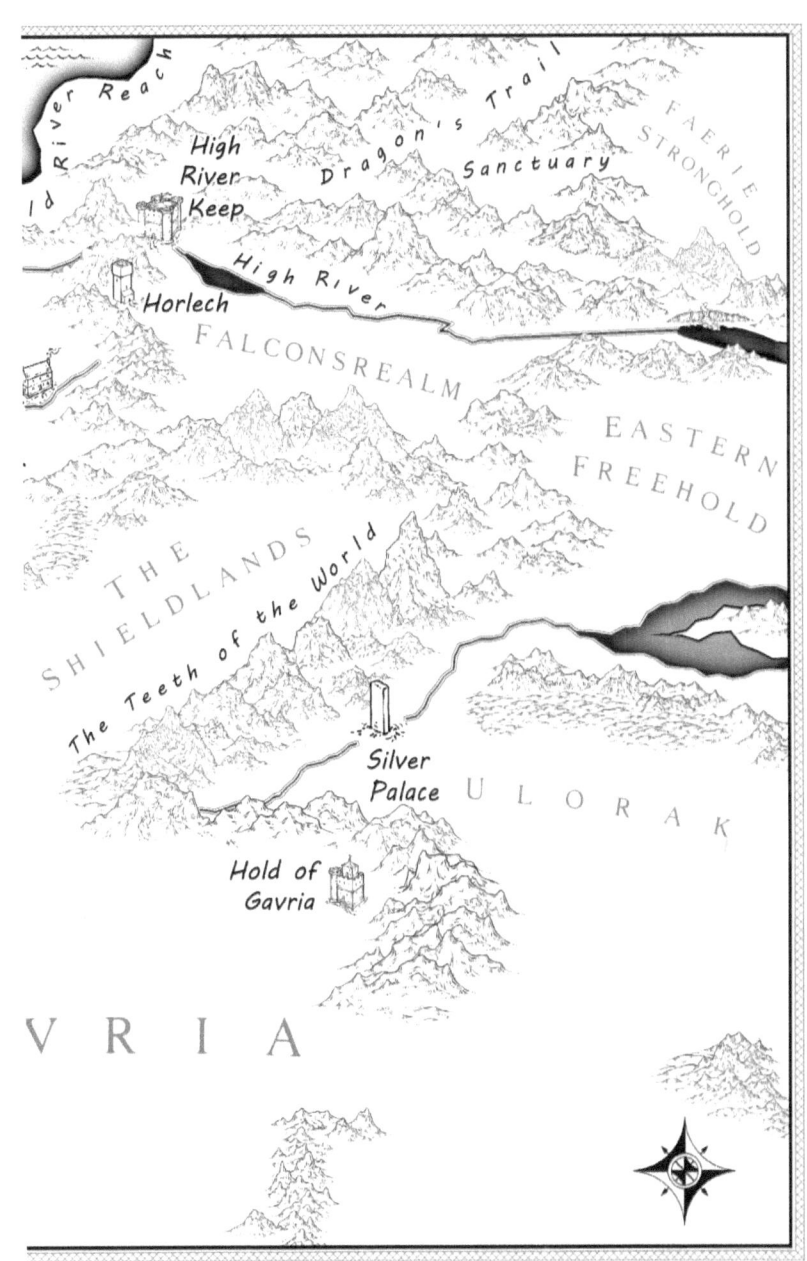